Shadow of the Eclipse

by

L. A. Kelley

Shadow of the Eclipse

Cover Art by *Abigail Owen*

The Wild Rose Press, Inc.
PO Box 708
Adams Basin, NY 14410-0708
Visit us at www.thewildrosepress.com

Publishing History
First Fantasy Rose Edition, 2020
Print ISBN 978-1-5092-3085-3
Digital ISBN 978-1-5092-3086-0

Published in the United States of America

With every breath, the air around Cal became hotter and more oppressive, pressing on his shoulders like a stifling blanket. Humidity dropped to nothing. Beads of sweat on his brow evaporated. Cal licked his dry, cracked lips and grimaced at the gritty feel of sand on his tongue.

Sand in a corn maze?

They turned a corner and stumbled into a clearing. In the center was an arbor that arched over a circle of flagstones on the ground. A glowing flame hovered above the stones, suspended in midair. Meg and Cal exchanged dumbfounded looks and stepped forward. The clarion note of a distant horn sounded a soldier's call to action. A surge of adrenaline flooded Cal's veins. He hadn't felt like this since his days on patrol with the Army. Unconsciously, Cal's hand went to his hip, reaching for the sword. He stared at his empty hand. *Sword?*

The flame grew larger and brighter, shooting through the arbor into the heavens.

"Cal!" Meg's voice sounded very far away.

"I'm here!" Cal reached for her, but the flame blinded him, blotting out the maze, blotting out the sun, blotting out the world.

Nothing remained but the roar of the cheering crowd.

Dedication

Nobody does it alone.
Many thanks to my friends and family
for their continued support,
and a special shout-out to Lara Parker,
the guru of grammar.

Part I: Penumbra

The scent of fresh blood drifted through the veil, and the Everdark howled in triumph. At long last, the proper cosmic forces neared alignment. An eon had passed since guardians forced the Everdark past the threshold of the gate and into the void, but this time nothing barred its entry. No call to arms from the other side, no warriors to deny access to the feeding grounds. The Everdark inhaled. Nothing existed beyond the gate but the sweet aroma of raw meat, stronger with each breath.

The Everdark paced in front of the gathering mist. The gate remained out of reach but not for long. Soon, hot, salty blood would course down its throat once more, with no god or man to stand in the way. The guardians had lost the knowledge of the route between worlds in the annals of time, but not the Everdark. The delicate crunch of human bones still held a pleasant memory.

****

"Morning, Cal. Don't tell me you're having hot coffee on a day like this. Is that your superpower? It's a bird, it's a plane, it's Callum MacGregor drinking scalding beverages in a single bound."

Cal wiped a hand across his sweaty brow and grinned at Joe Mendoza, owner of the Crossroads Inn. "Iced." He hefted a bakery bag and shook it. "My superpower is in the cruller. How's business?"

"Booked solid." Joe nodded at his own package. "Elaina sent me for packets of Amaranth's special tea blends. She decided to try an afternoon tea, and it's going so well, we may make it permanent. Trust my wife to seize every business opportunity."

"Becky asked for a few days off to help you and Elaina this weekend. You're not planning to steal my paralegal permanently are you?"

"Nope. For some reason, Mom enjoys her job. You must pay her better than I do," Joe said with a grin. He shaded his eyes to peer at a sky dotted with a scattering of wispy clouds. "What do you think of this heat? Crazy for late October, huh? Amaranth says it's because of the eclipse."

"My professional advice is don't take anything seriously said by a middle-aged woman with seven cats and a fairy figurine collection."

Joe's eyes twinkled. "Yesterday, she told Elaina bad omens are in the clouds."

"Uh-huh. Eclipses don't cause heat waves."

"If you say so, Cal," he said lightly. "They sure are good for business though."

"Eclipses are rare and folks are intrigued. Lucky for us, the town is in the dead center of the umbra."

"A year ago, I thought an umbra was a male umbrella instead of an eclipse's darkest shadow. Now, I'm liking it on social media." Joe gazed at Main Street, crowded with pedestrians. "Motels and campgrounds two hundred miles away are full. It was thoughtful of the eclipse to coincide with Crossroad's harvest festival. The grounds don't open until tomorrow and the buzz in town is that stores have already broken sales records. Hey, God," Joe called to the sky, "if your idea of evil omens is for everyone to turn an insane profit, please send more. The chamber of commerce backs you one hundred percent."

"Watch what you say, Joe," said Cal lightly. "You never know what demons are listening."

They said goodbye, and Cal walked the block to his law office. He regarded the shiny brass plaque for Callum MacGregor, Attorney at Law, with a half-smile and then paused to take a final look over his shoulder at Main Street. Long, thin shadows cast by the morning sun made black hash marks on the sidewalk. Strange to think in a few days the brightest object in the sky would disappear for nearly four minutes.

The door was unlocked, and the bells over the jamb jangled a cheerful welcome. Becky Mendoza looked up from her desk as she shut off her computer. "Morning, Cal."

"Morning. I just saw your son. Why are you here? You're supposed to be off today."

"Well, that's a lovely greeting to the world's best paralegal," she teased. "I wanted to finish the Emerson's paperwork for their closing. It's done, and I'm heading out unless you need me for something else."

"Nope. Any new appointments?"

"Not for today or the rest of the week. Everyone's mind is on the festival except for George Lydecker. He called and wants to revise his will."

Cal paused mid-sip and hurriedly gulped the mouthful of coffee. "Again? He changed it two weeks ago." An uneasy suspicion jelled. "Don't tell me..."

Becky snickered. "He's cutting out the nephew."

"He just put Dylan back in," Cal sputtered. "The wanker's only been with him a month. What did he do this time?"

"Something about the lyrics of his new rock anthem. I couldn't quite make out all of it. George's sentences run together when he rants, but I believe Dylan settled on a clever combination of a male body part, Tantric sexual position, and the name of George's mother. I calmed him down long enough to make an appointment in two weeks."

"Two weeks, eh?" grunted Cal. "Good. If I'm lucky, both will have a spontaneous attack of common sense, and George will cancel. Ever notice how people like George and Dylan see themselves as put-upon, but no one else does?"

"George is set in his ways but cut Dylan some slack. He's a good kid who's had a rough time of it. By the way," Becky added lightly, "wanker can be substituted nicely for each of the nouns in the title of Dylan's song. Should I suggest it?"

"Please don't. Anything else?"

"I left letters in your inbox for signatures and a draft of the ordinance on pole banners the town council sent for review."

"Thanks, Becky. You're the best."

"I tell you that daily." She grabbed her purse off the floor and gazed dreamily out the front window. "It's exciting, isn't it?"

"Yup, the shop owners on Main Street are celebrating. Joe practically did a backflip."

"Not just that. Of course, I'm glad for the uptick in business. Joe and Elaina have barely owned the place a year, and an inn thrives on repeat customers. Having

Crossroads in the center of the umbra brought great publicity for the town, and rooms are booked solid for the next two months. I mean the eclipse. I can't imagine what it will feel like when the sky goes black in the middle of the day."

"Creepy, I expect. Sunrise and sunset are absolutes. When something disrupts the cosmic pattern…well, no wonder ancient civilizations freaked. In parts of the world, folks believed the moon attacked the sun and banged pots and pans to frighten it away. To the ancient Chinese, the moon was a hungry dragon. Warriors shot cannons and arrows into the air to stop it from devouring the sun…" Cal shrugged at her amused expression. "History geek."

Becky chuckled. "It's reassuring to know a few brave souls watch out for the rest of us long enough for rituals to work their magic. You realize, of course, as a small-town lawyer, you're the closest thing we have to a champion of justice for the common man. Any plans to shoot at the moon?"

"Planning a quiet day at home with a pair of funky sunglasses. I'll watch the eclipse from the backyard in the comfort of my lawn chair, cold beer in hand if it stays this hot."

Becky raised an eyebrow. "You're not going to the festival? Everyone in town will be there. According to George, his corn maze is extra challenging this year. During a momentary lull in his tirade over Dylan, he even managed to say he erected a temporary arbor in the center for those who make it through. Can you imagine that from George? Local gossip says it's Amaranth's idea."

"Great. More fairy decor." Cal shifted on his feet.

"I'd feel weird ambling through a corn maze by myself. Amaranth can keep the reputation of town eccentric. I have a business to run."

Becky patted his arm. "You need to get out more."

"I date."

"Not enough. The breakup with Allison was a while ago."

"I don't obsess over Allison. A small town wasn't for her, and I was happy in Crossroads from the day I took over the practice from Isaac Bingham. Her job offer in Europe triggered the split, but if we were meant to be together, we'd have found a way." Becky regarded him with doubt, and he added, "Canceling the wedding was for the best. Speaking as a lawyer, breakups are painful, but divorce is worse and more expensive."

Becky put her hands on her hips. "So, dive into the dating pool before the good ones are taken. Tons of people will be there, including single ladies, both local and visitors."

Not a chance. By the stubborn set to Becky's expression, she was primed to argue while he wanted to drop the subject of dating forever. Cal slid effortlessly into his appeasing lawyer mode. "I appreciate your concern and promise to give it some thought."

"Don't think too much," Becky threw over her shoulder as she headed out the door. "I expect to see you there."

Cal sat in his office with the door ajar to listen for the jangly bells. Not that he expected walk-in traffic today with everyone's thoughts on the eclipse. He finished the cruller, signed the letters in his inbox, and flipped through the draft ordinance from Crossroads' town council. His gaze wandered out the window to the shadows on the sidewalk. Funny, how they appeared darker than usual today—long, spidery fingers reaching out to snatch at unsuspecting passersby.

Cal forced his eyes to stay on the page, struggling to get past the first paragraph. "Pole banner permits," he read, "may be issued for the following: public awareness, charitable fundraising..." His attention strayed to the window again. Cal drained the last of the iced coffee and shoved the papers aside. Maybe he should have added a shot of espresso. His concentration definitely lagged this morning or was he affected by burgeoning excitement for the eclipse? It sure shook up Crossroads. Not enough to please Allison though.

Sweet, sad pain tugged at his heart. They had a good thing through law school, but truth be told even then the end was in sight. Allison's eyes lit up at the prospect of a future partnership at a big legal firm, while his glazed over. She voiced support for his decision to move to Crossroads, but from that moment, an emotional curtain descended between them. It was over. They only needed the final goodbye. Her sudden job opportunity in London made it easy but no less painful.

Since then, Cal threw himself into his new responsibilities, but maybe Becky had a point. It might be time to try again. The jangle of the office bells startled him.

"Hello?" called a familiar voice from the reception area. "Anyone home?"

"In here!" Cal jumped from behind the desk and greeted Isaac Bingham with an outstretched hand. "Isaac, what a nice surprise. You look great. How's retirement?"

Despite the gray hair, the elderly man's grip was firm. "No regrets. Plenty of time for fun, and the grandkids keep me and Julia hopping. We have another one on the way. You look good, too. No second thoughts on taking over my practice or putting down roots in a small town?"

"No complaints of any kind except I have to pop a few extra-strength aspirin before every appointment with George Lydecker."

Isaac's eyes twinkled. "Trust me, his father was worse."

Cal ushered him to the leather armchairs used for client consultations. "Can I get you some water? I've got bottles in the fridge."

"No thanks, I'm fine."

"I suppose you're in town for the harvest festival and the eclipse?"

"Not exactly." Isaac studied the room with a pleased expression. "I like what you've done here; new paint, carpet." He nodded at the laptop on the desk. "Everything is up to date the way it should be. I've heard fine things about you from others in Crossroads. Now I see he was right all along, and I left my clients in good hands. He was always right…" Isaac's voice drifted away. He peered out the window with a distant expression as if captured in a bygone memory.

The clock on the bookcase ticked off the seconds. Cal cleared his throat. "Isaac?"

"Forgive me." Isaac shook his head with a laugh. "You must think I'm a crazy old coot. I came back to see you. I have something I've waited a long time to deliver."

Cal raised an eyebrow. "Oh?" Isaac reached into his pocket and handed him a voucher for a free funnel cake on the first day of the harvest festival. Cal's confusion deepened. "Um, thanks, but I wasn't planning to go—"

"I also bring a message. Strange," Isaac murmured with a half-smile. "I imagined this conversation many times over the years but now don't know where to begin." He cocked his head and gave Cal an appraising look. "Have you ever heard of the Lux Foundation?"

"Sure," said Cal. "I wouldn't be in Crossroads without it. After two years in the Army, I used the GI Bill to pay for college, but the Lux Foundation awarded me an additional scholarship and then another to law school after I graduated. The money covered every expense and when I passed the bar, the foundation provided a grant contingent on moving to a rural community. I hadn't considered a place like Crossroads before then. I got offers from big city law firms, but the idea of being my own boss suddenly appealed to me. Without the grant, I never would have come here; probably never even knew Crossroads existed."

"Do you remember applying for the scholarships or the grant?"

"Well, no," said Cal, "but I filled out dozens of financial aid packages, and heard the grant was from an anonymous donor. What's this about?"

"You never applied for anything from the Lux Foundation. Phillip Bingham was my grandfather and the founder. I'm on the board now. He died a long time ago, but earmarked funds for your education and the grant. He's the reason I approached you to take over my practice."

Cal blinked. *Isaac's grandfather?* "I don't understand. Why did he care about me?"

"I don't know, but that's not the strangest part." Isaac leaned forward. "The meeting with my grandfather to discuss your future took place thirty years before you were born."

Cal's mouth dropped open. "It's not possible. My parents hadn't even met."

"Hard to take in, right?" Isaac chuckled. "Me, too. I remember that conversation as if it was yesterday. I was the youngest grandchild, and we had a special bond. The day after passing the bar, he called me to his office and offered money to start my own practice if I did it in Crossroads. I had never heard of the place but was grateful and had no urge to live in a big city."

Isaac shifted in his chair. "Then he asked me to make a promise and keep it secret. 'Swear, Isaac,' he said, 'on pain of death, for that's what we face if the vow is broken.' I was shaken, to say the least, but Phillip Bingham was the kindest, most generous man I'd ever known. He never asked for favors lightly, so I agreed. Then he proceeded to fill me in on Callum MacGregor; birthdate, parents' names, college, the necessary facts to keep track over the years. Although, he was adamant that I maintain physical distance."

Cal gaped at him in disbelief. "The heat…maybe I should call someone."

"I don't have sunstroke, Cal, and this isn't a joke. He set aside money not to interfere with your life, but to smooth the rough patches with scholarships and the grant. He also told me to offer my practice in Crossroads as soon as you passed the bar. He said I'd be ready for retirement by then, and you'd be a damn good lawyer and jump at the chance to come here." Isaac chuckled. "He was right about that, too."

Cal sagged into the seat cushion. "This is crazy. How?"

Isaac said, "He knew the eclipse occurred this year. He gave me the date and said Crossroads was in the umbra. Your attendance at the harvest festival had paramount importance."

"Let me get this straight," sputtered Cal. "A man died before I was born but predicted my life. He paid for my law degree and smoothed the way to Crossroads for the sole purpose of going to a town party where I eat a funnel cake and wander aimlessly through a corn maze."

"Yes."

"That's insane."

"No argument, counselor, but the story gets better. Callum MacGregor wasn't the only not-yet-born person my grandfather needed to attend the Crossroads Harvest Festival."

****

So intent on the computer monitor, Meg didn't hear the footsteps behind her. She jumped as Chloe dropped a carton of folders in her inbox. "What's this stuff?" Meg asked.

"New accounts."

She peered at the names and her jaw tightened. "Those are old accounts and they're yours."

Chloe held out her hand and spread her fingers wide, examining the new French manicure. The odor of fresh nail polish wafted in the air. "I don't have time. Carter assigned me to a special project."

"Uh-huh."

"What's that supposed to mean?" Her voice dripped icicles.

"Nothing."

Chloe motioned to Carter Landon's door. "You forgot to sign the expenditures report. He wants to see you."

"I didn't forget I—" Chloe paid no attention. She flounced back to her desk and settled into the new ergonomically designed chair; leather upholstery, super expensive. Meg didn't have to ask the price. She already knew right down to the penny and sales tax, along with the cost of the bouquet of roses that appeared on Chloe's desk once a week.

Meg poked her head into the office of the Director of Purchasing and Control. "You want to see me?"

"Shut the door and take a seat. The expenditures report needs your signature." He handed her a file.

Meg flipped through the papers and a knot formed in her stomach. Landon hadn't made any of the requested changes. "I explained to you, I can't sign off when unauthorized expenditures appear on the company credit card."

"The expenditures were authorized by me."

"I found a weekly charge at a manicure salon and a flower shop listed under Miscellaneous Office Supplies."

"If management wishes to treat an employee for exceptional service," he said coolly, "that's none of your concern."

Exceptional service? That's a new phrase for banging the boss. "The card also had a trip to Las Vegas last month; two round-trip plane tickets, hotel accommodations—"

"Business conference. I took my wife."

Sure you did. "As I explained, I need receipts and a conference program—"

"As I explained, I must have thrown them out." His words were cold and brittle, and the knot in her stomach tightened.

"That's not the only discrepancy." Meg straightened her shoulders. "I can't sign this. My name is on the report. I'm responsible to company headquarters for its accuracy."

"Company headquarters didn't hire you. I did." Landon leaned forward, bearing down on his knuckles in a dominance display, like a great ape that happened to favor three-piece suits. "Let me give you some advice, Meg. Think of this office as my team. Players who support Team Landon are well-rewarded. Call it a signing bonus. They become MVPs and sent to the majors. Those who don't, never get to bat." He handed her a pen. "Be a team player, Meg. As long as the proper signatures are in place, headquarters doesn't care about the report. In the overall scheme of things, it's only a little money and after all, it isn't yours."

It isn't yours either. Your wife's family owns the firm.

She stared at the pen and then placed it on top of the file and slid both across the desk. "It's not my money, but it's my reputation on the line."

Landon's eyes narrowed. "I'm very disappointed in you, Meg, but I can't have an employee in the office refuse to play on Team Landon. Your services are no longer needed here. You're fired." Red-faced, Meg jumped from the chair. She flung open the door and stormed from his office. "Don't expect to have an easy time finding a new job in this town!" Landon bellowed from his desk. "Word gets around when you're not a team player."

Meg dumped the box of new files from the inbox on the floor, ignoring the startled expressions of her coworkers and the smirk from Chloe. She threw a few personal items inside and hurried away, cheeks burning as hushed whispers followed her out the door.

Twenty minutes later, Meg was in her apartment lobby. A man from a courier service stood near the stairwell, peering at the time display on his cell phone. *Must be nice to be paid by the hour.* Meg brushed past and went upstairs to her apartment. She set the box on the couch and paced the floor, fists clenching and unclenching. She should have told off Landon as soon as he fired her. Dirty, rotten SOB. She should have wiped that smirk off his face.

Meg pulled up short. Her eyes narrowed and she peered at the laptop on the desk. Surely, the first thing Landon did after firing her was to call IT and reset the passwords, especially the one that accessed accounting data. Of course, it was Wednesday afternoon when Landon always seemed preoccupied. Could it be because the charge card showed receipts for two dinners at Renaldo's Ristorante Italiano every Wednesday for the past month? The same night Chloe claimed to work late, yet, her inbox was as full as ever Thursday morning.

Her fingers froze on the keyboard. This wasn't like her. She took a steadying breath. "Geez, don't get your panties in a twist. You're not raffling off state secrets on the dark web. Skedaddle in there and don't get nabbed." She logged into the site and snickered when it opened immediately. Meg pulled up the digital copy of the expenditures report, highlighting the most interesting items. She retrieved Mrs. Landon's email address from her contact list. Nice of Landon to have thrown an office party at their big, swanky lake house on Labor Day weekend and have his wife handle the RSVPs. Meg composed a note to Mrs. Landon, explaining she needed the receipts from their recent trip to Las Vegas.

Mr. Landon can't find the paperwork but told me you went with him. Please ignore the charges for flowers and manicures. Mr. Landon said they were gifts for a staff member as a thank you for services rendered. That goes for the dinners at Renaldo's on Wednesday nights as well.

She attached the file. "Chill, girl. You're almost home." Landon's lake house had been chock full of pricey furnishings. Meg wondered idly how many he'd get in the divorce. Probably squat. His wife's cousin attended the party and Meg recalled she was a pit bull divorce attorney. She hit send and raised her arms. "Booyah!"

The enjoyable glow that came from sticking it to a loathsome human being faded. Meg logged out of the company website for good and sat back in the chair with a sigh. Unemployed again. The job had come along at the end of a long tiring search. Finding work had never been easy. Prospects panned out, one good job lost to corporate downsizing, another to mergers. Then a succession of employers with Landon's scruples who expected her to use creative accounting skills to cover their lies. She quit them, hunted for others. How long before potential employers eyed the job hopping on her résumé and refused to even grant an interview? Rotten luck seemed to dog her footsteps with half her life after college spent chasing a paycheck. Now the search had to begin once more.

Why was she a magnet for corporate malfeasance? Meg closed the laptop. Landon wasn't apt to give a glowing reference, and local employers would expect her to explain why she left a well-paying job. Would they believe her? Landon was sure to invent a story to cover his butt. Maybe it was time to try her luck in a new city—again.

Meg jumped at a knock on the door. The courier from the lobby handed her a large envelope. "I have a delivery for Meg Adler."

She grimaced. Severance papers so soon? Landon didn't waste any time. He probably suspected her answer and had them ready to go this morning. She scrawled her signature on his tablet.

He cleared his throat. "They sure were specific."

Meg blinked. "What?"

"The sender. I had orders to deliver the package at exactly 3:57 p.m. today and had to adjust my whole route."

"Oh, uh, sorry."

"No big deal, just wondering why so dead set on the time."

Meg gazed at the return address, bemused. The Lux Foundation? "Beats me."

She shut the door and plopped on the couch, shoving aside the box of odds and ends from the office. Her brows knit together in a puzzled frown. "What's the Lux Foundation?" She snorted. "If they want money from me, they're in for crushing disappointment."

Meg ripped open the package and spilled the contents onto her lap; a voucher for a free funnel cake on opening day at something called the Crossroads Harvest Festival, a pamphlet for the Crossroads Inn, and a sealed envelope. Written on the front was her name in a series of decorative calligraphic swirls. Meg fingered the envelope, heavyweight vellum with an ivory tint, hinting at both age and quality. "Who uses antique paper?" she murmured, frown deepening. "Let alone writes letters anymore in fancy longhand."

She pried up the flap with a fingernail and removed a folded sheet of the same antique vellum. At the top was *The Lux Foundation* embossed in gold.

Dear Meg,

The Lux Foundation is always on the hunt for people of exceptional character and abilities. I would like to discuss an employment opportunity in Crossroads that will not only be challenging, but also in society's best interest. Unfortunately, this is a limited time offer, and I'm unable to see you in person. I've taken the liberty of making a reservation under your name at the Crossroads Inn, all expenses paid, of course. Check in Thursday afternoon, and my representative will meet you Friday morning on the grounds of the harvest festival to present the particulars.

With fondest regards, Phillip Bingham.

****

Cal gawked at Isaac. "What do you mean you can't tell me?"

"Sorry, Cal," said Isaac. "My grandfather's instructions were specific. You will meet this person on Friday morning at the harvest festival, but I can't give you a name."

Cal narrowed his eyes. "Can't or won't."

"I'm afraid it's all I can say at the moment. I will add that my grandfather's intentions weren't meant to drive you crazy, although, you may believe that's the case. My opinion, for what it's worth, is he didn't wish to affect outcomes."

"What outcomes?" demanded Cal.

"He didn't go into detail but insisted events must proceed in a particular order that I had to maintain at all costs. He was adamant. No deviation was part of the promise I made to him." A smile tugged at Isaac's lips. "I'm almost in the dark as much as you. I have to admit, I'm eager for the end of this weekend. Whatever mission my grandfather devised for you and this other person has to conclude successfully by then."

Cal snorted. "Do I sense an 'or else'?"

"Let's hope not." A hint of apprehension flashed across the elderly man's face, and Cal shivered with an unexplained chill. He opened his mouth to speak, but Isaac jumped in. "Phillip Bingham was a man of exceptional character with a strong personal code of moral justice. He never lied or broke his word. Can I count on you to help me fulfill the final promise to my grandfather?"

Cal raised his hands in surrender. "Why not? I suppose the only way to find out what this insanity means is to go through with it. Good thing I didn't make other plans for the weekend."

Isaac rose from the chair, beaming a smile. "Excellent. Thank you for humoring an old man—two of them, if you count Phillip Bingham. Now, I must go. It's wonderful to see you again, Cal."

"You, too." They shook hands, and Cal escorted him to the door. "You dropped a bombshell today, Isaac, that's for damn sure."

"Not an easy thing to do at my age. Nice to hear I've still got the stuff."

As Isaac stepped over the threshold, Cal pulled him back. "Does this other person have my name or description?"

"No."

"The festival is spread out. Where do we meet?" Isaac remained silent, and Cal blew out an exasperated breath. "So, tomorrow morning two strangers wander the grounds on the off-chance they bump into each other and spontaneously realize they were both summoned by a dead man for the same mysterious reason—which you refuse to explain. Meanwhile, let's have funnel cake."

Isaac flashed a wily grin. "Like what you've done with the place, Cal. Keep up the good work."

Cal shut the door and leaned against the wall, shaking his head. No use in even pretending to work today. Not after that conversation. He pulled a sheet of paper from Becky's printer and wrote, *Closed for the festival. Back on Monday.* He taped the sign to the window, turned off the lights, and locked the door behind him. Cal walked home and changed from his suit and tie into jeans and a T-shirt. He switched on the TV. Local news reports held nothing but talk of the upcoming eclipse. He switched off the TV, picked up a computer tablet, and tried to concentrate on the Middle Ages history book he downloaded a few days ago. Cal had gotten to the halfway point, enjoying the author's colorful descriptions of a world long gone. But after five attempts to plow through the next chapter on Germany, he tossed the tablet aside.

The day dragged on and the antsy need to move suddenly captured his legs. He wandered through town, dodging pedestrians on the sidewalk, catching snatches of their excited chatter on the coming eclipse. Was one of them his mysterious contact? He peered into the faces of passing strangers searching for a clue, but not a flicker of recognition came his way.

Cal's path detoured to the edge of town and the festival grounds abutting the Lydecker farm. Harvest committee volunteers put on the finishing touches. They erected booths and tents days ago. Parking lots were defined, the play area awaited the first child, everything prepared for Friday's crowds. "And somewhere in that mess," Cal muttered, "I'm supposed to find you."

He skirted the festival site and reached the corn maze. Despite the recent heat wave, George's crop thrived, and the stalks towered overhead. The entrance was roped off, but Cal could see into the maze to the point where the path branched left and right. Most people being right-handed naturally turned to the right, an almost instinctive reaction. A breeze gusted through the fields, rustling the golden tassels.

To the left.

"What?" Cal spun in a half-circle, but no one was there. "Great," he snorted, "now you're hearing things."

The urge to keep moving disappeared, so Cal turned toward town. He crossed the street and ambled past the Crossroads Inn, owned by Becky's son Joe and his wife, Elaina. No wonder they were booked solid, the location was prime. Guests had an unimpeded view of both the festival activities and the cornfield. Cal stopped to wait for a car to pull into the inn's guest parking. The driver was a woman in her twenties with her hair pulled back in a ponytail. "Hope you have a reservation," he said to himself, "or you'll be sleeping in the corn maze."

****

Before Meg left Thursday morning, she considered the sweater. The weather had been unseasonably warm, but country nights could be cool, and Crossroads was far from the big city. She tossed the sweater on top of the other clothing and zipped the suitcase shut. Her hand froze on the grip. "This is crazy, the least rational decision you have ever made. The Crossroads Inn is probably a front for a cult of serial killers."

Maybe not, though, and she certainly needed the job. Suspicious after reading the letter yesterday, Meg immediately called the number on the pamphlet to verify the reservation. A cheerful woman named Becky answered and assured her everything was in order and the room would be ready on Thursday. Meg then checked the inn's website. Nicely designed, the pictures of the accommodations overflowed with charm. Plenty of five-star reviews, too, from happy guests.

The Lux Foundation was also legit. Meg stayed up late Wednesday doing her homework, and the online research led to the conclusion it was a respected charitable organization without a smidgen of scandal to taint decades of operation. Because it was privately funded, few details were available on internal operations. The website didn't list much besides several current projects, and she didn't find a single mention of Phillip Bingham. Nevertheless, legit charity review sites gave it the highest marks and gushing praise. By every account, the Lux Foundation was completely, totally, and one hundred percent honest, so well-run as to be a model for others. An organization where number crunchers didn't manipulate funds for personal gain but used them to help people and better society. The kind of place she always hoped to work.

What the hell did they want with her?

One way to find out. Meg hefted the suitcase. "Rationality be damned."

The sun barely peeked over the horizon as Meg started the car. She had mapped the route on the GPS. The drive was nearly five hundred miles, and her plan to arrive late that afternoon required an early start. By midday, Meg was far from the city and stopped to eat a quick picnic lunch. The weather was warm, and she tied her hair in a ponytail to keep it off her neck.

The noon hour passed, and the sun began the slow descent toward the horizon. The landscape changed to wooded rolling hills awash with vibrant autumn colors. After another two hours, Meg left the interstate for a county highway. Every hotel at the bottom of the exit ramp sported a neon No Vacancy sign. Tidy farms sprouted along the road. Finally, she reached Crossroads' town limits. She drove at a crawl on Main Street where hordes of pedestrians spilled over the sidewalks in a human tide. An overhead banner proclaimed *Harvest Festival, Friday, Saturday, Sunday.*

The Crossroads Inn was on the other side of town across from the fairgrounds and a large cornfield. Meg parked the car in the lot and grabbed her suitcase from the backseat.

"I'll get that." A man bounded down the stairs. "I

saw you pull in. I'm Joe Mendoza. You must be Meg Adler. We're expecting you." He took the suitcase and led her to the front desk and then introduced his mother, Becky, and wife, Elaina.

"Oh, yes," Becky said cheerfully. "We spoke on the phone. It's nice to meet you. The room is ready. Breakfast is included and served in the dining room."

"You have a table reserved for dinner at six tonight," added Elaina. "It's paid for, too."

"By Phillip Bingham?" asked Meg.

"Phillip? Don't recall anyone in the Bingham family named Phillip." Elaina slid across a guest register and handed Meg a pen. "Please sign right there…Isaac Bingham made the reservation a year ago. Are you a family friend?"

Meg froze, pen poised over the register. "A year ago?"

"Yes, right after Joe and I opened the inn. It was our first reservation, and a good thing, too. We're booked solid for the festival and the eclipse. We've been turning people away for months."

Meg stared at her. "Eclipse?" Elaina's words didn't sink in.

"Aren't you in town to see it?" said Joe with surprise. "A total solar eclipse coincides with the Crossroads Harvest Festival this year."

"No, I saw news reports on the eclipse, of course, but didn't realize this was the right spot, and I'm actually here on business…" *Stop babbling.* Meg scrawled her signature and gawked at Elaina. "Mr. Bingham made the reservation over a year ago. You're positive?"

"Yes, right before he left town."

Meg's voice dropped and she leaned forward. "Is he…is he strange?"

Elaina exchanged puzzled looks with the others and Becky jumped in. "Not in the least. Isaac is a lovely man. He had a law practice. I'm a paralegal and used to work for him before he retired. Haven't you met?"

"No, there was this letter and a meeting, but I don't know who…at the festival…funnel cake…" *Geez, stop babbling already.* "Um, the key?" Meg added weakly.

Elaina handed the key to her husband. "Joe will take the luggage and show you to the room."

Meg turned away with the definite impression a mental message flashed between the two women. The details weren't hard to guess.

Elaina: The only strange person around these parts is this chick.

Becky: Bless her soul, I hope she remembered to pack her medication.

Joe escorted Meg to the top floor. He unlocked the door, set the suitcase inside, and handed her the key. "You have the largest suite with the best view. If you need anything, please don't hesitate to tell me or one of the staff."

"Thank you. So, when is the eclipse?"

"Sunday at noon. You're staying, aren't you?"

"I'm not certain. It depends on how my meeting goes. By any chance, did Mr. Bingham leave a message for me?"

"No, sorry," he said. "Hope your business keeps you around to see the eclipse. You don't have to check out until Monday, and it would be a shame to miss it. When will any of us get the chance to be in the middle of something as strange as this again?"

"It's something strange, for sure," said Meg dryly.

Joe shut the door as he left. Meg surveyed the suite, and her nervous hesitancy evaporated as fast as an ice cube on a hot plate. "Wow. If this is corporate headquarters for a cult, sign me up."

Cozy oozed from every corner. The room had a quirky shape with odd angles, befitting an old inn. Against one wall was a large antique brass bed covered with a quilt. Meg sat on the mattress and gave an experimental bounce. A wide grin erupted across her face. The super cushy mattress certainly exceeded her modern standards of comfort. Tucked into an alcove were a loveseat, two armchairs, and a coffee table. Oil paintings as well as watercolors decorated the walls while a cherry sideboard held a vase of fresh flowers, a coffee maker, packets of teas, and a plate of sugar cookies. Their sweet vanilla scent perfumed the air better than any artificial freshener. The bathroom even had a clawfoot tub along with a large marble-tiled shower.

French doors to a balcony let in fading autumn light. Meg swung open the doors and stepped past a pair of rocking chairs, leaning her elbows on the railing. Across the road were the festival grounds, nestled against the entrance to a cornfield maze. Meg squinted. Some kind of structure stood in the middle. She wondered idly if she could determine the correct path through the maze from her vantage point, but the wind gusted and the waving, twisting stalks obscured the route.

Meg arched her back and stretched. Sitting in a car for hours left her muscles in knots. A stroll outside before dinner was just the ticket. She grabbed the sugar cookies off the plate and nibbled on them as she crossed the street. The main gate to the harvest festival was roped off and the entrance to the parking lot blocked with barrels. Most of the workers must have either gone home or to dinner.

Without people, the harvest festival grounds had an eerie silence—a ghost town preparing for a celebration. What do the dead celebrate? mused Meg. Were they envious of this world; bound to it, yet always apart? Maybe ghosts needed the living. Without people, the dead had no one to resent. Perhaps, the only thing a wandering spirit could hope for then was the end of days and nothing left to mourn.

Meg strolled past rows of corn and stopped at the entrance to the maze. Stalks reached high overhead, intercepting the last rays of the sun. In the murky half-light, their shadows intertwined and stretched as if to swallow the field, the harvest festival, and then the town.

"What secrets are you hiding?" she murmured.

A breeze kicked up a pile of dried leaves at her feet. The stalks swayed together in a whispery chorus, a muted conversation not quite audible to human ears. Despite the heat, Meg shivered and headed back to the inn where cheerful lights and tantalizing aromas beckoned her inside. She enjoyed an excellent dinner and added an extra-large tip to the paid-in-full check, courtesy of the enigmatic Isaac Bingham and his apparently imaginary relative, Phillip.

Meg returned to her room, made a cup of herbal tea, and took it to a rocking chair on the balcony. She settled down and sipped her drink, idly swaying to and fro. Stars twinkled in the velvety black sky. Across the road, the Crossroads Harvest Festival stood poised, awaiting Friday's crowds.

An air of excited anticipation filled her. Who would she meet at the festival? What was this mysterious offer in society's best interest? Who talked like that to describe a simple employment opportunity for a number cruncher? Her gaze drifted once more to the corn maze, but the pitch-black field revealed none of its secrets.

****

On Friday morning, Cal headed for the festival grounds, forcing his steps to maintain a brisk pace instead of breaking into a run. He hadn't slept well, mulling over Isaac's strange story most of the night. How could a person who died years before his birth have intimate details of his life, and why the interest in Cal MacGregor? The only logical conclusion was that Isaac was a liar and fed him a big chunk of baloney. Logical, yes, but that didn't jibe with the kind, honest, caring, man he knew and respected.

As opening time neared, Cal's excitement grew. Even if this turned out to be nothing more than a twisted joke, he wanted the punchline. He approached the Crossroads Inn and a young woman with hair pulled back in a ponytail bounded down the steps and joined the crowd streaming toward the fairgrounds. "Glad you didn't have to sleep in the corn maze," he said to himself.

Cal waited with burgeoning impatience through the blah-blah-blah speeches from town officials. He idly scanned the audience and spotted Ponytail again. She was by herself, shuffling back and forth on her feet. Unconsciously, he smiled. Ponytail appeared as impatient for the grounds to open as him. Finally, the last speaker walked to the podium, an astronomer from the state university. He was mercifully brief and invited people to stop by a booth to ask questions about the eclipse and pick up free viewing sunglasses.

"Remember," he added, "never peer directly at the eclipse without them. We'll have a screen for our telescope to project the big event. Meanwhile, at night you can watch the stars. The eclipse will be unforgettable, so keep your fingers crossed for cloudless skies on Sunday."

The festival opened. Cal walked past a few booths and then stopped short with a rueful shake of his head. Now what? Where was he supposed to go? Who was he supposed to find? He wandered aimlessly by games of chance, agriculture and livestock displays, and craft items for sale before his nose drew him to the heavy scent of fried food. He used the voucher for a funnel cake. The girl with the ponytail was there, too, at the back of the line. She rose on tiptoes, neck craning to search the crowd. She must have gotten separated from her friends.

Cal ambled past the last row of booths, nibbling the funnel cake. Its pillowy sweetness did nothing to quell the irritation rising with every step. He was hot and exasperated, Isaac's bizarre mission sounded crazier by the second. *What the hell am I doing here? I have no idea who I'm supposed to find. This is pointless. Go home.* He made an abrupt about-face and nearly smacked into Amaranth Goldstein. She stood motionless with her index fingers pressed to the sides of her temples.

"Oh, hi, Amaranth." Cal quickly licked his fingers

and brushed a crumb of powdered sugar off his shirt. "Didn't see you there. Enjoying the festival?"

Her face lit up. "Immensely. The metaphysical vibrations are screaming. Can you feel them?"

"Sorry, no."

"That's too bad, but some of us are more sensitive to elements from beyond the earthly plane than others. George's corn maze is throbbing with intense psychic fluctuations. The members in the chat room disagree, but I say they're every bit as powerful as the Astra Noctis in 1906."

"The what?"

"Astra Noctis—the rare time when the planetary confluences fall into proper celestial alignment and thins the boundary between our world and the other realms. Of course, that didn't coincide with an eclipse, so it wasn't nearly as powerful as the one will be on Sunday. Even so, I urged everyone in the chat room to stay on high alert." She glared in the direction of the corn maze. "I told George, and he only snorted at me."

With a great deal of effort, Cal didn't snicker. "I'm sure the confluences will work themselves out."

"Oh, no, they never do. Not without help." Amaranth grabbed his arm. "Everyone must be on guard against the confluence. What if the veil thins beyond renewal? Who around here is prepared for that?"

"I'm not sure," he said, wondering how to politely make a break for it and still retain her as a client.

"Exactly. No one is, but even that woman at the entrance to the maze agreed they were particularly strong."

I'll bet she did, and I'll bet she didn't roll her eyes

29

until after you left.

"I hoped to have Summer spread the word, but she seems to have disappeared. Will you mention it to people?"

"Um, okay." Cal gently removed her arm and nodded over his shoulder. "I'll go that way and you go the other. We'll cover more ground."

Amaranth beamed Cal such an air of gratitude guilt washed through him. It didn't last long as she hurried off without hesitation in the opposite direction. Cal skirted a booth and ducked out of sight before Amaranth circled back again. Straight ahead were rows of lush green corn, and Cal picked up the pace. The one place in the harvest festival he was sure not to run into Amaranth and her lunatic ideas was the maze. She had already covered that section.

As Cal neared the field, he heard muffled squeals of laughter and shuffling footsteps. The stalks rustled but grew so close together he couldn't make out the shapes of any people.

"Not that way!" laughed a girl. "You're running us in circles."

"I told you, I know where I'm going. Hey—wait up."

She laughed again. "Gotta catch me."

The voices died away, but they sounded suspiciously like Dylan Lydecker and Summer, Amaranth's daughter. Cal wondered idly if Dylan's appearance in his uncle's maze meant a change in his rock song's lyrics. If so, he had to credit Dylan with more sense than he thought possible or maybe it was Summer's steadying influence. While Dylan seemed to flounder since he moved here, Summer had already planned to attend the local college's agricultural program after graduation in the spring, and she was certainly pretty enough to draw any young man's attention.

Cal stopped short. The young woman with the ponytail was at the entrance to the maze. Was she the one Amaranth approached? She stood by herself, studying a group of people leaving the exit. Cal watched her, curiosity rising. *Who comes to a harvest festival alone—except an idiot like me on a wild goose chase?*

He froze. It couldn't be. Cal walked up to her, and she eyed him with clear anticipation. "Excuse me, are you by any chance waiting for someone..." He rubbed the nape of his neck. "I can't figure out how to say this and not sound crazy."

Her eyes widened. "Someone I don't know?"

He grinned and held out his hand. "Callum MacGregor, call me Cal."

"Megan Adler—Meg." She shook his hand. The warmth of her skin pressed against his brought a pleasant tingling sensation.

"So, Cal," Meg said. "Why meet here? What does this festival have to do with a job?" She flashed a cheeky grin. "I should warn you I don't work the carny circuit."

A job? An uneasy sensation settled in his gut. "I've no idea. I thought you knew why we were here."

"Me?" Meg pulled back her hand and color rose to her cheeks. "What is this? Some kind of sick joke? Who does this Phillip Bingham think he is, anyway?"

Cal gaped at her. "Phillip Bingham contacted you? Not Isaac?"

"I got a letter from him with a vague employment offer from the Lux Foundation along with an invitation to attend the Crossroads Harvest Festival." She wrinkled her brow. "It was a funny kind of letter on really old paper. The room at the inn was paid for by a man named Isaac Bingham, and I needed a job, so I figured what the hell. The instructions said a person would find me here to discuss the details. I assume that is you." Her voice tightened in anger. "Is Phillip Bingham the town lunatic?"

"No, but I'm sorry to tell you he's very much dead." Cal gave her a recap of his meeting with Isaac.

As Meg listened, her eyes widened in astonishment. "Phillip Bingham died decades ago? How could he know I'd lose my job this week and be desperate enough to jump at this crazy offer?"

Cal ran a hand through his hair. "How did he know either of us would even be born?"

Meg took a wary step back. "I'm not sure I believe you."

"I'm not sure I believe it myself. Listen, do you want to go somewhere and talk? Try to figure this out? I'll call Isaac, tell him we found each other, and demand an explanation."

Meg cocked her head toward the entrance of the corn maze. "Do you hear that? Someone called for help."

"Probably lost in the maze. George made it extra challenging this year."

"No, it's different." She sucked in a breath. "M-my name—I swear I heard my name."

A gust of wind rippled the stalks. They bent toward the entrance, fluttery hands beckoning them inside. Cal strained to hear past the whispery rustle of the leaves.

Almost as if they were voices...

"I'll check it out," he said. "Maybe someone fell and got hurt. Wait here—"

"Not a chance." Meg bolted into the maze, and Cal ran after her. They came to the first intersection, and she skidded to a halt. "Which way?"

"Left," Cal said without hesitation.

They dashed deeper into the field, now left, now right, now straight ahead. With each step, Cal's path became surer as if something pulled him with an invisible cord.

Meg puffed beside him. "How do you know which way to go?"

"I-I can't explain it."

With every breath, the air around Cal became hotter and more oppressive, pressing on his shoulders like a stifling blanket. Humidity dropped to nothing. Beads of sweat on his brow evaporated. Cal licked his dry, cracked lips and grimaced at the gritty feel of sand on his tongue.

Sand in a corn maze?

They turned a corner and stumbled into a clearing. In the center was an arbor that arched over a circle of flagstones on the ground. A glowing flame hovered above the stones, suspended in midair. Meg and Cal exchanged dumbfounded looks and stepped forward. The clarion note of a distant horn sounded a soldier's call to action. A surge of adrenaline flooded Cal's veins. He hadn't felt like this since his days on patrol with the Army. Unconsciously, Cal's hand went to his hip, reaching for the sword. He stared at his empty hand. *Sword?*

The flame grew larger and brighter, shooting through the arbor into the heavens.

"Cal!" Meg's voice sounded very far away.

"I'm here!" Cal reached for her, but the flame blinded him, blotting out the maze, blotting out the sun, blotting out the world.

Nothing remained but the roar of the cheering crowd.

Part II: Umbra

Chapter One

The crowd spilled outside the city gates lining both sides of the road. A roar went up as the army came in sight.

"The people love you, my lord," shouted Rammat.

Prince Ashur-etil-ilani acknowledged the cheers with a wave of his hand. "The people love a victory, and I happen to bring it."

"Not so, my lord. Their pride overflows at how easily you crushed Babylon's enemies and returned home with treasure to honor the gods."

"Easily?" His jaw tightened. "Tell that to my soldiers lying dead on the battlefield."

His aide-de-camp regarded him with surprise. "War always exacts a cost, lord. Thank the gods our enemies paid a higher price."

Ashur untied the goat bladder full of water from the saddle and swallowed deeply to wash the sand from his mouth. His eyes squinted in the brilliant sun as he scanned faces in the crowd. "None of the royal household are here."

"I dispatched a messenger this morning to the palace with word of the army's triumphant arrival. He returned to say King Ashurbanipal waits at the temple to offer thanks for his eldest son's safe return and accept the tributes of war for the great Marduk's blessings."

Tributes of war? Ashur shot a glance over his shoulder. A long line of men, horses, and wagons heavily laden with treasure stretched past the earthen dikes and irrigated fields outside the city gates. Many soldiers marched behind him, but far fewer than months ago when the campaign began. He grieved the loss of every one. Soon, the roars of the crowd would mix with the wails of new widows and their fatherless children. The only real tribute from war was blood and more war.

"You are deep in thought, my lord."

Ashur rubbed the back of his neck. No need to burden Rammat with his melancholy. "The road was long. Weariness is upon me."

Rammat jabbed him in the side. "We are home, my lord, and the palace concubines can do much to make a man forget his aches and pains."

Ashur grunted. "At the moment, I prefer a bath and a funnel cake."

Rammat shot him a puzzled expression. "Funnel cake?"

For an instant, blurred images flashed through the prince's mind; strange sights and smells, tall green stalks with yellow tassels, a bright light, and a woman with her hair gathered at the nape of her neck to resemble a horse's tail. Ashur reined his mount to a halt. What had happened?

"My lord?" Rammat regarded him with concern. "Are you ill?"

"No." Ashur forced a smile. "Simply enjoying the view of the city." He brushed away the remains of the disturbing vision. No, not a vision or illness, simply the effect of the heat and too many weary days on the trail. His aide appeared unconvinced, so Ashur dug his heels into the horse's sides. With a prancing sidestep, the stallion bounded ahead. "Let us not keep the king waiting."

The army thundered over the bridge spanning the great moat surrounding the city. Ashur took in the view of the massive lion-headed Ishtar Gate with pride. Covered in brilliant blue lapis lazuli glazed bricks, the façade glimmered under the rays of the sun. Babylon, the jewel of creation, the center of learning and culture, the city his father conquered, but spared. No other place on Earth approached its magnificence.

Ashur passed the towering outer wall, fifty royal cubits in width and two hundred in height and led his army down the main boulevard. A boisterous throng lined the streets, their shouts deafening as the treasure wagons came in sight. He passed the entrance to the palace and the Hanging Gardens and inhaled deeply. A whiff of sweet jasmine tickled his nostrils.

The Hanging Gardens were a masterpiece of engineering. Ascending terraces sloped up a hillside. The tier on tier effect created a giant amphitheater with the uppermost galley nearly fifty cubits high. Rich earth piled on each supported the roots of the largest trees. Ground level was planted with foliage of every kind, paved with brick walkways, and dotted with fountains. The designers determined to bring pleasure to any beholder, no matter where their sights fell.

Members of the king's household waved as his entourage passed. The shape of the sloped terraces allowed for construction of royal apartments strewn among the grounds as if they were so many blossoms.

Prince Ashur's own quarters were near the hidden screw-like lifting machines supplying water from the Tigris and Euphrates rivers. The designers kept the mechanics from the public's sight to maintain the picturesque view and increase the wonder of the garden. As a child, Ashur marveled at the complex engineering. When the time came to select marriage quarters, he chose to live by the sound of constantly running water. His late wife, Hassmira, voiced no complaint, but he sensed her disappointment with the small, less opulent chambers. She spent as little time there as possible and preferred the grandeur of the palace and socializing with ladies of the court.

Once past the Hanging Gardens, the streets widened to the Processional Way, a red and yellow brick-paved corridor over half a mile long. Enameled images of lions, bulls, dragons, and flowers adorned the walls on each side along with inscriptions containing prayers from the king to the Babylonian gods.

At the end of the Processional Way was the Temple of Marduk; a giant ziggurat built of clay and stone, with huge square towers and crenellated terraces. The sacred shrine at the top contained a statue of the great god and had a commanding view of the city. Underneath were elaborate halls, storehouses, living quarters, and holy sanctums to perform rituals to retain the favor of the divine.

Prince Ashur's heart quickened at the sight of his father. King Ashurbanipal waited at the entrance to the ziggurat, surrounded by members of the royal court and the priests and priestesses of the temple. Ashur reined in his horse and dismounted. He strode to his father and dropped to his knees. "My king. I return victorious with tribute for the temple."

King Ashurbanipal grasped Ashur by the shoulders. "Arise, my son." Ashur stood, and the king drew him into a warm embrace. "Welcome home. Your presence was sorely missed." He held him out to arm's length. "My heart rejoices to see you unharmed."

"Thank you, Father."

Ashur's fraternal twin, Prince Sin-sharish-kun, stepped forward and embraced him. "Welcome, brother," he murmured in his ear. "All of Babylon revels in your glory and does you honor. You are truly a worthy successor to our father."

A prickle of irritation inched up Ashur's spine. What was it in Sin's tone? Why did compliments from him always seem to bear the sting of hidden insults? "Thank you, brother."

The king clapped Ashur on the shoulder. "I'm sure you are weary from your travels. Let us have the high priest bless the gifts for the temple and then we can retire to the palace where the rest of the court awaits your arrival. I have commanded a banquet in your honor."

Ashur motioned for Rammat to have the men bring the temple's allotment, twenty chests filled with precious items and sparkling jewels. High Priest Balu-su stepped forward to receive the offerings. He thanked Marduk for Prince Ashur-etil-ilani's victory and safe return and then uttered prayers over the bounty. With the blessing complete, a coterie of priests and priestesses scurried to take the chests into the temple.

They scrambled to obey, and Ashur's lips twitched in a faint smile. *All the number crunchers are hopping today.* His smile faded. Number crunchers?

A young priestess knelt to lift the casket of pearls at Ashur's feet. As she rose, her eyes met his. An eerie rush of familiarity surged through Ashur as if he should have her name on his tongue. The priestess flushed. She turned quickly away and mounted the stairs. Ashur drew in a breath. Her hair was tightly gathered with a gold fastener at the base of her neck and resembled a horse's tail.

****

A lock fell into the damp ink on the papyrus and with an impatient tug Nemra bunched her hair at the neck and secured it with the gold fastener.

"There you are! Hurry, they're coming!" Tal-banit's squeal of excitement broke Nemra's concentration on the scroll. "Prince Ashur-etil-ilani is within sight of the main gate. The king arrived at the temple with his retinue, and High Priest Balu-su ordered the chosen of Marduk to assemble for the blessing and acceptance of the offerings." Her eyes held a dreamy gaze. "I wonder what treasures await?"

Nemra's attention returned to the column of figures. "They await Marduk, not any of us."

"At least you touch everything during the count," Tal-banit said with a pout.

"I keep records for the temple," said Nemra. "I don't own the tribute."

"But if the allotment is great, Balu-su will allow us to choose pieces for ourselves after securing the temple's share. Won't he?" Tal-banit added with concern.

"Yes, as is tradition. You better hurry."

"I'll wait for you."

Nemra bit back a sigh. She'd never finish with the

girl's constant chatter in her ear. "I must complete these calculations first. I'll be there shortly."

"Balu-su won't be happy if you're late," she warned over her shoulder.

"Plenty of time," Nemra murmured. "I don't even hear the crowd yet." She lifted her brush from the parchment and gazed contentedly out the window at the Hanging Gardens in the distance. Such a peaceful scene always made her work go faster. This was her favorite spot in the library although technically she broke a strict rule by being in a restricted area. The racks surrounding her climbed to the ceiling and held astrological scrolls, but they were only for the eyes of High Priest Balu-su.

I'm not looking at the scrolls. I'm seated at the desk, looking out the window.

Nemra bent her head to the parchment, tracing her finger along the row of recently entered figures. The numbers instantly ordered in her head, aligning in perfect harmony, the same as the stars in the sky. Numbers told her everything; the annual barley yield, the tonnage of ore from a copper mine, the contents of the caravans passing through the Ishtar Gate in a year. Numbers had wisdom hidden in their depths, and it was Nemra's duty to puzzle it out. With the proper numbers, a person could see into the future and learn whether Babylon's fields would produce enough crops to prevent starvation or which trade routes would prove to be the most profitable and bring the highest prices for goods at distant markets. Numbers even predicted the movement of the stars and the moon.

Or whether the sun will die, shrouding the world in eternal night.

Nemra shivered, briskly rubbing her hands up and down her bare arms, using friction to allay a sudden chill. Why did such a strange thought enter her head? She put aside the calculations. As she rose from the stool, her sandaled foot brushed against a soft object. Under the table was a papyrus roll bearing the official mark of Balu-su on the scroll bar. Nemra glanced around the room. Balu-su secured the sacred astrological charts to the shelves with locks and chains and he had the only key. On a shelf near the ceiling was a slight gap, wide enough to fit a single scroll. He must have worked on them earlier and this one fell unnoticed under the table.

Nemra reached for the scroll and her hand froze. Only Balu-su had the authority to touch sacred writings, but she certainly couldn't leave the scroll there. Nemra snatched it off the floor, and it fell open. One glimpse at the columns of figures and curiosity seized her. The high priest was in the process of updating the king's astrological chart. The scroll contained Balu-su's notations for the rotation of the five planets twirling among the stars in an endless celestial dance.

The numbers called to her as if they had a voice. Nemra glanced over her shoulder and then surrendered to temptation and examined the high priest's entries. The phases of the moon waxed and waned in comforting familiarity. Night always followed day and the track of the sun across Anu, the heavens. Two magical orbs, one cool and changing, one hot and constant, keeping evil at bay and the universe ordered in perfect harmony.

No. Not quite.

Her brows knit together in a frown. Was there an

error? Nemra did a series of quick calculations in her head and her distress deepened. To accept the high priest's mathematics threw the entire chart out of alignment and produced a different map for the sun and moon. The results were inconceivable, skewing the ordained path of celestial bodies. How had Balu-su not noticed?

Nemra gnawed at her lip. Balu-su, High Priest of Marduk and the kingdom's chief astrologer, didn't take kindly to corrections. Nor would he be pleased to learn she had been in a restricted area, but surely this information must be brought to his attention. Nemra's head jerked up at a roar from the crowd outside. She hurriedly rolled the scroll and then went to the nearest window overlooking the entrance to the temple. Directly below, the king and the royal retinue waited at the bottom of the steps. In the distance was Prince Ashur-etil-ilani on horseback, leading his troops along the Processional Way.

If she arrived late to the ceremony, Balu-su would scarcely hold his tongue. Nemra left the astrological chart on the table. She grabbed her accounting scroll, placed it in the workroom, and then ran to the temple entrance. Everyone's attention focused on the arrival of the prince. Nemra slipped into place behind Balu-su and exhaled a soft breath of relief. He turned his head and scowled in disapproval. "You are late, priestess."

By the gods, the man had the ears of a bat. She bowed her head. "I beg forgiveness. I was in the midst of accounting—"

The shouts of the crowd drowned out her words.

"I do not have time for excuses now," snapped Balu-su. "The prince approaches. Mind on your duties, priestess."

"Yes, lord." She gave thanks to the noisy raucous that interrupted what would surely have been one of Balu-su's tirades. Not that he hadn't set it aside for later. Balu-su never missed an opportunity to lecture an underling.

Nemra regarded the approach of Prince Ashur-etil-ilani with interest. She had only glimpsed him a few times since committing to the temple. He lacked the refined features of his brother who often visited Balu-su in his capacity as the king's representative. Though to her mind, his countenance reflected a noble bearing absent in his sibling, younger by only twenty minutes. Curious, the accident of fate. Had they held different positions in the womb, Prince Sin-sharish-kun would now receive the accolades of the temple and his brother relegated to an unimportant position in the palace.

Her heart softened as Prince Ashur-etil-ilani neared the steps. A rush of unexpected warmth lifted Nemra's spirits as if greeting the return of a friend who completed an arduous journey. She shook her head. Strange thoughts to have on the approach of nobility. They were rulers, nothing more.

The prince's procession halted in front of the royal entourage, and Balu-su descended the stairs in preparation for delivery of the blessing.

"The prince looks tired," Nemra whispered to Tal-banit.

She snickered. "He looks rich to me."

Balu-su did honor to Marduk and lauded Prince Ashur-etil-ilani for his safe return with tributes for the great god's temple. With formalities completed, he signaled first for the librarians to secure the scrolls and clay tablets. Along with royal treasuries, foreign libraries were always emptied during military campaigns and the contents brought as gifts to the temple. Preserving the wisdom of the world bestowed additional glory on Marduk.

With the library's new acquisitions removed, Balu-su signaled for the priests and priestesses to gather the treasure. Nemra scurried down the steps and bent over to pick up a casket of pearls at the feet of the prince. She stood up and their eyes met.

Corn-maze-fire-Cal.

Blood pounded in Nemra's ears. She turned away and stumbled up the stairs, gripping the handles of the casket so tightly, her knuckles were white. What was that? What had happened? For an instant, a terrifying spiral of words and images flooded her mind; a maze constructed from green stalks, fire, the face of a stranger, yet mirroring that of the prince. Him and not him. The man reached for her and called out a name.

"Meg," she whispered.

Not her own, alien on her tongue, but at the same time felt true. Had she gone mad? Nemra reached the portico at the top, fighting the urge to turn and peer at the prince again. Swallowing hard, she entered the temple and leaned against the cool stone, struggling to regain composure. The heat…it must be the heat. The temperature had been oppressive the past few days even this late in the season.

Tal-banit hurried to her side, balancing an ornamental bronze urn on her hip. "I watched him," she said softly. "His eyes followed you up the stairs."

Nemra's heart sank. Had Balu-su noticed her stumble? If so, a scathing rebuke was in store on her inability to show proper deference to the gods. "Balu-su?"

"No, Prince Ashur-etil-ilani."

Nemra blinked in surprise and drew herself up. "Don't be foolish. The prince has no interest in a priestess of the temple. Come, we must hurry to the counting room before Balu-su notes our absence. I am already due one lecture today and rather not have two."

They hurried to the inner staircase and continued to climb, passing living quarters for the clergy and their servants. Next was the entrance to majestic halls filled with scrolls and clay tablets, the great library of Babylon. Nemra came to the most heavily guarded section with the counting antechamber and the massive treasure room. Her attention strayed to the stairway leading to a trap door. The final floor directly overhead held the great pavilion at the top of the ziggurat where the power of Marduk on Earth resided.

Balu-su stood in the center of the counting antechamber, supervising the unloading of the treasure. Nemra deposited the casket of pearls and hurried to his side. "A fine offering, the richest yet."

The high priest's expression was impassive. "Not even a tenth of the spoils."

Was Balu-su disappointed with the prince? How much more did he expect? "Surely, Marduk's pleasure will be great," said Nemra. "He will bestow a multitude of blessings upon the city."

Balu-su grunted. "You may begin the count, priestess."

Nemra sat at a desk and a servant brought her an ink pot, brush, and papyrus, the first of many. Clerics emptied the casks and Nemra carefully noted their contents. Hours passed. Figures filled scrolls, and servants brought more.

One wooden box contained only a single item; a headpiece in a simple drawstring pouch. The front was polished blue enamel inset with an inlay of the sun made from golden glass beads, rays spread wide in welcoming arms. Next to the sun was a full moon of luminous nacre. More glass beads surrounded them both, clear this time, to resemble a scattering of stars in a daylight sky.

Nemra lifted the headpiece, gazing at it with a vague sense of disquiet. How strange to see the sun and the moon in the sky at the same time as the stars. She had never come across anything similar and, yet, it possessed an eerie familiarity. Despite exquisite craftsmanship, the headpiece had little value compared to the other treasures. Indeed, it was almost plain and had a flaw; two tips of the sun's rays had broken. She ran her thumb across the smooth inlaid surface and pulled back with a start. No flaw, but part of the intricate design. As if the artist wished to picture the moon in purposeful advance, slowly swallowing the light of the sun.

Nemra hastily returned the headpiece to the pouch. She entered the description and then remembered Balu-su's scroll and bit her lip. No doubt another lecture, but it couldn't be helped. "With pardon, High Priest. May I have a word?"

Balu-su halted his wanderings among the spoils and stood at her side. "Have you finished?"

"No, my Lord, but this morning I was in the library and noticed one of your scrolls on the floor."

"Which one?"

"An astrology chart. I picked it up."

His posture stiffened. "Why were you in a forbidden section?"

"Working on the harvest accounting," she added in a rush. "That room of the library is very quiet. I disturbed nothing, my lord."

Balu-su's face reddened. "The astrological charts are sacred and the sole dominion of the high priest. Touching them is forbidden."

Nemra bowed her head. "I ask pardon, Lord Balu-su, and meant no disrespect but couldn't leave a scroll of such high importance on the floor." She dared to look at him. "I-it was unsecured, and I happened to notice the calculations and a possible error."

To her surprise, a heated rebuke wasn't the high priest's immediate response. Instead, an undefined emotion passed across his face. "What did you see?"

Nemra squirmed under his hawkish gaze. "A number may have been entered incorrectly. The paths of the sun and the moon appeared…" She hunted for a word. "Illogical."

"I have never found fault with your calculations," Balu-su said coolly, "so I will recheck the scroll but forbid you from entering that section of the library again or speak of this to anyone. Astrological charts are not the concern of the lower clergy. Now, continue your duties."

"Yes, lord."

He returned to the treasure room. Nemra, bemused, began the count again. No shouting? No calling attention to her faults in front of others. The value of the tribute to the temple must have put the high priest in an exceptionally good mood. That wasn't the angry reaction she anticipated. Not at all.

Nemra completed the accounting late in the day. Temple guards carried the last of the containers into the treasure room and sealed the door. To Nemra's relief, Balu-su hurried away without a word. She stretched the cramps from her shoulders. While others went to the main hall to begin the celebratory feast, Nemra hesitated. The high priest expected his clerics to attend, but the long arduous day put her in the mood for quiet first. Surely, no one would notice her absence for a few minutes, long enough to enjoy a cup of spiced wine alone in her room.

A shortcut to her quarters led past the entrance to the library. The halls were quiet. The librarians had already left to attend the feast, no doubt discussing the size of their treasure allotment from Balu-su in comparison with the clergy. Her lips twisted in a wry smile. If it's one thing Babylonians were good at, it's number crunching.

Nemra stopped short. Number crunching? What a strange term. Where had she heard it before?

Up ahead, Balu-su exited the library with a scroll under his arm. Her heart skipped a beat. She ducked behind a pillar and peered with curiosity from the shadows. Was that the astrological scroll with the error? Did the high priest plan to check the calculations now?

Balu-su went directly to a portico across from the entrance to the library. In the center was a solid gold basin filled with oil and lit with an eternal flame to honor Marduk. He glanced around, and Nemra's eyes widened in disbelief as Balu-su tossed the scroll in the fire. The high priest turned his face away and stepped back as the flame spit and roared. Embers fluttered in a glowing trail to the ceiling. As the fire died, Balu-su fixed his attention on the basin until the flame returned to normal. Without a backward glance, he strode in the direction of the great hall.

Nemra pressed against the pillar, pulse racing, as the echo of Balu-su's sandaled feet died away. She darted into the library and went directly to the anteroom with the view of the Hanging Gardens. The astrological chart wasn't on the table. She peered overhead, but the empty space on the rack was still there. Balu-su hadn't returned the scroll.

"H-he took it to his quarters earlier," Nemra whispered to herself. "Of course, that must be it." With a sinking feeling, she left the library and ran to the portico. The scroll in the basin was nothing but ashes. Out of the corner of her eye, she spotted a scrap of burnt papyrus on the floor that miraculously escaped the flames. Nemra picked it up and gaped in shock at astrological figures inscribed in Balu-su's precise hand. Only one explanation was possible.

The High Priest of Marduk, steward of the Great God's will, willingly committed blasphemy by destroying a sacred scroll.

Chapter Two

Ashur emerged dripping from the bath. A slave handed him a linen cloth, heated by stones warmed in a fire. He wrapped himself as more slaves towel-dried his body and hair. By the gods, it was good to wash off the dirt. He had begun to smell worse than his horse.

Servants laid out finery for the reception, but Ashur dismissed everyone with a wave of his hand. After the constant company of raucous warriors these last months, he wished for only the quiet of his thoughts. Ashur slipped on the sandals, fringed tunic, and the new belt holding a jeweled dagger and sheath, the latter gifts from his father to celebrate his return.

A sweet floral scent tickled his nostrils, and he inhaled deeply. Night blooming jasmine from the Hanging Gardens grew outside his chamber, a scent that always reminded him of home. With the gods' continued blessings, peace would remain in Babylon and war nothing more than a distant memory.

One of his brother's servants entered the room and bowed low. "Forgive me the interruption, Your Highness, but Prince Sin-sharish-kun—"

"Sent you to tell me he is outside."

"Yes, lord."

So typical of Sin to dispatch a servant when a knock on the door from him sufficed. Like the scent of night blooming jasmine, some things never changed.

"Then I won't keep him."

Sin waited in the garden. "Father sent me to fetch you. Everyone has gathered in the great hall." His eyes went to the new belt and dagger. "A generous gift for Babylon's most able general."

"Thank you, Sin. How was life in the palace during my absence? Father mentioned in a dispatch you offered to assume his duties as liaison to the temple. That was thoughtful of you. Dealing with High Priest Balu-su can be…" He sought for a word that wasn't insulting.

"Taxing?" said his brother with a grin. "I can handle Balu-su and am happy to assist Father in a small manner to ease his burden. The mantle of kingship is heavy. It weighs upon him more each year. As the crown will not fall to me, I hope to find similar ways to ease your burden in the future, too."

"As ever, brother, I am grateful for your loyalty."

A cheering crowd greeted Ashur's arrival at the banquet hall. His father embraced him and led Ashur to a seat at his side. New additions from the treasure horde reserved for the palace already graced the table, masterly crafted bronze vessels holding sweetmeats and two glittering gold cups filled to the brim with spiced wine. One sat in front of the king and the other at Ashur's place. Servants scurried with trays offering selections of Babylon's finest provisions; meat, fish, and fowl roasted with marrows and onions. Bowls full of apples, figs, and pomegranates. Dishes of peas, beans, lettuces, and wild mushrooms with warm bread and fresh cheeses.

As Ashur ate his fill, the king requested details of the campaign. Ashur bit back a smile at the gleam in his father's eyes when talk turned to battle victories; the old warrior, no doubt, relived past glories while he listened to the accomplishments of his son. Although bound by blood and the destiny of monarchy, father and son had at least one glaring difference. Ashurbanipal reveled in the glory of war while Ashur-etil-ilani only wished for continued peace.

The king leaned toward him. "Now that you are home, my son, we must consider the future of the kingdom. The mourning period for Hassmira has long ended. I have sent the king of Elam the offer of a marriage contract between you and his daughter. Balu-su assured me the next full moon will be an auspicious time to bind our realms, and the gods will grant you many sons."

"As you wish, Father."

Ashur didn't ask the name of his future betrothed. He didn't care. The marriage would be arranged as was his wedding to Hassmira, a princess from a distant kingdom. He barely recalled her face now. They met on their wedding day and despite due diligence to produce an heir, none came before she died of a fever. In truth, his mourning period was due to court protocol rather than sentiment. He had no romantic feelings for Hassmira, and she made it plain once she bore an heir she had no jealousy if he turned his attention to concubines until her body recovered enough to have another child. Such was the life of members of the royal court. Each accepted their place and fulfilled expected duties.

His thoughts drifted to the throngs of women and children at the gates this morning and their joy at the return of soldier husbands, fathers, and sons. No woman cheered his return with love in her heart. Would his new wife mourn him as a man if his life ended on the battlefield, or would the bigger regret be the loss of status and prestige as royal protocol forced her to step aside for her son's wife to become the new queen? An image flashed through his mind of the priestess on the temple steps that morning. Would she grant obeisance easily to a new monarch? That her heart might be heavy at his death brought strange comfort.

Ashur rose from his seat. Such melancholy had no place at a celebration. "If you will excuse me, Father, the journey was long, and I shall retire early."

"As you wish, my son. We will speak again tomorrow."

Ashur exited the banquet hall. Overcome by sudden restlessness, he wandered off the path leading to his quarters and deeper into the garden. Everyone was at the celebration, and peaceful solitude soon enveloped him. The only sound was his soft footfalls and the soothing rustle of the leaves.

The moon shone bright, dappling plants on either side of the path with pure silver light. His steps took him to a pool ringed by date palms and he peered into the depths. The circular reflection of Sin glistened in the water; Sin, the God of the Moon, his brother's guiding deity. Ashur idly tossed in a pebble, and ripples shattered the image. As the water stilled, the orb reformed. Nothing stopped the moon except the return of the sun in the arms of Anu the following day. Such was the will of the gods.

In the distance, a horse neighed. The sound brought to Ashur's mind the young priestess of the temple, her hair bound to resemble a horse's tail. Hardly the style of fashionable ladies of the court. Her keen eyes reflected deep intelligence. They caught his gaze and, for a moment, it seemed as if a bridge built between them. What would he find if he crossed to the other side? Ashur had a strong suspicion this one wouldn't bow to conformity or mimic Hassmira and offer nothing but dutiful, silent compliance. This one had a spark. A spark could become a fire, and a fire could light the way.

Ashur's gaze lifted to the moon. "To what?"

The God Sin held no answer. Ashur snorted in disgust. "No doubt to a lecture from both Balu-su and Father for having improper thoughts about a priestess of the temple."

Crack.

Ashur froze at the snap of a twig. Someone was on the path. Footsteps moved lightly with barely a whisper of sound. No one should be here except members of the royal court and they attended the banquet.

Warrior instincts took control, and Ashur pulled the dagger from its sheath.

****

Hands shaking, Nemra stared at the scrap of writing clenched in her fist. How could this be? Her mind searched for an explanation but to no avail. High Priest Balu-su, the great god Marduk's voice on Earth, had deliberately destroyed a sacred scroll. Even if Balu-su found an error in the calculations, every member of the clergy understood the necessity of proper cleansing rites before consigning religious papyrus to the flames. Nemra shuddered. To ignore ritual was to court disaster and leave a door open for evil to enter the world.

Balu-su's action made no sense. Why suddenly

destroy a scroll with only one figure in error in a series of calculations? Nemra tucked the scrap in her tunic. She must think, but first the high priest expected her presence at the banquet. If she didn't arrive soon, he would surely send people to hunt for her. An ominous chill rippled through her body at the thought of Balu-su's private guards telling him they found her at the eternal flame outside the library.

Nemra hurried to the great hall. She took a deep breath to steady her nerves and paid her respects to the high priest. Balu-su regarded her coldly. "You are the last to arrive, priestess."

"I stopped to say a quick prayer to Marduk for continued blessings on the kingdom."

Balu-su grunted his approval. Nemra bowed low and scurried away, fighting to ignore the sensation his sharp eyes tracked her every move. Tal-banit waved her to a seat at the banquet table. Servants rushed to offer delicacies from bronze platters laden with food. Nemra selected a few ripe figs and nibbled absentmindedly.

"You haven't eaten much," scolded Tal-banit.

"I'm more tired than hungry. The tally was long today."

"Thank the gods. Then feasts such as this will not have to wait for new tribute."

"We live to serve the gods, Tal-banit, not ourselves."

"No one else minds luxury," she teased, "except you. Not even Balu-su. He announced clergy will receive part of the army's gifts to the temple. To show honor to Marduk's servants is to honor Marduk himself. I hope mine is a pearl necklace," she added with wishful yearning.

Nemra watched the high priest surrounded by attendants and courtiers. He sat as regally as any king, especially with new gold wristlets inset with rubies. They had the most value of the items recorded in the count today. Nemra rose from her seat.

"Where are you going?" asked Tal-banit. "The musicians and acrobats are ready to perform."

"After being confined to the counting room since early morning, I have a need for fresh air."

"Are you ill?" she said with concern. "I can send a servant to your quarters with a sleeping potion."

Nemra smiled. "I suffer from nothing a walk in the garden won't cure." She hurried from the main hall, out the temple, and into the gardens encircling the ziggurat. Her feet raced along a path, emotions awhirl, hardly aware of the route until she arrived at the far gate. She had to think, to keep moving, away from the temple and the dark cloud in her mind cast by Balu-su's actions. Nemra exited the grounds and followed the Processional Way. Here and there, the light of an oil lamp flickered from a window, the quiet punctuated by bursts of laughter from families in the middle of their own celebrations for the army's return.

Nemra shivered with sudden foreboding and stole a glance over her shoulder. Down the street, a shadow moved. She hitched up her tunic and quickened the pace while chiding her nervousness. None dared raise a hand against one of Marduk's chosen servants. The punishment was death. She reached the Hanging Gardens with a strong yearning to lose herself in its wonders. At this time of night, sentries barred entrance to outsiders, but a priestess of Marduk was welcome anywhere in Babylon. She nodded to the men at the gate. They stepped aside and bowed their heads as she passed.

Her feet wandered the paths until she found steps to an upper terrace. From there, the park stretched out before her and she gazed at it with pleasure. Although the grounds were unlit by torches, moonlight cast a silver glow. Nemra filled her lungs with the scent of fresh greenery. Surely, the Hanging Gardens were a marvel to behold. Her thoughts turned to her encounter on the temple steps that morning with the prince. He looked into her eyes and then the image appeared of strange green stalks with yellow tassels. Strange, yet familiar.

"Corn." Nemra rolled the word on her tongue. "It is corn. Where have I seen it before?" She peered around. Perhaps here on other visits. The garden held many specimens, including those from far-off lands. Of course, that was it. The sight of the prince brought the stalks to mind. She would visit again in daylight and ask one of the workers to show the corn to her.

On the other side of the gardens, lights blazed from the palace windows. The faint sounds of music and revelry drifted in the air. No doubt the celebration for the prince's safe homecoming would continue well into the night. Nemra resumed her stroll, musing on Prince Ashur-etil-ilani's arrival at the temple. His expression had been unnaturally pensive, not what she expected for a conquering general. What wistful thoughts occupied the mind of a hero returning in triumph to his homeland?

Nemra gazed at the palace. Whatever distracted his royal highness was most likely long forgotten. Courtiers surrounded him now, and he basked in their attention.

She stepped on a twig, and the brittle snap broke the quiet. Nemra startled as a figure of a man emerged from the shadows. He moved with the stealth of a hunting lion, and moonlight glistened on a drawn blade.

"Who are you?" he demanded.

She jumped back. One hand clutched at her tunic. "I am a daughter of the temple," she cried, "and mean no harm."

****

Ashur stared at her in surprise. "I saw you on the steps this morning for the blessing." He sheathed the dagger. "I beg forgiveness, priestess. I didn't expect to meet anyone here at this hour."

She bowed her head. "No forgiveness is necessary, Your Highness."

"Shouldn't you be at the temple for the celebration?"

She flashed a cheeky grin. "I might say the same of Your Highness. I didn't expect to greet another in the gardens."

Ashur chuckled. "Official celebrations are more wearying than days on the trail."

"I am of like mind. So, we both shirk our duties," she teased. "A fine example set for the citizens of Babylon."

The somberness in his heart eased. "If you promise not to tell my father," said Ashur lightly, "I vow not to speak a word of this to High Priest Balu-su."

"A promise I will gladly keep." She backed away. "I'm sorry to disturb you, Your Highness. I'll be on my way."

"Please stay, priestess." The thought of Nemra leaving brought another wave of melancholy. "I had sought solitude, but now find comfort in the company of a like-minded soul. Are you familiar with the design of the gardens?"

"Only a little. I accompanied Balu-su on several occasions to deliver reports to the king." Her nose wrinkled in disapproval. "He is always anxious to return to the temple and never deviates from the path."

"Then allow me to act as a guide, and we may wander where you choose."

"I am honored, Your Highness."

"Call me Ashur. I weary of titles, too, this night."

A rush of warmth came with her smile. "I am Nemra."

"Nemra." The sound of her name was unexpectedly pleasant. "What do you care to see?"

"Show me your favorite spot."

"This way, then, Nemra." Ashur led them to the reflecting pool with renewed lightness in his step. He plucked dates from a nearby palm. They sat the water's edge and ate the sweet fruit.

"Delicious." Nemra swallowed the last bite. "Truly a feast fit for a king. Even the moon god Sin shines his approval in the water."

"My brother's namesake, although Sin is not as fond of idle wanderings through the gardens as I am." Ashur dabbed his hands in the water, washing the stickiness from his fingers. "If only every monarch's duty was as sweet as sharing figs next to a pool."

A smile tugged Nemra's lips. "Can't a ruler snap his fingers and order a servant to do unpleasant tasks for him?"

"Ah, would that kingship was that simple."

She laughed. "What good is it, then?"

Ashur grinned. "I often wonder that myself. What of you, Nemra? Do you enjoy the obligations at the temple? Don't you ever wish to snap your fingers?"

The smile left her face. "Occasionally."

Ashur eyed her with interest. "What is your duty there?"

"I keep the accounts."

"Ah, a number cruncher."

Nemra's face paled. She jumped to her feet and regarded him with wide eyes. "Where did you hear that?"

Ashur stood, confused by her reaction. "I don't remember. The words simply came to me. Balu-su or my father must have used it once. Is it a name for those who keep the accounts at the temple?"

"No. I..." She swallowed hard. "I, too, know the word, but not how or when it was used. It feels as if I heard it in a dream."

"A dream," said Ashur in a hushed tone. "I, too, had thoughts today that seemed dreamlike."

She drew in a sharp breath. "Tell me."

Ashur hesitated. "They are of no importance. I have no wish to ruin pleasant conversation with random musings caused by fatigue and too many days on a hot, dusty trail."

Nemra placed a hand on his chest, eyes pleading. "Please, Cal. Tell me."

Cal? Warmth flowed from her touch. The longing to open his innermost thoughts spread through him as quickly as the heat from her hand. "I saw the back of a woman's head, her hair worn in the same fashion as yours, a tall plant, and then the word funnel cake came to mind. I hungered for one when I entered the city but can't recall where I've eaten it. No doubt on my travels. Strange," he mused. "I can almost taste it. The cake had a sweetness as bright on my tongue as the dates."

Nemra's hand dropped from Ashur's chest, stealing the warmth with her. She stepped back from the water's edge. "This plant was a tall, green stalk with long pods growing amongst the leaves. They had tassels that shined as if spun from gold."

Ashur gazed at her in disbelief. "How did you know?"

"I have seen the like."

"Not here. I have walked every inch of the Hanging Gardens. No such plant exists."

"Not in the garden. I, too, have had this vision. The plant's name is corn."

"Corn," he murmured. "What else did you see?"

"Fire, a maze," she stammered, "a man who was you but not you. I have a memory of hearing the word you used—number cruncher but not funnel cake." Her lips twitched with a faint smile. "It has a pleasing sound though."

"It did...it does." Ashur ran a shaky hand through his hair. "What happened to us?"

Nemra gazed at the moon. "Dreams hold their own magic. I believe we were both sent a message from the gods."

"A message?" he said. "But what does it mean? Should we consult Balu-su?"

"No!" Her retort was so sharp, Ashur startled. Even in moonlight, the flush rising to her cheeks was visible. "Our religious teachings tell us," said Nemra, "only the high priest is sent visions from the gods. Only he can interpret their meaning, but..."

Ashur narrowed his eyes. "You have doubts of his ability."

Nemra stared into the depths of the pool. "Not his ability, but perhaps, his motives. His actions today…" She rubbed her temples. "I must think."

Ashur caught a subtle motion out of the corner of his eye. On the lower terrace, shadows moved. Warrior instincts bleated an alarm. "Be still."

Nemra's voice dropped to a whisper. "What is it?"

"Men below."

"Guests leaving the banquet?"

Ashur slid his hand to the dagger. "No. They use stealth and didn't come from the direction of the palace. How did outsiders bypass the guards—?"

The silence broke with a scrape of metal against leather. More than one hand had just drawn a sword from the scabbard.

Chapter Three

Men in dark tunics rushed the stairs. Strips of cloth covered their faces, leaving only a narrow slit for their eyes.

"Go, now!" ordered Ashur.

Nemra grabbed his arm. "You can't fight them alone."

Ashur shoved Nemra behind him. "Bring help from the palace."

Heart pounding, Nemra raced away. From behind her came the tinny clash of metal on metal and then the slap of sandaled feet on the path. At least one of the attackers made it past the prince. She came to a series of narrow ledges planted with rosebushes that went to the lower level of the garden. Nemra scrambled over the side, ignoring the pain as thorns tore her skin. She jumped down each successive ledge to the bottom. The entrance to the palace was in sight.

"Guards!" Nemra shouted at the top of her lungs. "The prince is under attack."

A voice responded from the palace. "Who calls?"

"A priestess of Marduk." From behind her came a whistling twang and sharp pain grazed her arm. An arrow burrowed into the trunk of a date palm, the shaft quivering with intensity.

Royal guards raced toward her with swords drawn.

"Upper terrace at the reflecting pool," cried Nemra.

"Hurry!"

Their shouts and footsteps faded away. Quiet, so quiet. Nemra stared into the dark, straining to hear. Why no sounds of battle? Had help arrived too late to save Ashur?

People spilled from the banquet hall, crowding the entrance. At a harsh command, they stepped aside to let the king and Prince Sin-sharish-kun pass.

"What has happened?" demanded the king. His gaze fell on Nemra. "Priestess? Was that your cry?"

Nemra bowed. "Yes, Your Highness. I met the prince while walking in the garden. Armed men attacked us, and I ran for help."

The king shook with rage. "Thieves in my garden? How did they avoid the sentries?"

"I do not know, my lord. We saw no others."

He glared at Sin-sharish-kun. "Why are you here? Help your brother."

"The guards are with him," said the prince, "and I'm concerned for your safety, Father. More of those men may be near."

"Go to your brother," he barked. "I am not helpless."

"Yes, Father." The prince bowed low. His lips pressed together in a thin tight line and he hurried away.

The king turned his attention to Nemra. "Priestess," he said with concern, "you are injured."

"Naught but scratches, Your Highness. I fear the rosebushes suffered worse."

"That is not a scratch. Go with my servant. The palace healer will tend to you."

"If you please, Your Highness, I ask to wait here

until the guards send word the prince is safe."

A second contingent of men exited the palace. "With enemies upon us," said the king, "this is no place for a priestess of Marduk. Go." He barked an order to the men to follow and ran down the path.

The servant led Nemra to a couch in an inner chamber. A healer arrived with balm and dressings and gave her a draught to dull the pain. Servants rushed in offering food, but Nemra waved them away. She winced as the healer cleaned and bound her wounds. "The arrow slice is deep, priestess," he said. "I'm afraid it will leave a scar."

"A scar is preferable to an arrow through the heart. Any word of the prince?" she asked the servants. They shook their heads. Nemra rose from the couch. "Then I will find out for myself."

They rushed in horror to her side, offering assistance. "Priestess," blurted one, "we have orders from the king to attend to your comfort."

"You must rest," insisted the healer. "I will make a potion to aid your sleep."

Nemra gritted her teeth. "My thanks for your kind attention, but I refuse. Until I have answers on the prince's condition, I will certainly not sleep."

A servant nervously licked his lips. "My lady, the king wishes—"

"Enough!" Nemra's voice rose to an exasperated shout. "Either let me pass or bind me to a pillar. I warn you, neither the king nor Marduk will be pleased if you choose the latter."

With anxious glances, the servants backed away. Nemra returned to the banquet hall with the healer who refused to leave her side. Guards stationed at the door to the gardens barred her passage. "I'm sorry, priestess," said the captain. "I am under orders to allow no one outside the palace. It isn't safe."

"Please, priestess," begged the healer. "There is nothing more to do here. Come away."

Instead, Nemra paced back and forth under the watchful eye of the healer. Now and then, she glanced toward the gardens beyond, fearful of what she might see. Shadowed movement flickered among the trees, leaves rustled, and in the distance came the faint murmur of men's voices.

"Sit, priestess," said the healer. "You must rest."

Nemra waved him back with her hand and continued to pace. "By the great god Marduk," she shouted, "someone tell me what happened to the prince."

****

Ashur readied to face the attackers as Nemra dashed from his side. The last thing a force of armed assassins would expect was determined resistance from one man on a narrow ledge. With a battle cry, Ashur charged and grabbed a cluster of vines that spilled to the ground from an upper terrace. With one hand, he swung over the startled men. He slashed the dagger with the other and received a sharp cry of pain as a reward. Not a death stroke, but he drew first blood.

A powerful kick sent one of the attackers stumbling into the others, knocking them askew. Ashur landed lightly on the upper terrace. The men quickly regrouped to scramble after him. He dodged their sword thrusts, and then a man pulled a bow. Ashur threw himself to the ground as an arrow whistled past his ear.

"Leave him," snarled a voice. "Kill the girl."

Ashur raised his head and peered over the side. The archer tore along the path, with the rest of the band close behind. White hot rage flooded his veins. *They're not after me. They're after Nemra.* With a curse, he vaulted to the lower terrace and raced after them, dagger in hand, but they were already out of sight.

"My prince!" Rammat ran toward him on the path with a squad of royal guards and servants with torches.

"Here! We must return to the palace at once. A priestess of Marduk is in danger."

"Have no fear." Sin-sharish-kun stepped from the shadows. "The woman is safe and under guard at the palace. She warned us of an attack. What happened?"

Ashur breathed a sigh of relief. "Armed men by the pool. They disappeared into the gardens. Did you not see anyone?"

"No," said Sin, "the way to the palace is clear." Shouts came from distant corners of the Hanging Gardens. "Men search the grounds as we speak."

Ashur snatched a sword from one of the guards. "They may try to escape through the main gate."

Sin hesitated. "Father wishes you to return to the palace."

Ashur scowled at him. "I will not leave the gardens until I'm convinced Nemra is safe from their hands. Come!" Swords drawn, they advanced on the gate. The hairs on the back of Ashur's neck stood up. Something was wrong. No demands for identity came from men posted here. "Where are the guards?"

"My lord," called Rammat. "Over here. I found them."

The bodies lay against the wall. Ashur demanded a torch. He examined the dead with raging anger.

"Throats slit, arrows through the hearts, the attack was swift and clean. They had no time to protect themselves or sound the alarm." He stepped outside the wall. The Processional Way was empty, but fresh prints in a dusting of sand drew his attention. He dropped to one knee and brought the torch closer. One set of footsteps was small and light, others large and heavy, following closely on Nemra's trail.

"With many guests expected," said Rammat, "the gates remained open for the celebration. A perfect time to attack."

Sin peered over Ashur's shoulder. "The trail stops here. We can do no more tonight and should return to the palace." He ordered men to take the corpses away.

Ashur gave in with a glower. "As you wish. I will see for myself Nemra is unharmed." He ordered the guard tripled at the gate and men to search the Processional Way. Had assassins followed her trail from the temple?

"Who is this Nemra?" asked Sin.

"One of Marduk's chosen. The men were after her."

"A priestess of the temple?" he scoffed. "For what purpose, brother? To harm a priestess is to not only anger the king, but also the gods. What fool risks death on Earth and punishment beyond the last breath taken?"

"I don't know, but the men broke off the attack on me and pursued her."

"Or the theft more difficult than planned. They certainly didn't expect to find an armed prince, so simply wished the girl not to raise the alarm before they made their escape."

Ashur regarded him with doubt. "You believe they

69

were common thieves?"

Sin motioned to Ashur's dagger. "One treasure such as this can make a dozen men rich. Guests wore their finery to the celebration and are easy victims if they chanced to leave the palace and stroll in the gardens. A strange time for a priestess to visit," he mused. "Was she here to meet you?"

Arthur raised an eyebrow. "What reason do I have to meet a priestess alone at night?"

"She's quite lovely."

His voice tightened. "We had nothing other than a pleasant conversation. If you're suggesting more—"

"I apologize, brother," said Sin in a soothing tone. "I mean no insult to you or any friends from the temple."

The slight stress on the word *friends* tainted the sincerity of the apology. Ashur swallowed back a sharp retort. No doubt, Sin would deny any hidden meaning, and he was in no mood tonight for any of his brother's verbal games.

As they neared the palace, the king approached with the royal guard and embraced Ashur. "You are unharmed," he said with relief.

"Yes, Father. Thanks to your gift of the dagger." He described the attack and asked after Nemra.

"I had my personal healer see to her."

An icy chill wrapped Ashur's heart. "Nemra was wounded?" He turned on his brother. "Why didn't you tell me?"

"She is well-tended," said Sin mildly.

"With your permission, Father," said Ashur. "I will judge for myself."

"As you wish, my son."

He ran to the palace, blood nearly boiling. Those men dared touch Meg—no Nemra. He shook his head. *Her name is Nemra.*

He edged past the guards and up the steps to the hall. Nemra paced the room, fists clenched. "By the great god Marduk," she shouted, "someone tell me what happened to the prince?"

He stepped into the hall with a smile. "The prince is here and at your command."

"Ashur!" Her face lit up at his approach, and then she blushed. "I mean, Your Highness."

Ashur's gaze dropped to the bandage and the deep scratches on her arms and legs. His finger gently tucked an errant tress behind her ear that had escaped the clip. The touch of her skin once again ignited a pleasant glow within him. The tenseness he carried since the attack melted away, replaced with unexpected warmth and renewed anger against those who dared lay hands on Nemra. "Sit. You're in pain."

"The pain is nothing now that my prince is safe." The color in her cheeks deepened.

The king's healer bowed low. "She should rest, my lord. The king will not be pleased if she weakens."

Ashur hid a smile at the man's obvious concern not for Nemra's well-being, but his own standing in the palace. "I will tell my father you have done well. Leave us. I will tend to her comfort. If the king disapproves, he may direct his anger at me." The healer backed away, a mixture of gratitude and relief on his face. Ashur chided Nemra gently, "You are stubborn, Chosen of Marduk. See how you disrupt our quiet lives in the palace."

Her gentle laugh stirred his heart. "That was not

71

my intent. How may I make amends for my ungracious behavior, lord?"

"Sit with me so I know you rest and those in the palace will be safe from my father's wrath." Ashur led her to a cushioned bench.

"Did you catch the attackers?" she asked.

Ashur scowled. "Guards continue to search the gardens, but I believe they will find no trace of them. The men escaped, but not before slaughtering the sentries at the gate." He regarded her sharply. "These were not ordinary thieves but well-trained. Why were they after you?"

Nemra sat back in astonishment. "Clearly, you were the target."

"Not so. The leader halted the attack on me to order your death. Their tracks at the gate were on top of yours. They followed you into the gardens from the Processional Way."

She gasped. "I-I have no idea. I am of no importance."

"You are a daughter of Marduk and share in the wealth of the temple."

Nemra snorted in disbelief and touched the simple gold necklace around her neck, her one bit of jewelry. "I wear little finery, or are you thinking ransom from Balu-su? He guards the riches as if they were his own. He wouldn't part with a single gold coin to buy my release." She fingered the necklace with a look of apprehension. "Mere thieves wouldn't have known that."

"Those men wanted your death, not jewelry." His voice dropped. "They weren't brigands roaming the streets. They functioned as a unit and were as skillful in their actions as the guards in the palace, as deadly as any temple guards."

"Sent to assassinate me? Why?"

"I cannot say, but they had no fear to enter the grounds, and knew the guards' stations as if they were here before."

"Protecting Balu-su?" Nemra swallowed hard. "His personal guards swore their lives to him. His orders are unquestioned."

"Is there any reason why the high priest wants you silenced?"

"No, I—" Her face paled.

"Nemra?"

"I found something." Her hand reached inside her tunic and retrieved a singed scrap of parchment. "I watched Balu-su burn a sacred scroll."

Ashur peered at the numbers in confusion. "What is this?"

"The remains of an astrological chart. Touching the sacred scrolls is forbidden to anyone but Balu-su. I happened to see the numbers on this one and found an error in the calculations—at least, I thought it was an error. Now, I'm not certain. I brought it to Balu-su's attention during the count. Afterward, he burned the scroll in secret."

"Did you ask why?"

Nemra's face flushed. "I didn't dare. I was at the library at a time when I should have been elsewhere and am only a priestess. I have no right to question him. He has no obligation to answer me."

Ashur's voice rose in anger. "Then Balu-su will answer to me."

"Not concerning affairs of the temple. Even you

can't force the high priest to talk. To harm him in any way is sacrilege."

Ashur's gaze went to the parchment. "What did those numbers say to you?"

"If correct, they are an omen. Unimaginable evil nears Babylon, but why Balu-su shuts his eyes to the truth makes no sense." She drew in a sharp breath. "Perhaps his actions are the reason for our dreams."

"The gods won't speak to the high priest," he said, "and instead speak a warning to us. Why?"

Nemra shivered and tucked the bit of parchment in the folds of her tunic. "Perhaps they tried, but Balu-su refused to listen."

Ashur took her hand. "Nemra, if evil threatens Babylon, I must do everything in my power to stop it."

"You can't act alone, and the king will never sanction a move against Balu-su on the beliefs of a lowly priestess. We must prove sacrilege first. I need to return to the temple."

"Nemra, he tried to kill you."

"I have no reason to stay. Only at the temple can I discover the meaning behind Balu-su's actions and the gods' warnings."

Ashur's grip tightened on her fingers. "I can't protect you there."

Color deepened in her cheeks. "Ashur…"

Shouts from outside drew Ashur's attention. "The king is returning. We will speak of this again. Meanwhile—"

"We speak of this to no one. I understand."

Sin entered the hall first and gazed at their clasped hands. Ashur let go of Nemra, and they both rose to their feet.

The king followed with the royal guard. He went directly to Ashur. "We searched the gardens, but they vanished as quickly as they came." His expression grew dark. "They will not find easy entrance again. The gates will remain well-guarded." He turned to Nemra. "You have the thanks of the king."

Nemra bowed her head. "None are needed, Your Majesty. I am grateful to be of service but now must return to the temple."

"No need to hurry, priestess. Stay the night and rest. My servants will attend to you."

"Thank you for the kindness, Your Majesty, but my wounds are minor, and I have duties to perform."

"Father," said Ashur, "allow me to escort her safely to the temple."

"Very well, my son. Impress upon High Priest Balu-su the need to stay vigilant."

Ashur's eyes narrowed. "You can be sure of that."

Ashur called for Rammat and a squad of soldiers. Heavily armed men and horses met them at the palace gates. Ashur lifted Nemra onto the back of his own mount. "My horse is a warrior stallion but will carry you gently."

Nemra's smile renewed Ashur's anger at the marauders in the gardens. They tried to take Meg—Nemra—away from him. They must be found and punished, and if led by the high priest, so be it. Balu-su's station would not protect him.

A soldier brought Ashur a mount, and he swung into the saddle. As they rode along the Processional Way, Ashur's gaze swept the streets on either side searching for any hint of trouble, but the night was quiet. They entered the temple gate and stopped at the ziggurat's steps. Ashur dismounted and raised his hands to Nemra's waist. She placed her arms around his neck. Cradled in his strong grip, she slid lightly to the ground.

For an instant, they stood locked in each other's embrace. Ashur's breath caught in his throat as the moon cloaked them in its silver light, binding them together.

Balu-su exited the temple door and hurried down the ziggurat's steps. "Priestess, you survived the attack, thank the gods."

Ashur released Nemra, and the strange sensation of mystical bonds dissolved as she slipped from his side. He wanted nothing more than to pull her back in his arms.

"Marduk held me safely in his hands this night," said Nemra.

Ashur regarded Balu-su coolly. "How did you learn of the attack?"

The high priest hesitated slightly. "I received word from the palace."

"Indeed? Who sent it?"

He waved a dismissive hand. "One of the slaves." His sharp eyes peered at Nemra. "Your cheeks are flushed, priestess."

"Are they?" she said. "No doubt from my exertions."

"Yes, of course." He took her by the elbow. "Come inside and rest. You are safe now."

Ashur stepped forward. His hand resisted lightly on the grip of his dagger. "I leave Nemra under your care, Lord Balu-su. Keep a watchful eye for those who attacked us in the gardens in case they try again. Anyone who harms Nemra will answer to my blade. Is that understood?"

The high priest's lips formed a tight smile. "Be at peace, my lord. The well-being of those in the temple is my utmost concern."

Ashur mounted his horse. He watched Balu-su climb the stairs, Nemra at his side. The great gilded door swung shut behind them. One thought rang in the prince's head.

Liar.

Chapter Four

The door closed, and Balu-su's fingers tightened on Nemra's elbow. "Why were you in the Hanging Gardens at such a late hour?"

His touch on her bare skin sent a chill, and she pulled her arm away. "I felt the need to walk after a long day at the count."

"We have our own gardens."

"The palace grounds are always open to the servants of Marduk, and no better place exists then the Hanging Gardens of Babylon to refresh one's soul. Don't you agree?"

He grunted an unintelligible response, and then his tone sharpened. "Did you see the faces of the men that attacked?"

"No. They were covered." The urge soared to escape Balu-su's questions. "With respect, lord, I will retire to my chambers to rest."

"Until tomorrow, then, at the allotment of the temple's tribute to the clergy." He glanced at her bandaged arm. "If you aren't well enough to carry out official functions, I can have another make the notations for you."

"I will attend, my lord."

His keen eyes didn't waver. "We all rejoice at your safe return."

"Thank you, Lord Balu-su."

He signaled for the servants. They had kept their distance, but now rushed forward to escort Nemra to her quarters. *To offer assistance or prevent me from leaving again?* The temple's own healer arrived to change the bandage on her arm. Tal-banit entered with a servant carrying a tray of spiced wine. Nemra dismissed the healer and servant, but Tal-banit remained.

"Attacked by thieves on palace grounds," she said with a horrified gasp, "and then to escape with your lives. The gods truly smiled on you and the prince."

"Not so the guards."

"Their duty is to protect the royal family with their lives. They will surely receive a just reward in the afterlife."

"That's little comfort to wives made widows and children now orphaned. Tell me, why did you call them thieves?"

"Balu-su told us thieves tried to steal your jewelry."

"Did he?" Nemra mused. "Balu-su seems to know much."

Tal-banit cast a teasing glance at her. "How fortunate the prince was at your side. That's two meetings in one day."

"Sheer chance we both found need of fresh air this evening."

"If he was not a prince and you were not a priestess, it would be quite romantic."

Tal-banit's teasing brought a flutter of unease. Such thoughts should not be spoken. "Since we are, you may dismiss those foolish notions at once."

"As you wish." Tal-banit leaned forward with an

avid gleam in her eyes. "Will you still be at the division of the tribute tomorrow?"

"I have no reason to set aside official duties. The wounds are minor, and I will be well-rested by morning."

"Good." Tal-banit shifted in her seat. "The other clergy and I feared Balu-su might take it solely upon himself to perform the ceremony. Not that we question his abilities," she added in a rush, "but his estimation of value can be…that is, to say, an impartial allotment might not be his greatest concern…" Tal-banit beamed at her. "Your judgment is never in question. After all, you are in charge of the count and record the true worth of every piece. Especially the pearls. I noticed one string in particular."

As Tal-banit's idle chatter continued, Nemra rubbed her temples. She had no wish to listen to a catalog of riches from the treasure room. "Perhaps it's best we both rest for now and leave discussion of the tribute for tomorrow."

"Of course," said Tal-banit. "Sleep well, Nemra. May the gods favor you with pleasant dreams."

Nemra breathed a sigh of relief as the door closed behind Tal-banit and blessed silence descended on her chambers. Finally, she was alone with nothing but her thoughts for company. Weariness pressed upon her shoulders. Her footsteps dragged and thoughts muddied. Nemra staggered to the bed and shut her eyes. Ashur's face rose to mind. Warmth flooded her cheeks. They were no doubt flushed with color. Why did the mind of a priestess of Marduk turn to a prince? He was sworn to fulfill the obligations of a king while she was sworn to fulfill the obligations of Marduk's handmaiden.

The face of Ashur faded away. Nemra drifted to sleep.

****

The brilliant golden light of the sun caressed her skin. Skin that was hers but not hers. She stood with Ashur in the cornfield at the center of the maze. The warrior prince, but not the face of the prince. They had donned strange clothing. She wore the headpiece, he carried a black sword, the blade decorated with matching symbols.

"Now?" he said.

"Not yet."

Day turned to night.

All light extinguished.

The Everdark howled, "Come to me." Its maw gaped wide and drew the world toward its raging hunger. No escape for them. No escape for anyone. Nothing but a pit of eternal darkness.

Ashur took her hand. The sun, moon, and stars on the sword and crown began to glow.

"Now," she said.

They entered the dark.

****

Nemra's eyelids shot open. Her heart hammered against her ribs.

"Forgive me, my lady." The servant backed away from the bed. "I didn't mean to startle you. I have breakfast prepared and will draw your bath."

Nemra sat up. Cold sweat plastered the sheets to her skin. She drew in a deep steadying breath. *By the gods, what a dream.*

The servant regarded her with concern. "My lady,

are you ill?"

No need to alarm the servants over a nightmare. "No, it's simply the heat. I'm perfectly well but hungry. I'll dine on the balcony." Nemra swung her legs off the side of the bed, pleased she stood without trembling limbs. She sat at the table above the temple garden. As Nemra ate, her thoughts turned once again to the prince. Strange how he entered her dreams now, too. A smile twitched her lips. Strange but not unpleasant.

Servants removed the empty dishes, and Nemra entered the bathing chamber. She slipped into the water and relaxed with a sigh. Once clean and dry, she dismissed the servants. Alone in the room, her tranquil demeanor dissolved as images from the eerie dream resurfaced. The sensation grew again of being two people at the same time, Nemra the priestess and this other woman, but always Ashur at her side. The experience felt so real, not the sense of a normal dream, more like a vision.

Nemra drew in a breath. Could it be? Did the gods send a true omen? Earlier flashes showed random objects, unfamiliar words, and names. Disturbing, yes, but they brought no threat of doom. This one was different. She shivered.

This one came as a warning.

But of what? Her hands went cold. What was that thing in the maze? It had a name—Everdark, ravager of light and life. Nemra faithfully served the gods for years but never heard of such evil. Was it a demon? If such existed, surely Marduk would protect Babylon from this horror. A lowly priestess could do no more than ask for the god's blessing.

A troubling thought arose. What if the warning

came from Marduk? What if he expected more of her? Nemra walked onto the balcony and her gaze lifted to the sky. "I am your faithful attendant, ask what you will."

The god didn't answer.

A servant knocked at the door. "Balu-su is ready to begin the division of the tribute and commands your presence."

The high priest waited in the treasure room. "I have secured my personal allotment. The clergy may select from the rest."

Nemra cast a glance over the riches in the corner claimed as Balu-su's own. A rapid calculation in her head assessed the value at nearly five times more than the remainder.

Balu-su ordered servants to remove his new acquisitions, and he retired to his chambers. Nemra sat at the desk, preparing the scroll. She was entitled to make the first choice after Balu-su, but the sight of his horde left a sour taste in her mouth and no hunger for more shiny trinkets of her own. It was right that Marduk's faithful were rewarded, but today Balu-su acted as a greedy ruler rather than a priest.

Upon Balu-su's exit, the clergy filed in. Nemra's task was to note each selection and assure objects conformed to the temple's rules; higher ranking clergy received items with more worth, lower ranking less. Nemra faithfully recorded each gold cup or jeweled wristlet. With an elated expression, Tal-banit approached holding a lustrous strand of pearls. As Nemra marked the scroll, Tal-banit bent over and whispered in her ear, "You should choose before the best is taken."

After several hours, Nemra recorded the description and worth of the final object. The last priest left, eyes gleaming over a solid gold cup clasped tight to his chest. She was alone except for the guards who waited by the door to the vault. They eyed her with curiosity, no doubt wondering why she hadn't yet made her choice. With dull indifference, Nemra entered intent on taking the nearest item and then returning to her chambers. She paused to study the objects at her feet; small caskets with jewelry, silver plates, an assortment of enameled bowls. Any not selected by the clergy remained in the treasure room as the property of the temple.

What does it matter? Pick one.

Her hand reached for a simple gold bracelet and froze. In a corner lay the drawstring bag. The sun and moon headpiece had been hastily shoved aside by hands eager to paw through more splendid riches. Its unassuming nature called to her as if a voice in her head commanded, "Take me."

Nemra removed the headpiece from the sack. She slipped it on and gave her head a tentative shake. It sat snugly, a perfect fit, as if the maker custom-crafted it for her use alone. A vague sense of heat emanated from where metal touched her skin. Nemra took it off to examine it at arm's length. She ran a thumb across the unnatural depiction of the sun, moon, and stars in a daylight sky. Unnatural and yet correct.

This headpiece wasn't mere decoration, nor the idle fancy of an artisan's wealthy patron. Nor was it meant to rest upon a ruler's head, a symbol of earthly power. The longer Nemra held the headpiece, the more certain she was the artisan crafted it with a special purpose.

But what? Where did it come from?

Nemra returned it to the bag. She marked the scroll with her choice and signaled the guards to secure the door.

****

Ashur threw back the sheet with a scowl and got to his feet. No point in tossing and turning any more, sleep had fled his chamber for now. Not that sleep welcomed him with open arms last night. He was restless, closing his eyes and then waking with a start. Each time, memory tugged at snatches of dreams only to have them scatter as leaves from the garden path in a summer breeze. He rubbed the nape of his neck. All that remained now was a disquieting belief he left an important task undone.

The first rays of the sun washed the view outside his windows with a rosy hue. A servant entered with breakfast, and after dining, Ashur summoned Rammat to the treasure room for the final division of spoils for the army. They discussed the allotment and number of shares for those who earned additional rewards. Rammat sent for the men. Ashur stood by and watched as grateful soldiers collected their payments. *Blood money.* Ashur's thoughts strayed to sitting with Nemra by the pool. At least, those were pleasant.

After Rammat doled out the last gold coin, Ashur left the palace and entered the gardens. Would Nemra's company now ease his restless soul as it did last night? He walked to their reflecting pool. *Their pool?* What force drew him to her? The desire burned to see Nemra's face again, to revel in the same wondrous sense of connection. He had never experienced such a powerful bond with any woman; an uneasy suspicion rose that none could ever light the same fire. He gazed into the pool. What would it be like to pluck a flower from Nemra's garden?

You will never know.

His lips twisted in a wry smile. The gods surely had a sense of humor to bring him together with Nemra, an unattainable priestess of Marduk. Soon, he would have a new wife, one to bear his children, profess no contrary thoughts, and answer without question to Ashur's every beck and call. She would show gratitude because he showered her with riches and made her a queen. Marriage elevated her above the rest of the women in Babylon, and she would revel in her position. If asked, she'd profess her love for Ashur above all else, yet, freely offer concubines to keep him from her bed. A dutiful, proper, consort for a king.

Only yesterday, the thought of the wedding filled Ashur with indifference. Now he had a wistful longing for a woman at his side to behold him as a man before she bowed to him as a king.

"You have deep thoughts, brother." Sin ambled along the path. "I called and you didn't answer. Father wishes you to come." He cocked his head. "What so engages your attention at the pool?"

"Nothing of interest." He joined Sin and they walked toward the palace.

"Not even the memory of a loving gaze from a comely woman last evening?" said his brother lightly.

"Nemra is a priestess, Sin," he snapped, "not a concubine. Speak of her with respect."

"Of course, brother," he said in a soothing tone. "Don't be cross. It was merely an ill jest, although, anyone could see she had great concern for your safety."

"As she would with any person attacked in her presence."

"I only issue a warning. She is a priestess, but also a woman. It's possible her feelings run deep. It isn't wise to encourage such from one who can be neither wife nor concubine."

The thought that Nemra had a similar attraction to him filled Ashur with a sudden rush of pleasure. Just as quickly, he brushed it aside. Sin was correct. Any relationship with Nemra outside the confines of official duties was impossible. "Thank you for the concern, brother, but you are mistaken. Nothing exists between us. Do you have news of the attackers?"

"No. They vanished without a trace."

Or hide where we are forbidden to search.

"I doubled the guards at night," added Sin. "Thieves won't find an easy entry again."

Ashur scowled. "Entry was hardly easy, yet, they were able to slaughter trained men-at-arms. You still believe they were mere thieves even though nothing was taken."

Sin shrugged. "They lost the chance when you came upon them."

The king waited in the throne room and greeted Ashur warmly. "Good news, my son, the marriage is arranged."

Ashur blinked. "Marriage?"

"Yes. Messengers came this morning with the signed contract from the king of Elam. His daughter's caravan arrives within a month. What is it, Ashur? You seem disturbed."

"Forgive me, Father. My mind is preoccupied by the events of last evening."

"Yes, a most unfortunate incident. Happily, wedding preparations will take our thoughts off such unpleasantness. I must meet with Balu-su at the temple. He has to consult the astrological charts for the most opportune day and time to set the nuptials."

An urge grew in Ashur to be rid of the palace walls. "Allow me to go for you, Father."

"An excellent idea," said Sin. "You can check on the health of the priestess, too. No doubt she is well-rested from last evening."

Ashur gave him a sharp look, but nothing in Sin's expression hinted at any underlying meaning.

The king nodded his approval. "Ashur, impress upon the high priest the need to schedule the wedding as soon as possible after the princess arrives. He will be rewarded for a quick response. The kingdom needs an heir."

"Yes, Father." Ashur turned to leave.

Sin cocked his head. "Aren't you curious?"

"Of what?"

"Your new bride. You didn't ask anything about her—not even her name."

"Her father is the ruler of Elam. That's all I need to know."

"Quite right," huffed the king. "Ashur understands duty." The implication hung in the air. Sin did not.

Sin stiffened. "If I had more responsibility—"

"Your only responsibility is to support your king and do as he commands."

From the tightness in Sin's lips, he bit back strong words. Ashur had no wish to hear them escape and left for the stables. Would Sin never learn? It was best not to argue and simply respect the king's decisions.

An air of gloom settled on Ashur as his father's command echoed in his ears. The prospect of a second wedding with another woman who delighted more in the gifts bestowed than Ashur's company did nothing to lift his spirits. He swung into the saddle and trotted down the Processional Way to the temple. Upon arrival, a servant escorted him to Balu-su's chambers. Ashur cast an eye at the elaborate furnishings. Strange how he never noticed the riches surrounding the high priest before, suitable even for a prince.

Balu-su was effusive in his congratulations on the wedding announcement. His eyes glistened at the mention of the reward. "Please assure the king I will prepare the chart with due haste."

"Good. And how is Priestess Nemra?"

"Nemra?"

Balu-su's puzzled expression irked Ashur. "Has the high priest already forgotten the attackers wounded one of his own last evening?" *Or has the mention of added riches cast other thoughts from your mind?*

"Of course not, my lord," he murmured. "She is well."

How do you know? Did you even bother to ask her? "Summon Nemra. I will judge for myself."

"As you wish," he said in a clipped tone.

He dispatched a servant, and Nemra arrived clutching a cloth bag to her chest. Her gaze lit upon Ashur. The pleasure in her smile chased the gloom from his heart as did her assurance she was well.

"As your highness can see," said Balu-su, "she has suffered no ill effects. I will begin work on the chart for the king." His eagerness for Ashur to leave was plain.

"I am happy to escort the prince from the temple," said Nemra. Balu-su grunted his approval.

The door to the high priest's chambers closed behind them, and Ashur said lightly, "Is he always so charming?"

Nemra chuckled. "Yes, but after much prayer, Marduk granted me the patience to ignore his moods."

Ashur's steps slowed as they exited the temple. The thought of leaving Nemra's side so soon had him searching for a way to keep her at hand. He paused and cleared his throat. "The view of the temple grounds is pleasant from here."

"Have you ever visited our gardens? They aren't nearly as fine as those at the palace, but I am happy to show them to you."

He smiled at her. "I would enjoy that."

Nemra returned the smile. "This way then." They wandered over manicured paths to a lush flowerbed filled with color. A delicate scent tickled his nostrils. "You shared with me your favorite spot," she said. "This is mine."

Ashur's heart thrummed inside his chest. "Its loveliness suits you."

Pink tinted her cheeks. The scent increased in strength, and Ashur inhaled deeply, loathe to move. Did his enjoyment of the delicate floral bouquet keep him fixed to Nemra's side or had a different power bound them together? His hand twitched with the urge to pull her close and feel her body next to his. Ashur shifted on his feet. This was madness. He should not allow such thoughts of a priestess. He should return to the palace at once and forget he ever heard her name.

Ashur coughed and motioned to the drawstring bag. "What do you carry?"

"I recorded the temple's allotment this morning. This is my choice."

"May I see?"

She hesitated. "It has no importance."

"Please."

Nemra opened the pouch and tentatively removed a headpiece. "What do you think?" She seemed eager for his opinion.

Ashur raised an eyebrow and blurted his first thought. "Balu-su would never want this for his share."

Her eyes sparkled in amusement. "No, he wouldn't. It's not…it's not…"

"Expensive?"

Nemra's laughter filled his heart. "No, it isn't, but the design is unusual, don't you agree?"

"Very. I've never come across anything similar."

She peered at him with a questioning look. "Where did you find it?"

"Behind a sealed door in a palace. It sat on a pillar in an otherwise empty room. Strange," he added. "They must have deemed it important, but it's hardly the headpiece of a king." He touched a finger to the inlay of the sun.

****

They stood shoulder to shoulder, not dressed for battle, but the soldier in Ashur cried out war was in the air. The woman at his side wore the headpiece; not Nemra's face, not her clothes or body, but Nemra's heart and courage. Their spirits melded together, warriors chosen from the past joined those of the future, rising up to meet the enemy. Ashur peered at his empty hand. Where was the sword; sun, moon, and stars glowing on metal black as night? Fierce compulsion overcame him. He must find the sword before time ran out.

Too late.

Day became night.

The gate opened.

The Everdark emerged.

Night became eternal.

Chapter Five

Ashur sank to his knees, cradling his head in his hands. With a gasp, Nemra was at his side. "Ashur, are you ill?" She dropped the headpiece and gently pulled his hands from his stricken face. The undeniable truth hit her like a bolt of lightning sent from Anu. Ashur had a vision.

"I'm going mad." His voice was no more than a choked whisper.

"You are not mad," said Nemra. "This must be an object of great power. I, too, had a vision when I touched the headpiece."

Ashur gazed at her with wonder. He took her hands and cradled them tight against his chest. "How can this be?"

"I have no answer." Nemra felt the pounding of his heart. She described the people in the maze and the coming of the Everdark. "What did you see?"

Ashur staggered to his feet. "Much of the same. Another time, a distant place, two people who were as us, yet, different." He stared into the distance. "We stood in the center of a maze. Many hearts joined as one to confront a great evil that condemned Babylon to eternal darkness."

Nemra drew in a sharp breath. "We fought together."

"Yes." Ashur's gaze dropped to his sword hand.

"You wore the headpiece, and we both prepared for battle."

"Prepared, but not ready," she said. "Something is missing."

Ashur startled. "You feel it, too. In the vision, I wielded a black sword." He clenched his fist. "To confront this evil without the sword would be as if stepping upon the battlefield unarmed."

Nemra shuddered. "Or performing a ritual without the song of honor to the gods. They have given us a gift, Ashur, a warning of the future."

"The gods wish us to act." He shook his head. "I'm a soldier, Nemra, and have led armies, but I do not know how to proceed. Do we consult Balu-su?"

"No!" The word burst from her lips. "The high priest should speak for the gods, but I can't...I don't..." How could she explain her fear and the need to keep the visions secret?

"Good."

She blinked in surprise. "You will not argue?"

"We are of the same mind." Ashur brushed a finger lightly across her cheek. "I trust you. Not him."

Her heart raced at his gentle touch. "And I trust you and no one else." She swallowed hard. "Only the high priest is allowed direct contact with the gods and the right to interpret dreams. If the knowledge we kept these visions comes to Balu-su, he will declare blasphemy. He has the power to demand our deaths. I can't ask a future king to take such a risk."

"The gods asked us," said Ashur, "and we have answered. The question is what do the gods wish us to do?"

"I don't know." Nemra gazed at the azure blue sky.

The stars and moon were in hiding now, but still there, as constant as Anu. They revolved in an eternal cycle. "Our lives are joined to the sun, moon, and stars," she murmured. "We are born under them. We die under them. Their positions change in each season, but with the right numbers in the charts, the gods offer clues to the days ahead. The mathematical relationship between the celestial bodies is the handwriting of the divine. Reading the messages allows us to glimpse the future."

Balu-su's calculations danced through her head. They had no alignment—yet. Marduk sent the visions as a warning, but the message was incomplete. Only one way revealed the full truth. Nemra's excitement rose. "The answer lies with the scroll Balu-su thought to destroy. He found an omen in the numbers and hid the meaning, but it seems the gods wish us to understand."

"The scroll does little good when burnt to ashes."

"The piece remains with the most important calculations. Alone, the numbers say nothing, but Balu-su must complete a new chart for the royal nuptials. If I can gain access, compare the old segment of the scroll with the new, perhaps I'll see what he is so determined to keep hidden." Her expression clouded over. "He will never allow me to touch it."

"Once Balu-su completes the chart," said Ashur, "he presents it to the king. After the ceremony, it is placed in the royal treasury to become part of the bridal gifts. I can remove it for you to examine."

At the mention of the wedding, Nemra's heart gave a wistful tug. "What of the sword in our visions?"

"I've never seen such a weapon in my travels nor in the home of any noble in Babylon." Ashur rubbed his chin. "I would have heard if the sword was captured armament. Soldiers always talk, and word of such an unusual blade would surely reach my ears. Can it be in the treasure chamber at the temple?"

"No. I would have remembered any such description in the accounts, but the sword was part of the vision, so the gods deem it important."

"Fortunately," said Ashur dryly, "war has been good for Babylon. The sword may be part of my father's spoils and forgotten in a corner. I'll search the treasure room and the rest of the palace."

They looked at each other and the silence lengthened between them. Ashur shifted on his feet. "I should return to the palace or others may wonder at my absence."

Nemra stared at the ground. "Yes, you must have much to do before your new bride arrives. My congratulations on the upcoming wedding."

"It's hardly worthy of congratulations." His voice was gruff. "The marriage is merely an affair of state. I don't even know her name."

Nemra's heart pounded. "Surely, any woman would be honored to have such a noble husband."

"She will be rich and a queen," he said harshly. "No doubt, that is foremost in her mind."

"Then she is a fool." The words escaped her lips before Nemra called them back. "Forgive me, I-I have no right to speak thus."

Ashur took her hand. "Do not apologize. I value your thoughts—and your company, more than any other." He pressed her fingers to his lips.

His kiss left a blazing imprint on her skin, and Nemra's breath caught in her throat. *I am a priestess of*

Marduk, not meant for any man. I should pull my hand away. Nemra's body rooted in place, as a delicious fever claimed her. She read the longing in his eyes and knew hers reflected the same. His head bent toward Nemra and their lips met.

Desire blazed a fiery arrow to her heart. Even the brilliance of the summer sun didn't compare. Ashur pulled Nemra close and her arms went around him. Their bodies melded together, so tight she felt his beating heart through her tunic. Each rhythmic throb echoed hers, two hearts working as one. This man was meant for her. He belonged at her side.

Ashur can never be mine. He already belongs to another.

Cold despair doused the flame. She pushed back from his arms.

"Forgive me." Ashur's voice shook. "I had no right to take such liberties."

"I have nothing to forgive." Nemra swallowed hard. "What you took, I gave freely and with no regrets."

"Nor have I." His expression filled with bittersweet yearning that tugged at her heart. "My soul calls out for you, Nemra, as it's done for no other. The sight of your face, the feel of your lips on mine fills me with joy. I wish I had the power to bestow on you the honor of wife." He pulled her close again. "I have never wanted so much to be the son of a potter rather than a king."

His words wrapped around her heart, melting her resolve. "I will gladly take whatever you offer." *One word and I am yours. Here. Now.*

This time Ashur pushed away. "No. If I can't bring you honor, I vow never to bring shame, but you have my heart, Nemra. Always."

"And you mine, Ashur. Know that there will always be a woman in Babylon who values your life above the riches of the kingdom."

With a wistful smile, Ashur turned from her. Nemra watched as he disappeared down the path. She picked the headpiece off the ground and clutched it to her chest. Since childhood, she devoted her life to the service of the gods, never with a single misgiving.

Until now.

Why did his touch so easily open the door to a heart long since shuttered? Why had the gods brought such an unattainable man into her life? Why did it feel so right to have Ashur at her side and life so cold and empty when he was gone? The duties of a priestess of Marduk were all she ever wanted and now it seemed she lived a lie—as if her life meant to follow a different path. The Nemra in the vision had no doubts. She stood with purpose and focus, and the man with her had the strength and courage of Ashur.

The thought of the prince's upcoming wedding produced a rush of turbulent emotions. By the gods, she needed to distract her thoughts. Nemra's finger ran along the headpiece. Balu-su would have begun crafting a new astrological chart in the library to select the most auspicious wedding date, but Ashur had also delivered scrolls to the temple with the tribute to Marduk. Might she find a clue to the headpiece's purpose in one of them?

Nemra slipped the headpiece into the pouch and hurried to the library. "I wish to see the new scrolls. Are they catalogued?"

"Not yet." The librarian motioned across the great

room to a table that contained two piles of scrolls. "Trade accounts and court records."

"No astrological charts?"

"They are reserved for the eyes of the high priest."

"I'm well aware of the rules," she said smoothly. "I only wished to know if they had been removed so not to open one by mistake."

"Balu-su took them to the antechamber. They await his inspection after completion of the new nuptial chart for the king." He nodded toward the table. "Do you need assistance with those, priestess?"

"No. I merely wish to examine the scrolls to see if I must add notations to the temple's treasury accounts."

Nemra walked away before the librarian asked more questions. A quick review of the scrolls in the first pile brought nothing of interest, only lists of recent crop harvests and tax rolls. The second pile showed more promise. The descriptions of court proceedings also listed gifts to the royal treasury.

Nemra scoured the records. Little by little, frustration grew. None of the scrolls mentioned the headpiece. Despite the object's rather plain appearance, it must have had great importance. Why else was it concealed in a hidden chamber of the palace?

She drummed her fingers on the table, and her eyes went to the bag. The headpiece's decoration was celestial in nature. A more logical place to find an answer might be in astrological charts not court records, but to lay hands upon them was sacrilege.

Geez, don't get your panties in a twist. Skedaddle over there and don't get nabbed.

Nemra sat back with a start. Geez? Panties? Skedaddle? Nabbed? The strange words faded from her head as quickly as they arose.

She shot a glance at the entrance. The librarian was engrossed in a papyrus. Nemra grabbed the bag and made her way across the room, careful to avoid observation. Her heart hammered as she approached the section devoted to astrological charts and she froze at a scratching sound. Slipping behind a rack of papyri, Nemra crept noiselessly to the high priest's special collection. She poked her fingers between the slats of a shelf and carefully moved a scroll to the side. Balu-su sat ten feet away at the table by the window overlooking the garden. His back faced her with a sheet of papyrus stretched in front of him. He dabbed a stylus pen in an inkpot and marked the surface with notations.

Behind him on the floor was a large basket, pushed against the rack on the other side of Nemra's hiding place. She counted a dozen scrolls. The chipped paint on the scroll bars hinted at great age, but the markings weren't Assyrian, or any language she recognized from the library. These must be the new additions.

So close she could practically touch them…Nemra burned with frustration. She would never slip from the library with the whole basket, and Balu-su could lock the scrolls away at any time. Perhaps this plan was folly after all. Did even one hold a clue to the headpiece? She turned toward the door. She should leave.

Hold on there, cowgirl.

Nemra blinked, and the voice faded. It seemed to come from the basket. She squinted at a scroll bar with a dab of faded gold paint, a round shape with protruding rays. Was that a sun? Heat blazed through the hand holding the pouch as intense as if she waved it over a blacksmith's forge. Nemra bit her lip to keep from crying out. The pain vanished in an instant, and she drew in a shaky breath. The headpiece made the choice for her.

Dropping to her knees, Nemra reached a slender hand to the other side of the rack. A mantra played over in her head. *The gods wish me to do this…the gods wish me to do this.* Her fingers touched the scroll. Carefully, silently, Nemra eased it from the basket.

The rasp of chair legs against the stone floor sent her heart racing. Nemra whipped her hand back and froze, the forbidden scroll tight in her grasp. The scuff of sandaled feet neared. Between the slats, she glimpsed the bottom of Balu-su's robes. He stopped in front of the basket and her mouth went dry. From above came the clink of a chain. He replaced a scroll in the rack over his head and retrieved another. Footsteps retreated to the table. Chair legs moved again, followed by the wispy sound of papyrus unrolling.

Nemra tucked the scroll into her tunic. She backed away on hands and knees until the end of the row and then stood up and peered around the shelf. Balu-su hunched over the table. His attention focused on the new scroll, oblivious to all else. Nemra darted from the chamber. She scurried past the racks straining to hear any sound of pursuit. Nothing but hushed silence dogged her footsteps.

Chill, girl, came the voice in her head. *You're almost home.*

The phrases emitted a comforting familiarity. "Chill, girl," she whispered to herself. "You're almost home."

The librarian's back was still turned as Nemra scurried through the exit. She hurried to her quarters, secured the door, and then collapsed on the bed, heart pounding. She dug the scroll from her tunic and raised it high overhead. "Booyah, Marduk."

****

In late afternoon, Ashur headed to the treasury. Attending to official duties with his father kept him occupied most of the day. He appreciated the distractions as any free moment his thoughts drifted to the kiss with Nemra. By the gods, what possessed him? The kiss was tantamount to an unforgivable sin. To desire a priestess of Marduk was forbidden, but even now the taste of her lips remained, the feel of her body pressed against him brought a wild rush of passion. A sweet ache bloomed to see her face again. It took every ounce of strength to prevent his steps from turning toward the Processional Way.

Then what? Take Nemra from the temple and make her his concubine in the palace? That was the only life he could offer. Balu-su might issue a token protest, but a few gems from the royal treasury slipped into his hand would garner beaming approval from the high priest, of that Ashur had no doubt. He was also certain Nemra would come willingly. Even now his heart felt as if it sensed her exact location. He could point at the walls and say, "This way," as if one kiss forged a mystical chain, binding them together.

What of it? Should Nemra give up a life of honor to become no more than a possession in the palace? She would be a plaything of the king with no power of her own, and no status for their children, the children conceived by love instead of duty. Ashur clenched his fists. He must let her go and walk away. A life together in this time and place was impossible.

His heart filled with despair. "You're such a wanker," he muttered.

"My lord?" A palace guard eyed him with confusion.

Ashur blinked, unaware he uttered the strange words aloud. "Nothing." He entered the corridor to the treasury, irritation rising with every step. By the gods, what happened to him? If he didn't watch his tongue, word would get to the king his eldest son's mind was weak. Nothing would please Sin more. His lips twitched in a wry smile. *Now there's a wanker.*

Ashur arrived at the heavily defended treasury deep within the palace walls and ordered the guards to open the door. War proved profitable to the King of Babylon. Ashurbanipal and his son's conquests spilled into multiple chambers, laden with the riches of a dozen conquered monarchies.

Returning triumphant from a campaign with spoils to add to the kingdom's wealth always filled Ashur with pride, but now he surveyed the casks of gold and precious gems with listless apathy. Conquest was a future king's duty, the only way to ensure the safety of the kingdom, but the riches at his feet now appeared as little more than trifling baubles. He stared at them with growing unease. Could this fortune buy protection for the kingdom from evil? The answer was plain.

Evil couldn't be bribed. Evil must be faced head on and vanquished—and that required the right weapon.

Ashur scoured the riches in the main chamber, but nothing resembled the sword. He went through each antechamber. Some contained jeweled weapons similar to the dagger gifted by his father, but not one matched his vision. The gods sent him a message. The sword

103

was important, and the man in the center of the maze yielded it with a purpose. If Ashur was to defeat evil, he must do the same, but the weapon wasn't in Babylon. Of that, he had no doubt. Why did the gods send an incomplete warning? What use was it to him and Nemra?

At the thought of Nemra, his gaze went to a silver chain adorned with a single pearl. He picked it up and ran the links through his fingers. The modest necklace held no allure for a queen, but Nemra would surely approve, and it would look lovely on her.

"There you are."

Ashur turned with a start. "Sin, what are you doing here?"

"The household guards are under my direct command. They alert me when a person enters the treasury."

Ashur raised an eyebrow. "Spying on me?"

Sin drew himself up in affront. "Hardly, brother. The heir to Babylon has every right to be here, but after the attack in the gardens, I gave orders for my men to inform me of any who entered this section of the palace. We can't be too careful." He gazed around the chamber. "What are you searching for?"

Ashur blurted his first thought. "A welcome gift for my new bride."

"That?" he said scornfully. "It's more suited for a merchant's wife—perhaps even a priestess of the temple."

Ashur swallowed back a sharp retort. "Is it? I confess I have no eye for baubles." He tossed the chain in a basket.

"Allow me to make a choice then." Sin plucked a

large brilliant ruby from the shelf and handed it to him. "This one. She can have the palace jeweler craft it into a pendant. I guarantee she will be pleased."

Ashur tucked the ruby into a pocket of his tunic. "Thank you, Sin." He turned to leave.

"Irusha."

He stopped in his tracks. "What?"

"Your new bride's name," he said with an innocent air. "Irusha will be pleased."

Ashur strode from the treasury. "Wanker," he muttered under his breath.

Chapter Six

Nemra removed the scroll from the hiding place in her room, tucked behind a stack of clay tablets with records of household accounts. For two days, she maintained the same routine. After the evening meal and the completion of temple duties, Nemra hurried to her quarters, bolted the door, and pored over the scroll. Her one fear was Balu-su discovering the theft before she returned it to the library. So far, he focused on the new astrological chart for the nuptials, but he would finish that task soon. Meanwhile, Nemra struggled with a growing sense of urgency. Time was short.

Unrolling the scroll flat on the tabletop, she lit a candle, and peered once again at the markings. While they weren't Babylonian, the celestial depictions led her to conclude this certainly was an astrological chart. These figures weren't words, but numbers, and that was a language Nemra spoke fluently.

She checked and rechecked the earlier calculations. They were correct. The information on the scroll was ready for her to decipher and reveal the hidden meaning. With a linen cloth, Nemra dabbed the sweat from her brow. By the gods, the heat had intensified the last few days. Even nightfall brought little relief. Not a breath of wind stirred. The heat hung heavily in the air, slowing movements, muddying thoughts. She struggled to reach clarity with the numbers. The answer was within her grasp. All that remained was to interpret the final entry, but, so far, the significance eluded her...

The crown.

Nemra sat back with a start. Pulse racing, she stood and scanned the room. The door was barred, no one had entered and whispered in her ear. She stared at the drawstring pouch on the desk. She had kept the headpiece close while working on the scroll, finding strange comfort in its presence.

Her skin tingled with a strong compulsion to wear it once more. With shaking hands, she opened the bag and removed the headpiece—no, *the crown.* The celestial objects appeared brighter, lit with a fire of their own. Nemra placed the crown on her head. Gentle warmth radiated to her hands. She gazed at them in wonder and then trailed a fingertip across the scroll; adding, subtracting, multiplying, dividing. The calculations aligned in her head in perfect harmony, the hidden meaning now laid bare.

Nemra paled and clutched her tunic. "It can't be." She drew a steadying breath and reached inside the drawstring pouch again and retrieved the scrap rescued from the flames. She checked and rechecked the numbers against the notations on the mystical chart.

The fragment of burnt parchment fluttered from her shaking hand. She grasped the edge of the desk, caught in a mental whirlwind of dread and dismay. No doubt in her mind remained. *Balu-su knows.* He beheld the signs and read the awful truth; unspeakable evil approached Babylon. Instead of warning the faithful at the temple and rousing them to prayer, he chose to ignore the message in the stars. No—her anger at the high priest soared. He chose to hide it.

She rerolled the papyrus. Ashur must be warned, and the high priest confronted. Her theft of the scroll was sacrilege, but Balu-su's dedication to the service of Marduk was no longer trusted. Whatever the reason for his actions, he willingly led Babylon's inhabitants into imminent danger.

"Nemra." Tal-banit tapped on the door. "Balu-su has summoned the clergy to appear at once."

Nemra's heart skipped a beat. She removed the crown and opened the door, careful to block Tal-banit from entering. "For what purpose?"

She shot a nervous glance to the corridor and whispered, "He has the whole temple in an uproar. Balu-su finished the chart for the king and then discovered one of the astrological maps brought as tribute by the prince disappeared from the library. Surely, none of the faithful dared touch it, but Balu-su ordered everyone to the great hall while guards search our quarters."

Nemra steeled her nerves, fighting to scour any emotion from her face. "Where is Balu-su?"

"At the palace delivering the nuptial chart."

"Go. I'll meet you in the great hall."

Tal-banit regarded her with surprise. "You must come now."

"I'll be there shortly. Hurry."

Nemra waited until the sound of her footsteps disappeared. She placed the crown in the pouch, grabbed the scroll, and hurried to the first floor. Although most of the guards aided in the search, a few watched the main entrance. In the dark, Nemra slipped from a lower portico and then dashed across the grounds.

The guard at the exit to the Processional Way stopped her. "Balu-su commanded none to leave the temple grounds."

Heart pounding, Nemra held out the scroll. "The missing scroll was found and must be returned to him without delay." The guard appeared unsure, and Nemra squared her shoulders. "Do you defy the high priest?"

He bowed. "No, priestess. Open the gates!"

Nemra ran to the Hanging Gardens. Guards posted at the entrance barred her path. "The gardens are closed after dark by order of Prince Sin-sharish-kun."

"I am a priestess of Marduk," said Nemra, panting, "and have an urgent message for Prince Ashur-etil-ilani. Let me pass."

One murmured in the ear to another and then waved her through. When Nemra was in sight of the palace, she paused, suddenly unsure. A retinue of temple guards waited out front for Balu-su. They would surely question her, and she must speak with Ashur alone. Nemra turned and headed to the reflecting pool to wait until Balu-su departed.

****

Ashur sat on the bench gazing into the water. Perhaps Balu-su had finished with the king and left the palace by now. He had no wish for a chance meeting with the high priest. After the vision and his talk with Nemra, he didn't trust himself to hold either tongue or anger in check. The high priest had a secret, to be sure. If only Ashur had proof.

Unconsciously, his fist clenched as if in need of a weapon. The sword from the vision held importance, and it wasn't in the palace, or in possession of a Babylonian noble. Ashur had made discreet inquiries over the past days. No one owned such a blade with those markings or had ever heard of a black sword. Why had the gods sent an incomplete message? Why wasn't he clever enough to figure out the answer?

Ashur turned his head at the sound of footsteps along the path and his face lit with pleasure. "Nemra."

"Ashur. I thought you were in the palace. Balu-su arrived with the nuptial chart."

"It holds my father's interest," he said softly, "not mine. Something happened. I see it in your eyes."

Nemra held out a chart. "I found this in the library. It's one of the scrolls brought to the temple as tribute. I read the message." Even in moonlight, he noted the sickly pallor of her face. "Evil is upon the kingdom. Tomorrow the moon will swallow the sun at its highest point in the sky."

Ashur gaped at her. "That's impossible. Surely, the chart is in error."

"I wish to the gods that was so, but numbers always speak the truth to me and never lie. A dark shadow will sweep across Babylon at midday, blotting out the light. In that time, the wall between the worlds of humans and gods stretches thin. An evil presence hovers just beyond the boundary, searching for an opening to enter our domain. If it finds the way…" She shuddered. "The darkness will last forever. The sun will never return. The demon will feast until it consumes the last spark of life from every soul on Earth."

Ashur drew in a sharp breath. "How can we stop such great evil?"

Nemra hugged her arms tight to her chest. "This is beyond my role as priestess of the temple. I have no knowledge of such things."

"Does Balu-su?"

"Perhaps."

Ashur clenched his fists. "Yet, he chooses silence."

"He hid the truth from the clergy at the temple for reasons of his own, of that I'm certain."

Ashur took her hand; the cold intent of a warrior flooded his veins. "He will not hide the truth from me."

Sin met them at the palace steps. "My guards informed me Priestess Nemra had urgent words for you, brother." He shot a glance at their clasped hands.

"Is Balu-su with the king?" demanded Ashur.

"He returned to the temple with his retinue. You had no interest in the nuptial chart," he said lightly, "why consult the high priest now?"

Ashur scowled. "Nemra brought proof Balu-su is a traitor to Babylon."

The prince's eyes widened. "How can this be?" Nemra explained her findings. When she was done, Sin shook his head. "This is evil, indeed, brother. What will you do?"

"Balu-su must answer for his deceit."

"Drag him from his quarters?" Sin raised an eyebrow. "He has many guards. We won't easily subdue him."

"Ashur," said Nemra. "You cannot shed blood in the temple of Marduk and anger the gods."

Sin rested a hand on his brother's shoulder. "The priestess is right. Allow me to fetch him. I will go to the temple and explain you have examined the nuptial chart and require further discussion. Despite the late hour, he can't ignore a summons from a member of the royal family. Balu-su will be none the wiser. Once inside the palace gates, my guards will take him into custody with

111

no blood spilled in the temple."

"Very well. Meanwhile, I will inform Father—"

"We should question him first, Ashur," said Sin. He nodded his head toward Nemra. "I mean no disrespect, but the king is sure to take the word of Balu-su over a priestess. You know Father's mind. He will think us fools for even suspecting Marduk's high priest of treachery and dismiss her claims at once without bothering to hear evidence." Ashur wavered, and Sin added in a rush. "Once the king makes his decision, Balu-su will be free, and the chance to discover his true intent lost."

"I'll wait with Nemra in the gardens by the reflecting pool. Make haste," called Ashur as Sin hurried away. "I fear time is not on our side."

Ashur escorted Nemra to the bench by the pool. "It seems we are ever fated to meet here."

"If so," said Nemra with a smile, "it is a pleasant spot and almost puts my heart at ease."

The warmth of her smile dulled his anger at Balu-su, and instead he reveled in the comfort of Nemra's presence. A wisp of hair had escaped the clip. Ashur tucked it behind her ear. "All I need from life is to see your face."

Her smile faded as she gazed at the moon. "I fear for the future, Ashur."

"As do I." He shifted on the bench. "The sword isn't in the treasury, nor did I find any hint to its whereabouts." He stared at his open palm and his fingers curled around an imaginary grip. "I've never seen this weapon and yet swear it was made for me."

"If only we had more time."

Ashur raised her hand to his lips. "If only we had

more freedom. I would never allow you from my side."

Her voice dropped to a whisper. "A command willingly obeyed."

The bushes rustled. Ashur jumped to his feet, hand to the dagger at his side. "Who's there?"

Sin stepped into the open with a retinue of guards. "Peace, brother."

Ashur narrowed his eyes and moved in front of Nemra. "Why have you returned with such haste? Where is Balu-su?"

"There's been a change of plans." His voice was cold, the evil intent evident.

Ashur raised the dagger. "Traitor! Not another step."

"Drop the dagger or the girl dies first." Archers nocked their arrows.

"Ashur, go," cried Nemra. "You must warn the king."

He gave her a stricken look and tossed the dagger to the ground. Guards set upon them and bound Ashur's and Nemra's arms and legs with cords. Ashur struggled helplessly as another placed a gag over his mouth, fiery hatred surging at his brother's treachery.

"Twenty minutes," said Sin mildly. "That's all that separates a future king from a lowly prince, always judged by his father to be second-best. Not skill, not ability, nothing mattered except that Ashur-etil-ilani was firstborn." Sin picked up Ashur's dagger and his gaze went to the palace. "I'd be a fool to let a mere twenty minutes stand in the way of a kingdom."

Ashur staggered from a sharp blow to the head. His last sight before losing consciousness was Nemra being dragged away.

****

Nemra groaned. Her eyelids fluttered open. Sunlight streamed through windows and she blinked in the bright light. The heat was stifling, and her head throbbed. Bleary-eyed, she gazed at her surroundings and drew in a sharp breath. She was in the holiest chamber at the pinnacle of the ziggurat where the clergy performed the most sacred rites to Marduk and made offerings to the great god. On the floor was the pouch and the scroll. Ashur laid at her feet, a puddle of blood from a head wound staining the immaculate stone floor crimson. Her gag was gone, and she cried out his name, but the prince made no response.

Sick with fear, Nemra struggled to move, but her wrists were bound to the statue of the god.

"Help," she cried. "Someone help us."

The trap door in front of the altar opened, and High Priest Balu-su emerged with Ashur's dagger in his hand. "Good, you're awake, priestess," he said mildly. "Save your voice, no one can hear you. The temple guards brought you to the chamber. They are far below and loyal to me and won't permit anyone to pass."

Her whole body trembled with rage. "No thieves attacked us in the Hanging Gardens that night. Your men tried to kill us both."

"You saw the scroll and forced my hand," he said. "I couldn't have a warning spread to the palace before I was ready to act."

Nemra struggled to free her wrists, ignoring the pain as tough leather cords cut her skin. "Do your men know you're a traitor to Babylon, a blasphemer of the gods?"

"They only know what I choose to tell them,"

Balu-su said mildly. "A priestess of Marduk, no more than a shameful whore of Babylon, seduced Ashur-etil-ilani and convinced him to murder Ashurbanipal and make her his queen."

Nemra gasped. "The king is dead?"

"Not yet, but soon, and by a son's hand." His sandaled foot prodded Ashur's side. "Not his, of course, but his brother's. The firstborn's dagger, a loving gift from his father, will be found embedded in the king's heart as soon as we finish here."

"Who will believe your lies?" she scoffed. "No one in the kingdom doubts Ashur is loyal to his father."

He regarded her with contempt. "Palace security is Prince Sin-sharish-kun's concern. He hand-picked the guards and they swore loyalty to him as the temple guards did to me. The new king will have the backing of both. None will dare to stand against him. Sin-sharish-kun will describe how he came upon the horrific crime and chased the murderers to the temple. They begged sanctuary. I refused, and they were killed."

Nemra glared at him. "This isn't a plan of opportunity. You and the prince have been plotting the takeover of Babylon."

A faint smile twisted his lips. "For quite some time. The prince needed the support of the temple, and the alignment of the planets showed me the opportune moment. No one has the power to stop us." His eyes narrowed. "You should have kept out of this, priestess."

"This is insanity, Balu-su," said Nemra. "You see what's coming. I read the charts. You deliberately hid the truth. Today, at the highest point of the sun, day turns into night. A monstrous evil prepares to ravage the world unless we stop it."

Balu-su leaned toward her, and Nemra shrunk from the hunger in his eyes. He licked his lips like a lion poised over the kill. "Not a faceless evil," he said, "but a new god to replace the old, one filled with ancient power, trapped beyond the mystic veil. Yes, I read the signs. He will share his power with anyone who offers an escape route to our world."

The horror of his infamy rocked Nemra to her core. "Fool, have you learned nothing as high priest? If clergy perform proper rites, a god may grant a request, but never does one share power. It is not in a god's nature."

Balu-su's complexion reddened and his hand closed around her neck. "Silence, whore. In exchange for help, the god will gift me powers and I'll become immortal. The faithful of this temple will no longer worship Marduk. They will worship me."

"And the new king?" she choked out. "Will he worship you, too? Or doesn't he suspect what you have planned?"

With a wily smile, Balu-su released his hand from her throat. "The king's concerns rest with ruling the kingdom, not with religious affairs." He strode to the window, eyes squinting at the sun. "Midday is upon us, whore of Babylon. Can you feel it?" His voice trembled with excitement. "A new world is at hand. When the darkness is complete, a sacrifice to the god will thin the veil and reveal the gate. The deaths of a prince and a priestess will do nicely. See, even now the shadows lengthen."

The bright sunlight flooding the chamber dimmed, decreasing the stifling heat. Screams rose up from far below. Balu-su peered over the ledge at the city. "The citizens of Babylon watch the moon devour the sun and wail in terror." His expression filled with contempt. "Have you noticed from this great height how people resemble frightened ants? Kick the sand and they scurry to and fro. See how they gather at the gates to the temple grounds and call upon their high priest to intercede with the gods. Help is coming," he said with disdain. "Bow your heads, bend your knees, and worship me."

Shadows thickened and spread, deepening the chill in the room. Blood raced through Nemra's veins as an unearthly pounding echoed within the stone walls.

Something approached, moving and circling and watching. Evil stalked right outside the veil, searching for the entrance to the world. Nemra strained at the bonds, slicing her wrists but to no avail. Blood dripped from her wounds and fell on the pouch at her feet.

From inside came a faint glow.

Balu-su strode from the window, triumph on his face, the dagger in his raised hand. He kicked aside the pouch. "The time has come, priestess, to greet our new god."

With a roar, Ashur staggered to his feet. Blood streaming down his face, he lunged at the high priest. Nemra screamed as Balu-su plunged the dagger into Ashur. "Too late, my prince."

Ashur stumbled back. With a battle cry, he yanked the dagger free and hurled it at the high priest. Stunned, Balu-su swayed on his feet, clutching the hilt protruding from his chest. "No...no..." He coughed, blood dribbled from the corner of his lips. Ashur lumbered toward him, his expression contorted with

117

rage. The priest's eyes widened in horror. He raised his hands in defense, but Ashur knocked them aside. One arm wrapped around Balu-su's neck. One sharp twist and the high priest collapsed with a thud on the floor.

Ashur yanked the dagger from Balu-su. He fell against Nemra and sliced the cords from her wrists. With a cry, she caught Ashur as his legs gave out and she eased him to the ground. The glow from inside the pouch was the only light in the chamber now. Day had become night.

Nemra pressed a hand against the stab wound. Blood gushed between her fingers and she swallowed back a sob. "I must bring help—"

Ashur touched her cheek. "No…no time. I heard what Balu-su said. Must stop it…must…"

A bloodcurdling howl filled the air in a victory cry.

"It has the sacrifice…" Ashur choked out a breath, his face as pale as the moon. "It found the gate. Hurry, Nemra, protect our people." The spark faded from his eyes. "I will love you forever…" His hand dropped to his side.

"Ashur…" Nemra pressed her lips against his forehead. Grief threatened to still her heart.

In front of the statue of Marduk, the air shimmered and glowed. Mist appeared and formed a shadowy gate. Something rammed the surface, jarring it open a crack. "I am the Everdark," it roared. "My time has come."

Hatred forged purpose. Nemra tore the crown from the pouch and placed it on her head. The sun, moon, and stars shone with fiery internal light. Nemra slammed her hands against the gate. The heat was intense. Scorching agony raced up her arms. She bit her lip to keep from screaming and tasted blood.

The Everdark shrieked in frustrated rage. Again, and again, it hammered at the gate.

The crown blazed fire. *I cannot hold long,* came a voice in her head.

"Use my strength," Nemra commanded, clenching her teeth. "All of it. This…gate…will…not…open."

Life drained from Nemra. With each ragged breath torn from her lungs more slipped away. Soon her heart would still, all essence drained, yet Nemra held fast.

Forgive me, said the crown with woeful regret. *You will die.*

"My people will live."

The chamber went from black to gray. Outside came an exultant cry from the citizens of Babylon as the sun returned to the sky.

The howls from the Everdark weakened. Blood pounding in her ears, Nemra pushed with her remaining strength, but the gate refused to shut tight. A crack remained.

The shimmer faded. The veil between worlds reformed, but more fragile than before. "I have found a weakness," snarled the Everdark. "I see the gate now and wait until the alignment of forces returns. Ten years? Ten thousand? Time means nothing to me…" The voice faded away as the last of the mist disappeared.

Nemra sank to her knees. The crown dropped from her head and rolled across the floor. The fire extinguished from the sun, moon, and stars, a dull and lifeless headpiece once more. With her last bit of strength, Nemra crawled to Ashur's side and laid her head on his chest. Only a few beats remained for him now. The steady thrum from her own heart slowed and

119

weakened. Soon, it would stop, too.

Tears fell from her eyes. "The Everdark is defeated for now, my love. Your sacrifice was not in vain. Babylon is safe, but the monster will come again. No weapon can stand against it."

She raised her eyes to the statue of Marduk towering overhead. As the light in the chamber brightened to full day, her eyesight blurred and dimmed.

Faithful daughter of Marduk, faithful son of Babylon, the battle is ended. The arms of the eternal open wide.

"Do not judge me worthy to join you," she gasped out, "unless Ashur is at my side."

Sin-sharish-kun climbed out of the trap door, sword in hand. He eyed the bloody dagger on the floor and the body of the high priest. "My brother's handiwork, I presume." He tucked the dagger in his belt. "I have need of this."

Nemra lifted her head from Ashur's chest. "Marduk awaits Ashur and me. Enjoy your power. It won't last long." She spit on the prince. "The gods of Babylon curse you."

The prince raised his sword and ran through the whore of Babylon and Prince Ashur-etil-ilani, piercing both their hearts with a single stroke.

Once more the chamber went dark.

Chapter Seven

Cal moaned and rolled over. The pain had vanished. One hand went to his chest. No sticky blood remained on his tunic. "Nemra?" he whispered.

Tunic? Nemra?

Cal's eyelids flew open. "What the hell?" he sputtered at the sight of orderly rows of cornstalks overhead instead of the statue of Marduk. His hands briskly rubbed across his clothing and he sighed in relief. No tunic, but a T-shirt and jeans minus a stab wound.

Meg stirred beside him and let out a muffled groan. Cal struggled to a sitting position and his hand reached out and touched her arm. "Nem—Meg. Talk to me. Are you hurt?"

Meg's eyes opened. She regarded him with a bleary gaze. "Ashur?"

His heart skipped a beat. "Not quite. Y-you dreamt it, too?"

Meg blinked several times. "Cal?" She looked around and her eyes widened. "What the hell?"

He managed a shaky smile. "My sentiments exactly." He staggered up and helped Meg to her feet.

Meg gazed blankly ahead and then her expression filled with relief. "We were in…" She swallowed hard. "I thought we were in…"

"The temple of Marduk."

121

"I was Nemra. You were Ashur." Meg's face paled. She placed a hand on his chest. "That scumbag, Balu-su, stabbed you."

Cal slipped his hand over hers, smiling at the ferocity in her tone. "I'm okay."

"Good...that's good." A faint pink blush colored her cheeks. "I was worried. I-I mean Nemra was worried. I mean..." Her hand trembled. "Cal, what the hell? W-was that a dream? A nightmare?" She snorted. "What do you people put on the funnel cakes around here?"

"I could have sworn," he said dryly, "it was nothing more than an excess of powdered sugar, only now I'm not so sure of the white stuff." No mystical flames danced over the flagstones under the arbor any longer, but laughter and voices drew closer. "People are coming. Let's get out of here and go someplace quiet to talk."

Meg dropped her hand from his chest. "Fine with me. The farther from here, the better."

Cal led them through the maze, his steps never faltering. They reached the exit and Meg stopped, eyeing him with suspicion. "That was mighty quick. You didn't make one wrong turn. How did you know the way out?"

"I haven't a clue. I swear I'm in the dark as much as you."

Meg's eyes narrowed, and she took a step back. "I don't know you. I'm not sure I believe anything you say. I'm beginning to think I need to get away from here right now."

The idea of Meg leaving left Cal cold and empty. He stifled the urge to grab her arm and insist she stay.

He needed Meg at his side.

What's wrong with me? I'm not Ashur, she isn't Nemra.

Cal's shoulders sagged with sudden fatigue, and he drew a steadying breath. "Please don't go. I wouldn't believe me either if I were you, but I need to figure out what happened in the maze. I can't do it alone."

The indecision on her expression wavered. Her gaze drifted back to the rows of corn rippling in the warm breeze. "I can't either. What do you suggest?"

"I'm a lawyer." He wiped a hand across his sweaty brow. "Damn, it's hot. My office isn't far and it's air conditioned. I'll call Isaac and demand answers."

"If he refuses?"

"I'll find a way. Lawyers are good at uncovering hidden truths."

"So are accountants."

Cal blinked. "You work with numbers. So did..." He pressed his lips together.

"Nemra?" The stiffness in her posture relaxed. "Never thought I'd find common ground with a pagan priestess in a Babylonian temple. Okay, I'm in. Lead on, once more."

Cal hesitated, his attention fixed on people entering the maze. "I feel as if I shouldn't leave yet." He floundered to explain, struggling to find words to describe his tumult of conflicted emotions. "I don't know what I want...warn them of danger, maybe."

Meg's expression softened. "Protect them?"

Unconsciously, his hand dropped to his side as if to reach for a sword. "Yeah. I sound crazy, huh?"

"Not so much anymore, but I suspect whatever happened inside that maze was for our eyes alone." She snorted. "Thank you, Phillip Bingham and the Lux Foundation."

They walked across town to his office taking turns describing Ashur and Nemra's lives. "It was so real," said Cal in wonder. "I can close my eyes and still smell the flowers in the Hanging Gardens."

Meg elbowed him playfully in the side. "Admit it. Being a prince was cool."

Cal chuckled softly. "I can't deny the life had perks. I didn't cook my own meals, servants did the dirty laundry, and I never had to make my bed."

"What about the palace concubines?" she teased.

"Not my thing," he said. "Not Ashur's either, apparently. He was searching for love—and a good funnel cake."

"So was Nemra. She got these words and images but didn't understand them. Part of our lives bled through, but we couldn't hold onto the memories from here."

"Nemra the priestess and Meg Adler were both bean counters," Cal said lightly. "I guess some things are meant to be."

She grinned. "I guess so."

They arrived at Cal's office and he ushered her to his desk. "I'll call Isaac first..." He gawked at the time display on his cell phone.

"What's wrong?"

"We were only gone two hours," said Cal. "It felt like days." He dialed Isaac's number. "Voicemail," he muttered, "I'll leave a message...It's me. I found Meg, and you have a helluva lot of explaining to do. Call me back or I will hunt you down. You know I can." He hung up and dropped the cell in his pocket.

"You were a soldier." Meg stared at the wall where Cal displayed his diplomas along with the honorable discharge certificate.

"Yeah. Two years active duty in the Middle East."

"You didn't stay in the service."

"No. I finished my tour and used the GI benefits for college. I wanted a different life."

"So did Ashur," she mused. "He only knew Nemra a few days but loved her with all his heart." Her voice softened. "He died to protect her."

Cal's breath quickened. "Nemra stayed by his side to the very end. She must have loved Ashur very much, too."

"I did. I…I mean, she did," Meg stuttered, face reddening. "Nemra refused to pass into eternity without Ashur." Her hand clutched the neckline of her shirt. "Everything she experienced is still inside me. I feel her love for him. It was powerful, and yet they were doomed from the start."

"Ashur would have traded every jewel in the kingdom for a life with her."

Meg's eyes sought his. "I can't imagine loving a person you just met that much. Can you?"

Despite the air conditioning in the office, the temperature seemed to rise several degrees. The silence lengthened between them. Cal's hand twitched. He wanted to reach for Meg, pull her close. His hand stilled. He had no right. Instead, he said, "While we're waiting for Isaac to get back to us, we can do a little research."

Meg's hand dropped from the shirt to her side and her lips twitched in a faint smile. "I'm game. Frankly, I want to know if these people were real or at the very least confirm my hallucinogenic funnel cake theory."

Cal turned on the computer. "Then let me try." He pulled up a second chair next to his desk. "At least one person in that vision, or whatever the heck it was, existed."

Meg blinked. "Seriously?"

"Yup. Ashurbanipal was a king in ancient times." Cal typed in a search, amused by Meg's shocked expression. "I've always enjoyed reading history. It was my college major and I toyed with the idea of teaching until law pulled me in a different direction. If I recall my class on the Middle East correctly, he conquered Babylon...aha!" He stabbed his finger at the screen. "King Ashurbanipal and the Hanging Gardens of Babylon...He had two sons, Princes Ashur-etil-ilani and Sin-sharish-kun. A few records say they were twins, very unusual for them to have survived birth in that time period."

"According to this account," said Meg, scanning the entry, "after the death of the king, Prince Sin-sharish-kun seized the throne. Nothing about murdering his father or plotting with a high priest named Balu-su. They even state the cause of Ashur's death is only a possible murder instead of a fact."

"Records dating from ancient Babylon are sketchy," said Cal. "History has to be pieced together from different sources and no telling how much is accurate. The Hanging Gardens were destroyed long ago, so was the temple of Marduk, the library, and its records."

"Funny, but I'm bummed to hear that," said Meg with a wistful look. "It's as if I discovered my childhood home burnt to the ground and a place once

126

important to me is gone forever."

Cal continued to read. "Huh. Sin-sharish-kun didn't enjoy his rule for long. The author of this article states he died a year or so after seizing the throne, and speculates he was overthrown and murdered."

"Serves him right," grunted Meg. "Imagine, killing your own father and brother. Can you find anything on Nemra?"

"Let me see." Cal did a quick search and came up empty. "No, but that's no surprise."

Meg raised an eyebrow. "Why?"

"The few ancient writings that survive don't mention female names unless they were queens or goddesses. Sorry, but their contributions weren't considered important."

"That sounds like something my ex-boss would say." Meg jabbed him playfully in the shoulder. "Four billion years of evolution and men are still pigs."

"Yes, we are," Cal replied with good humor, "and on behalf of every bearer of a Y-chromosome, I wish to offer my deepest apologies for humanity's history of sexism and social injustice and add a heartfelt promise to do better in the future."

Meg burst out laughing. "On behalf of every woman on the planet, apology accepted." She shook her finger at him. "I'm holding you to your word, so fair warning. I'll have to keep an eye on you."

The suggestion brought Cal a pleasant tumble of emotions. "I'm okay with that."

Meg smiled faintly and turned the keyboard toward her. "Let's see if I can find the crown and sword." A search brought up nothing.

Cal rubbed his forehead. "We never saw the sword,

and Ashur was convinced it wasn't in the kingdom. The crown was so distinctive though. I really thought we'd find a listing of it in a museum."

"It might be in a private collection. That sword…" Meg mused. "It must be important, but why?"

Cal shifted in his seat. "Tell me I'm not crazy. Tell me you feel the truth, too."

Meg shivered. "Someone made the sword for use against that thing."

"The sword is a magical weapon," said Cal, "not for everyone, but a man like Ashur could wield it." He flexed his fingers. "I had a powerful urge to hold the sword in my hand—I mean his, but Ashur was right. It wasn't in Babylon." He shook his head. "I feel like a damn fool. Don't ask me to explain because I can't."

"I believe you," Meg said softly. "I had the same sensation with the crown. It called to me—to her." She smiled. "Geez, this pronoun thing is confusing." The smile faded and she turned her head away, but not before he glimpsed sadness in her eyes.

Cal touched her hand. "What is it?"

"They didn't have a chance. Ashur's sword was meant to weaken the Everdark enough for Nemra to close the gate. She couldn't shut it alone. At least, not all the way." Meg tensed. "The Everdark sits on the other side, gathering strength and waiting for the chance to try again."

"You don't know that."

"Don't I? Don't you?" Her eyes narrowed and she jerked her hand away. "You sense it, too."

"Maybe." Cal gestured to the monitor. "But I don't think we'll find any more answers here."

Meg swallowed hard. "In the maze?"

"Yeah, but I can't say I'm up for a return visit yet."

"Me, either." Meg shuddered. "I can still see that eerie fire hovering over the flagstones. Say, whose idea was the maze, anyway? Isaac Bingham?"

"Beats me. George Lydecker owns the farm and, as far as I know, the harvest festival always includes a maze, but I haven't lived in Crossroads long. George planted the corn, but I can't imagine him constructing a portal to another dimension, and the community college doesn't offer adult extension courses on demon slaying. At least, I don't think so." Cal sat up with a start. "Oh, crap. I may know someone who can shed a little light. My paralegal, Becky, told me Amaranth talked George into erecting the arbor."

"Who's Amaranth?"

"Local Earth Mother. Her real name is Debbie Goldstein. Amaranth grew up in Crossroads but left town a long time ago. She came back last year to open a teahouse and organic herb shop with her daughter, Summer. I saw Amaranth this morning at the festival. As a matter of fact, she said something strange, even for Amaranth." He frowned. "What was it now…She stopped me with a warning of confluences and a veil."

"She talked to me, too." Meg's eyes widened. "Hang on, you mean a veil between dimensions?" She jumped to her feet. "Where can we find her?"

"It's lunchtime." Cal pushed back his chair. "She must be back at the shop by now."

Amaranth's teahouse, Grow a Pear, was a short walk down Main Street. "What exactly do we say to her?" said Meg. "Let's face it, our story is whacked."

"I can talk to Amaranth without giving too much away. Actually, getting Amaranth to talk New Age stuff is no problem. Getting her to stop is another matter."

The shop had a screened porch in front. Two tabbies immediately wrapped themselves around Cal and Meg's ankles. "I see Isis and Osiris are on duty today. Amaranth's cats take turns."

Meg bent over to scratch their heads. "How many does she have?"

"Seven at last count, but the number comes and goes as she finds them homes. Amaranth is a sucker for strays."

A sign on the door said *Please Don't Let in the Cats.* They stepped inside the shop and Cal paused to inhale an appreciative breath. "Say what you will about Amaranth, it always smells great in here."

Meg gazed at the shelves filled with herbs and fresh plants, and then grinned. "She has a thing for fairy figurines too, I see."

Cal followed her gaze to a shelf in the corner with figurines made from assorted scrap metals. "Yeah, Amaranth welds garden sculptures, but don't mention them to her."

"Why? They're kind of cute."

"I made the mistake once, and she dragged me through the shop to introduce me to each one. They apparently have different personalities and prefer to choose their owner. Amaranth also names them." He nodded to a sculpture in the corner. "That's Piddlewinks. Amaranth insisted he wanted to go home with me, but Piddlewinks creeped me out."

Meg snickered. "Afraid he lusted after you?"

"Either that or he planned to murder me in my sleep. Plus, I refuse to spend hard earned cash on anything called Piddlewinks, so I passed." Cal peered around. "I don't see Amaranth or Summer. Hey, Dylan Lydecker is at the register."

"Related to George of the corn maze?"

"His nephew. Dylan's not a bad kid, but he's going through a rough patch. His mom is single and in the military. She was unexpectedly deployed overseas and couldn't take Dylan so sent him to George to finish his last year of high school. He had to leave his home and friends behind and start mid-term as a senior in a strange place. So far, all he and George have done is butt heads."

"Maybe he's another of Amaranth's strays hunting for a new home."

"Could be. Hey, Dylan," he called. "No school?"

"Closed for the festival."

"You working here now?"

"Helping out with the crowds," he mumbled, shuffling his feet.

And to escape Uncle George for a while? "I need to talk to Amaranth."

He motioned over his shoulder. "She's in the back."

The tearoom was in the rear of the shop, small with only eight tables. The lunch rush was over, and most of the customers had left. Summer cleared dishes from an empty table. "Two for lunch? We're almost ready to close the kitchen."

"Sure," said Cal. "Please ask your mom to join us when she has a chance."

"Okay. I'll let her know you're here. Take the table by the window."

They sat down and Cal motioned to the view of a lush garden outside. "The food here is excellent, totally

131

organic. Amaranth plans a different menu each day, depending on what she harvests from her garden or buys fresh at the local farmer's market." He leaned over the table and his voice dropped low. "Which reminds me, think twice about ordering her secret blend organic herb tea. I suspect the dried leaves she uses aren't chamomile."

Meg snickered. "After a day like today, it might be exactly what I need."

Summer returned with a basket of herb and cheese biscuits warm from the oven, bowls of homemade tomato soup and fresh garden salads. Meg shot Cal a wicked look and ordered two iced glasses of the special house blend organic tea.

They finished eating and Meg leaned back with a sigh. "Everything was delicious as promised, and..." she added with the mischievous grin, "the tea had an unusual flavor. I can't quite place it, but am totally refreshed—"

"Chamomile."

Amaranth waltzed across the floor with a friendly smile on her face. "Cal, it's so nice to see you again." She turned to Meg. "And who is this?"

"Meg Adler," said Cal, "a friend of mine."

"Oh, yes," said Amaranth. "We spoke at the entrance to the maze."

"I told Meg you designed the arbor..." Despite Cal's earlier assurances to Meg, he floundered on how to broach the subject of the maze without sounding like a lunatic.

"It was lovely," blurted Meg. "Very unusual."

Cal startled as Amaranth pulled an empty chair to Meg's side and peered at her with intensity. "How so?"

Meg shifted in her seat. "When I stood underneath, I thought I heard, um, sounds inside."

"Sounds," echoed Amaranth in a hushed tone.

Cal jumped in. "Yes, very interesting acoustics."

Meg nodded. "The acoustics, right, or uh, lights maybe? Lights in the maze—"

Without warning, Amaranth grabbed Meg's arm. "I knew it," she said with a happy crow. "You sense the confluences, too."

L. A. Kelley

Chapter Eight

Meg leaned away from the slightly crazed gleam in Amaranth's eyes. "Beg pardon," she said meekly.

"You're a sensitive, aren't you?" gushed Amaranth. "When I was in the kitchen, I felt an explosion of positive vibrations. It must have happened the instant you stepped into the shop." She wagged her finger at Cal. "Shame on you. You must be a sensitive, too, and pretended not to notice this morning. Why? Being in touch with the elemental spirits of life is a special gift. Don't hide. Shout it from the rooftops. Summer, come over here. Bring Dylan, he needs to hear this, too."

Dylan bounded over from the cash register. Summer set aside the broom she used to sweep the floor and pulled up a chair next to him.

Meg bit her lip at the horrified expression on Cal's face. Shouting from the rooftops that the button-down lawyer, entrusted with family secrets, spent his off-hours communing with mystical vibrations was not the best foundation to build a successful practice.

On the other hand, I'm a perfect stranger here and don't care what people think.

"To be honest," said Meg being anything but, "I'm the one who, uh, had the strange vibes in the maze. I told Cal, and he suggested we speak to you." She stifled a snicker at Cal's undisguised relief.

134

"Oh, I see." Amaranth patted Meg's arm. "Don't be alarmed by what you sensed. These are natural forces at work, and the convergences are particularly strong right now."

"You mentioned that before," said Cal. "What exactly is a convergence?"

"They occur where two ley lines meet," said Dylan. He smiled shyly at Summer. "She explained it to me."

Well, that clears up everything. Meg raised an eyebrow at Cal.

"Ley lines?" he said weakly.

Amaranth tsked. "Haven't you heard how Crossroads got its name?"

"I, uh, assumed it was, you know, a crossroad."

"Naturally, but a special kind. Oh, the Chamber of Commerce says the founders settled here to create a farming community, but those of us in tune with the astral plane know the true reason Crossroads is different. Ley lines are ancient channels of intense psychic energy encircling the globe. They connect the most mystical places on Earth."

"Like guitar strings, dude," said Dylan. "Vibrations."

"That's right," nodded Summer. "If you're sensitive and standing in the right spot, you can feel the psychic emanations pass right through you."

"So, a ley line goes through Crossroads," said Meg.

"Not just one, *three* intersect," said Amaranth. "They form the most powerful convergence on Earth. Usually, they're dormant, but lately…" Amaranth shivered. "The one in Crossroads is positively screaming. It's due to the influence of the upcoming eclipse, of course. Eclipses can exert tremendous psychic influence on the ley lines."

Meg and Cal exchanged an *ah-hah!* look. "Let me guess," said Meg. "The convergence is at the center of the maze under the arbor."

Amaranth beamed at her. "I knew you were sensitive. The ley lines intersect in that exact spot. I told George it was essential to build the arbor there so those seeking spiritual enlightenment could easily find the convergence. It took a little convincing, but he agreed."

Cal raised an eyebrow, his skepticism obvious. "George is okay with ley lines and stuff?"

Dylan blew out a disgusted snort, and Amaranth shot him a disapproving look. "That's enough, Dylan. You and George have your disagreements, but I've known him since high school. His mind is more open than you realize."

"Is that why he rolls his eyes every time you talk to him about going organic on the farm?"

"Nonsense, he does no such thing. George is simply a teensy set in his ways and needs gentle encouragement to embrace new ideas. He built the arbor when I asked, didn't he?"

"Maybe, Mom," said Summer coyly. "Mr. Lydecker wanted to impress someone."

"Honestly, Summer, I'm sure George was only being kind."

They were getting way off topic, so Meg broke in. "What are convergences good for?"

"Plenty of things," said Amaranth. "Mystics use them to seek guidance, others to peer into different dimensions on the metaphysical planes. Certain people can channel psychic visions of the future or make contact with the past."

"Really?" Cal leaned forward. "That's very interesting. You say it's possible to travel backward in time to another place?"

Amaranth paused as if to consider the question. "I picture it as a spiritual, rather than an actual physical journey. I've never done it myself but read accounts of others who had the ability to inhabit a different body—stepping into someone else's life for a bit, as it were."

"Wow, that sure sounds like fun," Cal said dryly. "But confusing, too, if you don't recall your true identity. The person in the past suddenly gets weird thoughts in his head and can't make heads or tails of them. I imagine he assumes he went crazy."

"It's not very practical either," said Meg tartly. "I spent a lot of time stumbling around trying to figure out what was going on." Amaranth, Dylan, and Summer peered at her with puzzled expressions. "I mean," she added in a rush, "I'd *probably* act that way."

"Me, too," said Cal with a twinkle in his eye.

"It would be so cool to travel with someone though," said Dylan. He shot Summer another smile.

"You really think it's possible, Mom?" asked Summer.

"I don't see why not. When hearts and minds unite us, time and distance is no obstacle."

The door chime halted further conversation. A new group of customers entered the shop, and Amaranth rose to her feet. "Lovely to meet you, Meg. Do stop in again soon and we can continue this fascinating discussion. It's so nice to talk to another sensitive." She waltzed away, calling over her shoulder to Cal. "Don't forget, I have a fairy waiting with your name on him."

Meg snickered as several customers shot curious glances at a red-faced Cal. She nudged his arm and whispered, "Let's get out of here before your entire practice flushes down the toilet."

"Good idea." Cal paid the bill and they left.

"Did you believe that stuff about ley lines and convergences?" said Meg.

"I don't know what's real anymore." Cal swiped a hand across his brow. "It sure hasn't gotten any cooler though."

They reached the entrance to the festival grounds, and Meg's heart skipped a beat. The sun's rays beat against her skin with fierce intensity—the same as the sun over Babylon. "I don't know either. Maybe I caught a case of mutated bird flu from the pigeons in the city and I'm actually not here but sweating out a fevered dream in my apartment." She gave him a hopeful look. "Will you come to the maze with me? I need to see it again."

"I won't leave your side. I swear it."

The fierce intensity in his words left Meg with a pleasant sensation that lingered as she edged through the crowds. Nervous butterflies fluttered in her stomach at the entrance to the maze. She glanced at Cal and the butterflies drifted away, replaced by confidence. Cal gave her his word, and he won't run no matter what. He wasn't that kind of man.

A laughing group darted past them and disappeared behind the lush stalks. Meg pulled up short, staring at the maze in confusion. "I-it doesn't give off the same vibe."

"No mystical voices calling your name?" said Cal. "Not for me either. It's so...so..." He wrinkled his brow.

"Normal?"

"Right. Maybe we broke it," he added dryly.

Meg stared at the rows of waving corn. "It's not broken. Even with those people inside, I can't shake the sense of emptiness, like a battery drained dry. Whatever crazy thing happened to us in there, it's gone. It's over." Her crushing disappointment surprised her. This was nuts. She died in there. Why wasn't she happy the maze didn't summon her again?

"Over..." Cal's shoulders sagged. "I guess we were only meant to take one trip to Babylon."

Meg rubbed her eyes, consumed by sudden fatigue. The emptiness emanating from the maze seemed to sap her energy reserve, too. "I suppose I should head back to the city. After all, I came here for a job. That hasn't changed, and I need to start the search again."

"Don't leave now." Cal regarded her with concern. "You're too tired to drive. At least wait until morning."

The lines around Cal's eyes hinted at his own underlying exhaustion. Meg managed a weak smile. "Okay, the room at the inn is paid for, so I'll stay the night. Get some rest, too. You had quite the day, murdered by your evil twin and all." Cal's expression brightened and rekindled those pleasant sensations in her.

"Good," he said. "I'll walk you to the inn."

They exited the fairgrounds. Awkward silence enveloped them at the inn's door. Cal plucked an errant strand of hair off Meg's face and tucked it behind her ear. "Better check that ponytail, part of it tried to escape. Nemra had the same problem." He shifted his feet. "Will I see you tomorrow?"

Meg felt a flush fill her cheeks. "I-I'm not sure, but I…that is to say, we, Nemra and I," she stammered, "want to thank you for stopping Balu-su. He would have killed her—us, before we faced the Everdark. Damn these pronouns."

Cal smiled. "No thanks necessary. Besides, Ashur stopped him, not me."

"Did he?" she said softly. "Ashur didn't act as a prince born to absolute rule and Nemra didn't act as if she were a priestess sworn to blind obedience to a pagan god. Makes you wonder what was real." Memories of Nemra and Ashur's kiss returned with a bang, and she found it difficult to keep her voice steady. "I still remember the feelings, good and bad, that went with her life."

"I'm the same with Ashur. He had powerful impressions of Nemra…" Cal clapped his mouth shut and took a step back. "Goodnight."

Meg nodded numbly. Fatigue swallowed even the energy necessary to respond. She lumbered up the stairs to her room, and collapsed on the bed, staring blankly at the ceiling. Unbidden, her thoughts drifted to the kiss between Nemra and Ashur. A passionate longing to feel it again raced through her body. Meg placed her hands on her cheeks. They were even hotter to the touch, practically scalding.

Meg squirmed on the bed. Cal had made his attraction clear. It wasn't difficult to imagine the sensation of his lips pressed to hers. All she had to do was run after him…

Reality shoved fantasy aside and kicked her in the pants. "Just a dream," she murmured wistfully. "He's not Ashur. This isn't Babylon. I can't love someone I just met."

What if you do?

"Then it's only remnants of Nemra's love for Ashur." Meg forced herself from the bed and opened her suitcase. Her heart was in big trouble. The smartest plan of action was to run away before it broke and leave Crossroads in the dust.

****

The Everdark shrieked in rage, and the world trembled under Cal's feet. "One battle is not a victory. No human can destroy my perfection. I am eternal."

Meg stood at his side. "I have sworn to the crown. The power answers to me."

The Everdark laughed and life balanced on the brink of extinction. "A mere trifle, a bauble, not enough to stand against a god."

The black sword hung in the air in front of Cal, blinding light radiated from the symbols on the blade. The mist slowly parted and the gate became visible once more. With a triumphant howl, the Everdark advanced.

Cal reached out his hand and grasped the hilt.

****

Cal rolled over with a groan and his eyelids fluttered open. He blinked in rapid succession, half expecting to see a sword floating near the ceiling. "Oh, man, what a night." He pushed himself up and swung his legs off the side of the bed. The scattered remnants of the nightmare clung to him like oily residue. He shook his head to rid the cobwebs. That sword...why did it infiltrate his dreams?

Why did Meg?

Cal picked up his cell phone from the nightstand

and glanced at the display. He slept late; it was past ten in the morning. Meg must be on her way to the city by now. He glared at the phone. He didn't even remember to ask for her number.

His shoulders sagged. Why should he? He barely knew her. Sure, they shared a weird dream, or possession, or whatever it was, but the longing stirring in his heart wasn't real.

Cal staggered into the shower and blasted the spray. The water struck his skin with the force of stinging needles, and he leaned against the cool tile. The minor discomfort was a welcome distraction from the confused feelings for Meg. This was crazy. He had been burned once by opening his heart and the urge to repeat the experience didn't exist. Any lingering desire for Meg must be a residual effect from Ashur's attraction to Nemra. Yet, it wasn't Nemra who infiltrated his dreams.

Cal toweled off and dressed. The lethargy capturing his limbs since he woke vanished with the water down the shower drain. His stomach growled. No wonder he was hungry. His last meal was yesterday's lunch.

Cal opened the refrigerator. He shifted around a few containers of leftovers, peering at them with lackluster interest. He grabbed his keys and headed out the door. Out-of-towners packed Main Street, every restaurant full with a long wait for a table. He wouldn't eat unless he returned to his apartment.

Of course, he had another option. Cal detoured to the fairgrounds. He bought a funnel cake and then ambled to a picnic table within sight of the maze. He finished eating, his attention never wavering from the

142

corn. Everything was normal again except for the unusual autumn heat; no hushed entreaties, no muted roar from a crowd, no mystical forces pulling him into the cornstalks. If anything, the air was unnaturally still, as if time paused to draw a breath, waiting with anticipation.

"Well?" Cal snarled. "What are you waiting for?"

****

Meg opened her eyes. Sunlight streamed through windows of the French doors. The room was exactly the same as last night with her neatly packed suitcase on the floor. Fatigue had overwhelmed her, and she never made it to the car, but after a good night's sleep, she had no more excuses. She showered and dressed and tossed the dirty clothes in her luggage, ready for her return trip to the city.

Yup, all ready. Better get on the road. Nothing to do here.

She paused, staring at the zipped-up case. Her stomach growled a hungry protest. Plenty of time to leave after breakfast, and thanks to Isaac the bill was already paid. A little voice inside her cried out in relief to have discovered a perfectly logical reason to delay checkout. Meg brushed it roughly aside. A close examination of her heart this morning was definitely not on the menu.

Joe greeted her cheerfully in the dining room. "Take any seat. We have our special pumpkin waffles today."

Two tables were open; one overlooked the garden and the other had a view of the harvest festival. Meg sat at the latter and watched the entrance to George Lydecker's corn maze. The festival grounds were open.

143

People headed inside wearing an assortment of shorts and tank tops, but nobody dressed to battle ancient evil. Nothing out of the ordinary. She stifled a snort. What did she expect to see? A doorway to hell with a welcome mat?

Meg tapped her foot, vague restlessness coursing through her, and she fought the urge to jump from her seat. Joe returned with breakfast, and the urge disappeared. Meg dug in and made short work of the waffles. After chasing the last few syrupy crumbs around her plate with the fork, she sat back in her seat and wiped her mouth with the napkin.

At once, the restlessness reappeared. *I should go upstairs and get my bags now. I should definitely leave.* Her gaze returned to the window, and she lingered over a second cup of coffee, overcome by unexplained lethargy. "Too many carbs," she muttered.

Becky came to the table. "How was everything?"

"Perfect," she said. An image of Cal floated to mind. *No, not perfect. He isn't here.*

"Oh, I almost forgot. Isaac left this for you." She reached into a pocket and handed her an envelope.

Meg stared at the familiar cream-colored vellum. Written on the front was Cal's name in elegant calligraphy.

"I offered to leave it for Cal at the office," said Becky, "but Isaac said you'd take it to him."

Meg's heart thumped. "When was Isaac here?"

"An hour or so ago."

She forced her voice to remain steady. "He didn't say anything else?"

"No. By the way, how's the job hunt going?"

The pressing need to move overwhelmed Meg, and

she jumped from her seat. "I'm not sure yet. I'll let you know."

"Do you need directions to Cal's office? He's probably there."

"No, he isn't," she called over her shoulder.

****

"Cal!"

Cal turned with a start. At the sight of Meg, a wide grin spread over his face. "I thought you left."

Her face was flushed, and she panted as if she ran from the inn. "I planned to but couldn't and then I got this from Becky." She held out a cream-colored envelope. "Isaac Bingham dropped it off this morning. I'm supposed to deliver it to you."

Cal took it, gaping at his name on the front. "That's not Isaac's handwriting."

"No, it's from Phillip Bingham. I recognize it from his letter to me. Becky thought you were in your office, but I knew you'd be here." Meg gave an excited hop on her toes. "Well, open it."

Cal broke the seal and removed a single sheet of paper, three words only.

Find the sword.

A breeze wafted through the fairgrounds, rippling the acres of corn. Meg's head turned toward the entrance to the maze, a flush tinted her cheeks. "I sense something."

Cal's muscles tensed, tightness wrapped around his chest as if a rope bound him tight. "I do, too. It's tugging me to the maze." He peered at Meg, a question in his eyes.

Her expression lit with excitement. "I'm game."

Meg took a step, and he pulled her back. "Hang on

a second. Nemra and Ashur are dead. Could be we're only doomed to repeat their final battle in the temple. I don't want you to go through that again." How could he explain this sense of dread? "I don't want to see your death again." His grip on her arm tightened. "I don't want to lose you in there."

Meg's expression softened. "I don't want to see Ashur's death either, but…"

"You have to go."

"Yes." She cocked her head and gave him an appraising look. "You do, too. Nothing I say will stop you. You're not a person to run from trouble or leave a job half-done."

Cal's lips twitched in a faint smile. "I could say the same for you." He held out his hand. "We do this together then, side by side. I swear I won't let go."

She placed her hand in his. "I swear I won't let go."

Meg's touch released a flood of strength and renewed purpose in Cal. They entered the maze, hands clasped tight. The tug on his chest strengthened. He led the way with determined steps, so sure of the route he could run it blindfolded.

They reached the center of the maze, vacant except for them. The breeze gusted, the air shimmered around the arbor, as if time and space rippled and bent in the wind. Inside the arbor, an ember burned bright and then blazed with the semblance of a second sun. The flame shot up, licking at the heavens.

Meg drew a deep breath. "Ready?"

"Ready." He held her hand tight. Nothing could tear him away.

Together, they stepped toward the fire. "When

hearts and minds unite us," Cal muttered under his breath, "time and distance are no obstacle."

The light vanished, and the world went dark.

Chapter Nine

Cal opened his eyes and blinked. Above his head, wispy sunlight filtered through a canopy of oak leaves cloaked in tendrils of fog. *Oak trees? Definitely not Babylon.* He stood in the center of a glade, his vision obscured. He touched his brow. A helmet? Cal raised a visor and ran his hands along his chest. He gaped at the clothing in disbelief; armored boots, a tunic with a coat of arms crossed by a baldric and underneath the tunic a linen shirt next to his skin. Between that…He poked a finger at his chest. *Chain mail? What the hell?*

Memories overwhelmed Cal in a rush and his pulse raced. *Meg? Where was Meg?* He scanned the surrounding woods in panic. He held her hand only a second ago and promised to never let go. Now she vanished. "Meg!" he yelled.

The brush rustled. "Meg, is that you?" Cal scrambled past bushes and nearly collided with the biggest horse he'd ever seen. The stallion had a pack lashed to the saddle. The coat of arms on the blanket underneath matched the pattern on his tunic. The horse stopped cropping grass, raised its head, and stepped toward him.

Cal hopped to the side. Metal boots or not, one of those dinner-plate sized hooves could mash his foot to pulp. "Whoa," said Cal. "Nice boy."

The stallion halted, nosed him gently, and

nickered.

With a raised eyebrow, Cal patted him on the neck. "You're mine? Great. Who the hell am I? Where the hell am I?" He surveyed his surroundings. Judging by his clothing, the horse, and the wooded landscape, a good guess was a knight in Europe during the early Middle Ages, maybe eleventh or twelfth century. Cal removed the helmet. Damn, it was hot. Chain mail didn't exactly breathe, and the leafy trees must mean he landed in the dead of summer. Cal swiped a hand across his forehead and brushed the indentation of a long scar. As with Ashur, he didn't have the same appearance. Meg might not either. At least this time his memories were intact, but how would he find her in this world? Cal's jaw set in a thin, tight line. His hand dropped to the baldric holding a scabbard and sword. He'd find her, no matter what, and nobody better damn well stand in his way. His fingers curled around the haft.

Cal blinked. "The sword!"

He pulled it from the scabbard and stifled a cry of disappointment—not the same one from Ashur's vision. Instead, his hand grasped a longsword, a fighting man's weapon, common for the upper ranks in the Middle Ages. It displayed fine craftsmanship, though, and must have cost the owner a pretty ducat or two.

His arm gave a practice swipe through the air. Muscles responded automatically as if they spent rigorous hours training for its use. At least the previous owner did, and the skill apparently stuck with him while he inhabited this borrowed body. "I remember who I am," he mused. "So, who the heck are you?"

Cal slid the blade into the scabbard and unfastened the pack. He rifled through a few articles of clothing on top and found a purse with a handful of silver and gold coins. He hefted it in his hands. His new self wasn't exactly rolling in dough. He dug deeper and came upon a letter. Under the signature was an impression made from a signet ring. At first, Cal peered at the letter in dismay. The highly calligraphic writing style bore no resemblance to modern languages. Without warning, the letters blurred. He blinked to clear his vision, and the words aligned to make sense.

The letter was a writ of passage signed by Drogo Ursenkrieg, the margrave of Augsburg, and addressed to Sir Roland de Bruche of Flanders. It offered employment to Sir Roland and permission to travel Augsburg's roads and enter the city gates.

"Roland de Bruche?" The name had a comfortable, familiar ring. "You're Roland de Bruche and you're going to see Drogo Ursenskrieg, the Margrave of Augsburg." Cal dug through his memory recalling scraps from the ebook he started to read. Augsburg was in Germany, which made perfect sense as a margrave was the German equivalent of a marquis, a member of the nobility.

Sir Roland was from Flanders but eager to work for a German margrave. He was probably a second or third son of lesser nobility. In the early Middle Ages, loyalty was fluid. Roland wouldn't inherit much from his family, so his only recourse was to join the church or seek his fortune with a wealthier liege. He'd chosen the latter.

Cal wrinkled his brow. "Augsburg, Augsburg, why does that sound familiar? Damn, I wish I read more of that book."

The stallion snorted and pawed the ground. His

ears flattened against his skull.

Hidden warrior instincts roared to the surface and screamed an alert. *We've got company.* Blood raced through Cal's veins. Muscles responded without conscious thought as he turned to face the unknown. His body struck a battle stance; legs apart, weight evenly balanced. His eyes narrowed. The position felt good. Natural.

A twig snapped, and another horse whinnied. Cal swung into the saddle and drew the sword. No one with honest intent ever snuck up on an armed man in this time period. He surrendered to every instinctive response ordering him to fight and allowed Sir Roland's muscle memory to take control. The stallion pranced a skittering sidestep, flanks tensing underneath Cal's legs.

Knees gripped tight, feet secure in the stirrups, sword raised high, Cal charged through the brush. Five masked men, two on horseback, faced him with swords drawn. A sixth masked man, smaller than the rest, stood in the rear. He glanced nervously over his shoulder and didn't have a sword.

The marauders' horses reared in surprise at the sneak attack. Cal's warrior's eye took in his opponents at a glance. Despite better numbers, these men were unarmored and not battle-trained. The advantage was his. His stallion lunged into one of the men on foot trampling him into the ground. Cal's sword ended another. With one kick to the head from his stallion's hoof, a third swordsman's neck jerked back, and he fell into the dirt, never to rise.

The riders quickly recovered from their surprise. With horses under control, they now came at him from two sides. He heard a tinny clank and felt the shock of a blade, but the chain mail stopped the thrust from reaching his flesh. His opponent was not so lucky. Four down, two to go.

Cal struck at the rider while his stallion shoved his weight at the other horse and threw it off balance. As the animal stumbled to regain its footing, the man reeled in the saddle. His sword arm dropped, exposing his heart. One quick thrust from Cal finished the fight.

Only the smallest member of the band remained. He bolted into the woods. Awash with Sir Roland's battle lust, Cal gave chase. He cut in front and leapt to the ground, sword in hand, ready to draw final blood.

The man fell to his knees. He pulled off the mask and clasped hands in prayer. "I yield, lord," he said, voice trembling. "Have mercy."

Cal blinked. Not a man, a boy.

Tears welled in his eyes and he stared at Cal's sword. "I yield, my lord. I beg you…"

Sir Roland's instincts bellowed in his head to run him through.

Shut the hell up. Cal lowered his sword. "What is your name, boy?"

He swallowed hard. "Tomman, my lord."

"How did you get mixed up with these brigands, Tomman?"

"My parents died of fever, lord, so I went to my uncle and pleaded for him to take me in."

"Who is your uncle?"

He licked his lips and motioned to a corpse on the ground.

"Ah, I see. Do you enjoy a life of crime, Tomman?"

His eyes filled with horror. "No, my lord. My uncle

put me to work in the stables. I have a deft hand with horses. When I learnt he and his men were thieves, I wanted to run, but…" Tomman swallowed hard. "I had nowhere to go, and Uncle swore to kill me if I ever tried. H-he forced me to come with them today to keep watch for the margrave's men who patrol this road. He said I would be baptized in blood and be one of them forever." He threw his arms around Cal's legs. "Forgive me, my lord," he moaned. "I have no wish to harm anyone."

"Okay, fine." Embarrassed, Cal patted him on the head. "You can let go now. I won't kill you."

Tomman's face lit up with joy. "Thank you, thank you. Please, lord, let me repay your mercy. I will do anything you ask."

Cal considered the eager boy at his feet. He could certainly use a guide. "I'm expected in Augsburg. Do you know the way?"

"Yes, my lord. I journeyed to the market often with my father." Tomman bowed his head. "I am your humble servant, lord, and devote my life to your comfort and well-being."

"That's not what I—oh, never mind." Arguing with the Middle Age mindset of honorable servitude would get him nowhere. "Let's go."

Tomman sprang up and ran toward the corpses. Cal's assumption he'd offer to bury them proved in error. "You bested them in battle, my lord," shouted the boy. "Their possessions are yours. Allow me the honor of gathering them for you."

So much for chivalry. Stripping the dead apparently a time-honored tradition. Within a short while, five naked bodies sprawled on the ground.

Tomman secured their belongings to the two horses. The boy was practically brought to tears again when Cal told him he could keep one for his own.

They headed to Augsburg at a canter. As with the earlier battle, the muscle memory in Cal's borrowed body took control. He relaxed and balanced automatically, steadying in the seat, rhythmically swaying with the gentle bounce of the stallion. Cal's optimism soared. He had retained Roland's skills and could call upon Tomman's familiarity with the area when needed. This new identity was going to work. Now, all he had to do was find Meg and the sword.

"Have we far until we reach Augsburg?" Cal asked.

"No, lord…" Tomman reddened. "I do not know your name, lord."

"Sir Roland de Bruche of Flanders."

"We will come to the gates before nightfall, Sir Roland." He tilted his head and gave Cal a questioning look. "Flanders is many leagues. Have you journeyed long?"

"It seems," Cal said dryly, "as if I have traveled for years." He shifted in the saddle. "As a matter of fact, I've lost track of time. What is today?"

"Tis the seventh morn ere the ides of August."

What? As if in answer, a date popped into his mind, August seventh. *Thank you, Sir Roland.* Something pricked at a buried memory in relation to the date…what was it? Cal lifted a hand to scratch his head and then remembered he wore the helmet. He brushed the annoying sensation aside. "My, my," he said in an offhanded manner, "so far into summer."

"Yes, lord." Tomman wiped his brow. "And such

heat."

"That's unusual for these parts?"

"The farmers say they have never seen such weather."

"So…" He paused. "You're a bright lad. Do you know the year?"

Tomman blinked. "The year?"

"Yes, yes, what year is it?"

"Why, tis 1133."

Augsburg, 1133? The irritating jab returned as Cal frantically tried to recall every scrap of Middle Age history. Why was that place and date so familiar? The elusive answer came to him in a flash.

"Oh, hell," he muttered.

****

Meg's head jerked up. She blinked. "What the hell?"

Across from her was a girl dressed as a damsel in a Renaissance fair. She held a needle threaded with yarn. Her fingers poised over a frame with a half-stitched needlepoint tapestry and she gaped at Meg. "Lady Clare?"

Lady Clare? This isn't Babylon. At least, I have my memories, but where am I now?

The girl cleared her throat. "My lady?"

"What? Oh, never mind." Like the girl, Meg held a needle and sat at a frame. "It's nothing. Stuck my finger." The girl went back to her work. Meg poked the needle in the cloth and stared down at her body. The hem of her dress brushed the floor. The design was similar to the girl's outfit but with subtle differences. Meg touched her neck. She wore a gold chain adorned with a ruby pendant. Attached to a belt around her waist was a large keyring. Meg shot the girl a sideways glance. Who was this kid? She couldn't be more than fifteen. Sister? Friend? Servant? Cosplayer?

I have my name, at least—good old Lady Clare. Meg's eyes widened. *Where was Cal?* Except for the girl, she was alone in the room. Other needlepoint tapestries hung on the walls, but in contrast to those Meg had seen in museums these weren't old. Outside a nearby window was farmland. The chamber had two doors. One was open, and she glimpsed a bed. Was this a private drawing room? She and her companion sat next to the hearth of a large stone fireplace with logs on the grate, but no fire. Speaking of fire…

Geez, it's hot. Despite a breeze from the windows, the air was stifling. Her hands went to her head, and she gave her hair a little pat. A metallic circlet held in place a piece of silk. Her hair had been bound up in a tight coil at the base of her neck. Meg flapped her hand in front of her face to create a breeze and then froze, staring at the gold band on the third finger of her left hand. *Oh, crap.*

The girl sighed. "I pray we have a break in the weather soon."

"Uh, yes, it sure is hot." Meg couldn't tear her attention from the ring. "My…uh, my husband…"

The girl reached over and patted her hand. "I'm so sorry for your loss, Lady Clare."

"He's dead." Without thinking, Meg chuckled, and the girl's eyes widened. "I mean," Meg stammered. "It gives me great comfort to remember he is now with the angels in paradise."

"I'm certain he is, my lady."

Meg considered her words carefully and then

heaved an exaggerated sigh. "It seems like he's been gone forever. How long has it been?"

"Near a month since you received the letter from Duke Frederick. It was only a few weeks after my arrival." She shot her a shy look. "I am most grateful you took me in."

"Think nothing of it. You've been a great comfort in this trying time." The girl flushed with pleasure. "So, this letter," said Meg. "I can't recall where I put it."

"I saw you place it in the jewelry case, my lady. Shall I fetch it for you?"

"Yes, thanks."

The girl scampered to a bureau and retrieved an intricately carved box. The lid was locked. After a moment of panic aware the girl's eyes were upon her, Meg remembered the keyring on her belt. She chose the smallest key and stifled a sigh of relief when it fit. The letter rested on top of an array of shiny coins and jewelry.

Meg opened the letter and her stomach tightened in a knot at the sight of the illegible scrawl. She was a moment away from calling up a few phony tears and asking the girl to read it to her when something in her head clicked into place. The letter had been written in May to Lady Clare of Kuneburg from Frederick II, Duke of Swabia. Her husband, Johannes, (so that was the bugger's name) had died in April fighting the Turks in the service of Pope Innocent II.

Judging by the heat, it was the middle of summer, July or August. Lady Clare was only a few months widowed, but no grief crept through her emotions to Meg. Although, she received definite affectionate vibes about the girl. Lady Clare enjoyed her company.

Arranged marriages were the norm in this time period with women considered more property than person. Did Lady Clare have remorse or relief at her husband's death?

The girl rose to answer a knock at the door. "Good morrow, Herlinde," said a man. "I have the accounts ready for her ladyship." The girl turned to Meg. "Do you wish to see Wilhelm now, Lady Clare?"

Aha! Two more names. "Let Wilhelm in, Herlinde." They sat at the desk and went over the receipts. It didn't take too much effort to deduce Wilhelm was the steward. Sir Johannes' little fiefdom wasn't an empire but appeared to provide a comfortable living with income from vassals' farms, a brewery, and the estate's own holdings. Meg dismissed Wilhelm and then did a closer examination of the entries, flipping through previous pages. The records were hardly modern spreadsheets. Nevertheless, they presented a detailed record of the life of a woman of the manor, if one knew how to read the story in the numbers.

Meg ran her fingers down the columns, regarding the totals with approval. Clare kept careful track of expenditures. Her eyes were drawn to a notation on Herlinde's arrival. She wasn't a relative. Clare recently added her to the household and paid for a pair of shoes as the girl's were worn beyond repair. Meg idly read through other household purchases and found payments to a stonemason for several grave markers. Even for the upper class, life in the Middle Ages was hard at best.

A closer examination of the receipts showed cash flow on the rise every year since 1123, the date Clare's name first appeared in the record book. At that time, Clare wed Johannes and took charge of the household.

Also listed was the value of the dowry delivered with the marriage contract signed on her fourteenth birthday.

Meg sat back in her chair. Clare married at fourteen? She gave a mental shrug. Oh, well, it's not as if she had college and a career in her future. Marriage or the nunnery was the only option for a girl back then. Curiosity rose, and she cast a surreptitious glance across the room at Herlinde. "If you hadn't come to me, what would have happened to you?"

The girl's face paled. "I had no family. My father's debts after he died left no money for a dowry. If you hadn't taken me in…" She swallowed hard.

The pained expression told Meg everything. Begging or prostitution and an early death. A groundswell of twenty-first century righteous indignation overcame Meg's discretion, demanding release. "Dowry's stink," she raged. "A woman should be valued for her brains alone and not on how much cash she brings to a husband. Man, I am never reading a historical romance again. That chivalry crap is nothing, but male propaganda…"

Herlinde stared at her, mouth agape.

Yeah. The Middle Ages is probably not the best place to fire up a feminist revolution. "I'm sorry, Herlinde. I didn't mean to shout. I get angry at how difficult a woman's position can be with very little choice."

Herlinde relaxed. "Indeed, my lady."

Meg peered at the jewelry box. She removed a small leather drawstring bag filled with silver coins. She handed them to Herlinde along with the necklace and ruby pendant from her neck. "Take these."

"M-my lady," she stuttered. "I-I couldn't…"

"I insist. If you ever decide to leave here, you now have something of your own to take with you."

To Meg's embarrassment, Herlinde fell to her knees with tears in her eyes and clasped the hem of Meg's dress to her cheek. "I will never leave unless you send me away."

"T-that's great." Flustered, Meg ordered the girl to her feet. "But now you have your own money to use as you will."

Herlinde clutched the bag of coins to her chest and gazed at the necklace in wonder. "Are you certain of this?" She licked her lips. "I was told it was a gift upon the signing of your marriage contract..." Herlinde's voice dropped to a whisper. "From the man who is said to be my lady's father."

Meg raised an eyebrow. *The man who is said to be my father? An interesting way to phrase paternity unless...oh.* "Who have you heard my father to be?" Herlinde appeared hesitant to speak and Meg tapped her foot. "Well?"

"King Henry."

Meg blinked. "Of England?"

"Forgive me," blurted Herlinde. "I mean no disrespect. You are truly of noble birth, even if that birth wasn't...that is, to say, not quite..." She swallowed hard.

"Legitimate." Meg laughed. *Well, well. I'm a royal bastard.*

"My lady?" said Herlinde, puzzled by Meg's reaction.

She patted Herlinde's arm. "Think no more on it. My father gave me the necklace and I can do with it whatever I please, but perhaps it's best to keep the gift our little secret. Tuck it away with the coins."

"Yes, my lady. You are not the only person born off the sheets of a marriage bed," she added warmly, "but your nobility is far greater than any bearer of a royal title."

"Thank you, Herlinde." Meg's attention returned to the account book. She still had no clue how to find Cal—or if he even made it to this time period. Her heart gave a gentle tug. No, he was here. He'd search for her, too. She felt it.

Her eyes lingered over entries listing the money spent to send Johannes to fight in a stupid skirmish for Pope Innocent II. Between warhorses, armor, travel expenses, and supplies, outfitting knights to slaughter in the name of God definitely wasn't cheap. Even death didn't stop the bills. Johannes was buried where he fell, but Lady Clare authorized payment for a marker in the family chapel. Other notations for the chapel caught Meg's eye. She had commissioned a carpenter to construct a box soon after her arrival at Kuneburg. Clare had written one word in the margin in her neat, precise lettering: *swert*. Meg's mind did a simultaneous translation.

Sword.

Meg's heart pounded. She slammed shut the account book.

Herlinde jumped. "Finished, my lady? Do you care for refreshments? I can fetch us wine."

Meg eyed her askance. "You're not old enough to drink—never mind," she muttered. "Forgot where I was. Everyone drinks here."

"Lady Clare?"

Meg flashed a smile. "Actually, I'm in the mood

L. A. Kelley

for fresh air. Why don't we take a walk around the grounds? Perhaps, a stroll to the chapel?"

They passed servants in the halls that bobbed a curtsy or bowed when she passed. Meg nodded and smiled, all the while clinging to Herlinde's arm and hoping no one asked any questions. Once outside, she peered around with interest. This wasn't Buckingham Palace. The estate and manor house more closely resembled a prosperous working farm than regal quarters. Was Clare happy here? Did she expect more from marriage or was life in a middling fiefdom the best the bastard daughter of a king could hope for? Still, as far as the Middle Ages was concerned this was comfortable. When her husband left, Clare attained a level of autonomy that must be rare. How would that change now that she was a widow?

I hope I'm not here long enough to find out.

In contrast to Babylon, the gardens were practical rather than scenic and supplied the kitchen with fresh fruit and vegetables in season. Meg didn't have a green thumb, but some of the leafy stuff appeared wilted. She wiped her brow. It must be the heat.

They strolled on a gravel path to a tidy graveyard. In the center was a stone structure, with a crest that said Kuneburg emblazed over the door. This was the family chapel. Near the entrance were three smaller markers newer than the others. Each one had a cross carved over the figure of a praying angel. Meg read the dates and names; two boys age five and three, and a girl age one. They sounded so familiar...She nearly stumbled, overcome by a surge of grief.

Herlinde's grip tightened on her arm. "My heart aches for your loss, my lady."

The horror of her words sank in. These were Clare's children.

Meg swallowed hard, forcing aside Clare's heartbreak. A few rapid calculations and she determined Clare had her first child at sixteen and her last at twenty. Then her husband left her to manage on her own with three small children while he rode off to seek glory. One by one the children died, succumbing to disease or accident, but did that bring Johannes home? Not a chance. He was having too much fun slaughtering perfect strangers. When Meg considered Johannes, she had no echo of loss from Clare, but the woman had deeply loved those children.

Meg's hands clenched. Cal would never abandon a wife and children in a stupid pursuit for riches and fame. She tore her gaze from the heartbreaking tableau of the three little graves. The chapel door was locked. She used a key and stepped inside. Two narrow windows let in faint light, and she paused as her eyes adjusted to the gloom. The room was small and plain with only two wooden benches and a raised dais. On top, next to a wooden cross, was a rectangular object covered by a white cloth embroidered with the family crest. Meg ran her fingertips across the tight stitching admiring the delicate work. Her hands had never made anything so fine, but Clare's did.

Meg yanked off the cloth to reveal a box. She opened the lid and pressed her lips together to stifle a triumphant cry. Inside was a sword, identical to the one Ashur described to Nemra in his vision. It had a pitch-black metal blade inlaid with shapes of a golden sun, silver moon, and stars.

"A most unusual design," said Herlinde, peering

163

over her shoulder, "and I've never seen such metal. It's much shorter than other weaponry. I do not judge it useful for a knight on horseback."

"No," said Meg. "It's made for a different type of battle. Did I, uh, ever mention how my husband came by it?"

Herlinde regarded her with confusion. "You said it was part of your dowry."

"Oh, yes, of course," Meg stammered. "I meant to say, did I ever mention when it came into my family's possession?"

"Only that it was during the First Crusade." She eyed Meg with a puzzled air. "'Tis a fine sword, but Sir Johannes didn't take it when he left."

"No, he didn't," said Meg. "A sword can choose the right man to wield it. Johannes wasn't that man." Her fingers hovered over the blade expecting a reaction, a perception of power, similar to what she felt when the crown was near. To Meg's disappointment, nothing intruded on her senses. She rested her hand on the blade and only cold hard metal met her touch.

She gripped the haft and raised it from the dais. An uneasy sensation traveled up her arm, and she put it down. The weight was wrong. The balance was wrong. The feel in her hand was wrong. No wonder Johannes left it here. He couldn't fight with it. Neither could Meg nor anyone else. The sword had already chosen its master. Had it decided over a thousand years ago and waited all this time for Cal to return? For surely the sword was meant for him as the crown was meant for her. There were only two teensy problems—no Cal and no crown.

Meg shifted on her feet, edginess growing along

with certainty. Whatever power sent her to this time and place, also imbedded a warning. The veil had begun to thin again. The Everdark wasn't dead. It stalked the recesses of time hunting for the entrance to this world, and she and Cal had only a few days to act. Meg grabbed the sword and strode from the chapel with Herlinde scampering at her heels. She paused by the gravestones of Clare's children and sent a mental plea toward the horizon. *Cal, where are you?*

No answer came, but a feeling of eager anticipation rose within Meg. The sword's haft pulsed steadily as if to echo her heartbeat. No—the sword linked to Cal. The beat was his. Cal was near, and he searched for her, too. The sword would draw him as the crown once drew her. All Meg had to do was wait.

A dust cloud appeared on the horizon. Herlinde squinted. "Riders approach."

Meg grinned. *That was fast.*

Herlinde drew in a sharp breath. "They bear the standard of your liege, the One-Eyed Duke. My lady, it's as we feared. They've come to take you to Lord Frederick and force a new marriage contract."

Oh crap.

Meg darted back into the chapel, snatched the cloth off the altar, and wrapped the sword. "We need to return to my chambers." With the sword tucked tight under her arm, Meg ran to the manor house with Herlinde at her side. She went straight to the bedroom and shoved the sword under the covers. From outside the window came the frantic pounding of hoofbeats. They stopped in front of the manor. With a deep breath to steady her nerves, Meg smoothed her dress and gave a quick pat to her hair. "Let's meet our guests."

Meg descended the staircase as someone rapped loudly on the door. Wilhelm opened it and was nearly trampled as a squad of armed men rushed inside. One stepped forward with a bearing of arrogant authority. "I bring word from Duke Frederick. He summons Lady Clare of Kuneburg to Ulm." His hand rested on the hilt of his sword, intentions plain. "We leave at once. The carriage awaits."

Herlinde drew herself up. "Barking orders is no way to address Lady Clare."

The servants clustered around Meg in a protective stance muttering agreement, and Meg regarded them with a mixture of gratitude and concern. These people were loyal but not an army. If they confronted trained soldiers, they'd die. She didn't know whether the surge of anger belonged to her or Clare and didn't much care.

Meg stepped forward and jabbed the captain of the guard in the chest with her finger. He took a startled step back. "Listen up, bucko, because I'm only going to say this once. I'll go with you, but I have to get my stuff first."

He gaped at her. "Stuff?"

"Yes," she snapped. "Stuff, lady things. I'm not leaving without them, so you can wait right here until I finished packing. Am I going of my own free will or as a prisoner traveling to Ulm with only the clothes on my back?"

His eyes narrowed. "I have my orders."

"You may station a guard outside my door if it makes you feel better," she said sweetly, "but if any man dares enter my bedroom, I'll be sure to mention the insult to my father. Am I clear?"

Herlinde stepped to Meg's side, nothing but cold

hard intent in her expression. "I will accompany Lady Clare on the journey to see she is well-attended."

Before the captain could respond, Meg took Herlinde's arm, hitched up her skirt, and scampered up the stairs. The captain barked an order and one of guards followed them.

Meg ushered Herlinde into the chamber and slammed the door in the guard's face. "Set one toe over this threshold," she shouted, "and my father will cut out your heart and feed it to you with a spoon."

Amusement shone from Herlinde's eyes. "Would he truly?"

Meg grinned. "Probably not, he has a kingdom to run, but I've had experience handling powerful bullies. The trick is to agree to their face and work behind their backs. So, let's pack fast. I have an idea the captain isn't a patient man."

Herlinde opened a large chest and then went to an armoire to fetch clothing. "Get your things," said Meg. "I'll do these." Herlinde scampered away. Meg fetched the sword and placed it in the chest. She threw several dresses on top and then peered around. What else did Lady Clare need? Her gaze fell on the jewelry case and she packed it, too. Herlinde returned with an armload of her own clothing.

"This marriage contract..." said Meg. "It's a bit sudden after the death of my husband."

Herlinde snorted. "And most improper. The duke ignores protocol in his thirst to bind the daughter of King Henry to a member of his family."

So, poor Clare was a political pawn, which meant she was now a political pawn. Meg shut the chest and ordered the guard at the door to load it on the carriage.

"See that you don't drop it." Meg glared at him and added in her most threatening tone, "Or else." She was pleased to note a hint of apprehension in his eyes.

Meg hurried downstairs with Herlinde at her side. With the crook of her finger, she summoned Wilhelm and handed him the keyring. "I trust you to care for everything until I return."

Wilhelm took the keys and bowed low. "Yes, my lady." As he straightened, his gaze met hers. No words were spoken, but the meaning in his eyes was clear. He feared this was a one-way trip for Lady Clare. Despite the heat, a chill ran through Meg.

A carriage drawn by two horses waited outside. It had a canvas roof with flaps on the side raised to circulate the air and was more wagon than fancy conveyance. "Cinderella would hardly approve," she muttered.

"Cinderella?" asked Herlinde.

"This girl I met at a ball. She had family troubles, too."

The guardsmen helped them inside and Meg and Herlinde settled on a padded bench seat. The men loaded the chest and latched the rear gate. With the crack of the driver's whip, the wagon rolled away surrounded by their armed escort.

Escort or jailors? Either way, she wasn't getting out of this until the carriage reached Ulm. And then a medieval marriage? Meg squared her shoulders. Thanks, but no thanks. If it came to that, she'd find a way to escape and then hunt for Cal. She had the sword. Maybe Cal had found the crown. The crown and the sword had to work together to defeat the Everdark. Whatever magic created those objects called through the channels of time for two people to wield them, and Meg and Cal chose to answer. That's why the door didn't shut completely in Babylon; two warriors needed two weapons.

Meg gazed at the trunk, flushed with triumph. The sword fell easily into her hands. Everything happened so fast since her arrival, she had no time to think of the crown, but now she conjured a picture in her mind's eye. While inhabiting the body of Nemra, power coursed from the crown to Meg and forged a link. Had the crown survived the centuries and did the bond continue to hold strong as she inhabited Lady Clare?

Meg opened her mind—yes! A prickly tingle danced at the edge of awareness. The crown wasn't destroyed; only unlike at the Temple of Marduk, the connection now stretched thin. Almost as if...Rocked by the truth, Meg gripped the side of the bench to keep steady. "Oh, no," she whispered.

The crown was in the Middle East, thousands of miles from her, with no way to lay hands on it before the Everdark arrived.

Chapter Ten

Cal shifted in his saddle. Wait—the date couldn't be right. None of the facts from history fit. "Oh, hell," he muttered again.

"My lord?"

"Nothing, Tomman. Let's go." Cal pushed worried thoughts aside. Maybe on the way to Augsburg, he'd figure out what went wrong. He spurred his horse to a canter.

The sun rose in the sky. Morning mist burnt away, and they came upon a road. Cal wrinkled his nose at a strong stench. Judging by the ruts and the pungent odor of fresh dung piles, horses and oxcarts were frequent travelers. The route wove past peasants working fields of grain, small orchards, and here and there a thatched cottage nestled in a garden. After several hours of riding, the horses rounded a bend, and ahead loomed stout stone walls encircling a city.

Tomman waved a hand. "Augsburg, Sir Roland."

Despite the heat, Cal suppressed a shiver and mumbled another curse under his breath. Why hadn't he finished that damn ebook? The details he recalled were few, but enough to keep the scowl on his face. Although the author admitted facts from the time period were sketchy, scholars generally believed during an eclipse in 1133, Frederick II, Duke of Swabia, launched an attack against Augsburg. He quickly overcame the city's defenses, slaughtering citizens with abandon. The capture of the city was a minor note, an unimportant battle in Europe's long bloody history, only memorable because of the eclipse. People in the Middle Ages had seen it as an omen after the fact, but one monk wrote a local account. Cal's ebook had the picture of a woodcutting that depicted Augsburg's populace with hands raised in supplication. Underneath was a caption, and words buried in the back of Cal's mind leapt forward. *Very many stars were seen near the sun; many hearts were transfixed, despairing of the light. The face of the world was sad, terrible, black.*

The eclipse was an evil omen, for sure, but not for the battle of Augsburg. The Everdark waited for centuries until the veil thinned enough to escape. That time once again drew near, and Cal must be headed right into the thick of it. There was only one problem. According to the book, the date of the eclipse was August 2, 1133. The danger had already passed.

"Troubled thoughts, my lord?" Tomman regarded him with concern.

"No." Cal forced the scowl from his face. "Has there been an eclipse lately?"

"Eclipse?"

"Yes, you know, the sun disappearing from the sky…" Cal stopped at the boy's horrified expression.

Tomman made a quick sign of the cross. "No, my lord. I have naught seen such terrible magic."

"Never mind," Cal blurted. "Tell me of Duke Frederick. I am from Flanders and have little knowledge of local affairs."

The boy relaxed. "He is a powerful lord. The duke stood for election as king of Germany with the backing of his younger brother Conrad of Swabia and several houses, but he lost to Lothar, the present king. It is said Lothar has the support of the Holy See and the Pope will crown him Emperor soon."

"Frederick will have to bow even lower to him then," said Cal. "I'll bet that put his panties in a twist."

"My lord?"

"Skip it."

"My lord?"

Cal sighed. "Nothing. Has Duke Frederick been seen hereabouts lately?"

"I do not know, my lord."

They halted in front of a squad of heavily armed men guarding the open gates of the city. On top of the wall, archers with longbows scrutinized them with cold intent.

"What knight requests entry?" demanded a captain of the guard, hand resting on his sword hilt.

"Sir Roland de Bruche, summoned by the margrave." Cal showed them the letter.

The captain ordered the soldiers aside. Cal entered the market square to an immediate assault on his senses, overwhelmed by conflicting input from both his mind and Roland. The smell on the road was nothing compared to the un-deodorized bodies in town, not to mention the proliferation of livestock offered for sale. Vendors of chickens, pigs, goats, and horses shared space with fishmongers and butchers. Cal stifled a gag while the Roland part didn't appear to notice any of it. Cal gave a mental shrug. *What the hell. Go with the flow.* He ceded his sensory input to the Roland part and with each hoofbeat smells dissipated and faded into the background.

Augsburg was loud, too. Cal once rejected big city life and the cacophony of sirens, horns, and engines. New York in midtown rush hour was noisy, but had nothing on the earsplitting racket of whinnies, baas, clucks, and hee-haws in the market square. The strident clatter of hooves and cart wheels on cobblestone streets blended with the yells of human vendors hawking their wares. A city in the Middle Ages was one hot noisy mess. Why didn't historians record a massive crisis of deafness among senior citizens?

Oh, right. There were hardly any. Most everyone died by forty.

The most common language was Germanic, but apparently Roland was well educated. Cal's ear had no trouble discerning archaic versions of French, Italian, English, with a Latin word or two thrown in for good measure. Although part of the Holy Roman Empire, the polyglot population was no surprise. Augsburg was on a heavily traveled trade route between Munich and Stuttgart and attracted merchants from far and wide. The location on the river Lech gave the city an important commercial connection to the greater Danube whose waters sliced their way through half of Europe before emptying into the Black Sea. The strategic position and economic potential made Augsburg a tempting target and often put it in the crosshairs of political strife.

Cal and Tomman stopped at a stone structure at the city center. It was hardly the fairytale image of a castle, but rather a heavily fortified keep. Cal dismounted, and two servants at the door rushed to take the horses.

"Go with them," said Cal to Tomman. "Make certain the horses are well-tended. Sell the spoils in the market. Keep a third for yourself and find clothing more suitable for my squire." He whispered in his ear, "See what you can learn of Duke Frederick and his activities—discreetly."

The boy's eyes sparkled with understanding. "Yes, my lord."

Another servant led Cal inside where thick stone walls brought a bit of relief from the heat. They went directly to a large hall. He ushered Cal inside and then left. At one end, a massive stone fireplace with the carved signet of the margrave above the mantel took up most of the wall. No logs burned today, but doubtless a fire roared in the winter to cut the bitter chill. Intricate tapestries covered the walls, adding warmth and insulation. Only the very rich were able to afford such luxuries. Tapestries were a graphic display of the margrave's wealth as liege of a prosperous city. Unfortunately, that same wealth proved a constant temptation to others.

The servant returned with a tray. He placed a pitcher of wine and plates of sausages, roasted vegetables, bread, and cheese at a table. No utensils, of course, Cal ate with his knife and fingers, pleasantly surprised by the meal's taste. The wine was a tad sour, but the sausages would have been a big hit at any twenty-first century barbeque. Sanitation methods being what they were, Cal didn't dwell on the recipe. He finished eating and drummed his fingers on the table. How long had he been here? An hour? Two? Sunbeams streaming in the windows had shifted position, but without the convenience of a clock, marking the passage of time proved difficult.

The servant entered again and cried, "Lord Drogo

Ursenkrieg, Margrave of Augsburg."

Cal jumped to his feet as a man strode into the hall with purposeful intent. He wore princely raiment and a scowl. A pendant dangled from a heavy gold chain around his neck. It bore the identical signet as the one over the fireplace except his was encircled by rubies. The symbol of office announced to all, "I'm way better than you." Lord Drogo glowered at the servant. He bowed low and shut the door.

Cal bowed as well. "My lord."

Drogo regarded him with a piercing glare. "You have a reputation, Sir Roland. I hear you are a man who isn't afraid to bloody his hands."

Ah, so I'm a mercenary knight. That's cool. "There are five bodies in the forest who readily agree with you. They attempted robbery and failed."

"I have also learned you deported yourself well with King Roger of Sicily in the Battle of Nocera."

Cal modestly inclined his head. *If you say so.*

"A great pity," continued the margrave, "the battle ended in defeat and any hopes of acquired land lost with it. My guards noted your arrival laden with the spoils of combat and questioned your servant. He said you were attacked and laid waste to the men without assistance. Is that so?"

"Yes, my lord." He gave an offhanded wave. "They were mere brigands."

"Even so, the odds were impressive." Drogo narrowed his eyes. "Did you not recall my instructions to come alone?"

Not so cool. Drogo seemed as if he'd gladly punt Tomman off the nearest parapet. "The boy is loyal to me, my lord, and will hold his tongue."

175

"I expect you will make certain of that." His words sent a chill through Cal. "I am in need of a man with your particular skills. The rewards for success are great. Roland de Bruche is a youngest son with neither land nor fortune to call his own, fated to inherit only a name. Serve me well and you will find riches far greater than any trifles in the petty holdings of your father. Fail the assignment and you will meet your death."

"Then I will not fail, Lord Drogo."

The margrave's sharp eyes raked over Cal and his expression at last indicated approval. "Augsburg attracts merchants from across the empire and has many enemies jealous of the city's wealth. My forces have fended off attacks from those tempted by the riches within these walls."

"Not to mention," said Cal, "they lust after the city's strategic location both on a river to the Danube and the road between Stuttgart and Munich."

The margrave nodded. "Good. You understand my position. Recently, I learned of a new threat to the safety of Augsburg. A knight sworn liege to Duke Frederick died leaving a wife but no heirs. As such, Lady Clare of Kuneburg is under Frederick's governance. While Kuneburg is not a powerful holding, the woman is the bastard daughter of King Henry I of England and a highly sought-after prize. Being denied the kingship, Frederick now wishes to expand his influence in other ways. Rumors reached me he plans to increase his forces and marry the widow off to a cousin, thus giving him a tie to the English crown."

Drogo sneered. "King Henry has sired more bastards than flies on a dung heap but has seen them well wed and provided backing to their political allies.

If the marriage takes place, Henry may bolster Frederick's plans to expand his territory, and Augsburg will be the first to fall." A ferocious gleam shone from Drogo's eyes. "I will not have this marriage take place. Is my *full* intent clear?"

Hell, no. A hidden meaning lurked behind the margrave's words. Did he want to secure this woman's hand for himself or an ally of Augsburg? *Whatever. Best to feign understanding. This guy isn't the explaining type.* "Yes, my lord."

Cal's acknowledgement seemed to please him. "I received word Duke Frederick dispatched soldiers to escort Lady Clare to his castle at Ulm. You leave with first light. Do not fail me, sir knight."

"No, my lord."

The margrave reached into his tunic and tossed Cal a bag of coins. "This will ease your way. The rest is up to you." He strode from the room without a backward glance.

Cal stared at the bag. "The rest of what?" he said, rubbing the back of his neck. Terrific. First mercenary knight, now kidnapper, and still no sign of Meg. He brightened. His stolen life drove him toward Ulm. Perhaps, Meg was there with this Lady Clare character.

King Henry? A flicker of a passage from the book jabbed at his subconscious and then disappeared. Oh, well, maybe it would jar loose before he reached Ulm. "Lady Clare," he said, cheerfully, "prepare to be kidnapped."

A servant stationed outside the hall showed him to spacious quarters with a bed and unlit fireplace. Tomman was already there. On the floor were clean rushes with a blanket thrown on top. The boy's freshly purchased meagre possessions were alongside. Cal raised an eyebrow. His new squire obviously expected to sleep on the floor at the foot of Cal's bed. Sir Roland's memories weren't taken aback in the least. This must be luxurious accommodations for him according to Middle Age standards. Tomman certainly seemed pleased.

"The horses are well-tended, Sir Roland," said Tomman. "I sold the spoils in the market." He drew himself up and held out a bag of coins. "You were not cheated. I bartered a fair price."

Cal hid a smile at his intensity. "I'm sure of that. I trust you to hold the coins for me and guard them well."

Tomman's expression lit up. "Yes, my lord."

Cal's gratitude for Tomman's assistance increased as the boy removed his armor. No wonder knights had servants, he'd have never gotten the fastenings released himself. Cal sighed when finally stripped to linen undergarments. Tomman was certainly helpful, but kidnapping was dangerous work. Cal toyed with the idea of leaving him behind and then decided against it. His knowledge of the world was invaluable. Instead, he'd find a way to keep the boy safe when the Everdark arrived.

"I have a mission from the margrave," said Cal. "We leave first thing tomorrow for Ulm. Did you learn anything of Duke Frederick?"

"There was much talk in the market. Merchants recently arrived from Ulm did more in trade than usual due to the vast number of the duke's men in the city. Many sold double the amount in foodstuffs and horses."

"As if to outfit an army," mused Cal.

Tomman raised an eyebrow. "You think Duke

Frederick plans an attack?" His voice dropped to a whisper. "It is said he is discontent with current holdings."

Cal snorted in disgust. "Men such as the duke generally want more and are never satisfied with what they have."

"I should want a *little* more," said Tomman, "so I am able to keep a wife and land of my own."

Cal chuckled. "Aren't you a bit young to think of marriage?"

"I'm fifteen, sir," he protested. "My father took the bands at this age. And you, Sir Roland, don't you long for someone?"

An image of Meg popped into his mind. Unconsciously, Cal smiled.

"Ah," said Tomman. "The answer is writ on your face. Is she of noble birth?"

"She is quite noble, and the rest is none of your business."

"I see now. You swore fealty to the margrave to acquire a fortune great enough to win the lady's hand." His expression turned serious. "A noble endeavor, my lord. I will serve you well." Tomman got right to work, bringing hot water for Cal's washing and then busied himself polishing boots until Cal chased him to the bed of rushes with instructions to rouse him before dawn.

****

The wait was nearly over. Claws sank into the mist and grasped for the other side. Too far. The Everdark drew back with a snarl and inhaled, searching for the enemy's scent. Yes, there it was. Millennia ago, the Everdark's magnificent glory spread upon the Earth until forced into this prison by vile magic, but now the guardians dwindled from many to a puny few. They had taken the Everdark by surprise in Babylon, and it tasted bitter defeat.

The monster flexed its claws. Not this time. This time the gate had a crack.

****

Cal woke with a start, sweat beaded on his forehead.

"Sir Roland, daybreak is nearly upon us." Tomman peered at Cal with concern. "Are you ill, lord?"

"No, I'm fine." What was there to say? The end of the world was coming, but he had no way to stop it?

Tomman had scrounged bread and sausages from the kitchen to eat on the road. Cal sighed. Damn, he missed morning coffee. As the sun's first rays peeked over the horizon, they rode through the now quiet city, barely stirring for a new day. Once past the gates, Cal spurred his horse to a canter. He shot a glance over his shoulder as Augsburg faded into the distance. Echoes of the disturbing dream rang though his mind. Soon, more than half the citizenry would die, goods and finery looted to fill Duke Frederick's coffers. Not that the duke would live long enough to enjoy his conquest. Unless he stopped the Everdark, Frederick and his army were doomed, too.

Cal shook his head. The date. What was wrong with the date? He was positive the fall of Augsburg occurred August second, but it obviously hadn't since the city was still in one piece. Of course, history was muddy in this time period. Dates may not be exact...

He straightened in the saddle and focused his attention on the road ahead. No distractions now. He had to concentrate on finding Meg first and then the sword and crown. Fortunately, Tomman knew the route. "Tis heavy with merchants, my lord. We need only follow and will arrive in Ulm on the morrow."

The boy's knowledge was accurate. With full daylight came the sight of others packed for travel; many were merchants, but other men had the demeanor of battled-hardened soldiers. They stopped to eat at midday and then as the sun began to set took lodging at an inn. Dinner was at a long communal dining table in the company of other travelers, convenient for eavesdropping. Cal caught snatches of conversation. Apparently, word spread the duke was hiring and some were on their way to join his army.

Cal stifled a grin. That information opened a new possibility.

Chapter Eleven

Meg grunted as the wagon hit another rut. Sheesh, did the driver aim for each one on purpose or was the road that crappy? A glimpse out the tarp confirmed the worst—the road was that crappy. The pace slowed as the sun set, but the shine of the nearly full moon allowed them to continue to travel. She tried to nap on the bench, but the herky-jerky ride kept jolting her awake. By morning, she felt as if she spent the night in a bumper car. Meg rubbed her rump. Whoever said carriage rides were romantic was a dirty dog liar.

The driver shouted, "Whoa," and the wagon halted. Meg poked her head out from the tarp. They had stopped again to water the horses at a stream.

"Come on," she ordered Herlinde. "Let's stretch our legs."

The captain glared at her and opened his mouth as if to order them to stay in the wagon. Meg matched him glare for glare, confident he was bluster and bluff. She was no expert in the subtleties of medieval society, but no mere captain of the guard would defy the wishes of his lord and lay hands on a royal, even if she was a bastard. Of that, Meg was certain.

The captain held his tongue but shot scowls her way until they clambered inside. Despite his distrust, Meg had no intention of running. She'd never get far on foot and refused to abandon the sword tucked safely in the bottom of the chest. Plus, she had no idea where to go and had Herlinde to consider. Any escape attempt included the girl. These men were bound to take their anger out on her if Meg disappeared.

After several hours, they reached a main road. Villages were more frequent. Other travelers joined them; oxcarts and wagons, men on horseback, and peasants laden with goods for market. As the sun dipped toward the horizon, Meg got her first view of Ulm. Her heart gave an anxious flutter as the cart rattled past the heavily manned gates. Soldiers filled the streets, not to mention the city crowded with vendors. Leaving unnoticed wouldn't be easy. They rode past stone and timber dwellings through the bustling market and then up a slight incline to the fortified keep.

The medieval pipeline must have passed news of her arrival to the duke. A servant waited at the entrance. "His lordship will see Lady Clare alone."

Herlinde shot her a nervous glance. Meg patted her arm and ordered her to stay with the trunk. The servant hustled Meg inside to the elaborately carved door of a private chamber. He swung it open and announced. "Lady Clare of Kuneburg." She drew a deep steadying breath to calm her nerves and entered.

A man stood peering out a window, his hands clasped behind his back. He wore a tunic embroidered with gold lacework and fancy stitching. When the servant shut the door, he turned to face her. He had a patch over one eye while the other regarded her with ruthless intent. "Lady Clare."

Despite a disability, his stance screamed, "I am the local badass." A part of her in tune with Clare's emotions bleated a warning. *Show no fear. The duke only respects strength.* Meg curtsied. "Lord Frederick."

"I have considered affairs of state since the death of Sir Johannes and decided to see you settled in a new marriage. As your liege, I wrote a contract for my cousin, Sir Waltrud of Heisen. He agreed to the terms." The duke motioned to a paper on a table. "It only awaits your signature for the marriage to take place."

Meg's first instinct was to lash out at her treatment as a piece of property, but something held her back. A part of her mind understood anger got nowhere with the duke, and he'd even see it as a sign of weakness. Meg was no expert in medieval law, but apparently retained Clare's sensibilities of how the world operated. In this day and age, a woman's worth was bound to family connections and any money she brought to the table. For that, Clare whispered in her ear, the duke needed her alive and well.

Meg gave him a warm smile. Both she and Clare understood once one surrendered to a bully, a woman was never free. "I'm grateful for your concern," she said, "but must decline. My husband is barely cold in his grave."

The one visible eye narrowed. "This is not a discussion, Lady Clare."

"No. I understand it is a command, but I cannot consent to this marriage so near the death of my husband. We may broach the subject again after he has been dead a year."

The duke's face hardened. "I don't intend to waste a year while you feign to be in mourning. We both recognize this marriage as political as your last. This contract will be signed."

"Not today," Meg said coolly, "and certainly not

by me." She noted with satisfaction the little throbbing vein in his temple.

Duke Frederick strode across the room and stopped nearly toe to toe with Meg. "I have been in contact with King Henry. He agrees this alliance benefits his position and mine. Your father will not be pleased by your decision. This marriage will take place, Lady Clare. You will remain here until the contract is signed."

The duke loomed over her, but Meg refused to give an inch. "Then I will be a guest for quite some time and expect to be treated as the daughter of a king."

"The *bastard* daughter of a king," he sputtered with a glower. "Your father's acknowledgement of your birth granted rank and status, but at marriage I became your liege. Your loyalty is to me alone. I suggest your mind dwell on that. My cousin will arrive in the morning. At that time, I expect the marriage contract signed. If not, you will find these walls less hospitable." Red-faced, the duke stormed to the door and yanked it open. "Take Lady Clare to her quarters," he roared, "and see to it she isn't disturbed."

Two guards entered and led Meg up a central staircase to a room at the end of a hallway. One of the guards unlocked the door. To her relief, Herlinde was inside with the trunk, and rushed into Meg's arms. "My lady, I was so worried."

"I'm fine," she said, touched by the girl's devotion. The door behind her slammed shut, and a key turned in the lock.

"What said Duke Frederick?" asked Herlinde. Meg described the meeting, and she bristled at the name of Waltrud of Heisen. "He's twice your age, fat, dull-

185

witted, with the deportment of a swine, and the countenance of a turnip. Certainly, not worthy to be your husband. He has already seen three wives laid in the ground. It is said they died peacefully with a smile on their faces, grateful to at last be free of marital duties."

Meg chuckled. "I don't plan to be number four, but for the moment I'm stuck here. On the plus side, it's not a dungeon, but I fear that may change quickly. The duke isn't a patient man." Meg regarded the girl kindly. "I wish you would have stayed in Kuneburg. At least, you'd be safe."

Herlinde squared her shoulders. "Whatever happens, I will never abandon you."

"Thanks," she said with a warm smile. "It's nice to know one person here is on my side." Meg went to the window. The pane had been flung open to let in a warm breeze. She leaned on her elbows and peered over the sill. The room was thirty feet up and in the rear of the keep. She wrinkled her nose. Near the stables, by the smell, and out of sight of the main gate. The setting sun cast long thin shadows across the grounds. Even in the fading light, Meg easily spotted two guards directly below her. Not exactly overwhelming security, but then again, Duke Frederick expected a woman to bend easily to his will. There must be a way to escape. All she had to do was leave a locked room, pass the guards, and find a way out of the city.

Yeah, that's all. There were no bars on the window, but also no rope or ladder. Despite the longer hair style, she wasn't Rapunzel.

As Meg stood at the window, her mind conceived and discarded a dozen different escape plans. She blew out her cheeks in frustration. None of them proved satisfactory although she wasn't defenseless. The sword was at hand, and having a sharp, pointy object brought comfort. Granted, it was meant to fight the Everdark, but none of the guards knew that.

Pins and needles jabbed the nape of her neck. Meg briskly rubbed her skin, but the weird sensation refused to subside, almost as if a person poked her with a desperate need to attract attention...Geez, it was annoying. Meg froze and then turned to stare at the chest. She opened the lid and tossed out the clothing.

Herlinde peered at her, wide-eyed. "You brought the sword. For what purpose?"

Meg touched the haft and jerked back at a mild electric shock. She shook her hand to ease the sting. "I don't know. The sword has a mind of its own."

****

The buzz rang in Cal's head all day, not strident, barely a whisper, but enough for him to notice. He hadn't bothered to wear the helmet after they left the inn and secured it to his saddle; the armor alone nearly broiled him in this heat. Sir Roland's instincts tried to drown out his twenty-first century complaints; a knight didn't discard chain mail because he was hot. Cal ignored him.

Now, in the late afternoon Cal rubbed his ears in annoyance. What was that? Did Sir Roland have tinnitus? The sensation was like an annoying itch he couldn't scratch.

They arrived at Ulm. Cal stated his business to a soldier at the gates, and he granted passage to the inner keep. "I am Sir Roland de Bruche," he announced to a servant at the door. "I wish to offer my service to

Frederick II, Duke of Swabia." The man ushered him inside, and Cal brushed away the irritating buzz. No time for distractions when he had a duke to schmooze.

Duke Frederick greeted him with a scowl instead of a smile. Cal received the distinct impression this was his usual facial expression. Margrave Ursenskrieg was a merchant prince with an imposing personality, but this one-eyed warrior was born and bred to the sword. His uncovered eye narrowed, raking Cal from head to toe in silent scrutiny. "I have heard your name, sir knight. You are of Flanders."

"Yes, my lord."

"Your recent service?"

"King Roger of Sicily in the Battle of Nocera."

"The battle fought against Emperor Lothair's allies." His tone held a hint of interest. "It was said his forces were unstoppable."

Not a fan of Lothair, eh? Cal sneered. "Not, unstoppable, simply more numerous. A greater contingent could have soundly defeated them."

"So, you have no qualms to meet Lothair's forces on the battlefield again."

"On the contrary, my lord." Cal threw in a bit of swagger. "I am eager for it."

The scowl remained, but the single eye regarded him with greater favor. "I accept your service, Sir Roland of Bruche. Kneel."

Cal dropped to his knees.

"Do you swear service to me as your liege and to defend the house of the Duke of Swabia with your life?"

"I do."

Sir Roland's instincts had lain dormant and now

shouted an internal warning, "Brace thyself."

The blow to the head from Duke Frederick nearly knocked Cal on his rear. The ceremonial smack or coleé was used to seal the deal when a knight swore fealty and a lord accepted. Cal's books had described it as a tap on the cheek, but apparently the duke took his coleé seriously.

Cal's stoic response must have met with the duke's approval because he ordered him to rise and report to the barracks. With a deep bow, Cal backed away and hurried out the door. Tomman waited on the other side. "I took the liberty of finding the barracks already, my lord. I knew the duke would accept you."

"Your confidence in my abilities is a great comfort." As soon as Cal set one foot over the keep's threshold, he drew up short. The itch exploded into an eerie compulsion that snagged him like a bear trap and jerked him to a halt. He eyed the central stairway. Something up there beckoned to him, a clarion call he mustn't deny.

The sword.

His fingers curled as if they already held the grip. It was here in the keep. He felt it as readily as the mail shirt, but the keep was a busy place. Servants hurried to and fro. Would anyone notice if he took a casual stroll upstairs? Probably.

"Sir Roland?" said Tomman.

Cal pulled him aside and said quietly, "I have to go upstairs now without attracting attention."

Tomman nodded with a crafty look. "The servant's stairway, my lord."

There were advantages to having a loyal squire Cal decided. One simply gave an order and never had to

189

explain the reasoning. Cal followed Tomman to the far end of the keep. A curtain across a narrow stairway hid a passage for servants to travel between floors from the sight of the privileged. They began the ascent and the compulsion strengthened. Cal reached the second floor and it prodded him higher. The sword was up another flight.

Cal stopped on the third-floor landing and strained his ears to listen. From nearby came the sound of shuffling feet. He parted the curtain a crack. Down the hall was a guard in front of a door. The man had no chain mail, but a good stout sword at his side and no doubt the skill to use it. The compulsion became a blaring command in Cal's head. The sword was in that room. It took every piece of self-control to keep from charging at him, sword drawn. Despite Sir Roland's skill, Cal preferred to avoid combat and the chance of the guard crying out for reinforcements.

He studied his opponent's stance. Tough as nails, but used to following orders, and completely unversed in the same modern martial arts holds he learned in the military.

Cal whispered to Tomman, "Wait here."

He strode down the corridor. The guard spotted him at once. He drew his sword and pointed it at Cal's heart. "Halt—"

"Where is other guard?" demanded Cal in his most arrogant tone. He stopped in front of the man, the sword point nearly touching his chest.

The guard's harsh visage displayed a shade of confusion. "What other man?"

"Are you deaf?" spit out Cal. "The duke ordered two men on guard at all times."

His confusion deepened. The sword point wavered. "I had no orders—"

Cal glared. "Someone's head will roll." With one hand, he brushed aside the sword. "Put that away, fool. I supposed the door isn't even locked."

"Not so, m'lord." He rammed the sword back in the scabbard and hurriedly brought out a keyring. "I locked it myself."

"Good," said Cal. "That's what I wanted to hear." He kneed him in the groin. The guard doubled over, Cal grabbed him in a choke hold, and twisted the sword from his hand. Fifteen seconds later, he slumped to the ground. Cal signaled for Tomman.

The boy's scampered to his side, eyes gleaming. "A clever ruse, my lord."

"Thanks." He snatched the keyring from the floor. "Grab his arms and drag him inside."

"What's in this chamber?" Tomman whispered.

Cal unlocked the door. "A sword, I hope."

"For the margrave?" Tomman grunted as he tugged on the guard.

"No, for me."

Cal pushed open the door and stepped into the room. "Stop right there," said a woman behind him. He felt a sharp poke in the back of the neck.

Cal froze. "I mean you no harm."

"Yeah, that's what they all say."

The voice wasn't familiar in the least, but that tone…Cal turned around. A woman held the black sword steady with two hands, her expression one of deadly intent. A girl stood next to her, eyes wide with fear.

"I said," growled the woman, "don't move."

The face and bodily features were wrong. Cal peered into her eyes, heart hammering. She didn't look like Meg. She didn't sound like Meg, but damn it, the truth practically smacked him upside the head. His lips parted in a wide grin. "Meg!"

The woman gasped. "Cal." With a joyful whoop, she lowered the sword, threw herself into his arms and planted the most exuberant kiss he'd ever received right on his lips.

Chapter Twelve

Meg's arms encircled Cal, lips pressed tight to his, holding his body close.

Herlinde coughed.

Meg pulled back with a start, heart thrumming in her ribcage. The temperature appeared to have risen in the room by several degrees. "Sorry," she stammered. "I-I'm just so happy to see you."

"Don't apologize." Cal smiled and brushed a gentle hand across her cheek. "I'm happy to see you, too."

The sensation of heat in her face deepened and cascaded through the rest of her body, settling pleasantly a few degrees south of the border. "How did you find me?"

Cal nodded at the sword. "Actually, that brought me here. We have a connection."

Herlinde coughed again. "Lady Clare?"

Cal's mouth dropped open. "You're Lady Clare of Kuneburg? The Margrave of Augsburg sent me to kidnap you."

"Well, that's mighty convenient," said Meg lightly. "I hope you have a plan for getting out of here because if I have to marry the duke's fat cousin Waltrud the turnip, I'm gonna be ticked."

The mention of a forced marriage brought a scowl to Cal's face. His dropped his hand to the sword hilt. "Big fat turnip cousin Waltrud will have to get past me first."

The anger in his response provoked a smile from Meg. The distant recesses of her mind echoed with Lady Clare's cheering approval.

At Meg's kiss, Tomman stopped dragging the soldier across the room and gaped at them. Understanding now flooded his expression and he beamed at Cal. "Ah, Sir Roland, you found your lady."

Meg raised an eyebrow. "Sir Roland?"

"That's enough, Tomman," said Cal in a rush. "Meg, maybe this isn't the best place to swap stories."

"Right." She held out the sword with a cheeky grin. "Here, I kept it warm for you."

"Hang onto it until we escape. It won't fit in my scabbard and a black sword is bound to raise eyebrows." He nodded to the guard as Tomman stuffed him forcibly under the bed. "Has the same guy been outside the whole time?"

"No. This isn't one of the men who brought us here. A little while ago, we heard footsteps, voices, and jingling keys. This man let in a servant with a supper tray and then told her to return in the morning to fetch it."

"Good. That was probably the changing of the guard. If we're lucky, we have a few hours before his replacement arrives."

"Where do we go?"

"Let's escape then figure it out—Tomman, we need a way past the gate for the four of us."

"A wagon," answered Tomman without hesitation. "The sun is well past the horizon and nearly time for vespers, but we must move quickly. The guards shut the gates soon after."

"Take the duke's carriage," chirped Herlinde. "Lady Clare can hide under the bench. If the stablemen ask questions, I will tell them my lady signed the marriage contract and sent me to Kuneburg to retrieve wedding garments. The soldiers will have no doubt, especially with a knight as an escort."

As Meg wrapped the sword in the embroidered cloth, her eyes lit on the jewelry box, and an overwhelming urge came from Lady Clare to keep it from Duke Frederick's hands. Meg gave Herlinde the box. She locked the door with the guard's key and followed Cal down the back stairway to the first floor. Footsteps shuffled past the curtain and they pressed flat against the wall. When they faded, Cal motioned them out an open window, and they dropped to the ground. From nearby, came a Latin chant that Meg's internal Lady Clare recognized as vespers. Tomman led them to a courtyard and then a narrow alleyway that he assured them went to the stables.

Meg sniffed. Judging by her nose, the boy was right. The scent of horses was strong. When they were in sight of the stables, Meg hid behind a stack of barrels while Cal took Herlinde and Tomman with him.

Time passed and shadows lengthened. Meg scrunched into a ball in her hiding place, fighting the urge to run after Cal. How long had he been gone? Life was damned inconvenient without a watch. A muscle cramp shot through her leg and she shifted position. What was keeping them? Her grip tightened on the sword. If anything happened to Cal…

Her thoughts drifted to the kiss and her cheeks burned. What was she thinking? This was not rational, calculating Meg. She had her share of relationships, but never threw herself at a man, especially practically a stranger. Not that Cal felt like a stranger, and he seemed to enjoy the kiss as much as she did.

Wagon wheels slowed to a stop next to her and Meg peeked from behind the barrel. Hitched to the carriage were two horses with Tomman at the reins. Cal jumped from his mount. After a wary glance around, he lowered the rear gate and boosted Meg inside. Herlinde had shed her cloak and spread it across the bench so the cloth dropped in front, puddling on the floorboards. She raised one end. Underneath the bench was the jewelry box. "My lady," she whispered, beckoning her.

Meg scrunched against the side of the wagon, clutching the sword and box tight to her chest. Herlinde dropped the cloak and then shifted in her seat and spread her own skirts wide, effectively blocking any casual scrutiny.

Lying in tight quarters on a hard wooden floor as a wagon bounced along a cobblestone street was not the most comfortable position. Meg's head banged against the slats every time the wheels hit a bump, and Ulm had plenty of those. Her finger tugged at the neckline of her dress. The air was stuffy and the heat stifling.

Confined in dark, cramped quarters and unable to see was maddening. Had they passed the gate? A harsh voice called a halt and Meg's heart pounded.

"That's the duke's carriage, boy." Meg held her breath as the canvas tarp whipped back. "Who are you?"

"Herlinde, good sir. Lady Clare of Kuneburg sent me to fetch her wedding raiment. The marriage contract is signed."

Hoof beats stopped at the carriage gate. "What's

the delay?" barked Cal. "Lady Clare's servant must be on her way." His voice rose to an arrogant shout. "Perhaps you'd care to explain to Duke Frederick why the marriage to his cousin must be delayed because you refused to allow her to collect finery for the ceremony."

With a soft whoosh, the flap dropped in place. Meg blew out a breath as the wagon moved again. The infernal bounce eased for a few seconds as they passed the gate and the wheels rolled over the wooden planks of the drawbridge.

Tomman called out. "Get up there." The reins snapped. The horses went from a trot to a gallop.

They were free of the city, but the transition from cobblestones to a rutted road didn't lessen Meg's discomfort. The horses quickened gait only added to the shaking. With each jolt, she bit back a cry. Before long, Meg's body was sore and bruised, her head dizzy from the heat. The cloak lifted, and Herlinde dropped to her knees. She peered under the seat and held out her hand to Meg. "Come out, my lady. We are no longer in sight of Ulm."

"That's easier said than done," said Meg with a groan. She took Herlinde's hand, and the girl dragged her from under the bench. Meg let go of the sword and jewelry box. She wiped a hand across her sweaty brow. Not sweat—blood. She banged her head hard. Herlinde dabbed at the wound with a handkerchief. "I'm fine, Herlinde. Help me up." Meg placed an arm around the girl's shoulders and staggered to the padded bench.

Eventually, the wagon slowed to a halt. The gate lowered and Cal jumped inside. He went right to Meg and cupped her face in gentle hands, peering at her with an anxious gaze. "I'm sorry for the rough ride." He took the handkerchief from Herlinde and pressed it gently against her forehead. "You're hurt."

Meg smiled and placed her hand on top of his. "Knocked around pretty good, but I'm okay. Thanks for getting me out of there."

He returned the smile. "Anytime."

Tomman called from the front seat. "What direction, my lord? To Kuneburg?"

"It has no protection from the duke," said Meg. "Augsburg?"

A cloud passed over Cal's face. "Yeah, there may be a problem with that." He turned to Herlinde. "Go sit with Tomman. M—I mean, Lady Clare and I will speak privately."

Herlinde hesitated, and Meg patted her arm. "Do as he says. Sir, uh…" She stared at him blankly, his new identity escaped her.

Cal whispered an aside, "Roland."

"Right. Sir Roland and I are old friends."

Herlinde's eyes gleamed. "So I suspected from your greeting, my lady."

As soon as Herlinde scampered into the front seat, Meg turned to Cal with a grin. "I have to say, with that scar and chain mail and the way you took care of the guard and all, you're kind of a badass."

Cal chuckled. "New style I'm trying out. Like it?"

"Honestly, I prefer button-down lawyers to dukes and knights. I take it you had no problem getting past the gate?"

"The duke's soldiers are more focused on people entering than leaving. Frederick has no reason to check on Clare, so he won't learn of the escape for a while. Since it's the height of summer, the sun won't set until

late and with the moon we can continue on our way…"
A shadow fell across his face.

"To meet the Everdark." Meg's voice dropped.
"It's coming soon, isn't it?" She shivered. "I feel it. Do
you?"

He gave a terse nod. "Yes, but here's the problem,
Meg. According to history, an eclipse occurred across
Europe at noon, August 2, 1133. The event became
famous because it coincided with the departure of King
Henry I of England for Normandy. Henry died in
Normandy a year or so later and in hindsight people
took the earlier eclipse as a bad omen."

"Dear old Dad's on the way out?" asked Meg.
"Can't say I'll shed a tear since he agreed to marry
Clare to a turnip, but the eclipse must signal the arrival
of the Everdark."

"I agree, but a lesser known second event also
coincided with the eclipse. The city of Augsburg was
sacked and the inhabitants slaughtered by Duke
Frederick, but August second has passed. It's nearly the
middle of the month. The city stands, the eclipse didn't
occur, and there's no hell on Earth so the Everdark
didn't escape." Cal rubbed the back of his neck. "I can't
shake the idea I'm missing something obvious…"

"Is it the date?" said Meg. "Are you sure the
eclipse was the second? Maybe it was later in the
month."

"Later date…" The annoying little poke at his
memory finally jarred loose a fact. "Oh no. How could I
have been so stupid?"

"What is it?" asked Meg.

"The dates," blurted Cal. "They changed. In the
Middle Ages, people used the Julian calendar proposed

by Julius Caesar in ancient Rome, but the length of the year was off by eleven minutes. Over the centuries, the added time screwed up Easter's location. It was no longer in the spring. In the 1500s, Pope Gregory amended the calendar to stick Easter back where it belonged. It's the same one we use now and has an eleven-day difference. According to the Julian calendar, today is August 10, 1133."

Meg felt the blood rush from her face. "But it's really July thirty-first, two days before the eclipse and the return of the Everdark." She swallowed hard. "In Augsburg?"

"Everything seems to point us there." Cal glowered. "Which will reach us first? The Everdark or Duke Frederick?"

Meg shuddered. "I don't suppose we can warn Augsburg."

"It won't do any good," he said softly. "The margrave won't believe our story of the Everdark and even if he did, Duke Frederick's forces are too great. The city is already lost because, well, history says it happened."

"So many people are going to die."

Cal put an arm around her shoulder. "I'm afraid so, and in very unpleasant ways. I wish I could tell you otherwise."

Meg leaned against him. Even with hard chain mail, Cal's comforting warmth sank into her. She wondered if his heart beat as loudly as hers. "Thanks for not sugar-coating the truth."

"You can handle it," he said with assurance.

"It's Augsburg," said Meg. "That's where the veil thins, and where the Everdark tries to break through the gate. That's where we have to go."

****

Cal's gaze went to the sword on the floor. "We have to be sure." The draw was even stronger now. The mystical clarion called to him with an underlying urgency that rubbed like sandpaper against his skin.

He unwrapped the sword. As his hand curled around the hilt, a link formed at his touch; man to metal, as if the blade had been forged for his use alone. He held it in front of his eyes, testing the balance. The feel was perfect. This was more than a mere weapon, closer to an extension of his arm. The magical forces infused in its creation answered to him alone. The sword slept all these years waiting for the right person. If Cal accepted the responsibility, there was no turning back.

Do you accept the challenge, no matter the cost?

Cal's grip tightened. *I accept.* As if he threw an internal lever, the connection anchored in place.

"Where to?" he murmured. The blade jerked in his hand, pointing down the road.

A sense of gathering energy plucked at his hand. *The battle is upon us?*

"Not yet, but soon."

I wait. The energy stilled.

"We were right," said Cal, "and don't have a lot of time. The sword wants to go to Augsburg. The Everdark appears there."

Meg gnawed her lip. "That's a problem. I don't know about Tomman, but Herlinde is fanatically loyal. She won't leave Lady Clare, and I can't drag the poor thing to a massacre."

"Tomman is the same. We'll find a way to get

them out of the city before the Everdark arrives or Frederick shows with his army."

"Then we better hurry."

Cal grabbed her arm. "Wait a minute. Do you have the crown?"

"Not exactly."

He gaped at her. "What do you mean, not exactly? The crown and the sword have to be together. If it's in Kuneburg, we have to go there first."

Meg shook off his grip. "It's not in Kuneburg. I'm certain."

"Then where is it?"

She glanced away. "Probably in Augsburg."

"Probably?" he sputtered. "A monster will be there in less than two days. Probably isn't good enough. I'll go to Augsburg. Take Tomman and Herlinde with you to Kuneburg."

"Not a chance. I'm going with you."

"The crown is your weapon. You can't fight unarmed. No way will I let you—"

"Hold on there," said Meg with a stubborn set to her jaw. "We made the decision together. We entered the maze together. Whatever happens, we finish together. Besides, you can't stop me. What are you going to do? Tie me to a tree? Return me to Duke Frederick with a heartfelt apology for my kidnapping? You won't have time to say "My bad" before he lops off your head."

Cal's shoulders sagged. "I can't keep you safe if you don't find the crown."

The fire left Meg's eyes. Warmth and gratitude and perhaps a more powerful emotion replaced it. "You can't protect me here," she said softly. "The women in this time period are more property than person. They're never safe. I want to go home to coffee shops and funnel cakes and the right to vote and indoor plumbing and the freedom to choose my own path in life. I can't see any route to the future other than the one that brought us here. As far as we know, the only way back is to face the Everdark first, and that means going to Augsburg."

"Meg." He was a lawyer, damn it, trained in logical discourse. Where were the right words to convince her to stay behind? "We can't be sure…"

"No more arguments, counsellor." Her expression softened. "Besides, I'd rather die fighting that thing with you at my side than living here to a ripe old age in a castle married to a fat, ugly turnip."

Cal smiled and took her hands. "I'd never let you marry a turnip."

Meg laughed. "Thank you. True chivalry isn't dead. So, what do you say we get going? Time is wasting, sir knight."

Her laugh lightened his heart. Cal wrapped the sword back in the cloth and carried it to his horse. After securing it to the saddle, he mounted and called to Tomman. "We ride hard and continue through the night. We must reach Augsburg with due haste."

"Yes, my lord."

Herlinde crawled into the back with Meg. Tomman slapped the reins against the horses, and they took off at a gallop. The sun inched below the horizon, but a nearly full moon rose in the sky shining on them with pure silver light. They stopped occasionally to rest the horses. Cal searched for an opportunity to speak privately with Meg, but Tomman and Herlinde always hovered nearby. From snatches of whispered conversation, he got the impression each believed Cal was on a knightly quest to rescue his one true love from a forced marriage. Their frequent approving glances meant the mission met with their favor, and he had no intention of spilling the truth. They wouldn't believe it anyway. He barely did himself.

The ruse sat well with the remnants of Sir Roland. His medieval blood boiled at the thought of a woman with Lady's Clare's spirit and beauty lying with a man as repulsive as cousin Waltrud. Cal's twenty-first century sensibilities were right there with him but not for the same reason. It wasn't the visage of Lady Clare who occupied his thoughts, but the idea of Meg in danger that fired his blood.

A sense of pressing danger grew inside him. He and Meg were slowly being squeezed between impossible odds; on one side was Duke Frederick's forces and on the other was the Everdark. At the same time, the pull toward Augsburg strengthened with each mile, and the relentless tug pressed Cal to maintain speed. As they tore through the countryside, he glanced at the moon. Only one small missing sliver kept it from full phase. In two days, the solar eclipse began with the Everdark clawing at the veil.

Moonbeams gave way to gray shadows and then rosy pink dawn. They reached Augsburg's gates, open to admit travelers and merchants. Before Cal entered the city, he cast one last look over his shoulder and blew out a breath of relief. No sign yet of Duke Frederick and his forces.

The captain of the guard hailed Cal. "We have orders to watch for your arrival. A message was sent to

Lord Drogo. He expects you to report at once."

The carriage rolled through the bustling city streets and stopped in front of the keep. Meg stretched her arms over her head and groaned. "Finally. That was *not* a comfortable ride. I swear I'm one big bruise."

"The margrave will see to your comfort, my lady," said Herlinde.

"He'd better. I'm not in a ladylike mood."

Cal dismounted and helped Herlinde out of the carriage first. Then Meg placed her hands on his shoulders, he put his on her waist and lifted her to the ground. They stood with their arms around each other until Herlinde cleared her throat.

"So," said Meg, taking a step back from Cal, "what kind of guy is this margrave?"

"A city-state ruler is the Al Capone of the Middle Ages. Lord Drogo is a businessman but controls his own mini empire and nothing stands in his way. He wanted Lady Clare's marriage stopped for political reasons—a tie however slight to the King of England only advances Duke Frederick's power. What about the crown?" asked Cal. "Can you sense it yet?"

Meg shifted her feet. "Yes."

Cal's eyes narrowed in suspicion. "It's in Augsburg?"

"No."

Cal gawked at her. "Where is it then?"

"My best guess is somewhere in the Middle East."

He grabbed her arm. "What!"

"It's not here. It's never been here."

"You told me..." Cal sputtered in anger. "I assumed..."

"You assumed wrong."

Her calm demeanor stoked his anger. "You shouldn't be here unarmed. I should have forced you to return to Kuneburg." Frustration and despair barreled into him at once. "You have no weapon."

"It doesn't change a thing. The fight belongs to both of us." Her hand touched his cheek. "I won't leave you," she said tenderly.

Cal placed his hand on top of hers. "Meg…"

The door to the keep opened. A servant stepped out and called, "The margrave awaits."

Cal motioned to Tomman. "See to the horses and then return." His voice dropped to a whisper. "Don't let the sword out of your sight." Tomman nodded.

Meg pulled Herlinde to the side. "Hold tight to the jewelry box."

Cal and Meg followed the servant to the main hall. The margrave stood in front of the fireplace. He glowered at Meg and then turned his attention to Cal. Something was wrong. He certainly didn't broadcast warm and fuzzy vibes. In fact, he seemed angry.

"I did not expect your return with such haste, Sir Roland." Lord Drogo spit out the words between clenched teeth. "And *with* Lady Clare."

The truth hit Cal with a bang. Lord Drogo didn't expect to see Lady Clare in Augsburg. Even worse, he didn't want to see her in Augsburg. Cal had missed a subtle medieval inference at their last meeting, and the horrible knowledge of the margrave's real mission became plain.

He didn't send Sir Roland to kidnap Lady Clare. He sent him to kill her.

Chapter Thirteen

Meg looked from Cal to the margrave. This wasn't good. The margrave certainly didn't act like a boss whose employee completed a successful business transaction. Granted, she was the transaction, but then why was he furious to see her in the flesh?

Well, when it came to powerful men, money always did the talking.

"My thanks to you, Lord Drogo," Meg said. "I am beholden for your knight's rescue, as is my father. He will surely show his gratitude to Augsburg."

The margrave's eyes narrowed. "Will he? You speak with certainty I cannot claim. My sources say the marriage alliance with Duke Frederick was much desired by both parties."

"Not so, my lord," said Meg in a rush. "The duke had such desires, but my father did not."

"Indeed," Cal added. "Lady Clare informed me King Henry did not approve. That was why I brought her to you with all haste. Augsburg may benefit at the expense of the duke."

The margrave paused as if to consider Cal's soothing words and then shot him a disbelieving look. "Why should the king disapprove? He gladly wed her to a liege of Frederick before."

"The situation has changed since then. King Henry believes his daughter's marriage now to Frederick's cousin will bring him too much power. The duke," Cal said with a wily expression, "is an ambitious man."

The margrave rubbed his chin. "The king's only legitimate son died several years ago. Henry has no male heir."

Meg jumped in. "That's right. My father's eventual death is bound to cause contention among any parties that can claim even a tenuous link to the throne. He mentioned in one of his letters he fears Duke Frederick's ambitions extend beyond the channel."

"Into England itself?" muttered the margrave. "It's possible. Frederick's lust for control of the Germanic territories has no bounds. His greed may extend to King Henry's domain." He regarded Meg with sharp eyes. "You suggest an alliance with Augsburg by marriage?"

Meg startled. *Is that what I said?*

"She does, my lord," said Cal with conviction.

I do?

"It will benefit Kuneburg," added Cal, "and a marriage alliance with Augsburg curtails Duke Frederick's ambitions."

"What you say has merit for the city," mused Lord Drogo. His anger with Cal appeared to have cooled. "Any marriage needs approval from the king. I wish no grievance with Henry."

"My father has no objection," said Meg. "The last letter said he wanted closer ties to Augsburg."

"King Henry sets sail from England in two days to inspect properties in Normandy," added Cal. "He can be approached then."

The suspicion returned to the margrave's expression. "How did you learn of this?"

"I told him," blurted Meg. "The letter also said

he'd be in the area and wanted to drop in."

The margrave's brow furrowed. "Area? Drop in?"

"Visit," said Cal hurriedly. "He intends to visit Lady Clare."

"I have heard talk," said the margrave with interest, "of Henry's impeding voyage across the channel."

"My father will be so pleased," added Meg, "to learn a knight of Augsburg snatched me from Duke Frederick's clutches." She beamed at the margrave. His scowl was now more of a grimace, probably the closest thing he had to a happy face.

"I will consider your words." Lord Drogo whipped open the door and barked at one of the waiting servants to take Lady Clare to guest quarters.

Meg ignored the aches and pains of her travels and made a graceful curtsy. "Thank you, my lord."

He growled an acknowledgement and turned to Cal. "Sir knight," he bit out between clenched teeth, "you will remain."

Meg followed the servant, and the door closed behind them. She paused, an anxious knot in her stomach. What was going on? Cal had been sent to kidnap her. Well, she was properly kidnapped, but for some reason that ticked off the margrave. Was he mad enough to banish Cal from Augsburg or execute him on the spot? The knot tightened.

The servant beckoned to her. "My lady, this way."

Meg tore her gaze from the door and followed him to an antechamber. Herlinde waited, clutching the jewelry box tight to her chest. "Did all go well?" she asked anxiously.

"For now."

"Where is Sir Roland?"

209

"My guess is getting a royal ass-chewing for taking matters into his own hands."

"My lady?"

"He remained to speak with the margrave."

The servant led them to spacious quarters. To Meg's amusement, Herlinde ordered him to bring food and wine and then dismissed him with an imperious wave of the hand. The servant didn't appear to care and was probably used to getting ordered about, even by a slip of a girl. After the man bowed low and left, Meg tried the door and the handle turned freely. She peeked outside, relieved to see no guards. At least, she wasn't a prisoner this time, not that escape was in her plans. The only thing that occupied her thoughts was Cal and the approach of the Everdark.

Meg shut the door and leaned against it, her knees suddenly weak with relief. They found each other. No matter what happened, at least they'd face it together.

"He has a striking countenance, my lady." Herlinde's eyes sparkled.

Meg blinked. "The margrave?"

She giggled. "Sir Roland, of course. To have made such a bold and daring rescue for his lady speaks well of his courage and nobility of spirit."

"I'm not...I mean he isn't." The heat rose to her cheeks. "We're old friends."

Herlinde cast an innocent gaze at the ceiling. "I have never greeted an old friend so warmly."

"Um, yes, but he was gone for years...to the, uh, Holy Land doing, uh, the knightly things that they do there." She felt more color rise to her cheeks. "I was only pleased to see he returned safely."

"You even have nicknames for each other." Her

voice dropped to a whisper. "Did you use them when you passed love billets, so others did not suspect the truth? Fear not, my lady," she added in a rush, "I will keep your secret to my death."

Meg stifled a sigh. *I give up.*

****

"Explain your disobedience, knight," barked the margrave, "before I have your head served to me on a platter."

"Forgive me, my lord," said Cal. "When I heard Lady Clare's tale, I believed her escape was in Augsburg's best interests."

"We shall see," grunted the margrave. "Yet, I am unclear how you learned of King Henry's disapproval of the marriage." His eyes narrowed in suspicion. "She merely told you."

Cal thought fast. "Yes, my lord. We met many years ago at my father's house. Once I dispatched the guard at her chambers, Lady Clare said Duke Frederick held her prisoner and appealed for assistance. Again, my lord, in the best interest of Augsburg—"

"Yes, yes." The margrave waved his hand. "So you say, but I'm wondering if it isn't in the best interest of Sir Roland de Bruche as well. A marriage between you and Lady Clare would bring both rank and land."

Cal startled. "My lord," he sputtered, "I had no such intent—"

"Perhaps, not at the time." Drogo's eyes narrowed. "But the idea has merit. The lady must be wed to curtail Frederick's ambitions. Kuneburg is not an extensive fiefdom but, by all accounts, profitable under Lady Clare's hand. Of course, her real value is her connection, however tenuous, to the English crown.

Henry breeds like a rutting boar but has shown generosity to his bastards and their alliances. No one doubts your lineage. You are a proven knight of noble family, and I am your liege. Upon marriage, she and her holdings will also be bound to me. I assume you are not averse to bedding the woman?"

Cal's lips twitched in an unconscious smile. "No, my lord."

"And the lady? Will she wed so near the death of her husband?"

The margrave's harsh tone left no doubt this time in Cal's mind of the words' true meaning. Agree or die. "Lady Clare will have no objection."

Lord Drogo rubbed his chin. "Once Henry lands in Normandy, Frederick can press his intentions in person, and may sway the king's mind. It is in Augsburg's best interest to have no delay in the ceremony, then. The wedding will be on the morrow. I will prepare the marriage contract for signature." He called for another servant, barked a flurry of orders, and then turned to Cal. "You may inform Lady Clare of my decision."

Cal bowed. "Yes, my lord." He hurried out the door. When he requested directions to Lady Clare's chamber, a servant regarded him with such shock he quickly back peddled and said he simply wished to send a message for her to meet with him. With a suspicious glare, she scurried away. A few minutes later, Meg descended the stairs with Herlinde at her side. She gave Cal a helpless look that translated as "Herlinde won't leave me alone."

Cal offered Meg his arm. "Care for a stroll in the courtyard?"

She smiled. "That sounds lovely."

Cal turned to Herlinde. "Find Tomman and bring him to me."

Herlinde regarded Cal with suspicion, and Meg made a shooing motion. "Do as Sir Roland says." As she scampered away, Meg rolled her eyes. "She's a sweet kid, but frankly I'm sick of the constant hovering. She's driving me nuts."

"Yeah. I'm fed up at being eyeballed by every female here as if I'm a sex-crazed lowlife ready to jump on the first woman to pass by."

Meg's eyes twinkled. "You haven't checked yourself out in a mirror lately. With that scar, Sir Roland can easily make the cover of Serial Killer Monthly. Besides…" She elbowed him playfully in the side. "It's the Middle Ages. All men are pigs."

Cal grinned. "I recall apologizing to you once before for every male in recorded history."

"Okay," she chuckled. "I'll cut you some slack." Her voice dropped. "How'd it go with the margrave?"

"A few interesting developments." he said. "Let's sit and talk." He led her to a bench in the middle of the courtyard under the shade of a stately oak tree. Cal shifted his feet. "What's your opinion of shotgun weddings?"

Meg raised an eyebrow. "I have a feeling I'm supposed to be in favor of them."

Cal related his conversation with the margrave. "I'm sorry, Meg. This is awkward for both of us, but I didn't have a choice. If we want to stay in Augsburg long enough for the eclipse, we have to accede to the margrave's wishes."

"Actually," mused Meg, "this works for me. I've been trying to come up with a way to get Herlinde out of the city before either the Everdark or Frederick and his army arrives. The marriage is a perfect excuse. After the ceremony, I'll send her immediately to Kuneburg with orders for the servants to prepare for the arrival of Lady Clare and her new husband. That's a logical thing to do, right?"

"Makes sense," said Cal, "and it works for me, too. Herlinde can't travel alone, so Tomman will go with her. Fortunately," he added lightly, "we already stole a nice carriage."

Meg burst out in laughter. "I'm sorry," she said. "I may be a royal in a margrave's castle, but this isn't the storybook wedding I pictured as a little girl. It's more of a cut and dried business arrangement. The Brothers Grimm were a couple of liars."

"Despite being a lawyer," said Cal with a grin, "I can't say I ever considered a contractual marriage for my wedding either."

Meg shifted in her seat. "You had wedding plans?"

"Once. Never made it to the altar though. Allison and I…well, we didn't work out." Cal sat back. "Funny, that's the first time I've said that out loud and felt nothing but relief. The marriage would have failed. We were wrong for each other and needed different things."

"Such as?"

"From the beginning, Allison had her eye on a high-paying job and the excitement of life in a big city. I did too, at first, but deep down I had this itch to build relationships with clients, get to know them as friends, and see how I made a difference in their lives. I guess I wanted a place like Crossroads."

Meg flashed a teasing smile. "Bet you're having second thoughts about a quiet life in a small town now."

"No." Cal's gaze met hers and his heart unexpectedly skipped a beat. "Despite everything—no, but I wish I could send you away from Augsburg before the Everdark arrives. The crown—"

"Isn't here," Meg said firmly, "but I am, and you can't get rid of me that easily." Pink slightly tinted her cheeks. "So, I suppose you have to marry me."

"This is beyond awkward," said Cal gently, "but we only have to keep up the charade for a while. The Everdark will be here soon and, with luck, we won't need the crown. I can kill it with the sword, and then we return to the twenty-first century."

The question hung in the air between them. *And if we don't?*

To Cal, the answer was plain. *We'll be stuck in the Middle Ages where life is short and brutal, especially for women. Meg will be lucky to make it past thirty.* The muscles in Cal's jaw tightened. A surge of protective anger raced through him. He'd find a way to get her home even if it meant staying behind.

As if Meg read his thoughts, she rested a gentle hand on his. "I won't go anywhere without you."

"Meg…"

"Suck it." Her tone brooked no argument. "We're in this together."

Cal's fingers entwined with hers. "Together."

"Sir Roland!" Tomman entered the courtyard. He carried the linen wrapped sword and a scabbard. Herlinde was with him. She took one glance at their joined hands. Her lips pressed together, and she shot Cal a medieval stink eye. Cal sighed and let go.

Meg snickered. "Told you, even the girls here

know men are pigs." She jumped in before Herlinde forced her way onto the bench between them. "Sir Roland and I are to be wed tomorrow."

The disapproval in Herlinde's expression instantly disappeared and she clasped her hands together in delight. "Oh, my lady, such excellent news." Herlinde snatched Meg's arm, yanking her abruptly to her feet. "But tomorrow?" She clucked in disapproval. "We have so much to do."

Meg blinked. "We do?"

"Of course." Herlinde tapped her lip. "Wedding raiment must be prepared. I suppose we can borrow suitable garments from a lady in the margrave's court, and then there is the preparation of the bridal chamber…" She tightened her grip on Meg's arm and jerked her toward the keep. "You should not set sight on the groom the day before the wedding," she scolded. "It's bad luck."

"Wait…" Meg looked at Cal with desperation in her eyes. "We haven't finished discussing that person coming to see us…where and how do we greet him?" Herlinde's fierce grip towed her across the courtyard while she gushed a stream of happy chatter on wedding preparations.

Cal grinned at Meg's dismay. "I'll poke around. Meanwhile, don't fight the system."

"Easy for you to say," Meg sputtered.

"Congratulations, Sir Roland," said Tomman. "You won your lady. I knew you could do it."

"Thank you, Tomman." Cal clapped him on the shoulder. "I couldn't have managed the rescue without your help." The boy flushed at the praise. "I see you found a scabbard for the sword."

"Yes, Sir Roland. I purchased it in the market. The leather is old and worn, but the blade will fit." He regarded the scabbard with haughty disdain. "This will have to do until my lord can have one made more suitable to his new station as liege of Kuneburg. The margrave has issued instructions for you to be quartered in the keep instead of the barracks. I will show you to your chambers and we can also begin wedding preparations."

Cal blinked. "What preparations?"

"Surely, you jest, Sir Roland." He wrinkled his nose. "You have spent many days on the road."

Cal chuckled. "Not exactly smelling like a rose, am I?"

"No, and the leather needs polishing and suitable raiment attained and—"

"Spare me the details, just lead me to the chamber."

"This way, Sir Roland."

The room had several windows offering a nice cross breeze that gave some relief from the stifling heat. Cal ran a finger around his neckline. The chain mail wasn't helping. Tomman removed the armor and Cal stretched his arms over his head to work the kinks from his muscles.

News traveled fast in the keep. A knock at the door produced servants with clean clothing, hot water, food and wine. After eating, Cal stripped off his dirty clothes for servants to wash and got an eyeful of Sir Roland's body. The musculature was similar to his, but despite military service Cal wasn't covered in scars. Sir Roland had led a very aggressive lifestyle.

Not for long. Sorry, Roland. Cal had a tug of

217

regret. The Everdark's arrival didn't bode well for Cal or the body he inhabited. Without warning, a savage battle cry issued from the deep recesses of his mind. He gazed at the linen wrapped sword on the bed. Had Sir Roland heard and consented? After all, he was the youngest son; an itinerant knight with no prospects, due to inherit nothing from his family but a name. A good death on a field of honor would be an acceptable end for such a man. Cal clenched his fist. Neither the modern man nor the medieval knight planned to run from the Everdark.

But what about Lady Clare? And Meg? She didn't have the crown, and no possible way to retrieve it by morning. Cal rubbed himself dry briskly. He had to protect her.

Tomman sat at the hearth polishing Cal's boots. "The sword is a most unusual design. May I ask how Lady Clare came by it?"

"Um, it was with her family for a long time."

The boy nodded approval. "A family treasure, gifted to you for the marriage. The lady holds my lord in high esteem. Herlinde had doubts as to your intentions, but," he said smugly, "I told her she was wrong."

"Thank you. You have proven to be an excellent squire." Tomman flushed with pleasure. "As a matter of fact," added Cal, "I have an important assignment for you."

"Anything, my lord."

"Directly after the wedding tomorrow, escort Herlinde to Kuneburg. Lady Clare wishes her sent ahead to prepare for our arrival. Stay off the main roads and make sure to avoid any of the duke's men. Can you do that for me?"

Tomman drew himself up. "Of course, my lord." He examined the shine on the boots. By his satisfied expression, their new gleaming appearance was to his liking. He nodded at the scabbard on the bed. "It needs polishing."

Cal tossed him the scabbard and then removed the linen wrapping the sword. His fingers curled around the haft. Once more he marveled at the comfortable fit. An electric shock raced up his arm. Cal tried to open his fingers, but they remained clenched tight around the hilt. This time the sun, moon, and stars emitted a pure white light.

The battlefield is near. I watch.

The light faded until only a remnant of energy tingled against his palm. The sword was charged and ready, the magic needed only Cal's command to activate.

"Sweet Jesus, protect us." Tomman gawked at the sword. His tan skin was ashy gray and wide-eyed terror erased his cheerful smile. "M-my lord?"

"It's all right, Tomman," Cal soothed. "Don't be afraid." His mind searched desperately for a medieval explanation to calm the boy before he passed out. "This blade was, um, blessed by a saint to vanquish a great evil."

The boy licked his lips, eyes wide. "Which saint?"

"Which saint?" Cal latched onto the first name to come to him. "Saint George."

Tomman crossed himself and drew a shuddering breath. Color returned to his cheeks. "I have heard the tale. Saint George slew a dragon." He gasped. "Does such a creature lurk near Augsburg?"

219

"Yes, right, a dragon, but this must be our secret. Swear you will not speak of the sword to anyone."

"Y-yes, my lord," he stammered, "but if a dragon comes, you surely need the help of every man in the city to slay such a fearsome creature."

"No. This, uh, dragon can only be destroyed with this sword, and I am the only one who can wield it. Any other who fights, no matter how well-armed, will die."

Tomman crossed himself again. "Saint George came to you in a holy vision."

"Yes, and the vision must stay our secret, too."

"What of Lady Clare?"

"She is my concern."

The boy's eyes lit with understanding. "Saint George rescued a maiden. The dragon comes for Lady Clare and you are sworn to protect her." He coughed. "She has been wed and is not a maiden."

"Right, well, contrary to the story, dragons aren't only attracted to maidens. They seek to devour women of exceptional courage to, uh, bolster, their strength."

"I see the truth of it now," he said in a solemn tone. "Lady Clare's nobility draws the dragon, but she refuses to run or hide and thus endanger others."

"Exactly, so she will lure the dragon and I will slay it, but she wishes Herlinde safely out of harm's way first. The girl is loyal. She won't leave her side and is bound to be killed. You will do this for me and not speak a word to Herlinde of the true reason she must go to Kuneburg."

"Yes, Sir Roland." Tomman squared his shoulders. "It is an honor to serve such a noble knight."

The piercing intensity in his voice touched Cal. He clapped Tomman on the shoulder. "Thank you." He rubbed a hand over his eyes at a sudden wave of fatigue. Was it the burden of the sword, or merely the compounded exertions of the past few days? No matter, he couldn't remain on his feet much longer. "We rest for now. Tomorrow is likely to be a day neither one of us forgets."

Chapter Fourteen

Meg walked through the maze, Nemra at one side and Clare at the other. "Time grows short, sister," they said in chorus.

Meg's hand touched her bare head. "I don't have the crown. I can't shut the gate."

"No, but whatever strength we retained through the annals of years is yours to wield."

"Will it be enough?"

The sorrow in Nemra's eyes gave the answer. "You can still run," said Clare. "Save yourself."

Meg regarded them with disbelief. "Leave Cal to fight alone—not a chance."

Clare smiled in approval. "Then, sister, we will do what we can."

From nearby came a strident howl. "The veil thins," said Nemra. "The Everdark scents blood."

****

Meg's eyes shot open. The eerie dream dissolved into misty fragments, but the underlying truth remained. The Everdark was on the way, and she didn't have the crown.

"I'm sorry, my lady." Herlinde hovered over her. "I did not mean to jar you from sleep."

"No problem." Meg shook off the mental turbulence. *Suck it up. All Herlinde needs to see is a happy face.* She sat up and stretched. Bright light filtered through the narrow windows. "It's late."

"You were so weary from the hardship of the journey, I had not the heart to wake you sooner. The margrave sent word the marriage contract is prepared. The wedding will be in the keep's private chapel after sex and before vespers."

After sex? What the heck? "What did you say?"

"Sext, my lady."

Meg received an impression of ghostly laughter, and then Lady Clare's whisper, *Sext is noon prayers*.

"Oh, right."

"We have plenty of time to make ready for Sir Roland. I vow he will be awestruck at the first sight of you."

My wedding day to Cal. Her heart unexpectedly fluttered, and she stifled her feelings with a harsh dose of reality. The ceremony was for Lady Clare and Sir Roland. She threw aside the covers and got to her feet. A wreath of fresh flowers lay on a table. "From the margrave?"

"From Sir Roland," said Herlinde. Her eyes shone with approval.

Color rose to Meg's cheeks. "He was here?"

"No, Tomman delivered them. He said Sir Roland picked the flowers himself and Tomman wove them into a wreath for you to wear. Sir Roland had no gift for your wedding day but wanted to offer something. His appearance is rough," Herlinde said coyly, "but I believe he will prove to be a tender husband."

Heat flooded Meg's cheeks, but she said nothing. The flowers weren't the only gift. The margrave's wife sent a clean shift. Servants knocked on the door toting basins of hot water. After Meg bathed, Herlinde helped her to dress. The girl attempted to plait Meg's hair in a bun, but she shooed her away. It was so long and added too much weight at the neck. Meg selected a clip from the jewelry box and secured her hair in a ponytail.

Herlinde eyed her with doubt. "Tis not the fashion, my lady."

"I'll start a new one."

Herlinde place the wreath on Meg's head and then stepped back to admire the effect. She sighed. "You are truly beautiful."

Meg smiled. "Thank you."

Herlinde's hands flew to her cheeks and she gasped. "My lady we forgot the ring for the ceremony. You can use your wedding band, but what of Sir Roland?"

Meg poked through the contents of the jewelry box and pulled out a gold signet ring inset with two sapphires. "This will do."

"A gift from your father, judging by the signet," said Herlinde with evident approval. "Sir Roland will be pleased."

A servant knocked on the door to announce the margrave waited in the chapel. Meg hurried downstairs with giddy anticipation. Her heart beat wildly, and she paused at the entrance to draw a steadying breath. *Stop it. This isn't your real wedding.*

Herlinde opened the door. At the altar was the margrave, a priest, Cal, and Tomman. Off to the side was a small table with the contract, a quill pen, ink, lit candle, and a chunk of red wax. Despite the fact Cal wore the face of Sir Roland, the warm and welcoming smile seemed to come directly from him. He wore a clean linen shirt and doublet. The sword was in a scabbard, the leather polished to a brilliant shine. Meg signed her name to the contract as Lady Clare of Kuneburg. Cal added his as Sir Roland de Bruche. With the final finishing stroke, Meg's heart gave a giddy leap, and she shifted her feet, forcing them to remain still. They wanted to dance of their own accord. *Cut it out. This isn't real.*

The margrave melted a bit of wax over the contract and pressed his signet ring into it to leave an imprint. He motioned for the priest. Cal held out his hand to Meg for her ring. He leaned over and whispered lightly, "I like your hair." She took the ring off her finger, cursing herself for not being able to control a slight tremble in her hands as she placed it in his palm. If Cal noticed, he gave no sign.

The priest ordered them to clasp hands. Sir Roland's skin was rough and calloused and yet, comforting warmth seeped from his fingers into her. The ceremony was in Latin. Her mind had no trouble translating but Meg had difficulty focusing on the words. The heat from Cal's hand spread to her arm, then shoulder, flowing through her body with a variety of delightful sensations.

"Roland de Bruche," said the priest, "vis accípere Clare of Kuneburg, hic præséntem in tuam legítimam uxórem iuxta ritum sanctaæ matris Ecclésiæ?" *Roland de Bruche, do you take Clare of Kuneburg as your wife in accordance with the rites of our holy mother, the church?*

"Volo." *I do.* Cal slipped Clare's old wedding ring on Meg's finger. His hand must have warmed the metal because now the ring carried heat of its own.

"Clare of Kuneburg, vis accípere Roland de Bruche

hic præséntern in tuum legítimum marítum iuxta ritum sanctæ matris Ecclésiæ?" *Clare of Kuneburg, do you take Roland de Bruche as your husband in accordance with the rites of our holy mother, the church?*

"Volo." Clare's breath caught in her throat as she put the signet ring on Cal.

The priest pronounced them man and wife. *Oscula sponsam.* Kiss the bride.

Cal leaned forward. Meg's heart drummed against her ribs as their lips touched. A yearning deep inside reached out as she surrendered to the kiss. *Don't let go of this man, embrace what he offers.*

Was that Clare's voice or her own? The kiss ended, their lips parted, but the longing to feel them pressed against her remained. Meg pulled back, her mind jumbled at the wave of desire for a man she barely knew. What had gotten into her? Life had always been so rational, never letting her heart rule her head. Clare's emotions must have affected her. The poor woman had a lonely life joined with a husband she didn't love. She lost her children and the young Sir Roland could no doubt give her more. Perhaps, she even sensed kindness in him, or did that come from Cal? He was a kind man, to be sure. His treatment of Tomman was testament to that.

Meg drew herself up. Cal certainly didn't yearn for someone he barely met. He couldn't. Neither did she.

Yes, that's it. Rational thinking never let her down.

The margrave's natural demeanor could freeze boiling water, but he wasn't devoid of civility. He led the wedding party to the main hall where dinner was laid out on long communal tables. His family and courtiers joined them. Dishes came and went, minstrels played, toasts given to the couple's happiness. All in all, thought Meg, not a bad reception. She sat next to Cal, but exchanged few words, as there was no chance for privacy in a room full of people.

After several hours, Lord Ursenkrieg ended the festivities by shooting Cal a hard look. "I expect your marriage obligations to conclude forthwith. We will discuss your service to me as the new liege of Kuneburg on the morrow."

"Very good, my lord."

He bowed to the margrave and Meg curtsied. Out of the corner of her eye, Meg caught a hint of amusement in Cal's expression. *So much for romance.* He offered his arm and led her from the hall. Tomman and Herlinde followed behind them.

"Are you certain, you wish me to go ahead to Kuneburg, my lady?" said Herlinde.

"Yes. Sir Roland and I will leave as soon as the details of Kuneburg's alliance with Augsburg are settled. Everything must be prepared for my new husband's arrival." She patted Herlinde on the shoulder. "I trust no one else with this important duty."

Meg and Cal saw them to the stables. Tomman helped Herlinde board the wagon. He appeared unusually solemn, and when he bid goodbye to Cal, his voice held a slight quaver.

"Do you think they'll make it?" said Meg as the carriage rolled out of sight.

"We gave them a chance. It's all we can do."

"Is it my imagination or was Tomman worried?"

"I had to tell him about the Everdark."

Meg gasped. "What did he say?"

"Not here." He held out his arm. "I guess we're

227

expected to go to my chambers now, and well…you know."

Meg chuckled. "Right. Marriage obligations." She took his arm. "People are bound to wonder if we don't go upstairs."

Servants had lit candles, bathing the room in a soft glow. The bed was laid out with fresh linens, rose petals and aromatic herbs sprinkled on the sheets. "Smells nice, anyway," said Meg. Her breath quickened with a sudden image of Cal naked on those very sheets. Despite the warmth of the weather, the subsequent hot rush that went from her toes to her head wasn't disagreeable in the least. Meg tore her attention from the bed.

Cal elbowed her playfully in the side. "Do you feel as weird as I do?"

"At this moment, probably more." She turned away, so he couldn't see her flush. "Actually, I'm getting these screaming positive vibes from Clare, rather overwhelming really. She definitely approves of the marriage to Sir Roland." Positive vibes was a huge understatement. Clare would have no objection if she and Cal dove into those rose petals and made like rabbits. A disconcerting thought arose Clare might not be wholly responsible for Meg's own whirling emotions. She gave the sheets a brisk shake. The rose petals fluttered in a delicate shower to the floor. "That should convince Lord Drogo we fulfilled our obligations."

Cal picked up a flower petal. "I'm not sure Roland is convinced. He's blasting a lot of positive vibes about Clare, too."

"Don't you mean for her family connections and

property?" she teased. "Roland's no dummy."

Cal flicked the petal to the floor. "He appreciates his good fortune, but it's not only that. Clare is smart, brave, and kind. He admired her at once and his feelings have only deepened. Of course, that's not Clare. That's you." His voice softened. "For a bean counter, you're pretty cool."

"Thanks. So are you for a button-down lawyer." The silence lengthened between them, and Meg coughed. "You said you told Tomman about the sword…"

"Right. I touched it when he was in the room with me, and the symbols on the blade glowed. It's charged now and ready for the dragon."

"Dragon?"

"Tomman was frightened. I had to make up a story fast, so I said a dragon would come for Lady Clare. The sword was holy, blessed by Saint George, and I had sworn to defend her from the creature."

She snickered. "Saint George Lydecker?"

The corners of his eyes crinkled in amusement. "It was the first saint's name to pop into my head. Luckily, Tomman was familiar with the legend."

"That's explains his anxious attitude." Meg shrugged. "A dragon is as good an explanation as any. Nemra feared it might be a demon. I don't know how to describe the Everdark other than stone cold evil. If history repeats itself, the veil appears when the eclipse begins. Any idea where?"

"No, but I'm sure it will be somewhere in the keep. The sword can sense the exact location." Cal glanced at the bed. "It's late. Why don't you get some rest?" A smile twitched his lips. "After all, the servants expect to see rumpled sheets in the morning."

Meg touched his arm. "You want to talk about tomorrow?"

The smile left his face. "Why? We've been through this before."

"Yes, but you didn't have the sword."

"And you had the crown." He turned his head away. "The gate won't shut without it."

"I'm facing the Everdark. You can't stop me from coming with you."

Cal's jaw tightened. "Then there's nothing to discuss. Get to bed. I'll see you in the morning." He motioned to two chairs. "I can make myself comfortable over there."

"We're in the Middle Ages," protested Meg, "but my twenty-first century mentality has no problem sharing the bed without, well, getting too cozy."

Cal shifted his feet. "Sir Roland's desires are practically bursting at the seams. I don't want to take the chance he might...that is, he has expectations." Words appeared to elude him, but to Meg the meaning came through clear.

"I understand." *Sir Roland's desires are powerful, not yours.* Sorrow pierced Meg's heart, but she forced a smile. "I'm having the same problem reining in Clare. It's probably best for both our sakes if we keep some distance."

"Goodnight then."

"Goodnight." Clare kicked off her shoes and lay on the bed, and Cal blew out the candles.

Chapter Fifteen

Cal stood at the window, moonlight cast a silver glow on the room. Meg had fallen asleep, her face relaxed, expression at peace. His emotions, on the other hand, were a raging hurricane. Longing for her flooded every vein in his body. What would it be like to crawl under the sheets, slide the clip off her long hair and bury his fingers in its softness? The kiss at the altar wasn't enough. He could taste her lips, imagine his naked body pressed against her, hear Meg sigh in pleasure as he whispered her name.

Cut it out! Cal stifled a groan. Those passions belonged to Sir Roland. Meg experienced them, too, with Lady Clare, so his yearning for her was merely a crazy side effect of the magic that brought them here.

Is it really? prodded the little voice in his head. Then why did he see Meg's face when he gazed at Clare. Why did he hear her voice? The Lady of Kuneburg was a stranger, but Meg's courage and warmth drew him as if he were a magnet and she the North Star.

Not for long. Tomorrow, Meg would stand by his side with no way to protect herself. If he couldn't kill the Everdark with the sword, it would break free and he'd watch her die. Cal scowled at the moon, that damn full moon that without fail would shortly devour the sun. His jaw tightened. Not on his watch. When the eclipse began, he'd slip away from her and meet the Everdark alone. If he lived, great. If he died, so be it. With luck, the spell would collapse and send her home. If not…he preferred not to consider the alternative.

Cal turned from the window and sat in a chair with the sword across his lap. The room was too dark to see Meg clearly. The only sound to break the absolute silence was her soft breathing. Whether he made it back alive to Crossroads didn't matter to him, but Meg would not face that creature. Sir Roland growled his mental approval. Cal settled against the back of the chair and closed his eyes. Hours passed, sleep came in fits and starts. His body was already primed for a fight; a modern and ancient warrior's skills joined together, eager for battle and both ready for the day to begin.

The dark gave way to shadows. Faint pink light tinted the east. The sun rose higher, brightening the chamber. Cal stood and stretched. Meg stirred in the bed. Her head turned to him and she smiled. "Good morning."

"Good morning. Sleep well?"

Meg threw off the covers and got out of bed. "I did, actually. No weird dreams."

A knock sounded on the door and servants entered with breakfast. One set down a pitcher and shot an approving glance at the rumpled bedcovers as he scurried away. Meg snickered. "Gone to report to the margrave on the successful completion of marital obligations, I assume."

Cal chuckled. He peeked into the pitcher and heaved a sigh. "Beer. Damn, I'd kill for a cup of coffee right now."

Neither had an appetite. Cal strapped on the sword.

They stood at the window watching shadows contract across the courtyard as the sun rose in the sky. Hours passed, and it neared the highpoint. Noon was nearly upon them. Without warning, an icy prickle raced up Cal's spine. He looked at Meg. Her face was pale.

"It's close," she whispered. "Cal—"

A creak at the door cut off her words. That part of the room was in shadow with barely enough illumination to note the slow rise and fall of the latch. Cal put a finger to his lips and drew the sword. One hand raised the weapon, preparing to strike. With the other, he yanked open the door to reveal the startled faces of Tomman and Herlinde. "What are you doing here?" he barked. He pulled them inside and shut the door. "Tomman, I ordered you to take her to Kuneburg."

"I refused," said Herlinde stoutly, "especially after he told me of the dragon."

"Tomman!"

The boy's face reddened. "I-it slipped out, and we had to return, my lord, to warn you Duke Frederick and his men are on the march to Augsburg."

Meg drew in a breath. "How far?"

"Less than half a day."

From the corridor came the sound of heavy footsteps, and Sir Roland's alarm bells clanged. Cal shoved the sword into Meg's hands. "Hide this." He motioned Tomman and Herlinde to a large armoire. "Get in."

Tomman and Herlinde jumped inside, and Meg stuffed the sword under the sheets. An instant later, a half dozen armed guards stormed into the room.

"What's the meaning of this?" demanded Cal.

"You are summoned before the margrave," said the captain of the guards. He ordered the soldiers to take Cal away and stationed a man at the door. "She is not to leave. No one is to enter."

They grabbed Cal's arms and marched him down several flights of steps. This wasn't good. They definitely weren't headed for a friendly chat in the main hall. Sir Roland's warrior blood surged through his veins, and Cal struggled against their grips. "Where are you taking me?" he roared.

"Silence!" A blow to the head from the captain sent stars dancing before his eyes. They dragged Cal to an empty cell in a dungeon below the keep and chained him to the wall. The jailer locked the door and left with the duke's men.

Cal was alone, the only light from a flickering torch in a sconce on the wall. He strained against the chains, but to no avail. The Everdark was on the way and he wasn't going anywhere. At least he had presence of mind to leave Meg the sword.

A sick feeling settled in his stomach. *It won't protect her. I'm the only one who can wield it against the Everdark.*

The guard opened the cell. Behind him was the margrave and a squad of his men. Apparently, the guard didn't step aside fast enough because the margrave shoved him against the wall and strode up to Cal with smoldering fury in his eyes. "Duke Frederick marches on Augsburg. As we speak, his army nears the gates. He sent word demanding I hand over Lady Clare. It seems I underestimated his eagerness to forge a bond with Henry."

Cal blew out a snort of disbelief. "This marriage

wasn't of enough importance to prompt an attack."

"Frederick has a way of turning things to his advantage. He needed an excuse to sack Augsburg. The kidnapping gave him one."

Cal gripped the chains. "Release me. I promised to serve and will defend Augsburg's walls."

The margrave's jaw tightened. "I have other uses for you. I sent word to my allies and only need delay the duke until they arrive." He reached into his tunic and pulled out the marriage contract. He touched it to the torch on the wall, and the parchment burst into flames. "My emissaries are on the way to inform Frederick I was unaware of the kidnapping and your treachery. No marriage took place. I dispatched my guards to return Lady Clare to the duke's custody."

"The priest…"

A humorless smile twitched at his lips. "Saw nothing, so it is Lady Clare's word against mine. I informed the duke you are my prisoner and await his instructions. I suspect he wishes to deal with you himself and that is the only reason I kept you alive. Enjoy a heartbeat while you can," he growled. "I expect it won't last long."

"My lord!" A guard raced into the dungeon out of breath. "Lady Clare is gone."

The margrave's expression twisted in rage. "Where is she?"

"I have no idea," said Cal, "and if I did, I wouldn't tell you."

The margrave stormed to the cell door. "Come with me," he roared to the guards. "Search the grounds. She can't be far." He turned to the jailer. "I've decided Sir Roland is more trouble than he's worth. Kill him and throw the body over the wall as my gift to the duke."

****

Meg pressed her ear to the door. The key turned in the lock and then footsteps faded down the hall. She ushered Tomman and Herlinde out of the armoire. "Keep quiet. There is a guard outside."

"My lady," whispered Herlinde, "the duke will be here soon."

Her voice hardened. "The duke is the lesser concern."

Herlinde paled. "The dragon."

"Yes." Meg retrieved the sword from under the bedcoverings. "I must get this weapon to Sir Roland, and no arguments, Herlinde. Sir Roland and I have sworn to slay the dragon. It was, uh, a command from Saint George himself, but first we have to get out of here."

Tomman's hand went to his sword. "I only need a distraction."

Meg hesitated; a vague recollection came to mind that a member of the Adler side of her family hailed from central Europe. What if the guy at the door was a great-great-multiple great-grandfather who hadn't had time to perform his marital obligations? Meg scanned the room and her eyes lit on the jewelry case. "I have an idea." She dug through the jewels and removed a long string of pearls. Using the sword, Meg slit the string holding the necklace together and then clasped the ends tight to keep the pearls from spilling. She handed the jewelry case to Herlinde and the sword to Tomman. "I prefer not to kill anyone, so hit him on the head. That's an order." Even though both appeared grievously disappointed, they scurried obediently behind the door.

Meg called to the guard. "Open up. I have an urgent message for the margrave."

A key turned in the lock and he stepped inside, suspicion marking his features. "What is it?"

"I have information that will stop Duke Frederick's attack…oh, dear." Meg released the string and jumped back as pearls tumbled from her hand. She bent to pick them up. "Well, don't just stand there, fool," she snapped in her most imperious manner. "Help me."

Meg's spirits soared as he immediately crouched down. Nothing was more useful to an escape plan than dealing with the blind obedience of people under the thumb of rigid authority. They never questioned orders. Herlinde stepped from behind the door and whammed the guard so hard in the back of the head, the wood on the box made a cracking sound. The man dropped to his knees. With a gleeful light in his eyes, Tomman clocked him once with his sword's hilt, and he keeled over. Tomman would have had another go if Meg hadn't grabbed his arm. "Stop. He's out cold. Let's find Roland."

"How, my lady?" asked Herlinde. "He could be anywhere."

Meg took the sword from Tomman. "The sword can sense him."

The blade quivered in her hand. The tip lowered and pointed at the floor.

Tomman sucked in a breath. "The dungeon."

The keep was in a panicked uproar as word spread of the approach of the duke's army. From outside came a cacophony of screams, shouts, and the whinny of horses. People rushed past with fearful expressions, so intent on their purpose, they paid no mind to three strangers running through the halls. To Meg's relief, no guards were in sight; most able-bodied men had already left to defend Augsburg's gates.

They reached a staircase, and the sword continued to point straight down. Although the symbols remained unlit, Meg's fingers sensed heat radiating from the blade. The warning was obvious. Danger closed in on them. On the first floor, Meg paused and drew them into the shadowed alcove, backs pressed flat against the wall. She peeked out and spotted the margrave exiting another staircase at the end of the corridor with an expression that screamed, "Kill." His complexion was beet red and he grimaced as if trying to chew through chain mail. Her pulse raced as he stormed their way, but the margrave passed their hiding place, his men racing to keep up.

The sword hilt vibrated in Meg's hand, buzzing against her skin. Cal was close. "Lead on," she whispered. The sword pointed to the staircase the margrave just vacated.

****

The jailer regarded Cal with cold intent.

"I don't suppose," said Cal mildly, "I can convince you my freedom is in Augsburg's best interest?"

He pulled his sword from the scabbard.

Cal's eyes narrowed. "Didn't think so." He took in the jailer's stance. The blade was not a knight's longsword and less than two feet in length. The man wasn't tall either, maybe five foot four. He had a short reach while Sir Roland was over six feet. Combat in this day and age meant getting within stabbing distance of an opponent. Resistance from an unarmed man chained to the wall was the last thing on his mind. Cal grasped the links attached to the manacles and tensed.

"I'll make it quick," said the jailor. He pointed the sword at Cal's heart.

"Thanks. I appreciate it." With a savage kick, Cal's foot connected with the man's groin. The jailer dropped the weapon and doubled over, shrieking in pain. Cal wrapped his legs around the man's neck, locked them together, and squeezed. Years of horseback riding gave Sir Roland thigh muscles as strong as steel bands.

Cal gritted his teeth and held on as the jailer pummeled his legs in a desperate attempt to break free. After thirty seconds, the man's face turned blue, and he went limp. Panting, Cal released his grip, and the jailor slumped to the floor. Cal stretched his arm as far as the chains allowed, just shy of the keyring. He hooked his boot under the man's belt and gritted his teeth. With a grunt, he managed to shift him a few inches closer. This guy was short but no lightweight. Cal's fingertips brushed the keys.

The guard stirred and groaned. He cast a bleary eye on Cal. "Kill you…" he wheezed. "Kill you slow…"

"I don't think so." Meg strode into the cell with Tomman and Herlinde. She yanked the keys off the belt.

"Meg," said Cal with a grin, "you have perfect timing."

The jailer shambled woozily to his knees and made a grab for his weapon, but Tomman whammed him with the sword hilt and he crumpled in a heap.

"You'll be pleased to hear," said Meg as she unlocked Cal's manacles, "that Tomman is very good at hitting people over the head and knocking them senseless. Herlinde, that's enough. He's no longer a

239

danger." At her command, the girl stopped kicking the unconscious jailer in the ribs.

Cal brushed a stray hair from Meg's face. "Are you okay? I was worried."

Pink rose to her cheeks and her lips parted in a broad smile. "I'm fine. You?"

As if a wildfire suddenly flared in the dank cell, her smile filled him with warmth. "Better now that you're with me."

Meg took the sword from Tomman and handed it to Cal. "It's been calling for you."

"Calling...?" He touched the hilt. An electric charge shot up his arm, and the symbols on the blade ignited in brilliant white radiance. No explanation was necessary. The battle was nearly upon him. Adrenaline flooded Cal's veins, and his heart raced. The magic bound the sword to him as securely as a second skin. With each passing second, his sense of the Everdark intensified. The eclipse would arrive any minute, and the creature clawed at the veil, searching for the gate. "It's time to go, Meg. Let's get out of here."

"Where to?" she asked.

Cal gazed at the sword. His weapon, his power, but not hers. Hers was lost in a distant land, forgotten and buried under desert sands. *Forgive me, Meg. The fight is mine.* He motioned to the passageway. "That way. We have to get to higher ground before the eclipse begins."

At the top of the stairs, the bright light of a noon summer sun poured through a window. Cal paused by the dungeon guardroom. It was vacant, the men already at the walls. Not one of them suspected the real danger to Augsburg was closer than that. How could they possibly know a creature lurked barely a heartbeat away poised to rip apart the world?

"Herlinde," said Meg. "This fight isn't yours, but my jewelry is. Use it to build a good life with Tomman. He's a fine young man."

"He'll keep you safe," said Cal. "Tomman, in a few minutes the sun will disappear. Don't be frightened. It's Saint George's doing. In the panic, get out of Augsburg before the gates close. Swear to me to care for her."

Tomman swallowed hard. "I swear, my lord."

Herlinde threw her arms around Meg. "Will I ever see you again?"

"No," she said. "Our time here is done, but yours isn't. My last command to you is have a happy life. Go."

The girl wiped her tears and nodded numbly. "I will pray for you both." Tomman offered Herlinde his hand. She clasped it and they raced away.

Shadows lengthened. The light of the sun dimmed.

Here, said the sword. *Now.*

Meg stepped past the doorway and watched Herlinde and Tomman disappear around a corner. She turned to Cal and met his gaze. As if she read his thoughts, sudden understanding flooded her expression. "No!" She lunged for him.

Cal slammed the door and slid a locking bolt in place sealing it tight. "I'm sorry, Meg."

She pounded on the other side. "Damn it, Cal. Don't do this to me."

"I won't let you face that thing."

"You can't kill it alone. I'm part of this, too. You need me—"

His voice softened. He placed his palm flat against the wood. "I need you alive."

"Cal..." she cried out with a strangled sob. "Don't..."

The light through the windows dimmed, but the sun, moon, and stars on the sword shimmered, cutting through the gathering dark with fiery brilliance.

Confused shouts came from outside. "The sky! Do you see? What is happening to the sky?" The shadows deepened. The cries turned to terrified screams as the unthinkable occurred. The moon broke the chain binding it to the night. Bit by bit, it devoured the once steady, constant sun.

Light faded from the window. The misty border between two dimensions stretched and thinned. A rectangle of air shimmered with a hazy glow and the gate appeared. The crack was visible, no more than the width of a thumb. Peering through the other side, a shining eye glittered in the dark. The Everdark shrieked in triumph. "Your god awakens. Bow to me."

Cal tightened his grip on the sword, and warrior's blood flooded his veins. "Never."

"Then feed my hunger."

A glistening talon wormed through the crack, widening the opening ever so slightly. Cal coughed as fetid stench poured into the room. More tentacle than limb, a spiky clawed projection shot from the dark. Cal lunged at the Everdark, the markings on the blade flared to solar brilliance. The sword struck a talon. The bones in his arms vibrated at the shock of making contact and pain rocketed to his jaw. The sword deflected but grazed the creature's skin. The tentacle recoiled. The Everdark's high-pitched screech drove through Cal's eardrums like a rusty nail.

First blood! Roland's triumphant battle cry rang in his head. Cal sneered. "Felt that, didn't you?"

"Alone?" The grating rasp of the Everdark dripped scorn. "No mortal can stop me alone. You are nothing more than a meddler in my plans."

"Yeah," he muttered, "but I'll bet I can still tick you off."

In a flash, the tentacle snaked through the slit between worlds and widened the crack a fraction of an inch. It bobbed and weaved through the air in a mesmerizing dance. Cal lunged and scored another hit, a deeper slice this time, but the Everdark held its ground. Black ooze dripped from the wound, droplets spattered the paving stones and raised an oily, acrid fog.

Meg pounded on the other side of door. "Damn you, Cal. Let me in."

"A female," hissed the Everdark. "Her essence is familiar. We have met at the gate before, but I sense a lack in her now." It burst out in raucous laughter. "She has lost the crown in the annals of time and cannot stand against me. Weak human, foolish human. I will tear out her heart in front of you. The last sound you hear will be the crunch of her bones before her life force joins with mine."

With lightning speed, the tentacle struck the door to the guardroom and blasted it to pieces. A primal roar exploded from Cal's throat as he charged the Everdark, slashing again and again. The acidic blood ate through his clothes, sizzling his flesh, tainting his blood with poison. Agony ripped through his body, but Cal brushed aside the searing pain. The voice of Ashur joined Roland and together they shouted, *Attack!*

L. A. Kelley

Sweat streamed down Cal's face as he rained blow after flow on the creature. The poison reached his chest, his lungs burned with each breath. Soon, it would reach his heart. The darkness outside the window lightened to gray and Cal reveled in a rush of triumph. A few more seconds and the brilliance of the sun would sever the bridge between worlds.

With a savage thrust, the sword penetrated the Everdark's steely hide. The shock drove the tentacle into the opening. The monster howled in rage and pummeled the gate. It bowed outward straining at the hinge.

Cal's eyesight dimmed. Excruciating pressure encased his heart, squeezing ever tighter. He dropped the sword and fell to his knees.

Meg staggered over the shattered pieces of the door, blood pouring from a wound in her head. She threw herself at the gate, arms stretched wide, using her body to cover the crack. Her jaw muscles clenched with the strain of keeping the two sides together.

A tentacle shot from the veil, impaling her through the chest. "Release me!" The Everdark's roar shook the stone walls.

"Never," she choked out.

A single ray of sunlight pierced the gloom. The air shimmered. The howls of the Everdark faded as the gate vanished once more. Meg collapsed, blood gushing from the wound, staining the wedding shift bright red.

Cal crawled to her side, every breath misery. He took her hand.

Meg's eyelids fluttered shut. "I couldn't close the gate."

Cal laid his head next to hers. "I didn't kill it."

"You shouldn't have...locked me out." Meg exhaled a final breath.

Cal blinked as a sunbeam hit his eyes, and then the world went black.

Chapter Sixteen

The pain was gone. Meg rolled over with a groan, blinked, and opened her eyes. No stone walls loomed overhead, nothing but brilliant sunshine and blue skies. Blue skies and a blurry face. She blinked again to clear her vision…Amaranth Goldstein?

Amaranth peered at her with concern. "Are you hurt?"

"No, I'm fine I—" Her pulse raced. "Cal! Where's Cal? He was right next to me." She struggled to get up.

"Easy, dear." Amaranth helped Meg to her feet and motioned over her shoulder. "He's right there with George and doesn't appear injured either." She eyed her sharply. "What happened?"

Meg staggered to where Cal lay on the ground. His chest rose and fell, and she exhaled a sigh of relief.

He mumbled something, but the only recognizable word was "Meg."

"He's coming to," said George.

The fog lifted from Meg's head and she tightened her jaw. Cal shut her out. She stepped back. "I don't want to talk to him."

Amaranth placed an arm around her shoulders. "Let me take you to the inn."

"Go to my house," said George. "Dylan is there, and he can call the paramedics. Heat must have gotten to you two. Although, I can't say you two look like you have heat stroke."

"I don't have heat stroke," sputtered Meg, "and don't need an ambulance. Cal and I are fine."

"It's not the heat, George," said Amaranth firmly. "I've been telling you that's merely a symptom of the confluence." She took Meg's arm. "You could use a nice cup of my herbal tea. I gave a packet to George to sooth his nerves, but I suspect he has plenty left."

George wrinkled his nose. "It tastes like boiled grass. I prefer coffee. At least the beans are legal."

Amaranth ignored him. "George, bring Cal to the house as soon as he's awake. I'm sure he'll be anxious to see Meg."

"I'm not sure I'm anxious to see him," said Meg tartly.

They exited the maze. Meg turned toward the inn, but Amaranth grabbed her arm in a firm grip. Really firm. Honestly, she'd have to wrestle her to the ground to break free, and Meg suddenly drained of energy. She gave in and let Amaranth lead her away. They cut across the fields to the tidy farmhouse. Dylan sat on the porch swing next to Summer, and he jumped to his feet as they approached.

"Dylan," said Amaranth, "go make a pot of my special herb tea and a cup of coffee for your uncle. He'll be along soon."

They went to the kitchen. Meg sank into a chair. The heavy cloud of weariness settled on her shoulders. She gazed at her hands, fighting a sense of disconnect. A few minutes ago, she was surrounded by stone walls with a monster clawing at a mystic gate. She rubbed her temples with a sigh.

"Headache?" said Summer with sympathy. She

handed a steaming cup to Meg. "Mom's tea will fix that right up."

Meg took a sip. The brew had a refreshing taste with a hint of fruit and a minty undertone. With each swallow, her headache faded away. She cocked her head at Amaranth. "Are you sure there's nothing illegal in this?"

Amaranth winked. "I didn't say that." She leaned across the table. "Now would you care to tell us what really happened in that maze?"

"The heat—"

"It wasn't the heat."

Meg shifted in her seat under Amaranth's piercing gaze. "I don't know how to explain in any way that makes sense."

Amaranth nodded and gave her a perceptive smile. "You crossed the veil."

Meg gawked at her. "How did you—?"

"Meg!" Cal burst through the door out of breath with George on his heels. "Are you hurt?"

"I'm perfectly fine, Mr. MacGregor," she said between clenched teeth. "Fortunately, I've returned in one piece and won't be forced to marry a turnip after all."

George raised an eyebrow. "Turnip?"

Cal took her hand. "Meg, please listen—"

She yanked her hand away, blood near boiling. "You shut the door. You locked me out. How dare you after everything that has happened? It was my fight as much as yours."

"You didn't have the crown," Cal said. "No weapons, no protection. The Everdark was right there, hammering at the gate…" He sank into the chair next to her. "I'm sorry." His voice dropped to near whisper. "I only knew if you entered the room, you'd never leave, and I couldn't bear to watch it kill you again."

The agony in his expression tore at Meg's heart. "You think it was easy for me on the other side of the door not knowing what happened to you? Damn it, Cal." She swallowed hard. "I thought I'd never see you again."

Cal held her hand once more, and this time Meg didn't pull away. "Am I forgiven?"

"Maybe." Her lips formed a faint smile. "But I reserve the right to smack you later."

"I won't even duck," he said with a grin.

Meg's smile vanished. "The gate opened farther. I couldn't close it. When the eclipse arrives tomorrow, the Everdark will break through and hunt. So many people at the festival…they don't stand a chance."

His grip tightened on her hand. "We'll face it together."

Her heart skipped a beat. "Together."

The room had gone unnaturally quiet. Amaranth, Summer, and Dylan watched Meg and Cal in rapt amazement while George gaped in open-mouthed disbelief. He pulled a cell phone from his pocket. "I'm calling 911. You both need medical help."

Dylan stood and yanked the phone away. "No, they don't."

He lunged at him. "Give me that."

"No!" He held the phone out of reach. "Can't you see what's going on—"

"I won't buy into this New Age garbage—"

"Quiet!" Amaranth's shout cut through the argument. "Now, both of you sit and listen." They plopped into the chairs, and she glared at George. "You sensed something strange happening here. You're the one that broke off our conversation and ran for the maze saying you had to check on something. Why?"

"Maybe," he grumbled. "I couldn't stand to hear any more confluence nonsense."

"George…"

"All right, Deb," he snapped. "I'll listen."

"How many times must I tell you my name is Amaranth now? Will you listen with an open mind?"

He grunted. "I'll try."

Amaranth regarded him with a pleased expression. "That's the George I remember." For a moment, the sourness on his face lifted, and Meg caught the hint of a smile. Amaranth turned to her. "Tell us what happened and don't be concerned with logic or sense."

Meg looked at Cal. "We should give them the whole story."

Cal grimaced. "Okay, why not? George already thinks I'm crazy, but he's only one client and if the Everdark breaks through tomorrow, I won't have to worry about growing my legal practice any longer."

They took turns, starting from the beginning. No one interrupted. Amaranth, Summer, and Dylan sat fixed in spellbound attention. Meg couldn't place George's emotions; perhaps a mixture of incredulity, awe, and shock. The last thing she expected was his reaction when they finished.

George burst out laughing and slapped a hand on the table. "Well, I'll be damned. Phillip Bingham, you old son of a bitch."

Cal gaped at him. "You knew Phillip Bingham?"

"Never met the man, but he had an unexpected

influence on my life. My parents died in a car accident right after I graduated high school. I took over the farm but had debts to pay and responsibility for my kid sister."

Amaranth patted his hand. "I remember. You were going to sell and move away from Crossroads." She turned to Cal and Meg. "I left town, but George stayed and accepted responsibility for Dylan's mom who was a little girl at the time. George gave up college. He gave up everything to raise her."

George shrugged. "She's family."

Cal regarded him with respect. "I didn't know that. It must have been hard."

"Felt like the right thing to do," he mumbled. "Anyway, I was barely eighteen. The bank refused to loan a kid any money to keep the farm going, but a good offer came from a developer. I had all but signed the sale papers when out of the blue Isaac Bingham called. He said his grandfather, Phillip, had been an old friend of my parents. He left instructions for the Lux Foundation to offer a business grant if the family was ever in financial straits. The money was enough to pay off debts and buy new equipment. If it hadn't been for Phillip Bingham, Lydecker Farm wouldn't be in business today.

"Funny thing," George mused. "Later, I went through my parents' paperwork. They kept meticulous business records. Isaac was their lawyer, but I never found a single mention of a man named Phillip Bingham."

"Phillip wanted the land available to build the maze here," said Cal in a hushed tone. "It's as if he had a window into the future."

"Forget Phillip Bingham," said Summer. "What are we going to do to stop the Everdark? It's coming tomorrow."

Meg stared at her. "You believe us?"

"Of course, we do," said Amaranth. "I told you the confluence was particularly strong." George snorted, and Amaranth shook a finger at him. "You can't deny what happened, George. We were alone in the maze, and then suddenly Cal and Meg were under the arbor."

"Could have hidden in the corn," he grumbled, "and jumped out when we faced the other direction."

Cal ran a hand through his hair. "I'm having a hard time with this too, George. It sounds crazy, but believe me that thing will be here tomorrow, and we don't have any way to stop it."

"We can try," piped up Meg, "if we have the sword and crown. We were sent back in time to find them and activate their power. They're ready and waiting for us now." She turned to Cal with a hopeful look. "Do you sense the sword?"

"No. The crown?"

She dropped her gaze to the table. "No."

"Perhaps," said Amaranth, "the bond between you will strengthen as the Everdark draws near. You'll sense them then."

"What if the sword is still in Europe or the crown in the Middle East?" said Meg. "We can't get them to Crossroads by tomorrow."

Dylan jumped from his seat. "Hang, on…" He ran out of the room and returned to the table a moment later with a laptop. "Tell me everything you can about this sword and crown."

"Meg and I tried a search," said Cal.

"Let me give it a shot. I'm good with computers." They described the artifacts while Dylan entered search parameters. Summer peered over his shoulder offering suggestions as they scoured the internet.

"Amaranth," asked Meg, "how often do these confluences occur?"

"Hard to say. There's no set schedule. Two have already happened since the turn of this century, perhaps ten in the past hundred years."

"Ten?" said Cal. "Sir Roland and Lady Clare lived almost nine hundred years ago. Dozens of confluences may have passed since then. Why didn't the Everdark break through?"

"Maybe other people got hold of either the sword or crown and stopped it."

Cal shook his head. "No. I can't tell you why, but I'm positive once Meg and I, well, activated them, the sword and crown were only meant for us—no matter what bodies we inhabited."

"I agree," said Meg. "We're linked."

Amaranth thought for a second. "It must have to do with the eclipse then. I'll bet each time you were drawn to the past coincided with the date of a confluence during an eclipse. I can check." She pulled out her cell phone. "Someone in Mind Over Matter will have the answer. The message boards are humming. Everyone has been in a tizzy since the announcement of the latest confluence."

"Mind Over Matter?" said Cal.

"It's an online social group for those in touch with our spiritual essences. Our motto is 'If you have a closed mind, your opinion doesn't matter." Amaranth sent a text and a few minutes later her phone chimed.

She read the message and her eyes lit up. "Ah, that was fast. I have an answer from The Prince of Darkness."

Meg blinked. "Satan texts?"

"No, that's his screen name. Kevin is an astronomer at Lowell Observatory in Arizona. It's on a ley line, you know. Lovely man." Her voice dropped. "He claims his family has gone totally organic, but I have doubts. He once posted a dessert recipe from his wife that called for boxed cake mix. Can you imagine?"

George sighed. "You're rambling."

"Sorry," she said, "Kevin says the occurrence of an eclipse and a confluence at the same time is exceedingly rare. Dates are sketchy in ancient times, but his calculations suggest an early dual event occurred sometime during the Assyrian Empire."

"That puts it in the time of Nemra and Ashur," mused Cal.

Amaranth continued to read. "He says the last recorded eclipse to occur within a confluence was 1133 AD. Hmm…this is interesting. The next one is tomorrow."

"That's why the Everdark never showed," said Meg. She gazed out the window at the maze. "It had to wait all these years for the next chance."

"It's the last one," said Amaranth, peering at the phone's screen. "According to Kevin, this is the most powerful one yet, a real earth-shaker. There won't be another instance of both a full solar eclipse coinciding with a confluence of this same magnitude. If the gate doesn't open tomorrow, it never will. If it does…"

"The gate never shuts," said Meg. "The Everdark comes bursting through, and the world ends." An anxious knot formed in her stomach. "Cal, we have to find the sword and crown by noon tomorrow when the eclipse begins."

"Aw, this is crazy," muttered George.

Amaranth folded her arms and regarded him with disapproval. "You're free to go if the conversation is not to your liking."

"This is my house, Deb," he sputtered.

"Amaranth."

He gritted his teeth and made a gurgling sound.

"I may have found something." Dylan turned the laptop to face the others. "Take a look at this."

On the screen was a grainy newspaper photograph from the *San Francisco Chronicle* of a man about thirty, dressed in the period of the early 1900s. He stood next to a fireplace in a room crammed with paintings, statues, and other objects of art. The caption underneath read "Mr. Robert Huntington returns from Europe in time for the spring season."

"According to the article," said Dylan, "Robert Huntington was a rich antiques dealer. He got back from a trip in Europe where he bought a bunch of paintings and sculptures and stuff. The reporter who wrote the interview talks mostly about Huntington's big purchases but check out the last sentence."

Meg peered at the screen. "It says along with paintings and sculpture, Mr. Huntington also purchased a few historical curiosities including a Babylonian headpiece, which he planned to offer for sale." She sucked in a breath. "Can it be?"

"Dylan," asked Cal, "did you find other references to the crown or any mention of a black sword?"

"Sorry, nothing."

Cal squinted at the heading on the top of the

newspaper. "Oh no."

"What is it?" asked Meg.

"The date of the article is March 18, 1906. A month later the San Francisco earthquake hit, and the city was destroyed."

Chapter Seventeen

Meg's shoulders sagged. "The crown can't be gone." A sensation of crushing defeat lodged in her chest.

"Simply because the trail went cold from there," said Cal, gently, "doesn't mean the crown was destroyed. Huntington was an antiques dealer. A private collector may have purchased it from him before the earthquake."

"That won't do us any good, and the article doesn't even mention the sword. Why were we sent back twice only to reach a dead end?" Meg shivered. Why was Cal so calm? Couldn't he feel the coming horror?

"Because this isn't a dead end," said Amaranth kindly. "We simply can't see the whole picture, yet."

"We don't have much time to figure it out," added Summer with a worried expression. Dylan reached over and took her hand.

Cal rubbed his chin. "You think the Bingham family bought them?"

"Is there a directory from that time?" asked George. He had stomped off to the corner with a sour look as the rest huddled around the laptop but now edged back to the table. George shifted his feet, obviously ill at ease as they turned toward him. "Maybe Phillip Bingham is in it. I'm just saying," he mumbled, "it's a starting point."

Amaranth beamed at him. "That's a wonderful idea, George."

"Was Phillip even alive back then?" asked Cal. "It was a long time ago."

"Hang on," said Dylan, hovering over the keyboard. "I downloaded a copy of a book called the *Crocker-Langley San Francisco Directory*. This issue was published in 1906, a few months before the quake."

"Telephone directory?" Cal frowned. "It'll be mighty thin. Telephones were rare."

"No, it has addresses for both businesses and people." Dylan scrolled through several pages. "No Binghams in San Francisco." He turned to his uncle. "Do you remember any other names in the family?" George shook his head.

"Isaac can tell us." Cal whipped out his phone, retrieved the number, and scowled. "Straight to voicemail. For whatever reason, we can't count on him for help."

Meg gripped the edge of the table to steady her shaking hands. *Why are we just talking? Why is everyone so calm when the end of the world is a few hours away?* She waved an arm at the computer screen. "Find Phillip Bingham," she said, "don't find him. What does it matter? Even if we knew for a fact Phillip Bingham was alive and had the sword and crown in 1906, it doesn't get them to Crossroads by tomorrow." She turned to Cal. The tightness in her throat made it hard to speak. "We can't save anybody."

Cal leaned toward her, but Meg pushed back the chair. "I need some air." She bolted from the farmhouse, racing past the corn until she reached the start of the maze. Groups of people entered and left, laughing, enjoying the day. Her footsteps lagged, breaths came in ragged pants. *Get out of here*, her mind screamed to them. *Run and never stop.*

Even that wouldn't save anyone. No place on Earth was safe from the Everdark. She stared mindlessly at the crowds. *How can I warn them the world will erupt in flames?*

A gentle arm draped across her shoulders. "I'm here, Meg."

She leaned against Cal, tears stinging her eyes. "Not for much longer. Haven't you heard the world ends on Sunday?"

"We're not dead yet, and I'm at your side for as long as you need me."

The tightness in her chest eased. She blinked back the tears. "Aren't you afraid?"

"Yes, but I'm also hungry and tired and can't think straight anymore. You must be the same. Come on, I'll buy you a corndog."

Meg chuckled. "A corndog? That's so normal. Nothing in the past two days has been normal."

"Which is exactly why we need a corndog right now."

Meg smiled. "And a funnel cake."

"Was there ever any doubt?"

Cal brought the food, and they sat at a picnic table to eat. "What is it about you," Meg teased as she picked at the funnel cake, "that makes me crave junk food?"

Cal grinned. "Feeling better?"

"A little." Her attention wandered to the cornfield. "What did we accomplish? What was the point?"

"Hey, we prevented the destruction of the world twice. So far, we're batting a thousand. Not to mention, the optimist in me says because of our actions, Tomman and Herlinde lived happily ever after."

"I hope so, too," said Meg. "I want to believe they got out of Augsburg, bought a nice farm in the country, and built a future with each other."

"My great aunt," mused Cal, "was heavily into genealogy. She traced the MacGregor family roots as far back as the 1400s in Scotland. Before losing track, she discovered a lone family branch that emigrated from Germany."

Meg's eyes widened. "You're not saying…"

Cal shrugged. "I have no evidence but like to think I helped plant the family tree in fertile soil. At the time we disappeared from Augsburg, it was still possible for a boy from humble beginnings to make his way to knighthood. Herlinde had the jewelry case, and they were both smart and strong. Who knows where one of their descendants landed today; maybe even sitting at a picnic table eating a corndog?"

Meg shifted in her seat. "One of my grandmothers emigrated from Lebanon. It's not that far from Babylon. I suppose there's a slim possibility an ancestor stumbled upon the crown and the family kept it safe until Huntington brought it to America—if he ever did."

Cal flashed a grin. "Well, you're certainly a wellspring of optimism."

His gently teasing tone made her smile. "I'm a math geek. I prefer numbers and facts instead of supposition. Rationality is encoded in my DNA."

"So is spunk. You're spunky, Adler, in whatever persona you inhabit. Don't forget that."

The warmth in Cal's eyes drew her in. Heat rose to

her cheeks. Meg fought the urge to cover them with her hands and hide any hint of a flush.

Memories arose of the stolen kisses between Nemra and Ashur, the wedding kiss of Clare and Roland. Her pulse raced remembering his lips pressed against hers. At each time, a kiss bound two lives together. Both Nemra and Clare's hearts willingly pledged to men they barely knew.

So did mine.

Meg glanced away from Cal. *This is ridiculous. It's not rational. I've only known Cal a few days. These emotions are remnants from intercepted lives. The romantic notions Cal and I shared in different times and places rightfully belong to other people. Whatever I feel for him now can't be real.*

Can it?

Stay focused, stay rational. Don't give into what isn't real. Meg rubbed a hand across the back of her neck. Exhaustion wrapped around her with the weight of a heavy cloak, sinking into her bones, muddying her thoughts.

Cal placed a hand over hers. "You're exhausted. I'll walk you to the inn."

Meg sat up straight and drew her hand away. "No, I can't sleep. There's something I need to do." Meg regarded him with a helpless expression. "Though I don't know what it is."

Cal rose to his feet. "We'll go back to my office. Dylan is still doing research at the farmhouse and promised to call if he uncovers anything else. We can do the same."

Meg nodded numbly. They crossed the fairground to Main Street. Cal led her to the office and motioned to the couch against the wall. "Why don't you put your feet up for a few minutes? I've done it myself when I've had long days and late meetings and didn't want to schlep back to my place. It's pretty comfy."

"Not yet. Look for them first." She didn't need to explain. Cal went right to the laptop. A fruitless search revealed nothing more on Sir Roland or Lady Clare. Meg swallowed hard. "Did our actions cause the attack on Augsburg? Did those people die because Roland rescued Lady Clare? Were they even real?"

"I believe they were real," said Cal gently. He waved a hand at the computer screen. "All this means is that Clare and Roland's marriage, their very existence didn't affect recorded history. Duke Frederick sacked lots of cities. Maybe he used the marriage as an excuse, maybe not. The records don't say, but nothing we did could have altered his plans. That wasn't why we were there. Frederick wanted the riches of Augsburg, so he took them."

Meg shivered. "We can't change the past."

"No, I'm sorry, but we stopped the Everdark even though it cost Clare and Roland their lives."

Meg gazed at Cal and her heart skipped a beat. "The sacrifice was okay with Clare. She didn't have a happy life. She didn't love her first husband, and he didn't love her. She had to watch her children die one by one. She found a measure of contentment as the lady of the manor, but I sensed she wanted more. Clare willingly gave her heart to Roland. I'm sure of it. I believe she saw the hero in him and wanted to be at his side." Meg turned away. "They could have been happy." Her voice caught in her throat.

"If it's any consolation," said Cal, "Roland had the

same feelings for Clare. It wasn't just a marriage of convenience for him. He loved her." His expression filled with sympathy. "Get some rest now."

"Okay. You should, too. Your day wasn't any easier than mine."

Cal motioned to his computer. "I'll read up on the earthquake. San Francisco was devastated, but a lot of first-hand reports exist. I can try to dig up more information on Huntington or Phillip Bingham."

Meg kicked off her shoes and lay on the couch. "Okay. I'll close my eyes for a few minutes." Through the heavy fog of lethargy, her mind whirled, pulling her back from the edge of sleep. The Everdark was coming. Stay awake.

Rest, sister. Nemra's soft voice filled her head. *Strength is needed.*

The battle is not finished, said Clare. *Not for you. Not for us.*

Meg eyes fluttered shut. "The crown," she whispered.

Nemra and Clare's voices called together. *The crown binds us. Our strength is yours. But another danger threatens the existence of the crown and sword before the summons to the final battle.*

Meg stirred on the couch. *Who dares?*

Protect the crown. The voices of Nemra and Clare died away.

I swear. Meg stepped over the edge and fell into sleep.

****

Cal looked up from the computer screen. Meg stirred and muttered "crown" in her sleep. He rose from the chair and went over to her. "Don't worry," he said in a hushed voice. "Everything will be okay. I promise."

Would it? Anger surged. His grandmother would have scoffed and called that a piecrust promise; easily made, easily broken. From where he stood, the future was bleak and no vow to Meg changed that. The only certainty was the Everdark would come tomorrow, and he had no way to stop it. He couldn't keep her safe.

Meg relaxed; her breaths were slow and regular, her face peaceful, the trials of Nemra and Lady Clare erased from her expression as she drifted in quiet slumber. Cal rested his hand gently on Meg's brow, fighting the urge to kiss her, ease her pain. His hand dropped to his side. He didn't have the right. He returned to the desk and sank into the chair, ignoring his desire to take Meg in his arms and escape from Crossroads. Run fast and far as possible and never look back.

What was the point? There was no escape from the Everdark.

Cal had loved once before, but the feelings for Allison didn't approach the desire to open his heart to Meg. Not even close. He shook his head. Perhaps he only channeled Ashur's and Roland's feelings. Those men loved briefly, but deeply, right down to their souls. How could the love he felt for Meg be as real, too? Things like that only happened in fairytales, not in the real world.

He focused on the computer screen and concentrated on unearthing more details on Huntington. His frustration built when search after search yielded no results. Perhaps he died in the quake with so many others or escaped San Francisco and never returned.

Cal changed direction and pulled articles on the quake. Although the shock waves and upheavals collapsed buildings, the real devastation was from fire. The mains ripped apart and, with no water to douse the flames, the whole city nearly burned to the ground. He shuddered. People who lived in San Francisco at the time must have thought the end of the world was at hand.

Cal rubbed his eyes and arched his back to ease the kinks in his muscles. A glance out the window showed downtown Crossroads shrouded in darkness. For an instant, his heart raced, and then the truth set in; not an eclipse but night. He'd been at the computer for hours, his eyes burned from staring at the screen searching desperately for answers. He leaned back in the chair and closed his eyes. All he needed was a short break…

****

To Cal's right was Ashur, to his left, Roland. The three of them stood in the center of the maze. Although the bright light of day beat down on their heads, the moon inched ever closer to the sun. Very soon, the veil thinned for the final time. Their warnings filled his head. *Be prepared. Another craves the power at your command but has no conception of the devastation unleashed by ignorance of the truth.*

"Someone else wants to use the sword?" Cal's jaw tightened. "I don't have it."

The sword is bound to you, to us. Follow the call.

Across the center of the maze the two hazy figures of Nemra and Lady Clare stood next to Meg.

Cal regarded her with a wistful pang in his heart. "She's not mine."

Apart we are nothing, together we are one.

The earth trembled; a violent upheaval threw Cal to the ground. Giant fissures opened in the earth and from deep inside issued a strident howl.

Protect what is ours, brother.

A crack formed underneath him, and he tumbled into the abyss.

****

Cal awoke with a start, heart pounding against his ribcage.

Meg stood over him, a gentle hand on his shoulder. "I'm sorry. I didn't mean to startle you. Did you have a nightmare?"

Cal ran a shaky hand through his damp hair. "Yeah, a doozy." He took a deep breath to steady his racing heartbeat.

Meg smiled wanly. "I know the feeling. I've recently had a few myself."

Cal pushed back his chair and stood. Pale morning light streamed through the window. His throat tightened. "It's dawn."

"Yes. The day of the eclipse." She motioned to the computer. "Did you find anything helpful in there?"

"No. Meg, I'm so sorry."

"Don't torture yourself." She laid a hand on his arm. "I'm not any help either."

He placed his hand on top of hers. "You have been to me. More than I can say." Her smile went straight to his heart. Cal jumped at a sharp rap on the outside door. He scowled. "Can't they read the sign? The office is closed."

"Maybe it's Dylan."

On the floor in the waiting room was a cream-colored envelope shoved through the mail slot. Written on the front was *Cal and Meg* in elegant calligraphy. Meg snatched it up while Cal whipped open the door. "Come on, Isaac," he shouted, "quit playing around..." The street was empty. In the distance, the sound of a car engine faded away. Cal slammed the door shut. "He's gone."

Meg tore open the envelope and Cal peered over her shoulder. Inside was a sheet of old vellum. The message was two words only. "Find me," she said. Underneath was the now familiar signature of Phillip Bingham.

Cal snorted in disgust. "How the hell do we find a dead man—?" An electric tingle pricked his skin. Once more, the eerie sensation of a mystical rope tightened around his chest, drawing him to the door.

Meg clutched his arm. "We find Phillip, the same way we found the others?"

"You sense it, too?"

She nodded; an eager light shone in her eyes. "I'm ready."

Without a word, they ran from the office. The loop closed, the knot tightened, drawing Cal forward with greater speed. Mystical voices whispered in his ear. *Hurry. Time is short.*

The fairground wasn't open yet, but without hesitation Cal and Meg skirted the barriers. They entered the maze, tearing past waving cornstalks, the route etched in memory. At the last turn, the flagstone pavilion came in sight. The air above the arbor shimmered with an iridescent glow and burst into flame. In the distance was the toll of a clanging bell. Cal drew Meg to a halt and held out his hand. "No matter the time or place, no matter the circumstances, I

267

will find you."

She grasped his hand, holding tight. "I will find you."

Together they entered the light.

Chapter Eighteen

"Did you find her?"

Meg blinked. She sat at a small round table covered by a purple cloth embroidered with gold astrological signs. From outside the room came the muted clang of a bell. In front of Meg was a clear crystal ball on a decorative mahogany pedestal. The curtains in the room were drawn; the only light came from several flickering candles. Their heat added to the uncomfortably stuffy atmosphere.

A young woman sat on the other side of the table, twisting a handkerchief in her gloved hands. She wore an old-fashioned shirtwaist dress, straw hat, and a small drawstring purse dangled from her wrist. "Madame Marushka?"

Meg gaped at her. "What?"

"The candles," she said in an awed voice. "T-they flickered. Did you make contact with her?"

"Her?" Meg stared at the crystal ball and understanding flooded in. "Um, I can't seem to reach…" *Who?* She pushed back from the table and gaped at her own clothing, a billowing purple silk robe decorated with the same symbols as the tablecloth. She put her hands to her head. A turban? On the third finger of her left hand was a gold band.

Oh crap.

A gust of wind fluttered the curtains. Heart

L. A. Kelley

pounding, Meg jumped to her feet. In the dim candlelight, a wispy see-through figure solidified in front of her. Cal peered in confusion and then his eyes appeared to gain focus. Transparent eyes. Ghostly eyes. His lips parted in a broad grin. "Meg! You're different, but I'd recognize you anywhere. Hey, this is convenient. My memories are intact and you're right here with me, although, I don't have a clue of my identity in this place. Any idea where or who we are?"

Meg gripped the side of the table for support. *Cal is dead. He can't be dead. I can see him, hear him.*

Cal regarded her with concern. "Meg, are you okay?"

"Cal..." Meg swallowed hard. "I-I'm fine and you're the same...sort of."

"I am? That's strange."

"Her name was Clara," said the woman, puzzled. "Who's Cal?"

Cal turned in surprise to the young woman and then back to Meg. "Who's she? What's going on?"

Meg whispered an aside, "She can't see you."

"Why not—?" Cal glanced down at his semi-transparent form and his eyes widened in horror. "I'm a ghost?" He stretched out an arm to Meg. She reached for him and her fingers passed through his hand.

The woman rose from the table and tugged at Meg's sleeve. "I don't understand. Did you find Clara? May I speak with her?"

"No, I-I'm sorry..." Meg tore her attention from Cal and swallowed hard to steady her nerves. "Y-you have to leave. The spirits aren't cooperating today."

"But I must contact Clara." Her voice quavered. "It's been so hard on us. I need to hear she's in a better

270

place and approves of my decision. I'm not sure I did the right thing."

Although Meg's heart went out to the woman's evident distress, she slipped a hand under her elbow and led her firmly to the door. "I promise we'll try again another day, but you must go now. I can't convince the spirits to speak. There's a, um, blockage in the astral plane. You understand."

The woman's expression implied she clearly didn't. Meg opened the parlor door. A teenage boy sat on a bench in the hallway, and he jumped to his feet and demanded, "Well?"

The woman shook her head. "She can't reach her today."

He glared at Meg. "Told you she was a phony."

"Don't be rude," the woman scolded. "Apologize to Madame Marushka."

He didn't. Instead, the red-faced boy flung open the front door and muttered under his breath, "Bet she reached quick enough for the cash." Affixed to the outer side of the door was a shiny brass plaque: *Madame Marushka, spiritualist. Readings by appointment only.*

Meg filled with guilt. "I'm sorry."

He sneered at her. "Yeah, I bet. We should call the coppers on you. I'm sure they'd be happy to hear about your little scam."

"That's enough," said the woman. "They told me at the lecture spiritual communication can't be rushed, and Madame Marushka has been very helpful." She turned to Meg. "When can we try again?"

"Don't give her more money!" protested the boy.

"I don't need more," said Meg quickly. "As a

matter of fact, I'll refund everything you paid me." She patted her flowy robe. *Damn it, no pockets.* "If you give me minute…"

"Oh, no, I can't possibly," said the woman. "You helped so much already. When can I return for another reading?" The boy blew out his cheeks in disgust.

Meg flustered. "I'll call you when the, uh, astral plane returns."

"Call?"

"Her clothes," said Cal. "The time period is early 1900s. She probably doesn't have a phone."

"Call *on* you," blurted Meg. "I'll call *on* you as soon as the astral plane comes back."

The boy snorted, "Don't hold your breath." He hustled the woman out the front door.

Meg stood on the threshold and watched them leave. The boy and his mother headed down a steep hill to join a queue of people on the corner waiting to board a cable car. He glanced over his shoulder at Meg and gave her a dirty look. She shut the door and leaned against the wall with a sigh.

"If I'm the ghost," said Cal in a teasing tone, "how come you have the white face? Come on, let's go back to the parlor. You look as if you need to sit."

They went inside, and Meg slumped into the chair. She took off the turban and tossed it on the table. "I don't know what I expected when we entered the maze, but it sure wasn't this. How do you feel?"

"Perfectly normal, not like a ghost. Although to be honest, I don't have a clue how a ghost is supposed to feel."

Meg swallowed hard. *Cal's not dead. I won't believe he's gone.* "Good. You're not dead, then."

His tone softened. "Meg…"

"You're not dead," she snapped. "Don't say it. Don't think it. I refuse to believe it. We'll find a way out of here together."

"Sure we will," he said with a smile. "So, that means according to the note we need to find Phillip Bingham."

"Yeah, but how? There weren't any Binghams in that directory."

"You're the psychic. Although, if you want my legal opinion, I'd say the kid was right and Madame Marushka is a con artist."

"I agree." Meg glowered at the crystal ball. "I feel awful. I don't have a tingle of psychic energy, and that woman is clearly desperate for help. She came to Madame Marushka and got taken. Her clothes weren't fancy. I don't think she has a lot of money."

"It's not your fault," said Cal gently.

"Seems like it," she grumbled. "What do we do now?"

"Well, we don't know Phillip Bingham's location, yet, but we have a starting point. From the cable car and the look of the street outside, we must be in San Francisco in the early nineteen hundreds."

"Go ahead, say it," said Meg wryly. "You mean at the time of the earthquake."

"Yeah, I'm trying not to focus on that. According to the newspaper article Dylan found, Robert Huntington may have the crown, so we start there. Confirming his possession might lead us one step closer to either the sword or Phillip."

"Okay, so how do we find Huntington?" She twisted the ring on her finger. "I'd prefer to track him down before hubby gets home."

"His address is probably in that book Dylan found. We can buy a copy, but we need cash. Madame Marushka must have a stash and we need the date to find out how much time until the earthquake hits. I have a bad feeling it's close." He glowered at his hands. "I'm sorry. You have to do the heavy lifting this trip. I'm not much help."

"Hey, you didn't ask to be a ghost." Her voice softened. "I'm glad you're with me."

"So am I."

The warmth in his tone brought a flush to Meg's cheeks. She held his gaze, and the heat increased. Meg jumped from the chair and whipped open the curtains. "Let's bring a little light in here. It's reminds me of a dungeon and I just came from one of those. It wasn't any fun."

"Blow out the candles, too," said Cal with a grin. "They make me nervous. Remember, a fire followed the earthquake, and one of us is already a ghost."

Sunlight flooded the room crammed full of furnishings and several leafy ferns in large oriental pots. Sepia photographs of ancient temple ruins decorated the walls along with schlocky paintings of dewy-eyed angels, glowing saints, and Grecian maidens with urns prancing around ivied columns. In one corner was a small writing desk with an open book. "It's for appointments," said Meg. "The entry says 10 a.m., Tessie Stanhope." She glanced at a mantel clock on a bookcase. The hands pointed to 10:22. "She must be the woman who just left." Cal grimaced and Meg regarded him with sympathy. "Don't say it. You hoped her name was Bingham. Me, too."

"I suppose it was too much to ask. What's the date?"

"April 17th."

Cal ran a hand through his hair. "Damn. The earthquake is less than twenty-four hours from now."

Meg opened the drawer and pawed at the contents. "Writing stuff...I don't see any cash, but here are a couple of reference letters from out of town attesting to her skill. Hmm...the handwriting is similar. I wonder if she wrote them herself." She snorted in disgust. "Can you believe this chick even has business cards? Madame Marushka, private readings by appointment only." She pulled out two more items. "Hey, we're in luck. Madame Marushka has a map and a copy of that guide Dylan found."

"This room is very public," said Cal. "She holds séances and other psychic readings, and that means lots of different people coming in and out. She would have tucked the cash away in another room where clients aren't allowed."

Meg shed the robes and tossed them over the chair. Underneath, she wore a white shirt with a high collar and a long dark blue skirt. She tugged at the waistband and grimaced. "I can barely breathe in this corset. I swear to God, if we ever get out of here, I'll never wear anything but jeans and a T-shirt again."

The door in the parlor led to a dining room and then a kitchen. "The kitchen is clean," said Meg. "Only a few pots and pans and they look barely used."

"She might have recently moved to San Francisco. The plaque on the door seems new, so did the map and guide."

They climbed a narrow staircase to the second

floor. The first door led to a bathroom and the second to a bedroom. Meg stopped in front of a full-length mirror, studying the image of the stranger reflected back. Madame Marushka had dark hair and appeared to be in her early forties. It was hard to tell for sure though. People in the past aged so much faster.

"It's strange," murmured Cal, peering over her shoulder. "It's not your face, but I see you hiding in there. I prefer the original."

"Thanks," said Meg with a grin. "I prefer the original, solid Cal, too."

Besides the mirror, the room had a bed, nightstand, dressing table, and large armoire. Meg opened a drawer in the dressing table and pounced on a black drawstring bag similar to the one carried by Tessie Stanhope. "Hah! Found her purse. She has ten bucks in bills and change and more of those business cards." Meg set it aside and pulled out a small rectangular booklet. "It's a savings passbook with an account number and Marushka's name and address. I guess no one frets over identity theft here." She ran a finger down the deposits. "You're right. Marushka is a recent arrival. She opened an account at the Mutual Savings Bank of San Francisco on Market Street less than two months ago. It's funny though," she mused. "I don't get any sense of this woman, no leftover emotional residue, no voices in my head. It's like she's gone—and I mean really gone."

"You mean her spirit was completely evicted to make room for yours?"

"Yes, and for some reason, I'm not sorry either. I get the distinct impression she wasn't a nice person and someone or something passed judgement on her. The psychic business paid well though. Madame Marushka made regular deposits. Her savings total two hundred and ninety-seven dollars."

"That's a healthy chunk of cash for this time period."

Meg opened the armoire and pawed through an assortment of lady's garments. "That's weird, no men's clothing. Maybe she's a widow."

Cal chuckled. "You can relax. My guess is there's no Mr. Marushka and never has been. Single women back then didn't get a lot of personal freedom, but the actions of a widow weren't as closely scrutinized. I'm willing to bet Marushka isn't her real name either."

"Great. I'm losing this." Meg removed the wedding ring and tossed it in the drawer. "You'd think at least a few of Marushka's clients would check out her claims."

"How? Few phones, no computers, everything done slowly and only by mail. With a con artist, it's all appearances, like those phony references. As long as Madame Marushka put on a good show people wouldn't get suspicious. She could keep the scam going for a while."

"That kid wasn't fooled." Meg scowled into the mirror. "I hate liars."

"Don't dwell on Marushka," said Cal gently. "Tomorrow, her scam ends forever when San Francisco is destroyed."

"You're right, plus I have the funny feeling wherever she went was a one-way trip." Meg sighed. "It's too late for Tessie Stanhope though. She already lost her money."

"I tell you what," Cal soothed. "We'll deal with Huntington first and then return the money to the Stanhopes."

"With a little extra." Meg took a blank withdrawal slip from between the pages of the passbook. After a few practices on notepaper, she copied the signature and entered the amount of $293.00.

"Not wiping her out?" said Cal in amusement.

"Nope. Just in case Marushka makes it back, I'll leave a few bucks for the cable car." She tapped the pen on the desk with a puzzled expression. "I use a credit card for purchases and an occasional ATM when I need cash. I've only been inside a bank a few times."

"If you're asking me if tellers in this time period use a secret handshake with clients, I've no clue. I do most of my banking online, too."

"I guess we'll find out." Meg dropped the passbook and the slip in the purse. "I'm better now. Sticking it to a jerk always improves my mood."

"Remind me not to get on your bad side."

"Not a chance. You're one of the good guys." Cal smiled and Meg's heart fluttered.

"Open the map," he said. "We'll head to the bank first."

"The bank, then Tessie..." Meg's eyes widened. "Oh, no. I don't have an address for her—hang on. I forgot the guide." She thumbed through it and frowned. "Only a few Stanhopes and no Tessie. Maybe one of the men listed is her husband."

"We'll check them out later. Does the book have an address for Huntington?"

"One Robert Huntington lives on California Street. Let's hope he's the guy." Meg opened the map.

"According to this," said Cal, "the bank is only a few blocks away. Huntington lives on Nob Hill, so he must be doing well for himself. We can catch a cable car."

Meg folded the map. "I have to do one more thing before we go, and you wait in the parlor. I don't care if it makes me a social pariah, but if I don't lose this corset, I'm going to die."

Cal chuckled and drifted through the wall. A moment later, his muffled voice came from the hall. "Hey, that was fun."

Before leaving the apartment, Meg took Madame Marushka's purse and slipped on a hat, gloves, and jacket from a coatrack by the front door. She walked outside and paused on the steps to take in the surroundings. San Francisco was noisy. A cable car clanged. Cars rumbled past tooting their horns. Horse-drawn carriages and bicycles clattered over cobblestone streets. Meg wrinkled her nose. "The cities in this time period still stink."

"Yeah," said Cal. "Not many have cars yet, so plenty of horse manure and sewage systems aren't the greatest."

They headed down the hill. The Mutual Savings Bank of San Francisco was housed in a large stately building around the corner. "Nice place," said Meg. "Fancier than the margraves' keep."

"They used to call big banks like this money palaces," said Cal. "Having an ornate building gave depositors the impression their money was safe. Madame Marushka certainly approved."

"The margrave would have, too." Meg gazed at the marble columns and frescoed ceiling. All this grandeur...for an instant she tensed and then relaxed and bit back a smile. She had just come face to face with a monster and a bank made her antsy. Meg went to a teller and handed him the withdrawal slip and the passbook. An anxious thought popped into her head and she blurted, "I don't have ID."

The teller gave her a quizzical look. "ID?"

"They don't have IDs," said Cal in a rush. "No drivers licenses, no social security numbers."

Meg flashed a smile to the teller and fanned her face. "I had no idee it would be so warm out today. No idee a'tall."

"Yes, Mrs. Marushka." He left his seat and returned a moment later with a three by five signature card from a file cabinet behind the tellers. He compared the two. Meg's heart pounded, and then he counted out the money, placed it in a bank envelope, and slid it across the counter.

"Thankee," she chirped.

Cal burst out in a laugh as they walked to the door. "He's peering your way and scratching his head."

"Stop snickering."

"Stop talking to yourself," he teased. "I'm a ghost. I can do whatever I want."

They caught a cable car at the corner, crowded with noontime passengers. A chubby man in a bowler hat quickly offered his seat to Meg and grabbed an overhead strap. The bell clanged, and they began to move uphill.

Cal walked through the man and stood next to her. "You're smiling."

"Can't help it. This is fun." Nearby passengers shot a curious glance at the woman who addressed the chubby man's backside. Meg bit her lip and made a mental note. *Don't chat with the Invisible Man in public.*

Twenty minutes later, they stood in front of Robert Huntington's house, a three-story Victorian on a slight rise. The roofline had gables and turrets punctuated with eyebrow windows that appeared to scowl at human Meg and ghostly Cal. "Nice digs," said Meg. "He must be loaded."

"What are you going to say?" asked Cal.

Meg climbed the steps to an elegant front door with an ornate brass knocker and dug one of Madame Marushka's business cards from her purse. "Not a clue. Maybe I can talk him into a reading." Her brow furrowed in a frown. "I don't sense the crown. When I was Nemra and Lady Clare, I got a definite tingle, even when it was far away. Of course, nearly 800 years has passed. Can you pinpoint the sword?"

"Hey, I'm a ghost, remember. I can't even grip a doorknob. I'm not sure I can sense anything in this reality."

"That explains you, but why me? Is the crown still in the Middle East? Maybe we're wrong about Huntington."

"No. There's a reason we were brought to each time period." Cal cocked his head at Meg. "Do you think the crown is in Babylon?"

Was it? "No." Meg gave her head an adamant shake. "I can't explain it. I don't sense anything, but I'm sure the crown is in San Francisco, and I choose to believe the sword is here, too." She eyed him with a sheepish expression. "I'm chock full of wishful thinking today."

Cal shrugged. "It's good enough for me."

Meg rapped sharply with the brass knocker. A few seconds later, the handle turned, and Tessie Stanhope opened the door. Meg's mouth dropped open. "What are you doing here?"

Tessie wore an apron over her dress and seemed startled to see Meg. "I'm sure I mentioned I'm Mr. Huntington's housekeeper. Why are you here?" Her eyes lit up. "Did you contact Clara?" She glanced over her shoulder and added softly. "I can't speak with you now."

"Actually, I came to see Mr. Huntington."

The excitement in Tessie's expression changed to doubt. "He only sees people by appointment, and I'm afraid…" Pink colored her cheeks.

"I'm not his type?"

"I don't mean any insult," she said. "Mr. Huntington buys and sells antiques and only cultivates exclusive clientele."

"Antiques, eh," said Cal in Meg's ear. "Good. He's the right guy."

"Don't worry about it," said Meg cheerfully to Tessie. "Despite Mr. Huntington's money, I don't think he's my type either." Tessie pressed her lips together as if to hide a smile. Meg handed her a business card. "Give it a shot anyway. I heard Mr. Huntington possesses an ancient Babylonian crown engraved with a sun, moon and stars. By any chance have you seen it?"

"No, but I've only worked for Mr. Huntington a few weeks. I believe he acquired an ancient headpiece on a recent trip to Europe."

A door off the hall flung open, and a man came out who matched the picture from the newspaper. Huntington gave Meg a rapid once over, and she practically heard the wheels turning. *No money or social status. Definitely not worth my time.*

"What's this, Tessie?" he barked.

She handed him the card. "Madame Marushka wishes to speak with you—"

"Marushka?" He dismissed Meg with a disparaging wave of the hand. "I see clients by appointment only and my calendar is currently booked." The implication was clear. *I'm always booked to people with no money.*

"But sir," said Tessie, "she asked to see an ancient headpiece."

Huntington raised his eyebrows at Meg. "Indeed?"

"Yes," said Meg. "Does it have a sun, moon, and stars?"

The eyebrows lowered and drew together in suspicion. "How do you know the design? I've shown it to no one."

"My spirit guide described it."

With a snort, he gave Tessie an accusing look. "You told her."

"No, sir," she insisted. "I've never seen it. Madame Marushka is a very powerful spiritualist."

"Spiritualist?" he scoffed. Huntington appeared ready to slam the door in Meg's face. She braced herself to argue, but then something seemed to pique his curiosity. "Perhaps, we should talk in my study." He ushered her inside and closed the door.

"A telephone," said Cal, eyeing the desk. "Not bad for 1906."

"Now the truth," said Huntington. "How did you learn of the headpiece?"

Cal snorted. "He's got some attitude. I don't trust him. Find the crown fast and get out of here. Ask him if he has the sword, too."

Meg sent a shut-up glare to Cal. Having someone

yakking in her ear was really distracting. "As I said Mr. Huntington, my spirit guide told me you are in possession of an unusual headpiece. I was curious and hoped to see it for myself."

"You've provoked my curiosity, too. A spirit guide, you say?" His voice dripped disbelief.

"Yes. His name is Cal. He knew about the crown," Meg said smugly, "and he was right."

"Crown?"

"Yes."

"Not a headpiece," he murmured and then added gruffly, "I don't believe in such nonsense as communing with spirits."

"And yet," she said pleasantly, "a spirit brought me here. May I see it?"

"Why? It is merely a curiosity that captured my fancy and has little value."

Cal snorted. "That's a big, fat lie. He's hiding something. Man, I wish I had him on the stand."

"I have an interest in antiquities, no matter the worth," said Meg, hunting for an answer that didn't sound too nutty. "Objects can retain a spiritual essence…" She shifted her feet. An infinitesimal tug drew her attention, a mental itch she couldn't scratch. *Over here against the wall*, it seemed to say. With a wild hunch, Meg pointed to a tall standing safe. "The crown is in there."

Huntington gaped at her.

"It's there, isn't it?" said Meg with rising excitement. "Will you show it to me, or is there a reason to keep it hidden?"

His shoulders stiffened slightly. "Of course not."

"Well, then?" prodded Meg.

With a hint of annoyance in his features, Huntington went to the safe. He shot a suspicious glance over his shoulder and used his body to block the dial. Meg hung back, gazing innocently at the ceiling, feigning disinterest. Meanwhile, Cal squatted next to the safe, watching in undisguised glee as Huntington entered the combination. "Right seventeen, left twenty-two, right five."

With a soft click, the tumblers slid in place. Huntington opened the door and removed a bulky object wrapped in linen and placed it on the desk. Meg's heart skipped a beat as he flung off the cloth. The crown was black with tarnish and layers of grime, the glory of the symbols obscured to anyone—except to a person who already forged a mystical link. A deep yearning to touch the crown coursed through her. Without conscious thought, she brushed the rim with her finger. A tiny spark of life pricked her skin.

Meg's pulse raced and she stifled a cry of triumph. The crown wasn't dead, only sleeping. For centuries, it had waited patiently for the Everdark's return, and for Meg to wake it in time to meet the final challenge. *Be patient a while longer. The Everdark isn't due to return for over a century.*

A faint voice, barely a whisper, echoed in her mind. *I wait.* The spark of life went dormant once more.

"You recognize the symbols?"

Meg jerked back to reality at Huntington's question. "Recognize?" she said. "Well, they're obviously the sun, moon, and stars."

"It has such a unique pattern. I've bought and sold rarities for years and never found anything with a similar design."

285

"Is that so?" said Meg with an innocent expression. "How interesting. You never came across a sword with identical markings?"

"No." Huntington stepped toward her. "Why are you really here?"

"As I said, I have an interest in relics. Cal described the crown, and I came to see it."

"Yes," he sniffed, "your spirit guide. What a convenient answer to any question." His jaw clenched. "Oliver sent you, didn't he?"

Meg drew herself up. "I have no idea who you mean."

"Don't you? Oliver prefers the company of lunatics, but as a businessman, he's not a complete fool. He must have gotten wind of my purchase and stumbled upon a customer hunting for that same design. Probably, one of his lunatic associates. Tell him, I won't sell." A crafty look crossed his face. "But if he introduces the buyer to me, I'll give him a nominal finder's fee."

"No one sent me here," said Meg. "I have no interest in the crown other than an appreciation for ancient spiritual artifacts. As far as I know, it has no great worth."

"In that case, I'll smash it to pieces." Huntington tossed the crown on the carpet and raised his leg over the top.

"No!"

Huntington smiled slyly. He returned the crown to the safe and spun the dial. "If you don't work for Oliver, why the interest, and don't give me more of that spiritualism claptrap. Does it have hidden value? What do those symbols mean?"

Cal tensed. "Meg, it's time to go."

Meg took a step back. "I have no idea."

With a sudden move, he grabbed her wrist. "I'm sure you do, Madame Marushka."

Meg struggled to get free. "Let go of me or you'll be sorry."

"Get your hands off her!" Cal took a swing at Huntington, but his fist passed right through his jaw.

"Maybe the object is stolen," he mused. "Is there a reward for its return? Tell me or we'll have a nice little chat with the police. I have friends on the force, Madame Marushka, if that's even your real name. A stay in prison might loosen your tongue."

Meg kicked Huntington's shin and he stumbled back with a yelp. Hitching up her skirt, she tore from the parlor and out the front door. "This outfit," she panted, "isn't made for a fast getaway."

"Follow me." Cal beckoned Meg to the yard next door and she ducked behind a clump of hydrangeas while Cal watched the house.

"What do you see?" said Meg.

"Huntington is on the stoop scanning the street and rubbing his ankle." Cal chuckled. "He's ticked."

"Humph, serves him right."

"He went inside and shut the door. Wait here a few minutes until I'm sure it's safe." He peered at the red marks on her wrist and glowered. "He hurt you."

Meg rubbed her skin. "I'm fine. Trust me. His shin is a lot worse. These are tough leather shoes with pointy toes."

Cal reached out to brush a stray lock of hair from her cheek, but it didn't move. His voice tightened. "Meg…"

"If you're going to apologize for not jumping to the rescue," she said gently, "save your breath. You didn't choose to come here as a ghost."

He scowled. "This sucks. I can't help if you run into trouble."

"You already helped. You got the combination to the safe."

"But Huntington doesn't have the sword."

"Yeah, but he mentioned this guy Oliver who was interested in objects with those symbols. He might have an idea. We can hang around here to get a word with Tessie about him, and then once night falls snatch the crown."

Cal grinned. "You act mighty eager to turn to a life of crime."

Meg's lips twisted in scorn. "I get Huntington. He figures I'm frightened away for good. Breaking and entering is the last thing a man such as him suspects from a poor, weak, little woman. I only hope I have the chance to kick him in the shin again."

"My sentiments exactly," said Cal.

"I knew it!" A boy jumped from behind a nearby tree. "You're a couple of crooks."

Chapter Nineteen

Meg gawked at him. "You're Tessie's kid. What are you doing here? Did you follow me?"

He folded his arms and regarded her smugly. "Aunt Tessie had to work. I told her I was going to school and then doubled-backed to watch your place. I figured to catch you in a scam, and I was right."

Meg stared at him. "Tessie is your aunt."

"Wait a minute," said Cal. "He said 'crooks' as in plural." His eyes widened. "He can see me."

The boy peered directly at Cal and sneered. "Of course, I can see you. I'm not blind or stupid."

Cal and Meg exchanged startled looks. "Are you thinking what I'm thinking?" said Cal.

Meg turned to the boy. "By any chance, is your name Phillip Bingham?"

"You know dang well it is," he snapped. "Aunt Tessie told you. You need to brush up on your flimflam, lady, if you forgot that much about your mark so soon."

"Meg," said Cal, "we can't talk here."

Phillip snarled. "You're not going anywhere until I get my aunt's money back." He held out his hand. "That'll be five bucks—plus interest."

"I like this kid," said Cal with a grin.

Phillip's eyes narrowed. "I can always yell for Mr. Huntington. I'll bet he'd pay plenty to hear you plan to rob his joint." He drew in a deep breath.

"How does a few hundred dollars sound instead?" said Meg. She reached into her purse and pulled out the envelope from the bank and handed it to him. "I planned to give this to your aunt."

Phillip opened the envelope and his eyes narrowed in suspicion. "What's the catch?"

"No catch," insisted Cal.

"Another scam, I'll bet," he snorted out. "The money is probably phony."

Cal eyed him in amusement. "Geez, you're suspicious."

"I know the way the world works, mac." Phillip's face reddened, and he balled his fists. "The rich don't care a penny for the poor. Well, nobody's making a sucker out of Aunt Tessie while I'm around." Despite his smaller size, Phillip threw a jab at Cal's jaw. The fist passed right through. Phillip's mouth dropped open. He poked Cal in the chest with a finger and got the same result. The blood drained from his complexion. He licked his lips. "You're a…you're a…"

"Yeah, I'm a ghost," said Cal, "but don't be frightened, I won't hurt—hey!"

Phillip dropped the envelope and bolted down the street.

"After him," shouted Meg. "I can't run very fast in this damn skirt."

Cal took off. After three blocks of racing up one of San Francisco's steep hills, Phillip finally slowed to a walk and then sagged against a fence drawing in ragged breaths. He gaped in horror as Cal glided up to him.

"I never figured being a ghost had an upside," said Cal lightly, "but it does. Since, I don't breathe, I can't get winded."

Phillip shot a wild-eyed look around the street as if searching for the best avenue of escape.

"No point in running," said Cal. "I can do this all day."

"W-what do you want from me?"

The boy's terror sent a rush of guilt through him. "First, I want to apologize. I'm very sorry I frightened you and have no wish to cause you or your aunt any harm." Cal cocked his head. "Do I sound like an evil spirit?"

Phillip's breathing slowed, and his expression shed the crazed look of a cornered animal. "No," he said. "I didn't reckon ghosts talked at all."

"Well, I'm not your usual ghost. At least, I don't think I am. The fact is Meg and I are here because we need your help."

"Who's Meg?"

"I am." Meg puffed up beside them, fanning her face. "Man, these hills are killer and Madame Marushka's stupid shoes are no help. They are definitely not made for jogging."

Phillip's eyes narrowed again. "If you ain't Madame Marushka, who are you?"

"Phillip," said Cal kindly, "we have a long story and can't talk here." He motioned to several pedestrians who shot curious glances in their direction. "No one can see me except you and Meg. Right now, the only thought going through folks' heads is why is that boy talking to thin air? If you don't want a reputation as the local lunatic, we need to find a better place."

Meg linked her arm with Phillip's. This wasn't the wily old man who sent them on this crazy journey, but an angry kid wanting to do right by his aunt Tessie. "Please, Phillip. I know what it's like to feel like Alice suddenly dropped down the rabbit hole, but Cal and I can help you and Tessie." She held the envelope out to him. "I swear the money is good."

"Also," Cal added with a grin, "it's a heck of a story. Aren't you curious?"

The last bit of wariness left Phillip's expression and a faint smile twitched his lips. "I reckon I am at that. We can talk at home. Aunt Tessie won't get off work for a few hours."

They boarded a cable car at the corner. Meg sat next to Phillip while Cal stood in the aisle. Phillip gulped every time an unwary passenger walked through him to find a seat.

"Where are your parents?" asked Meg.

"Pa died years back. Aunt Tessie is Ma's kid sister. She moved in with us when Ma got sick." A wave of wistfulness passed over his face. "She died a few weeks ago."

Meg patted his arm. "I'm so sorry. Was Clara your mother?"

"Yes. Ma ailed a long time, and we had to sell everything to pay the bills. After she was gone, Aunt Tessie moved us to San Francisco to find work and a fresh start." His voice softened. "I'm grateful to her. I got no one else. Aunt Tessie's worried though. Money's tight, so I told her I'd quit school and get a job." The words spilled out in a rush. "Aunt Tessie got upset and thought she hadn't done right by me in coming here and wanted to talk to Ma, but I didn't trust you. I owe her so much…" He regarded Meg with a hopefully. "Is that money for real?"

"Cross my heart and hope to die, and every cent is for Tessie."

They exited the cable car. Tessie and Phillip lived in a four-story walk-up. While Phillip led the way upstairs, Cal hung back and whispered in her ear, "How much do we tell him?"

"Everything," she said. "He can handle it."

The tiny one-bedroom flat was crammed with several pieces of second-hand furniture but spotlessly clean. "Where do you sleep?" asked Meg.

Phillip motioned to the threadbare couch and drew himself up. "I don't mind. It's enough for me."

She laid a gentle hand on his shoulder. "Life will work out better for you, Phillip."

"But first," said Cal, "we have to solve some problems here."

They sat at a rickety kitchen table. Meg and Cal took turns telling their story from the beginning, filling in the details of their lives. Phillip said nothing, but the skepticism in his expression quickly changed to shock before finally freezing in astonishment.

"Now we've landed in San Francisco," said Meg, "and understand why. We were sent back to find Phillip Bingham's younger self. You must take possession of the sword and the crown and get them out of San Francisco before they're destroyed or buried in the rubble." She squeezed his shoulder. "So, what do you think of our cockamamie tale?"

Phillip ran a shaky hand through his hair. "It's something for sure...I really do all that?"

"And more," said Cal. "You become a great man."

"But how?" Phillip sputtered, "I'm nobody, a poor kid without a nickel to his name."

"Honestly," said Cal, "I don't have a clue. We never meet in the future, so I don't know your history, but you wouldn't be the first great man to start from scratch."

"Speaking of the future," said Meg. "You need to take down a few details of our lives so you can keep watch."

Phillip retrieved a pencil and paper. He jotted their birthdates and places, parents' names, schools, and social security numbers.

"What are those?" asked Phillip, scratching his head.

"Never mind now," said Cal. "They're not used until the 1930s, but you'll know what to do with them when the time comes. Something called the Depression hits then. The stock market tanks, but investments such as short sales and oil hold steady. Write down public utilities, foodstuffs, and electrical equipment, too. Electric Boat, Douglass, and Honeywell are good. Also, IBM and later Microsoft and Apple."

"Apple? You mean a fruit farm?"

Cal chuckled. "No. It's a computer."

"A what?"

"Machines," said Meg with a chuckle. "They don't come around until later but keep them in mind. None of this makes sense now, but it will."

Phillip stuffed the paper in his pocket. "You got no proof the sword and crown will kill the Everdark. The folks who made them didn't leave instructions."

"That's true," said Meg, "but perhaps those who forged the weapons were only supposed to create them and nothing more. Maybe certain people have a special gift to recognize evil and that ability gives them the chance to stop it. Just a chance, mind you. Guardians of the gate apparently come in all shapes, sizes, and talents."

"Like a pagan priestess and Babylonian soldier," said Cal, "or a Christian knight and lady of the manor. The Everdark is terrifying in any time period. A sensible person would have run, but they stood their ground."

"Their bodies didn't fight us," said Meg. "Neither did their minds. Deep inside, they knew what these mystic forces asked. They willingly offered their lives to keep the Everdark behind the gate. We do, too."

Phillip shuddered. "How will you get back? The last two times you faced the Everdark during an eclipse, but there isn't one."

"When we get the sword and crown," said Meg, "we hope to find the way."

"You still came," said Phillip in amazement, "even though you could die in San Francisco. Cal's a ghost, so he's already got one foot in the grave. My letters never say for a fact you win the last battle?"

"No," said Meg. "They're certainly cryptic, but Cal and I decided to enter the maze whatever the consequences."

Cal's gaze fell on Meg. "Whatever our fates, I have no regrets. I'm glad I'm here."

Meg flushed and smiled at him. "So am I."

Phillip blew out a snort of disgust. "You're both nuts."

Meg laughed. "No argument there."

Phillip's head turned to the window and shuddered. "The earthquake is really coming?"

"Yes," said Cal. "In our time period that much is

historic fact, and nothing Meg and I do here can change it. The city is hit on April 18, 1906, and this area will be nothing but rubble. You and Tessie must be far away before then."

"How am I going to talk her into that?"

"You don't." Meg gave Phillip a wily look. "Tessie came for Clara's advice, so Clara will convince her to leave San Francisco."

"Lie to Aunt Tessie?" Phillip bristled. "It's not right after what she's done for me and Ma."

"It will save her life and yours," said Cal. "If your mother was here, wouldn't she give her blessing? Don't you think she wants both of you safe from harm?"

Phillip regarded Cal with grudging respect. "I reckon she does. You got a slick way of talking people into things, mister."

Meg nudged Phillip playfully in the shoulder. "Cal's a lawyer. It's what they do. Dead or alive, they have a way with words—"

The floorboards shimmied with a vibrating rumble. Mouth dry, Meg grabbed the side of the table to hold steady as the chair bounced up and down. Behind her, china dishes rattled in a breakfront. After three seconds the trembling stopped, but Meg's heart continued to hammer against her ribs.

Phillip patted her hand. "That little shimmy weren't no big deal. It didn't even break a plate."

Meg licked her lips. "If that's a little shimmy, I don't want to be anywhere near this place come morning. Right Cal...Cal?" She turned to him and her face paled. One of Cal's hands clutched his neck as if gasping for breath. He stretched out the other and mouthed her name.

"Cal!" She lunged for his hand an instant before he faded away.

****

Cal hit the floor sending a shock wave through his body. Blood pounded in his ears and his heart drummed a ferocious beat. On the plus side, he continued to feel his heart. "Meg," he gasped. "That was something. Did you feel it, too?" He raised his head. "Meg?"

Meg and Phillip were gone along with the apartment. Instead of a bare hardwood floor, he landed on a thick Persian carpet. The strange octagonal room had no windows and was lit with electric wall sconces designed to resemble glowing torches. Painted on the ceiling was an artistic representation of the planets in a night sky complete with blazing comets. Sprinkled among the celestial objects were astrological symbols.

Cal staggered to his feet. In front of him was a man and a woman dressed in long flowing white robes. Each wore a wedding ring, and they stood next to a glass case resting on a pedestal. The man had a beaming smile and wielded a sword. His sword. Cal filled with righteous indignation. "Hey," he said, "that's mine." Neither the man nor woman reacted to the outburst. "So," he muttered. "You don't know I'm here." He gazed around the room, scrutinizing the mystic symbols with dawning comprehension. "Is this a séance? Are you trying to summon the dead?" He snorted. "I've got news for you, buddy, it worked."

The man lowered the sword and turned to the woman. "I was right," he chortled, his eyes sparkling with glee. "This is a spiritual artifact with enough latent psychic energy to power the incantation. I most certainly felt a tingle that time."

"I did, too," said the woman. "Are you positive it wasn't simply an earthquake?"

"Absolutely. My dear…" His voice quivered with excitement. "We're close to bridging the eternal divide, and then we can rub it in those scoffers' faces." He raised the sword. "Together with this, you and I will usher in a golden age of spiritual enlightenment for the benefit of mankind."

She gazed at him with loving tenderness. "I'm so proud. You deserve every accolade, not to mention, vindication for your hard work."

"Our hard work," he chided. "I couldn't have done it without you."

She smiled gently and patted his arm. "Are you strong enough to try again? Communion with the mystic plane is taxing."

"It is, but success brought me renewed energy. Now step back. These vibrations can be powerful." The woman moved against the wall. The man traced a circular outline in the air with the point of the sword. He muttered a chant under his breath in a strange sing-song language.

Cal's eyes narrowed. "This isn't a séance. What are you up to?" A hazy shape formed in the air. Cal peered at the man's face and then at the woman. Nothing distracted their rapt attention on the sword. "You don't see it."

A suspicion took root. In the distance, came a quavering howl. Cal's pulse raced, but the couple's focus on the sword didn't waver. "You don't hear it."

"It tingled again." The man's eyes widened. "My dear, I'm forging a channel to the other side."

"Think of it," said the woman with a happy sigh.

"Soon, we will have a way to communicate with loved ones who have passed beyond the veil. Imagine the wisdom they can impart. No one will ever fear death again."

The awful truth of their actions hit Cal like a brick. The couple had located the gate between two dimensions—a gate that, with the right magic, could swing both ways and open from either side.

"No, no, no, no, no!" Cal shouted in helpless rage. "Stop what you're doing. Listen to me, don't open the gate. A loved one isn't waiting there. You have to stop now!"

The man continued to rotate the tip of the sword. The hazy outline sharpened, and the strident howl swelled. Cal lunged and grabbed the blade. Painful sparks of energy shot up his arms and burned with scorching heat. The sword stopped the lazy circle.

"What's wrong, dear?" said the woman.

"It appears to be stuck." Both hands clenched the hilt as he struggled unsuccessfully to control the sword.

Cal gritted his teeth and held tight. "No you don't." Lightning rippled and danced around him. Tongues of fire licked his arms. The very air in the room crackled, filling his lungs, flooding his veins. "I said, drop it!"

With a cry, the man released the sword, and it fell on the carpet.

Cal sank to his knees, his legs no longer able to support him. His eyesight blurred and dimmed.

The woman rushed to the man's side. "Are you hurt?"

"No, my dear, I'm fine." The man rubbed his hands briskly together and gazed at the sword in wonder. "I experienced a strong electric discharge, and at the same time felt as if someone snatched the sword from my grasp."

She took his arm. "You're pale. Rest for a bit, mystic exertions are taxing. We searched for years to find the proper incantation to summon the portal. Surely, a few hours delay won't matter, and then we can celebrate together."

He smiled at her. "You're right. A few hours make no difference, and I need to be at my best." He retrieved the sword and placed it in the glass case.

"Wait..." Breathing hard, Cal struggled to rise. Every nerve ending in his body was on fire. "Listen to me. You don't understand the danger..." He grabbed for the man's leg, but his hand passed right through. The couple walked to the door, and the man paused on the threshold to peer back at the case. His brow furrowed.

"Listen to me," Cal yelled.

"My dear?" said the woman.

"It's nothing." He shut the door.

Ignoring the pain, Cal stumbled to the sword. "You sense I'm here, don't you? You called me to stop him. I tried..." He stretched out his hand and a knot of sick fear tightened in his stomach. The transparency was greater than before. "Oh, no," he said. "Not yet."

Without warning, the temperature plummeted. Cal's arms snapped to his sides as if pinned in place by an invisible rope. The bands tightened. He couldn't move, he couldn't breathe. A violent tug yanked him into the dark, and the room with the sword vanished.

Chapter Twenty

"Cal!" Meg lunged for Cal, but he disappeared.

Phillip gaped at her. "Where did he go?"

Meg's mouth dried. "I-I don't know."

Phillip licked his lips. "Has he…has he passed to the other side?"

"No, of course not." *Cal's not dead. I won't believe he's dead.* She squared her shoulders. "We're in this together. Cal made a promise and he's a man who always keeps his word. He won't leave me, and I won't leave him. He'll be back."

Phillip regarded her with a cheeky grin. "Sounds to me as if you're sweet on each other."

Meg shook a finger at him. "Sounds to me as if that's none of your business."

"He's sweet on you, too."

Heat rose to her cheeks. "Think so? We haven't exactly had a normal relationship so far. Each of us has been in the body of two previous lovers. Maybe he's channeling past emotions."

Phillip regarded her in disbelief. "The way he watches you? Pa proposed to Ma after only a week of courting. He said the first time he laid eyes on her he knew she was the one."

"That's romantic but not very sensible."

"Maybe so, but Ma said when it's right, you feel it. Don't you feel something?"

Meg's gaze went to the spot where Cal stood a moment before.

Phillip elbowed her in the side with a smug expression. "Knew it."

"I can't decide who's more annoying, you as a kid or an adult."

The door opened. Tessie paused on the threshold and gaped at Meg. "Madame Marushka, what are you doing here?"

"Aunt Tessie," said Phillip. "You're home early."

She shut the door. "Mr. Huntington left for a dinner engagement at his club, so I didn't need to prepare a meal." Her eyes narrowed. "Phillip, why aren't you in school?"

He nodded to Meg. "We had business."

"Madame?"

"Clara sent a message I needed to deliver in person."

Tessie's gaze darted around the room in eager anticipation. "She's here?"

"No." Meg shifted her feet. *Damn, I hate lying to her.* "It came through my spirit guide, Cal, but he had to leave…" Meg motioned to the table. "Please, sit. We have a lot to discuss."

"Is this a séance?" said Tessie. "Should we join hands? You don't have the crystal ball, but I can make tea for you to read the leaves."

Meg sniffed. "No, that stuff is garbage." Tessie raised an eyebrow, and Meg quickly added, "I used the crystal ball before, but now it's different. I have a spiritual link with Cal, and he guided me to Clara."

Tessie bit her lip. "Madame Marushka, I haven't received wages for this week and can't afford to pay, even for a message from Clara."

"You don't need to pay." Phillip pulled out the roll of bills and pressed them into her hand. "She's here to help us. She gave the money back and more."

Tessie gaped at the bills and drew in a breath. "I can't take this."

"It's not mine," said Meg. "It's a gift from Clara. She, uh…she, uh…" She appealed silently to Phillip.

"Gave her a tip on the ponies," he blurted.

"Gave me a tip on the ponies," echoed Meg, "so I placed a bet for you."

Tessie gawked at her. "Clara never gambled. She said it was a fool's pastime."

Meg plastered on her most beneficent smile. "Clara is absolutely right, so don't ever do it again. She insisted it was a onetime thing to help you and Phillip and wants your promise never to gamble."

"I promise," said Tessie, looking even more confused.

Meg narrowed her eyes at Phillip. "You, too."

He wore a half-smirk. "I promise."

She leaned across the table. "A gentleman never breaks a promise to a lady."

He blew out his cheeks. "Sheesh, I promise."

Tessie ran her fingers over the bills as if only touch guaranteed their existence. "You said Clara had a message."

"That's right." Meg took Tessie's hands and cupped them between hers. "What I'm about to say will be very hard to accept, but you must. Your lives depend on it. Tomorrow morning, just after five a.m., an earthquake will level San Francisco."

Phillip tugged on Meg's sleeve. "Tell her about the

water mains."

"Right," said Meg. "The quake ruptures the water mains. Fire spreads quickly, but there's no water to fight the flames. This part of the city is reduced to ash and rubble."

Tessie paled. "Surely, this can't be true."

"I'm afraid it is. Thousands of people will die, and San Francisco has to be rebuilt from the ground up. Clara wants you and Phillip long gone."

Tessie clutched at her neckline. "Can't we spread the alarm?"

"Who'd listen to us? Most people think I'm a fake."

"Not me," said Phillip stoutly. "Not anymore."

Tessie regarded him with surprise. "You've certainly changed your tune."

"Yes." His expression didn't hold a shred of doubt. "She speaks for Ma. I'm sure of it."

Meg's grip tightened on Tessie's hands, mustering every ounce of sincerity. "One thing I've learned is I only have the power to do so much. I can't change what will happen tomorrow. San Francisco's fate is sealed, but the future…" She drew a deep breath. "The future is unwritten, at least for you and Phillip, but you must leave tonight."

Tessie's troubled gaze went from Phillip to Meg. She leaned back in her seat and drew a shaky breath. "A-all right. We'll go."

Meg blew out a sigh of relief. "Good. With the money, you can buy train tickets and the chance to start fresh, but first we have to get two special items to take with you. Actually, they're for Phillip. Clara insists he have them. I take it you have the keys to Mr.

Huntington's house."

"Yes, of course. I'm his housekeeper." Her eyes narrowed. "Why?"

"Because one of the items Phillip needs in his possession is the crown inside Huntington's safe."

Tessie's gaped at her. "You expect me to steal from my employer?"

"No," said Meg weakly, "I'll steal them. I already have the combination. I only need you to open the back door, so I can get into the study."

Tessie dropped the wad of bills. Eyes blazing, she pushed from the table and jumped to her feet. "I'm not a thief. What trick are you playing here?"

"No trick," said Meg, rising from her seat. "This sounds crazy, but the crown has great spiritual power. It must get out of San Francisco and stay in Phillip's possession."

"You're not a real mystic." Tessie grabbed Phillip's hand and yanked him to her side. "You're a charlatan trying to use me for dirty work. Clara would never condone a theft, and I won't allow Phillip to turn to a life of crime. Why was I so stupid as to fall for your game?" She pointed to the door. "Go this instant before I summon the police."

"Please," said Meg. "I'm not a thief. I don't want the crown for myself. It must go to Phillip. He's meant to have it. It's the only way to stop..." She turned to Phillip in desperation. "I understand now. The sword and crown are your destiny as much as ours. They chose Cal and me to wield them, but you have the heart of a protector. You keep them safe before the final battle. Accept your destiny and convince her."

"What sword?" said Tessie with a hard look.

305

"More valuables for Phillip to steal?"

"My destiny," Phillip murmured.

"What nonsense has Madame Marushka put in your head?" said Tessie. "We're going to warn Mr. Huntington right now."

Phillip's expression set with determination, and he shook off her grip. "She's not a liar, Aunt Tessie. You have to listen. Mr. Huntington doesn't understand. He thinks the crown is nothing more than an old antique to sell, but it's a weapon. I have to keep the crown and the sword hidden and safe until they're needed in the future."

"Weapons?" she sputtered, her skepticism plain. "Against what?"

"Against evil." Phillip voice had a solemn timbre. "I understand now, too."

"Are you sure, Phillip?" said Meg. "It won't be easy. If you want to walk away…"

"No. I accept."

"Phillip, this is nonsense," scoffed Tessie.

"No." Phillip held her gaze, calm and controlled. "I used to think it was bunk but not anymore. The sword and the crown need a protector and I'm going to help them."

The hard edge in Tessie's expression softened, and indecision danced across her face. "Only this morning," she said softly, "you were angry at Madame Marushka."

"I've changed. Aunt Tessie, I owe you so much. Please trust me. Have I ever lied to you?"

Her voice dropped. "No."

Phillip placed a hand over his heart. "I swear on my parents' graves. I swear with all my heart, I'm not lying. I spoke with Cal, too."

Tessie paled. "Her spirit guide?"

"Yes. I saw him. He's real."

She glanced around. "Is he here now?"

"No."

"Please listen to Phillip," said Meg. "He has a gift allowing him to see things others can't. The spirits asked him to use it for the sake of the innocent, and now he's agreed." She placed a gentle hand on Tessie's arm. "This is a burden Phillip has to carry throughout his life. He's very brave, and you should be proud. I can say for a fact, any supernatural responsibility exacts a toll. It will be easier for Phillip to bear if he always had a sympathetic person in his corner, so will you help him? Help us?"

Tessie eyed Phillip with affection and tousled his hair with a wistful smile. "I've tried to do my best by you."

"You have, Aunt Tessie." He swallowed hard. "I'm grateful."

"Then I suppose I can't stop now." She turned to Meg. "What do you want from me, Madame Marushka?"

"First of all," she said with a grin, "call me Meg. All you have to do is open Huntington's door. I have the combination to the safe. Cal gave it to me."

Tessie blinked. "He did?"

"Spirit guides are ever so helpful. Has Huntington left the house yet?"

"Yes. He'll be at his club by now."

"What about the sword?" said Phillip. "We don't know where it is."

"I hope when Cal returns, he has an idea."

"If he doesn't?"

"One problem at a time." Meg turned to Tessie. "Don't worry about the police. You and Phillip will be long gone before Huntington discovers the robbery and raises the alarm. Besides, once the earthquakes hits, he'll be too busy running for his life to remember the crown."

"Can your spirit guide tell you if Mr. Huntington survives?" said Tessie.

"No, I'm sorry. There are thousands of deaths and injuries, but most of the population lives. He has a chance like everyone else, but I'm afraid he'll lose his house and possessions in the fire."

"Mr. Huntington is not the most sanguine of men," said Tessie, "but has been a good employer and I can't simply turn my back. I'll write a note explaining I'm resigning my position and leaving San Francisco because you warned of an earthquake. He'll see it when he returns." She held up her hand to stifle any argument. "He'll think me a fool, but I must try."

"Best not to argue with her," said Phillip. "She's stubborn."

"Suit yourself," said Meg. "Leave the note and whether Huntington chooses to believe will be up to him. Now, pack your things. You won't come back here again."

Tessie plucked several bills off the tabletop. "Phillip, run to the livery and engage a hansom carriage. I'll pay the driver to deliver our luggage to the train depot. The stationmaster can hold them for us."

The boy darted out the door. Meg helped Tessie pack two carpetbags and a large trunk, and then they dragged them to the living room to await Phillip's return. Meg flung her arms around her in a spontaneous hug. "I owe you a debt I can never repay. Thank you so much for believing me. There's no reason you should."

Tessie smiled shyly. "Phillip convinced me. Life has been hard for him these past months. He watched helplessly as Clara slipped from us. Since she died, he's seemed lost, not taken much interest in anything. Now it's as if he's lit with an inner fire. I think he would have helped you whether I agreed or not, so I'll stick close to keep an eye on him."

"I'm glad. Everyone needs a person who loves them in their corner."

Tessie's gaze drifted to the door. "Does it turn out well for Phillip?"

"If he gets the sword and crown out of San Francisco, then I believe so. Honestly, I can't see the perils he'll face after that or stumbling blocks in his way or even tell how to steer him clear of pain. I can only say the magic gave me a glimpse into one possible future for Phillip. If he follows the right track, he becomes a great man."

"That's good enough. A chance for him is all I ever hoped for, too." Tessie shot her a sideways glance. "Do you know what happens to me?"

Meg momentarily toyed with the idea of a comforting lie but shoved the thought away. This woman deserved the truth. "I'm sorry. I don't even know if you make it safely out of San Francisco tomorrow."

Tessie regarded her sharply. "That's not the answer I expected. You assured me in our readings if I took your advice, the years ahead shined bright."

"Let's just say Phillip isn't the only one to undergo

a change of heart in the last few hours." Meg took her hands. "Promise me never again to consult a spiritualist, fortune teller, or anyone else who claims to have special insights into the occult."

Tessie stared at her. "Funny words coming from you."

"There are more crooks out there then you can imagine, ready to take advantage of suckers. Their advice will only lead you astray. Don't try to contact Clara. She won't answer again and anyone who says otherwise is a liar. Her job is done, and she's moved on to her reward. Keep a rational head on your shoulders and avoid anything that smacks of mysticism. Listen to your heart instead and you and Phillip will do just fine."

Her lips twitched in a smile. "You are a very eccentric person, Meg, but I promise."

Phillip bounded in with the carriage driver. The man hefted the trunk and took it downstairs. Meg and Tessie followed with the two carpetbags. They loaded everything into the carriage and climbed inside. The driver let them off in front of Mr. Huntington's house and then continued with the luggage to the train station.

"You don't have your things," said Tessie to Meg as they walked to the house. "Shouldn't you pack?"

"I travel light," said Meg with a grin. "Now, let's get that crown."

Tessie unlocked the kitchen door and led them through the house to Huntington's office. Meg went directly to the safe. "Right seventeen," she muttered, "left twenty-two, right five…" She gripped the handle, gave a firm yank, and with a click, it opened. With a delighted cry, she pounced on the crown and ran a finger lovingly across the surface. "Long time, no see."

Was it imagination or did the crown seem happy to be back in her hands, too?

Phillip peered around her shoulder. "Is it okay?"

"I don't see any damage." Meg briskly rubbed her thumb over the sun. "She could use a bit of polish though."

Phillip snickered. "She?"

"Yeah," said Meg with a chuckle. "After all we've been through, I think of her as a friend with a mind of her own."

"Go to the kitchen, Phillip," said Tessie. "I have a tin of polish under the sink. Bring it to Meg along with a clean rag." Phillip scampered away.

Meg placed the crown on her head, and it settled with comforting familiarity. "It's good to have you back," she said.

Tessie sat at the desk and took a sheet of writing paper from the drawer. She dipped the pen in the inkwell and wrote a brief note. "I'll warn Mr. Huntington," she said with a troubled expression, "but when he sees the crown missing, he'll think I'm a common thief."

Meg shut the safe and spun the dial. "With luck, he won't notice until we're long gone."

"Don't be too sure." Huntington stepped into the library holding a gun.

Tessie paled. "Mr. Huntington, I can explain—"

"No need, I see exactly what's going on. You intend to rob me." He strode across the room and snatched the note off the desk. "An earthquake?" he mocked. "Do you really believe that ridiculous story would prevent me from calling the police? How fortunate I returned early. After Madame Marushka's visit, I couldn't shake the idea the crown had hidden worth, so I left the club and arrived in the middle of a robbery. I was right. The alignment of those symbols is a code, isn't it? They point to a treasure."

Meg glared at him. "It's not that kind of treasure. The crown is worthless to you."

He held out his hand. "I'll be the judge of that. Hand it to me."

Meg stepped back. "No."

"Fine, we'll let the police sort it out." He moved toward the phone on the desk.

"Mr. Huntington," Tessie pleaded, "please listen. San Francisco will be destroyed by an earthquake tomorrow—"

"I've had enough of your stupidity, woman," he snapped. "I don't care whether you swallow this drivel or are too weak-minded to see the truth of that charlatan but save the story for your cellmates at the jail. They'll find it quite entertaining."

Huntington reached for the telephone. With a roar, Phillip barreled into the room and rammed him. Meg lunged for the gun, but he recovered his balance and grabbed Phillip in a chokehold. He pressed the barrel to his head. "Don't," he spit out. The boy struggled futilely in his grip, face turning read. "Now, Tessie, if you'd be so kind as to summon the police before your nephew loses consciousness."

Meg's heart pounded. The cold metal of the crown warmed against her skin. "Don't move, Tessie." She stepped toward him. "Let him go, Huntington, I'm warning you."

"Don't be a fool," he scoffed. "How can you get the advantage of me?"

The heat blazed. Her lips formed a tight smile. "I'm not entirely sure, but I have an idea you won't enjoy what comes next."

Ashes fluttered past Meg's eyes. Centuries of grime and tarnish burnt away to reveal the crown's hidden glory. Huntington sucked in a breath. "Impossible."

"Not impossible," said Meg smartly, "just highly improbable. Put the gun down, please, and I'll explain."

Huntington's stunned gaze remained fixed to the crown. "A true magical artifact..." A wild light shown in his eyes. "What does it offer? Power? Riches?"

"Nothing to you. The crown answers to me alone."

The gun barrel moved from Phillip's head and pointed directly at Meg. "Then don't tempt me to see what happens if you stop breathing. Hand over the crown."

Chapter Twenty-One

Cloaked in darkness, wind roared past Cal's ears with the force of a hurricane, sucking air from his lungs, thoughts from his head. Without warning, the roar halted, and the mystic rope released. His arms and legs flailed, searching for footing. Then he heard a scream and tumbled into the light.

"What the hell..." Cal blinked. His eyes focused and his heart skipped a happy beat. Meg stood in front of him with a strangely wary look on her face. He was still here. He found her and wasn't sent back alone. "Meg—*oof.*"

Cal doubled over as Phillip rammed an elbow into his side. He dropped the gun. *Gun?* Phillip jumped on top, pummeling him with his fists. Cal grabbed his arms. "Cut it out. What the hell's wrong with you?"

Meg's eyes widened. "Cal! Phillip, get off him." She yanked the boy away by the collar.

Cal straightened, rubbing his stomach. "Of course, it's me. I...I..." He gaped at Phillip as the truth sank in. "I felt him." He poked Phillip in the shoulder. "I feel him." With a joyful shout, Meg threw her arms around his neck. Cal held her body tight, his voice caught in his throat. "Meg, my Meg, I feel you, too."

Meg swallowed hard. "I was afraid I lost you. I can't lose you."

Cal rested his cheek against her hair. All doubts

drifted away. This wasn't Ashur or Roland who held other women in their arms. He was Callum MacGregor and the only desire flooding his veins was for a bean counter named Meg Adler. "You won't. I swear. Never."

"Never?" Meg tilted up her head, a question in her eyes.

His head bent down to hers. Their lips met, a promise forged between them. "Sword or no sword," he murmured, "crown or no crown, I won't leave you, Meg. I love you, and if I have no future with you, then I have no future."

"I love you, too." Meg's lips parted in a brilliant smile. No sunshine ever lit his world so bright.

"Meg," asked Tessie, "why are you kissing Mr. Huntington?"

Cal drew back with a start. "Huntington?" Both Tessie and Phillip gawked at them. He gazed at his body, clad in the suit of an early twentieth century gentleman. "Oh."

Meg turned to Tessie and Phillip with a twinkle in her eye. "It's Cal, not Huntington."

"Cal?" gasped Tessie. "Your spirit guide?" She sagged against the desk.

Phillip peered sharply at Cal and then drew in a breath. "He sure is. Don't know how I know, don't know why, but he's in there."

Tessie raised an eyebrow at Meg. "It appears to me you commune deeper than on a spiritual plane."

Meg flushed. "Let's not get into that right now." She turned to Cal. "What happened? Where'd you go?"

"The sword brought me to it." He explained his visit to the circular room. "The crown must have reached out when you were in danger and pulled me here. I heard a scream."

"That was Huntington," said Phillip with a smirk.

Meg chuckled. "We came here to steal the crown, but Huntington walked in on us. I warned him if he tried to take her from me, he'd suffer the consequences. I can't say I expected this."

"Me, neither." Cal ran a hand through his hair. "We have a problem." He explained what he saw in the round room.

Meg shuddered. "That man tried to force open the gate."

"He has no clue," said Cal. "He thinks he's jumpstarting a spiritual golden age, but instead, he'll unleash the end of the world."

"How do we find him? In only a few hours the earthquake hits."

"I've no idea. Neither the man nor the woman used names, and the room had no windows. I could have been anywhere, even outside San Francisco."

Tessie tapped a finger on her chin. "I wonder…describe the man, please."

"Early thirties, brown eyes, brown hair brushed back, round glasses, about five foot eight."

"That sounds like Oliver Lydecker. The woman must be his wife, Stella."

Cal and Meg exchanged a startled glance. "Lydecker?" said Cal.

"Have you met?"

Meg coughed. "We ran into a distant family member. What does he do for a living?"

"Mr. Lydecker also deals in antiquities and is often at odds with Mr. Huntington. They belong to the same club, and you might even say they're rivals. Each one wishes to outdo the other when it comes to the purchase of unusual antiques although Mr. Lydecker's motive has nothing to do with profit."

Phillip rolled his eyes. "Mr. Lydecker is president of the fairies."

"I've explained before," scolded Tessie. "He isn't a fairy. Mr. Lydecker is the High Priest in the United Ancient Order of Druids."

Cal shot a glance at Meg. She appeared to be struggling to hold in a laugh.

"Have you heard of them?" asked Tessie. "The members have an interest in every form of spiritualism."

A disturbing image popped into Cal's head of George Lydecker in a toga prancing through his corn maze while strewing flower petals over his shoulder. He shoved it from his mind. "What can you tell me about them?"

"The order is a group of open-minded individuals. They reject the dogmatic constraints of puritanical religious thinking and aren't afraid to ask deep philosophical questions and search alternative beliefs for answers."

"I get it." Meg grinned and whispered an aside to Cal, "New Agers."

"While the order is a private organization," said Tessie, "I've attended public lectures in their hall on transcendentalism, mysticism, and spiritualism. They were so intriguing that I decided to consult a spiritualist to make contact with Clara. That's how I came to visit Meg."

"Have you seen the round room?" asked Cal.

L. A. Kelley

A shadow of doubt crossed Tessie's face. "If it's at the order's headquarters, it must be in the private sanctum only open to full members. I've never been there."

"Having a Lydecker pop up," mused Cal, "can't be a coincidence. My gut says the sword is at the order, but if I'm wrong…"

Meg punched him playfully in the arm. "I say let's go for it, or do you want to spend the rest of your life inside Robert Huntington?"

"Not a chance. Tessie, where's the order located?"

"Right across from city hall."

"Damn it," he muttered.

Meg raised an eyebrow. "What's the problem?"

"I hoped their building was in a safer neighborhood, but the earthquake completely destroys that part of the city, and we only have until daybreak. If Oliver Lydecker is George's ancestor, we must convince him to get out of San Francisco now. If he dies here…"

Meg's eyes widened. "George won't be born, and the maze never built. We better get going."

Cal motioned to her head with a grin. "Aren't you overdressed?"

"Oh, right." Meg removed the crown and wrapped it in the linen while Cal tucked the pistol into his waistband. "How are you feeling?" she whispered to Cal as they hurried to the cable car. "You still look pale but not as bad as when you were a ghost."

He rubbed his temples. "Okay, except for a bit of a headache. I don't get a peep from Huntington either, but I suppose that's not a surprise. He's not a warrior. I get the impression he's hunkered in a mental corner watching the show with horror. I'd pity him," Cal grunted, "except he pulled a gun on you. He could stand to suffer a little. Maybe it'll make a better man out of him. Any word from Marushka?"

"Still no sense of her." Meg's brow furrowed. "Madame Marushka wasn't a good person. She cheated and lied, and I can't shake the feeling that's not the worst of her sins. I'm sure now her spirit made a one-way trip when I arrived. The forces that brought us here passed judgement, but I doubt any of her customers will complain."

Except for the flickering gaslights, darkness cloaked the city. Fog rolled in bringing with it a heavy weight that settled on Cal's shoulders. By this time tomorrow, the earthquake would have destroyed every building in sight.

As if Meg sensed his inner turmoil, she slipped her hand in the crook of his arm. "We can't save them. We can't even warn the fire department about the busted water mains. If by some miracle they believed us, it's too late for them to do anything."

Cal placed a hand on top of hers. "It's painful to accept the sword and crown only allow us to fix so much."

"History can't change." Meg's wistful expression tugged at his heart.

"The big stuff anyway. I choose to believe we gave Herlinde and Tomman a shot."

Meg nodded at the two seated in front of them. "Tessie and Phillip, too. The past is written, but the future is an open door."

They reached city hall, and Tessie pointed across the street to a nondescript brick building. "That's it."

Cal raised an eyebrow and cocked his head at Meg. "Don't say it," she said with a chuckle. "I expected architecture more reminiscent of Marduk's temple, too." She nudged him in the side. "This has the air of a law office. You should feel at home."

"Or an accounting firm," he teased, "so right back at you. There's a light inside so Lydecker must be there. We have to get the sword before he tries to open the gate again."

They darted across the street, but the door was locked. "Now what?" asked Meg.

Cal knocked, but no one answered. "We can't stay here all night. Let's try the back." They hurried to the rear and found a heavy wooden door and several windows. "They're locked, too," said Cal.

A glass pane shattered as Tessie hurled a rock through the window. Phillip gawked at her.

"Well," she said tartly, "don't just stand there. Reach in and release the latch so we can crawl through—and mind you don't cut yourself."

He grinned. "Yes, ma'am."

They entered a foyer which led to a hallway lit with electric light fixtures in the ceiling.

"I don't hear any voices," said Meg.

"Me neither," said Cal. "Let's poke around."

The building had a large lecture hall and a library marked PRIVATE. Both were empty and neither had a circular shape. Phillip scratched his head. "Where'd they go?"

"Tessie," said Cal. "Any idea how we get to the order's private meeting room?"

"No," she said. "I've only been in the lecture hall and assumed the entrance was at the end of the corridor."

"The only things here," said Phillip, "are the way we came in and the library."

"What now?" asked Meg. "The Lydeckers didn't just disappear."

Cal stared at the library door. A tiny tug pulled on his chest. Pulse racing, he turned to the others. "The sword is close. I sense it." He cleared his mind, stepped inside the room, and took a deep breath. "Come out, come out, wherever you are." The slight tug angled to the floor. He scuffed his toe on the carpet. "It's underneath us in a basement. That's why I didn't see any windows."

"There's no obvious entrance," said Meg, "so the room must have a hidden staircase."

Cal closed his eyes. "Where are you?" he said under his breath.

Follow. The tug strengthened.

Cal opened his eyes and allowed the persistent pull to lead him to a bookcase with volumes on Eastern mysticism. He fingers trailed lightly across the leather spines. "Not this one...not this one..." As if a hand closed on his wrist, his fingers jerked to halt. "Here!" He yanked books from the shelf and tossed them aside. Behind them appeared to be nothing but solid oak.

Touch, said the voice in his head.

Cal pushed against the panel. With a muted click, the bookcase slid to the side. Electric lights illuminated a narrow staircase. "Yes! This way." Cal led the others down the stairs to a small antechamber. A door on the other side had carved images of the sun, moon, and stars scattered amidst an array of astrological symbols.

"Hear that?" said Tessie. "It sounds like a man

321

chanting."

Icy fingers plucked at Cal's skin. A warning screamed though his mind. *The ceremony has begun.* He flung open the door and charged inside. "Stop!" he shouted.

Lydecker and his wife stood in the center of the circular chamber wearing their white robes. Oliver held the sword in front; a tiny circle of mist hung suspended in the air at sword point. He faced Cal with an angry scowl. "Huntington, what are you doing here? This is a private club."

"I broke in. Sue me. You have to stop the ceremony. It isn't spreading enlightenment. You're going to open a gate to another dimension and release a monster called the Everdark."

The ground trembled, and Meg grabbed Cal's arm. "Cal—what if these rampant mystic forces weakened the fault line, and the Lydeckers' actions jumpstarted the earthquake?"

Mrs. Lydecker startled and glanced nervously at her husband. "Oliver?"

"Rubbish, Huntington," sputtered Lydecker. "I understand what I'm doing. You're not even a true believer. You've spewed nothing but insults about the order—"

The floor shook again, and the misty circle shimmered.

"Cal," said Meg, "The gate is still beyond the mist, but he's forcing it into existence. It'll form any second and show the Everdark the exit."

"Cal? Gate?" Lydecker's eyes narrowed in suspicion. "This is a flimflam. You want the sword for a buyer." He drew himself up. "It belongs to the order and isn't for sale."

"I'm trying to do this peacefully, Lydecker. Give me a chance to explain before someone gets hurt."

The misty circle began to spin.

"Listen to him!" Meg took the crown from the wrappings and placed it on her head. "It has the same symbols. They're meant to work together to keep the gate closed and prevent the Everdark's escape."

Mrs. Lydecker bit her lip. "Oliver, perhaps you should stop until we hear what they have to say."

Oliver cut her off with a wave of his hand and glared at Meg. "She's lying, Stella. I recognize this woman now. She's Madame Marushka, one of those fortunetelling charlatans ostracized by the order."

The floor trembled. The circle expanded, spinning faster and faster.

"Please, you have to believe them," cried Tessie.

"If you don't," said Phillip, "we're all goners."

"Mr. Lydecker," said Meg, "I don't have the power of a ley line here. Force the gate to appear, and I may not be able to keep it shut."

Stella pulled at her husband's sleeve. "How do they know about the existence of ley lines? Oliver, maybe you should…"

The misty circle glowed with a faint light. Oliver and Stella gawked in stunned amazement.

"You see it now, don't you," said Meg.

Cal pulled the gun. "Time's up to make nice, Oliver. I have very good reasons for keeping you and Stella safe, but I'm an excellent shot and can easily wound instead of kill. Trust me, it'll still hurt. Now drop the sword and stand aside."

For an instant, hesitation marked Lydecker's

expression and then he lunged at the spinning circle. "I must see what lies beyond." The sword tip pierced the ring. With a whoosh, the glowing mist burst into flames and the center turned pitch black. A demonic howl rent the air. Wind shrieked through the chamber like a vacuum, sucking them toward the ever-expanding rift between dimensions.

Stella screamed in terror. The symbols on the crown flared to brilliance. Cal dropped the gun and grabbed Lydecker around the waist. "Let go of the sword!"

"I-I can't." His expression transformed by horror. "Something's pulling me in."

Meg gripped the rim of the flaming circle with both hands, straining to keep it from expanding any farther. "Hurry! It's coming."

Cal gritted his teeth, fighting the wind. He reached over Lydecker's shoulder and grasped the blade. The razor-sharp edge sliced into his skin. Blood ran down the metal and absorbed into the symbols. They flickered and then burned steady with blinding light.

Power coursed through Cal's body. He tossed Lydecker aside and with both hands swung the sword at the circle. It rebounded with a shock wave that send stabbing pain through his arms. He gritted his teeth and struck again. Though the dark at the center of the circle shone the cracked gate and beyond that two glowing eyes.

Meg screamed as flames encircled her arms.

With a roar, Cal swung through the fire and the blade bit into the black. The circle exploded, knocking him aside. He dropped the sword. Meg collapsed to the floor, and the crown fell from her head.

"Meg!" Cal crawled to her side. "Answer me." Relief rushed through him when she groaned.

She rolled over and blinked. "I'm okay."

"You're hurt." Her hands were red and raw. Cal kissed her forehead.

She smiled at him. "The crown absorbed the worst of it." She glanced around. "Is the circle gone?"

"It went ka-blam," said Phillip. He and Tessie helped them to their feet. "That was quite a show."

Tessie drew in a shaky breath. "Something in there moved. I-It had eyes and saw us."

"The Everdark is trapped for now," said Cal. "We bought some time."

"Cal, the crack widened," said Meg with a shiver. "The gate won't stay shut much longer."

"It's okay." He gripped the sword. "We'll have another chance."

Oliver had his arm around his wife. His face was ashy pale. "I'm sorry." He swallowed hard. "I didn't realize…I was so sure…"

"Relax," said Cal. "We're safe for now."

Stella eyed him in amazement. "Mr. Huntington, how did you stop it? You've never been a believer."

"He's not Mr. Huntington," said Phillip.

"It's a long story," said Cal, "and best not told here. We need to go—" The room rocked with a tremor and his pulse raced. "Uh-oh, by any chance does anyone have the time?"

Oliver shed his robes. Underneath he wore a normal suit with a pocket watch on a chain. "It's 4:15."

"We've got to go now," said Cal. "The earthquake will hit in less than an hour."

"What earthquake?" said Stella.

325

"I'll explain on the way. Let's get out here." He ushered them to the door.

"Where are we going?" asked Lydecker.

"Train station—" As Cal's foot stepped over the threshold, a violent tug jerked him across the room. He slammed into the floor, dazed, his body wracked by waves of frigid cold. Meg dropped to her knees beside him, eyes wide with fear. "I'm okay," he soothed. "Knocked the wind out of me is all. What was that?"

"I'm not sure." Meg swallowed hard. "But that's not the only thing knocked out of you. Look at your hand."

Cal held his fingers to his face. The room was visible through them, his body now nothing more than a ghostly outline. He scrambled to his feet. Tessie, the Lydeckers, and Phillip had crossed the threshold without a problem. Huntington lay groaning on the floor with the sword next to him.

"W-who are you?" Oliver choked out.

"You see me?" said Cal.

"Not well, though." Tessie's voice shook.

Meg's eyes were wide with fear. "Cal, you're hazier than before."

Cal stumbled to the doorway, shivering. His legs were unnaturally heavy and trembled supporting his weight. He stretched out a hand. It reached as far as the door jamb and was roughly shoved back. He inhaled. With palms flat, he pushed against the invisible barrier but to no avail. The effort was draining, and he swayed on his feet. Meg put out a hand to presumably steady him and it passed right though him. Cal forced a weak smile. "I guess this is as far as I go."

A tumult of emotions passed over her face and then

fear drained away. Meg removed the crown. "This is as far as I go, too."

Cal's gaze softened. "The earthquake won't be fun."

"I've had worse deaths with you at my side."

Meg's loving smile drove the aching cold from Cal. She picked up the sword and handed it and the crown to Phillip. "You're the keeper. Make sure they stay hidden. Others may get wind of them and want the power for themselves. They won't understand their true purpose."

Phillip squared his shoulders. "I promise."

Tessie laid a hand on his shoulder. "I promise, too. I'll help him any way I can."

"Oliver," said Cal, "you've seen what will happen if the sword and crown fall into the wrong hands. That gate must never open."

Oliver took Stella's hand. "We'll help the boy and keep the secret. No one will ever learn from us what happened here."

"Phillip," said Cal, "take Huntington with you. Get to the station and catch the next train. The earthquake doesn't hit until 5:15, so you should have just enough time to escape San Francisco."

"No, we don't," said Oliver. "The trains don't start running until six o'clock."

Cal and Meg gaped at each other in horror. "Oh, no," she said in a choked voice. "What do we do now?"

"Our yacht in the harbor," blurted Stella. "We can escape by sea."

"Cal, Meg..." Phillip clutched the sword and crown to his chest. "There's so much I don't know."

"You'll do fine," said Cal. "I have absolute faith."

The earth shuddered again. Ceiling plaster cracked and fell to the floor. "Run!" yelled Meg.

Tessie hoisted a groggy Huntington to his feet, and they stumbled up the staircase with Oliver and Stella on their heels. Phillip brought up the rear and paused on the bottom step. "Good luck!" he called before racing after them.

Cal backed from the doorway, energy drained. His legs buckled, no longer able to support his weight.

"Cal…"

"It's okay," he said weakly. "I'm not in pain. I don't feel much of anything now. Sure I can't convince you to take a boat ride with the Lydeckers? The earthquake will be a hell of a show from the bay."

"Not a chance," said Meg.

She lay over him, and her body melded to his. Her heartbeat thrummed in his chest, her breath warm on his lips, her blood rushed through his veins, and a loving essence filled Cal. He sensed the rising tension in the earth as it neared the breaking point. The tectonic plates ground together, kinetic energies built to an unnatural high. The city balanced on the knife edge of cascading failure.

Cal's mind drifted away, the only mental lifeline to reality was the image of a face. "Meg…" He latched onto her essence. To her.

"Hush, now," she said with no fear in her voice. "It's almost time."

A deep, resonant rumble mushroomed to a roar. He flinched at the crunching, grinding bedlam of noise. The floor heaved, tossing Cal and Meg apart. Jagged cracks ripped through the building, tearing the walls asunder. Bricks and mortar crumbled like dry leaves.

Cal strained to call for Meg, but her name died on his lips.

Lights flickered and died, consciousness drifted away, and the world rent in half.

Part III: The Path of Totality

Meg opened her eyes. Sunlight streamed through the windows.

Windows?

She sat bolt upright, gawking at the familiar surroundings. She lay on the bed in her suite at the Crossroads Inn. She jumped to her feet. "Cal? Are you here?" No one answered.

Heart pounding, Meg ran downstairs. Becky stood at the front desk and greeted her with a smile. "Good morning."

"Was Cal here?" she blurted.

"No. Were you expecting him?"

"Yes, I…" Meg swallowed hard. "By any chance did Isaac Bingham leave another letter?"

"No, sorry, but they're probably at the fairgrounds. Glad you're up. You don't want to miss it."

"Miss it?"

Becky regarded her with a puzzle expression. "The eclipse. It's nearly noon." She held up her viewing sunglasses. "We're ready to go outside and watch—"

Meg raced from a dumbfounded Becky. People packed the fairgrounds. Meg shouldered her way through the crowd to the corn maze. The entrance was deserted. A stack of hay bales blocked access, and a sign tied to the front said, *Closed until after the eclipse.*

"Meg!"

Cal sprinted toward her, and Meg's heartbeat soared. She threw herself into his arms. "When I woke up at the inn and didn't see you…"

"I know. When I opened my eyes in my office and didn't see you…" He held her tight.

Meg swallowed back a lump in her throat. "You're solid again."

He nuzzled her hair and breathed a sigh. "And you're not buried under rubble."

Meg pulled back. "Did you get a note from Isaac?"

"Nothing." Cal's eyes widened. "You didn't either?"

A tidal wave of despair rushed over Meg. Without the sword and crown, they were doomed. "I thought for sure he'd meet us here. What happened to him? Where are the sword and crown?"

"Not with us." Cal's voice tightened. "Meg…"

She squared her shoulders. "I'm going in there with or without it."

"So am I." He took her hand. "Together." Not an ounce of hesitation tinted his words.

"Together." Meg's fears drifted away. She could face anything with Cal at her side. "The Everdark will regret the day he ever picked a fight in this cornfield."

They skirted hay bales and hurried through the maze. The paths were empty; not a single person in view. They reached the center where the noise of the fairground crowd dulled to no more than a distant murmur.

Not a whisper of breeze stirred the air. The heat clung with the force of a living thing, squeezing tight, stealing breath. The waving stalks etched tiny wispy shadows on the ground. Second by second, they contracted and grew fainter as the moon took bites of the sun. Meg's grip tightened on Cal. Totality was almost upon them, and so was the Everdark.

Her pulse raced as a low rumble echoed through the corn. The rumble became a roar—a clanking, mechanical roar. Meg's brow knitted in a puzzled frown. "That sounds like a…like a…"

Cal peered into the depths of the field. "Car engine?"

He yanked Meg aside as a pickup truck with George Lydecker at the wheel blasted through the corn, smashing stalks under its tires. Amaranth sat next to him in the front with Summer and Dylan in the bed. The truck fish-tailed to a halt at the arbor. George jumped out with a pry bar. Dylan and Summer vaulted from the bed toting shovels. George pried up flagstones from the ground and Amaranth chucked them side.

"George?" said Cal.

"I got a letter," he grunted, loosening a stone, "shoved under the door and addressed to me from my great-grandparents, two people I never met."

Cal gaped at him. "Oliver and Stella?"

"Yeah. They said you ran into them. Said a bunch of other crazy things, too."

Amaranth tossed the last stone on top of the pile. Dylan and Summer dug into the ground with a frenzy, pitching shovels full of dirt over their shoulders.

George wiped his brow. "Did you know the Lydeckers founded Crossroads? Oliver and Stella came from San Francisco right after the earthquake and bought the land. It was a strange occupation for a man who owned an antique store before and never showed any interest in farming, but it turned out they both had green thumbs. The Lydeckers started a family tradition with the first crop." He pointed to the ever-widening hole where Dylan and Summer frantically worked. "No matter what the economic circumstances, this one section of the field laid fallow, never plowed under any circumstance. My grandfather promised Oliver; my father promised my grandfather." George shrugged. "It sounded dumb, but I promised my father, too. That's why the center of the corn maze has always been in this spot."

Cal gaped at the hole. "Are you telling me—"

"Oliver and Stella's letter said Phillip Bingham buried two artifacts directly underneath the exact dead center of the flagstones. I was to dig them up for people named Callum MacGregor and Meg Adler. They'd be waiting in the maze." George shuffled his feet and his face flushed. "Well," he said brusquely, "I had to see what's under there, didn't I?"

Amaranth took his arm with a smile. "Of course, you did."

The tip of a shadow brushed Cal's shoe. He jumped aside as something as cold as ice raked his leg. Three quarters of the sun was eaten away, and the rest rapidly disappearing. The hair on the back of his neck rose as an eerie howl emanated from the depths of the cornfield and slowly advanced on their position. The air stilled and the faint rustle of the stalks disappeared. At the edge of the clearing, the air shimmered and then formed the hazy outline of a gate.

Clunk. Dylan's shovel hit a solid object. He and Summer exchanged looks of triumph and dropped to their knees to scoop dirt with their hands. Cal and the others joined them. Clumps flew from the hole to reveal a steamer truck secured with a rusty padlock. Despite the grime and extra wear and tear brought by decades of burial, two names carved into the surface were visible; Cal MacGregor and Meg Adler. Dylan placed the point of the shovel in the hasp and with a grunt pried off the padlock.

Shadows merged and covered the earth. The misty gate solidified, the color now a vibrant blood-red. A heavy blow from the other side jarred the crack another inch, wide enough to see two eyes peering through the dark.

Cal flung open the trunk. The crown and sword rested on a faded silk pillow. He grabbed the sword. Meg placed the crown on her head.

The moon swallowed the last of the sun.

The Everdark battered the gate, shrieking in triumph. With each blow, it opened farther.

Fire burst from the symbols on the crown and sword. The flames dove to the ground igniting the ley lines. Cal tightened his grip, their ancient power coursing through his veins.

Voices whispered in his head. *Are you ready, brother?*

At Cal's sides stood the spirits of Ashur and Roland, each with a ghostly mimic of the sword. Surrounding Meg were Nemra and Clare, crowns on their heads to match her own.

We are with you. We are one.

Cal shot a glance at Meg and a grim smile marked her lips. "Hell, yeah," he said. "We're ready."

The gate burst open. The spirits of Ashur and Roland joined with him. A primal battle cry tore from Cal's throat as he raised the sword and charged. A tentacle whipped out of the dark. He lunged and severed the appendage with one stroke. It hit the ground, blood spattering, and spewed a cloud of the same choking stench Cal remembered from the Margrave's keep. The ley lines flared, burning the poison to harmless mist. Another tentacle took its place. Cal sliced it off and a new one appeared. Stabbing and thrusting, the skill of Ashur and Roland guided his arm while the symbols on the black sword cut a fiery trail through the unnatural night. Cal halted the Everdark's advance at the threshold, but it was clearly visible now. Beneath the eyes was a gaping maw, not just a mouth but the entrance to a flaming pit where the agonies of its victims would feed the monster's hunger.

"I am immortal," the Everdark screamed. "You cannot destroy me. I sense your human weakness even now. Soon, you die and then I feast."

"Not before I take a few more parts of you with me, you slimy bastard." A roar of approval from Ashur and Roland went through his mind. Cal struck again and again, pouring his strength into the blade, the skill of two expert swordsmen at his command. Sweat dripped down his brow. He gritted his teeth, muscles burning with the effort to sustain the attack. The Everdark was right. He was mortal and even with the help of spirit warriors he couldn't fight forever. The end would come, and he'd make the final sacrifice. "But until that time," Cal spit out, "not one damn inch."

****

Meg stood with Nemra and Clare. They were ready. The symbols on their crowns burned with a fierce light cutting through the dark. Meg stepped into the center of the intersecting ley lines and stumbled, clutching her chest, as raw power flooded her body, too much for one person to control.

The spirits of Nemra and Clare entwined with hers. *We are here, sister. Three are now one. Our hands are yours to hold the magic. Gather it in.*

"Three are now one," Meg said. Untamed mystic forces crackled and danced around her. She opened her heart, opened her mind, drawing every last bit of mystic energy from the lines. Meg staggered as the powerful blast coursed through her body. The hands of Nemra and Clare grasped the shifting, turbulent waves. They guided them to the crown, adding their strength.

Meg added hers, too. "Every drop," she shouted.

The Everdark roared a mocking jeer, the brittle rasp cut sharp as midwinter ice. "I have met you before in other lives and other forms. You were no match for my glory then. You are no match now. Puny sack of flesh and bone, I cannot be killed by a human."

The words rang with bitter truth. The Everdark was immortal. "Show me the way," Meg said.

The voices of Nemra and Clare joined together. *Death is but a single option.*

Meg laughed. She faced the monster; not a shred of doubt, not a grain of fear. "You're right. Your darkness is eternal, but I can destroy the gate and trap you forever. Cal, now!"

He charged the Everdark, dodging tentacles and slashed the sword across its eyes. The creature shrieked and staggered back from the gate's threshold.

"You die first," it roared.

Tentacles whipped his body. Arms shaking, Cal held his ground.

Meg raised her arms. "Come to mama." The

collective energy in the crown blasted through her fingertips and stuck the gate, draining away its blood-red color. As it faded, the gate began to inch shut.

"No," the Everdark roared, "you cannot hold me." It rammed the gate.

Meg gritted her teeth as a shock wave barreled into her. "More power, I need more power." She drew from the heavens, the very earth under her feet. Lightning rippled from her arms to the gate, etching symbols of the sun, moon, and stars on the surface. The gap narrowed by half and continued to close...only a few more inches.

"No!" raged the Everdark. Waves of unbridled hate forged a bolt of mystic energy. It struck Cal in the chest and hurled him to Meg's feet.

The crown blazed with pure light. The gate slammed shut cutting off the Everdark's shriek. The symbols on the surface melted together, one shining mass burning hot and bright, blotting out everything else. The last bit of energy poured from Meg's hand, and the gate's outline shimmered and trembled. A fissure formed, spreading a spider web of cracks. An ear-shattering explosion flung Meg to the ground.

The energies of the ley lines stilled. Meg blinked, peering at the sky. A sliver of sun peeked from behind from the shadow of the moon. "Cal," she whispered.

No one answered, and her eyes closed.

****

Cool air brushed Meg's cheek. She opened her eyes and stared at a bright light; not the sun, but a mundane ceiling fixture. For a second, her thoughts were a muddy blur and then memories flooded in. "Cal!"

Amaranth scurried into view. "He's fine, my dear, and resting on the sofa. You're both back at the farmhouse."

Meg swung her feet off a loveseat. "You saw?"

"Saw and sensed it. Why, the psychic reverberations have yet to settle."

Summer shivered. "The thing nearly got out before Cal pushed it back and you destroyed the gate. It was horrible."

"Yeah," said Dylan with a shaky voice. "Man, I figured it was over for us."

"You didn't run," said Summer with a smile. "You stayed right by me."

He flushed. "I wouldn't leave you."

Cal lay sprawled on the sofa, eyes closed. On a coffee table were the sword and crown, symbols now devoid of any inner light. Meg stumbled to Cal's side and laid a hand on his chest, nearly crying out with relief at the strong, steady heartbeat.

Cal groaned and his eyelids fluttered open. His gaze focused on Meg and his expression lit with joy. "Hey, you."

Her heart skipped a beat. "Hey, yourself."

Cal sat up and pulled Meg into his arms. "I am never, ever, letting you go," he said.

"Suits me fine." The kiss was long. Hearts bound, never to be apart...they were only brought back to reality when someone coughed.

"Hush, George," chided Amaranth. "Give them a moment to themselves."

Meg and Cal got to their feet. "Is everyone okay?" said Cal.

Dylan grinned and waved a hand at sunlight

streaming through a window. "The world's still here."

Summer chuckled. "Apparently, what happens in a mystic maze stays in a mystic maze. After we brought you to the house, Dylan and I went to the fairgrounds. All everyone talked about was the amazing eclipse. No one noticed the near apocalypse."

"The temperature dropped," chirped Amaranth, "and a nice cool breeze blows through the fields. Fall has arrived at last."

"Sorry for the damage to the cornfield, George," said Cal. "Hope the little jaunt with the pickup didn't cause you to lose too much crop."

"I'll manage." He crammed his hand in his pockets. "Been thinking maybe I've been too set in my ways. Maybe it's time for a change, check out this organic thing. Don't know much about it though. Could be too much work for one person. If I had help..." He glanced at Dylan.

Dylan's eyes widened. "You want me to work for you?"

"Not *for* me *with* me, as a partner. The land needs another generation of Lydeckers to care for it. You can live here after high school and go to the local college."

"Do it, Dylan," said Summer. "We can both major in agriculture. Forget music. Your songs stink."

Dylan gaped at her. "Summer! You said they were great."

She flushed. "I was only being nice because it was cool having you around. Besides, I'm right. You like working with me in the garden."

"A talent for growing things, Dylan," said Amaranth, "is a gift to cherish. I'm not saying you and George will never butt heads, but I think you'll do well together." She grinned at George. "Dylan and I can both drive you crazy."

His gaze softened. "I reckon I could get used to that, too."

"Dylan, people always have to eat," said Summer. Color deepened in her cheeks. "Crossroads isn't the big city, but I'm happy here. I kind of hoped you would be, too."

Dylan smiled at her. "Actually, life in the sticks is way cooler than I imagined."

Cal's cell phone chirped with a text. He glanced at the display and then grabbed Meg's hand. "We have to go."

"Where."

"My office. Isaac Bingham is waiting for us."

George tossed him a keyring. "Take the truck." He slipped an arm around Amaranth's waist. "The rest of us have things to talk over."

Meg and Cal grabbed the sword and crown and went to the truck. They tore past the fairgrounds enjoying the cool breeze through the lowered windows as the sounds of the festival faded in the distance. An elderly man stood at the door to Cal's office with a grin on his face.

Cal jumped from the truck. "Isaac…" he sputtered.

Isaac chuckled. "I know. You can't decide whether to throttle me or thank me."

Meg hugged him. "Well, I can. Thanks."

"You're welcome, my dear. I must say I'm very glad to finally meet you in person." He regarded the sword and the crown. "So, those two are responsible for the fuss. I take it they did what they were supposed to do."

"Like a charm," said Cal.

"Good. By the way, Meg, the offer stands."

"What offer?"

"The job offer. The Lux Foundation is moving its headquarters to Crossroads. My grandfather assured me years ago you'd be an excellent choice to run it. We'll talk more when you're finished."

Cal raised an eyebrow. "Please don't tell me you have another letter." He took Meg's hand. "We haven't recovered from the last ones."

Isaac nodded at the office. "I brought the projector and screen and they're all set."

"Projector?" asked Meg.

He winked. "Old school like Grandpa. I kept the film all these years but promised him not to watch it until after the eclipse. It's ready to go. Just flick the switch."

"Watch what?" Cal asked.

"The last message. You and Meg call me when you're ready to talk. We'll have dinner at the inn. My treat." His eyes twinkled. "I advise you to get those door locks changed, Cal. You never know what sort of riffraff will wander in."

Cal and Meg hurried to the office. A screen stood in front of the couch. Across the room on the desk was an empty 35mm film canister next to an old projector, threaded and plugged in.

Cal flicked the power switch, and the reels spun. A grainy blur flashed by, and then an elderly man's face appeared onscreen. Elderly, but recognizable. Cal chuckled. "Phillip, you old devil."

Phillip tapped the lens and called, "Isaac, is this thing on?"

"Yes, Grandpa," said Isaac from out of camera range. "Go ahead and speak."

Phillip made a shooing motion, and a door closed. He peered into the camera and winked. "Hi, Cal. Hi, Meg. Bet you two never thought to see me again. I wish I could have watched the final battle, but that wasn't meant to be. No matter, you both succeeded and are alive and well. I can't see into the future, but some things don't have to be told. I feel them."

Phillip leaned forward. "I wanted to tell you how everything turned out. We escaped San Francisco safely. Stella calculated the position of the ley lines and we came here to found Crossroads. The Lydeckers took up farming, and Oliver vowed not to plant at the intersection of the ley lines. He made his family vow, too but never told them why. I buried the sword and crown in the field after it was time for me to leave town. I knew they'd be safe. The Lydeckers said they'd make sure they weren't disturbed and Lydeckers always keep their word. Oliver and Stella gave me a letter for their descendant, George." He nodded at the door. "I'll have Isaac deliver it to him at the right time."

He grinned. "Huntington turned out not to be such a bad sort. He remembered what happened and the experience changed him for the better. He and Aunt Tessie hit it off, married, and had a family. Huntington went into electrical equipment companies and utilities. He had a head for business and did well. I got my start with him and did better. They're both gone now, but a branch of their descendants, the Goldsteins, live in town."

Cal drew in a breath. "Amaranth."

"I only stayed in Crossroads a few years," Phillip

continued. "You were right, Meg. Having the responsibility for magical artifacts can be a burden at times, and I didn't wish to draw any attention to the town. So, I kept my distance and made a life elsewhere." He shifted in his seat. "This message is also by way of an apology. Cal, I had Isaac use connections in the Lux Foundation to get your fiancée the job overseas. He also kept on eye on you, Meg. I set aside funds for him to buy companies you worked for and cut your positions. I needed you both free and in Crossroads when the time was right. Besides," he added, "you were meant for each other. Even as a kid, I knew."

Cal slipped an arm around Meg's shoulders.

"So, I guess that's it. Thank you for setting my feet on this path. I married a remarkable woman and had a loving family. My life has been a grand adventure. Forgive me for any pain I caused. Be well. Be happy. This tape will self-destruct in five seconds." He laughed. "Sorry, couldn't resist…Isaac," he shouted, "get in here and shut this thing off." A door opened and the screen went dark.

Meg touched the projector. "I forgive you, Phillip."

Cal rose to his feet and offered Meg his hand. "So do I." He pulled her close. "I'm not a mystic either, but Phillip's right. Some futures are easy to predict."

"I see mine," said Meg. "It's got your name all over it."

"You took the words right out of my mouth."

She motioned to the sword and crown. "Think they'll call again?"

"If they do, we'll answer, but for now, I'm taking the night off."

343

"Good." Meg smiled coyly. "Because I have a vision of our near future that doesn't involve corn mazes or mystic quests." She wrapped her arms around his neck. "But perhaps a funnel cake after I'm done with you."

Cal gently removed the clip from her hair. "Was there ever any doubt?"

A word from the author...

I write fantasy and science fiction adventures with humor and a little romance because life is dull without them. My books don't have sexy naughty bits or gore so your mama would approve, but I add a touch of cheeky sass so maybe she wouldn't. The South is home; a place where the heat and humidity have driven everyone slightly mad. In my spare time I call in Bigfoot sightings to the Department of Fish and Wildlife. They are heartily sick of hearing from me.

I hope you enjoyed *Shadow of the Eclipse*. If so, please leave a review. No essay is necessary, just a few kind words will make my day. Thanks a ton. You're a peach.

~

Published by the Wild Rose Press:
The Naughty List
One Enchanted Evening
Second Chance City
Spirit Ridge
Good Bones
Shadow of the Eclipse

Other books by L. A. Kelley can be found at:
www.lakelley.com
or email:
l.a.kelley.author@gmail.com

Thank you for purchasing
this publication of The Wild Rose Press, Inc.

For questions or more information
contact us at
info@thewildrosepress.com.

The Wild Rose Press, Inc.
www.thewildrosepress.com